She gave a sigh of relief. How could she of all people, find herself alone in an empty salon with Julian Marquez taking a shower? A shower? She heard water running full force. The man is nuts. She knew that a lot of famous people were eccentric, but this was bizarre. He had shown up out of the blue, babbled a few pointless words, and then ended up in the shower. She didn't really know what she was supposed to do next because he was too unpredictable.

Nicole leaned back in the chair and closed her eyes. She could virtually feel the steam in the room, see the cascades of water running down his lean, sinewy frame, feel his strong, wet hands on her shoulders as he pulled her into the swirling mist.

The door opened and she nearly choked on her coffee as he stepped out naked, except for a towel tucked loosely around his waist. Short spirals of wet black hair clung to his forehead; his midnight eyes shimmered, along with the gleaming muscles on the exposed parts of his body. And what a body! Broad chest, flat, well-toned mid-section, and narrow hips.

Her mouth opened, closed, and issued forth no words. He gazed at her nonchalantly, as if it were the most natural scene in the world. "I'm gonna crash on the couch for a few minutes, wake me when you get ready to leave."

The words still did not come as she watched him vanish into the tiny lounge room and close the door. She slapped her palms against her face and screamed inwardly. What should she do? What should she say? It was even more apparent that the man was insane, drunk, or both. But who was really crazy? She couldn't deny that she was both offended and charmed by his behavior.

HAVANA SUNRISE

KYMBERLY HUNT

Genesis Press, Inc.

Indigo Love Stories

An imprint of Genesis Press, Inc.
Publishing Company

Genesis Press, Inc.
P.O. Box 101
Columbus, MS 39703

ISBN: 1-58571-182-9
Manufactured in the United States of America

First Edition

Visit us at www.genesis-press.com
or call at 1-888-Indigo-1

DEDICATION

This book is dedicated to the memory of my father, a musician and master of the art of verbal storytelling.

ACKNOWLEDGMENTS

Many thanks to:

The creator of all good things for allowing me to fulfill a childhood dream that had been put on hold for a long time.

The editors at Genesis Press.

My sister for sharing and listening to all my stories.

The creative writers at the Rockland Center for the Arts.

Denise, my e-mail buddy for being so positive and encouraging.

Norma, a friend and former co-worker, whom I've unfortunately lost track of, but who I will always remember for her fascinating Cuban tales.

And finally, to the musicians, artists, and writers of the world for providing endless inspiration.

PROLOGUE

Chicago: The past

"You know, babe, you're just as cold as ice…an ice princess living in your own little dream world. Whenever things don't go exactly the way you want them, you just chill out and drift off."

She knew it was childish to be harboring resentment over the words her husband had spoken the previous night, especially since he had apologized, but Nicole still felt upset. It was not the first time that he'd blamed her for the problems with the physical aspects of their relationship.

Brushing back stray locks of hair, she glared at the breakfast table. Two cereal bowls sat there surrounded by puddles of milk, and bits of soggy frosted flakes. There was even more on the floor. Honestly, she thought, the two of them needed troughs. Her son, Trey, was only three, but what was Warren's excuse?

Even worse was the fact that it was Sunday and Warren, who had recently been promoted to detective, now had less restrictive hours and was off duty the whole day. He could have cleaned up the mess instead of leaving it for her when she had to go to work in the afternoon. Nursing had been the occupation he'd encouraged her into and lately it seemed to be monopolizing all her time. Was it her fault that she was always tired?

Warren and Trey had left the house a half-hour ago on a jaunt to the local deli to pick up the paper. Trey was at that age where he had to be with his father wherever he went, and that thought caused a brief smile to cross Nicole's face. Warren had better get all he could out of it, because the day would come when he would be begging the boy to accompany him.

A loud knock on the door startled her and the smile vanished. It was probably Warren being obnoxious again. She'd told him so many times to use the bell, or better yet, use his key. How did he know that she wasn't in the shower, unable to answer the door?

"I'm coming!" she yelled, deliberately taking her time.

She flung open the door, expecting Trey to rush in, loudly announcing his presence, but standing there was Warren's detective partner, Eddie Garcia.

"Eddie," she started, flushing with embarrassment, patting at her disheveled hair. "Warren isn't home right now. He just stepped out a few minutes ago with…"

"Nicole," Eddie interrupted, fumbling for the rights words. "I…I'm afraid I have some bad news."

Nicole's hands dropped limply to her sides. She stared at him, noting that his normally boyish face had aged at least ten years. Waves of panic washed over her.

"Warren is in the hospital. He's been shot…"

"Shot!" she screamed. "How could that be? He wasn't on duty…he…oh my God. Where's my son? Trey…"

Eddie stepped in, placing his hands lightly yet firmly on her shoulders, drawing her closer to him. "Your son is fine. He wasn't hurt."

She broke free of him. "My God…I have to go…I…"

"I'm here for you," Eddie said, taking a deep breath. "I'll take you to the hospital."

The scene at the hospital was chaotic. An army of police officers in full uniform were gathered about, talking in hushed tones with paramedics and members of the trauma team. She could not see Warren because he was in surgery, but a nurse carried Trey to her. The little boy had a bewildered look on his face, and he immediately reached out and clung to her. Nicole felt dizzy with anguish as she noticed the traces of Warren's blood staining Trey's clothing.

She knew she should call her parents because they lived only fifteen minutes from the hospital, but at the moment she was in such a state of shock that she couldn't remember their number. When a doctor came out to inform her that Warren's prognosis did not look good, she barely comprehended his words.

Trey was starting to weigh a ton and his arms around her neck were practically strangling her, but she could not move. They were frozen, bonded by the worst kind of pain.

"It's going to be all right, baby," she soothed. "It's going to be all right. Mommy's here."

She felt Trey's hot tears sliding down the back of her neck, but he remained silent, as silent as the cold flakes of snow falling from the gray Chicago sky.

CHAPTER ONE

Miami: The present

It was another hectic night at Miami General Hospital. Nicole Evans was used to working the night shift, but tonight seemed even more hectic than normal. The demands of the sick were unending, and being short-staffed did not help. Most of her fellow nurses were doing double shifts and sheer exhaustion had set in. She longed for one quiet moment.

Her friend and co-worker, Maria Velasquez, blamed it on the full moon. Nicole found herself wondering if there was really some truth to that. There was definitely something weird about a full moon in Miami.

She glanced down at the chart before her and cringed. Julian Marquez was on that list, and it was time for a temperature check. She'd held off doing that, at least until his endless parade of visitors had checked out. They didn't seem to realize that the man was sick and should be resting. Just because he was famous didn't make him any less fragile than anyone else.

"Well, tonight's the night, Nicole."

"Huh?" Nicole looked up at her friend Maria, who was positively glowing. "Tonight? What's so special about tonight?"

"You get to meet Julian of course."

"Oh…is that all? He's just another patient," Nicole said.

"To you maybe. I got his autograph last night. I think he'll be checking out soon."

"Good. We could use some peace around here." Nicole put the chart down and adjusted her stethoscope.

"Well, come on…he's famous and he's got lots of friends and fans." Maria was undaunted.

"Those friends and fans are a pain. What happened to all the balloons and junk they sent him?"

"He gave them to the kids on the second floor. They loved it."

"How sweet of him," Nicole said flatly.

"Nikki, don't be like that. He is sweet, really," Maria insisted.

Nicole suddenly remembered Mrs. Jenkins in 433. She had requested a sleeping pill, and it was well past the fifteen minutes she'd told her. It was aggravating to be so short-staffed. Had everyone been in, she would not even have to worry about meeting Marquez.

"Excuse me while I go see about the patient in 433. I'll check Marquez after," she told Maria.

It wasn't until much later that she actually found herself approaching room 400. It was the solitary suite of course. Mr. Latin Pop Star definitely would not be sharing a room with anyone else. She had wanted so badly to ask Maria to attend to him, since she was so crazy about him, but Evelyn, the head nurse, had insisted that she be the one. Maybe she'd felt that Maria would lose all professionalism around him. Nicole rolled her eyes at the thought.

The door was ajar and she started to knock but didn't. Why should she? She didn't usually do it with the other patients. This was a hospital, not a hotel. The room was dimly lit, and the man who some women loved to swoon over, lay there with his eyes shut, looking vulnerable. What was the big deal? He was handsome, but there were a lot of handsome men in Miami. He had jet-black hair and a slightly darker than olive complexion. Mr. Macho also had long eyelashes that a lot of women would envy.

Cut it out! the voice inside her screamed. *Stop admiring him.* "Mr. Marquez," she said in her authoritative nurse's tone.

His eyes opened—the blackest eyes she had ever seen. They looked like twin onyx stones with a diamond sparkle in the center.

"Sorry to disturb you but it's time for a quick temperature check."

He nodded silently. There was something about the way he stared as she slid the thermometer into his mouth. Velvety eyebrows, sculpted lips—the man definitely had something going in the looks department.

She busied herself checking her watch, anything she could do except stare at that face. The thermometer beeped and she removed it.

"Good or bad?" he asked.

"Hmmm, kind of in-between actually. It's 101. That's better than before, but still a fever."

"I thought all this stuff I'm on was gonna work." He motioned toward the IV in his arm.

"It is, but you really need to rest more." She glanced at all the cards and flowers in the room. "You have too many friends."

He smiled. "I didn't know you could have too many."

Nice smile, perfect white teeth. *Caps, I'm sure,* she thought. *Well, he can afford it.* "Two or three friends should be enough," she said. "More than that and they're probably not really your friends."

"Is that how it is with you?"

She really didn't want to converse with him, but his slight Cuban accent was pleasant, musical almost. If his singing voice sounded as fine as his speaking one, he had to be pretty good.

"I have my family," she said. "That's enough."

"Family's good." He was looking at her hands, probably noting the lack of a ring.

"Well," she turned, "try to get some rest."

"You know, I'm really not tired. Could you just stay a few minutes and talk?"

Talk? Talk about what? the rude voice inside her head screamed silently. "I would love to, but we're short-staffed tonight and there are many patients. Maybe a sleeping pill would help."

He laughed. She hadn't really intended it as a joke, but he probably took her reply as sarcasm. The truth was she had absolutely nothing to talk to him about, and he should be all talked out anyway, since most of the time he was surrounded by fans and friends.

"Nicole," he said, reading her identification badge. "You have beautiful eyes, Nicole. Anyone ever tell you that you look like Tyra Banks?"

She felt herself blushing. *Oh, get over it! He acts that way with all women.*

"Goodnight, Mr. Marquez," she said, moving out the door.

"Buenas noches," he said softly.

Nicole spent the rest of the night intensely busy and trying to avoid Maria, but she was pounced upon just as she was about to leave the hospital. It was well after midnight.

"Nicole, tell me what you think about Julian," Maria said, speaking so rapidly that all the words seemed blended together.

"What do I think? Really, Maria, he's just a vain, spoiled man who talks too much."

Maria did not seem to hear her. "What did he say to you?"

She feigned a star-struck expression. "He told me I look like Tyra Banks."

"Oh my God...you mean he actually said it? What have I always been telling you?" Maria was excited.

"You told me I look like Vanessa Williams."

"Vanessa...Tyra...What's the difference? They're both beautiful."

"Maria, you are entirely too much," Nicole said with a laugh. "See you tomorrow. Hopefully the love of *your* life will be gone by then."

As she slid into the car, Nicole thought about her son. Trey was safely tucked away in bed and her sister had probably retired too, figuring it was pointless to wait up for her.

She eased out into traffic and reflected on Miami, the tropical city that never slept. It rivaled or even surpassed Chicago or New York, because the minute the sun went down, the city roared to life. It was always party time. She passed the trendy hotels and nightclubs. Why her sister Allyson had chosen to open a salon here still eluded her, but it beat Chicago, the city she'd fled three years ago.

Nicole still felt the pain when she remembered Warren Evans, her husband. They'd known each other since junior high, dated through high school and married a month after she'd graduated from college. Warren had joined the police force and managed to persuade her to take up nursing. They had both been eager to start a family and once she completed additional schooling, her added income helped buy a house.

She had always loathed his being a cop, but Warren, like a noble knight, felt that he personally had to contribute to making the world a safer place. Law enforcement became his means of doing it and he rapidly moved up the ranks to become an undercover detective within the vice division.

As if it were yesterday, she could still recall how proud he had been when Trey was born. They had both felt such joy when they heard their son's first words and saw his first toddling baby steps. They'd thoroughly enjoyed all the precious little moments, and mostly the innocence that was light years away from the other realm that Warren inhabited, a world filled with violence and total disregard for human life. It was that realm which had cruelly shattered their world three years ago when he had taken his last drive to the store with his son.

Warren had not died right away. He lingered brain-dead for two agonizing days, with her at his bedside. The funeral with both families and a massive police presence was a blur. The only thing Nicole could focus on was her overwhelming responsibility to protect Trey from any more pain. The three year old had been an eyewitness to the horror. The only mercy extended to them was that the assailant, a known drug dealer, had been apprehended.

It became evident in the following days that the once cheerful, chattering little boy was suddenly mute. Months and months of psychotherapy had no effect. Her parents and friends were extremely supportive, but Nicole knew she and Trey had to get away from Chicago, away from the pain. When Allyson, her older sister, told her that they could come down to Miami and share her condo, Nicole took the offer, sold the house, and fled south. Now, three years later, Trey was six and attending a private school for the handicapped, where he was learning sign language.

Nicole's thoughts returned to the present as she parked the car and entered the condo. Allyson had left a dim light on for her, and all was quiet except for the panting of their German shepherd, Shane, who'd abandoned his post at the foot of Trey's bed to greet her. She knelt to scratch the big dog behind his ears and he thanked her with a sloppy, wet tongue.

She automatically headed to the kitchen for a cup of herbal tea, but the clock glared indignantly down at her, reminding her that there were only a few hours left if she intended to get any sleep at all. She had to be awake in time to get Trey off to school. Tossing Shane a dog biscuit, she walked quietly down the hall and glanced into her son's room.

Trey's angelic face seemed to glow under the night-light that he refused to sleep without. Nicole involuntarily leaned very close to hear him breathing. Perhaps he would murmur something in his sleep—perhaps those quiet sounds would actually form words. But she heard only gentle exhalations. She kissed him on the cheek and though he moved a little, he did not awaken. Sighing outwardly, Nicole left for her room, under the watchful eyes of Shane.

Next morning, Trey sat at the breakfast table, waging a war between two plastic dinosaurs. When one had a collision with a glass of orange juice, Nicole quickly caught it before the juice spilled on the table.

"Trey, stop fooling around and start eating. You only have thirty minutes," she admonished him.

He nodded and took a second swallow of the cereal. He should eat more, she thought, noting that Trey was growing tall and skinny. He possessed the wide eyes and curly hair of his father, but he had her coloring. Despite his problem, all of his teachers had declared him to be very intelligent. If only he would let the world hear the sweet sound of his voice again.

The sound of the television coming from the living room distracted Nicole. Allyson was in there looking at the early morning news. Although her salon opened at seven a.m., she didn't usually go in until later—the privilege of being the owner.

They had less than fifteen minutes now. Trey leaped up from his chair and over went the glass she had so valiantly rescued a few minutes ago. "Trey!"

He flashed her his best "sorry, mom" look and bolted out of the kitchen. She ran after him, waving his clean shirt, and tackled him in the living room, wrestling him into it. Allyson turned her attention to them and laughed.

"What's so funny?" Nicole demanded, with a frazzled look.

"You and Trey…this routine you go through every morning."

"If you come up with a better way, let me in on it," Nicole said. She noted that Trey had his books and was about ready.

"Trey, come give me a hug good-bye," Allyson said.

He came to her and tolerated the obligatory hug. It was Nicole's turn to be amused now. Trey was arriving at the point where he thought he was getting too big to be hugged.

The trip took almost thirty minutes in typical Miami traffic. All the way she kept watching Trey out of the corner of her eye as he fidgeted and stared out the window. She would have to do something about the routine they'd fallen into. Working nights, because her supervisor had informed her that she still didn't have the seniority to get the preferred earlier shift, meant that after school she had to take Trey to Allyson's shop, where he spent the hours looking at television or doing homework in the little room in back, until Allyson took him home around nine. With the exception of her days off, she saw him only in the morning and when he was asleep. It was not an ideal arrangement.

The car radio was blabbering away in Spanish. She wasn't quite sure why she didn't just change the channel, but by the time she dropped Trey off, she realized she had left it on because it was making her think of Julian Marquez. She shuddered at the realization. *I must be getting really desperate,* she told herself. *I am intrigued and captivated by a man whose lifestyle bears no resemblance to anything I've ever known, or would even want to. I've never even heard him sing.* Her eyes drifted toward the local record store as she passed by. It was a good thing the place wasn't open yet or she would have stopped in to pick up one of his tapes.

Enough. It really didn't matter what she conjured up. When she came on duty tonight he would most likely be gone, out of sight and out of mind.

CHAPTER TWO

The doctor had informed Julian that he needed to remain in the hospital for at least two more days. Julian thought the request was totally unrealistic because it was Tuesday and he had to be in New York City over the weekend for a sold out, two-night gig at Radio City Music Hall. If this trivial illness forced him to cancel, it would be the first time in nine years of live performances. He was not thrilled at the prospect of disappointing his fans.

He had been touring all spring and summer in the United States, Europe, and numerous Latin American countries. It was mid-August now, and the tour was winding down, with only New York and his hometown show in Miami remaining. He needed to finish up unscathed.

Just yesterday, Luis, his brother-in-law and acting manager, had been quick to remind him about all the money riding on those engagements and how expensive a cancellation would be. As an afterthought, Luis had added that if he *really* was too sick to perform, it was his decision and it would just have to happen. Sometimes the mercenary attitude of his own family, the promoters and publicists got to him, but Julian knew that no one pushed him harder than he pushed himself.

The doctors called it pneumonia with complications, but he did not feel all that sick—nothing that a couple of shots of vodka couldn't cure. The roar of the crowd would supply the rest of the adrenaline needed to coast through those two nights. After that, he would have two weeks' rest before his final three shows at home.

The sunlight streaming through the window added to his headache, but he felt too tired to get up and pull down the shade. *Too tired to pull down a shade and you expect to be out of here today?* he questioned himself. He could try to make it this afternoon, but for some totally illogical reason he wanted to stay in the hospital long enough to see a certain nurse named Nicole again. He could not explain just what the attraction was. Her beautiful green eyes captivated him, but his fascination with her went beyond her beauty. There was something deep in those eyes, something sincere and haunting, unlike anything he'd ever seen in the vacant stares of the gorgeous creatures who constantly flitted in and out of his life.

Beautiful women were everywhere. They could fulfill his physical desires and look good hanging on his arm at social affairs, but lately Julian had become totally disillusioned with them. He was thirty-two years old and for the past five years his personal life had been hollow. He'd found himself envying ordinary men with regular jobs, who came home to wives and children and woke up in the same bed every morning. It was ironic that though he was considered a fantasy figure to many women, he had never really been emotionally involved with anyone.

"Julian," the voice of his current fling rang out as she entered the room. "How are you?" Jami Austin stood before him, lean and leggy with long blond hair and a Barbie doll face. She planted a kiss on his cheek and he flinched involuntarily, hoping there wasn't a shiny red lip mark remaining.

"I'm hanging in there," he said dryly. "Probably be out sometime today."

"Great!" She didn't seem to notice his apathy. "I came by early because I have a seven o'clock shoot on the beach." She opened a can of Diet Coke and took a sip.

Julian gazed at her wanly. "Is that breakfast?"

"I'm terrible," she said with an irritating giggle. "I didn't have time to eat, but I will later." She shook back her hair. "You're starting to look like your old self again."

My old self, Julian thought, taking it literally. Jami was a decade younger than he was, and at the moment he couldn't even recall at what event they had met.

Barbie doll sat on the chair near his bed and crossed her legs. The illusion of a skirt she wore was so short he was amazed that he couldn't see beyond her endless legs. Knowing her, she probably wasn't even wearing underwear. She glanced at her watch.

"Yeah, you better get moving," Julian said. "You haven't got much time."

She pouted. "If I didn't know better, I'd think you're trying to get rid of me." She reached up and traced his eyebrow lightly with her finger. "You're not doing that, are you?"

"Now what would ever make you think that?"

She'd barely opened her mouth to reply when the door burst open and in charged his half-sister Elena, prepared to take over and do battle with whatever stood in her path.

"Elena, why can't you knock? We could have been horizontal or something," Julian said.

"Wouldn't be the first time I walked in on some of your nonsense," Elena countered sarcastically.

Jami looked annoyed, but tried to cover it by giggling. Elena ignored her completely and continued talking to Julian, switching over to rapid-fire Spanish.

"Have you seen the doctor yet?"

"Yes, I saw him."

"Good. You will be leaving today. I have everything taken care of. You will go right home and stay there for the rest of this week. No running around, no interviews, nothing. You will stay on your medication and then it's on to New York."

"Julian, I'll catch you later," Jami mumbled, easing out of the room. She was no match for Elena and she was aware that Julian did not even notice her departure.

"Elena, you don't always have to tell me what to do. I know what's up. I know about New York," Julian said.

"Okay, but you've been even more absent-minded than usual lately. You know what? I think right now would be a good time for you to leave this hospital. It's early and we can get you out of here without the fans or the press knowing. We've been told by security that we can leave by the back exit. Luis will…"

"Elena!"

"What? Why are you yelling?"

"Because I can't get a word in. You're going on and on about this and that crap, and the truth is the doctor said I should stay here two more days."

"Julian, I'm only…" She stopped. "What? What did you say?"

"You heard me."

She folded her arms and fixed him with a scathing glare. "Okay, so that's what he said, but what are you going to do?"

"Leave, of course, but this evening and not right now."

"I'm going to speak to that doctor. What exactly did he tell you anyway?" Elena badgered.

"If you're going to speak with him, why are you asking me?"

She shook her head furiously. "You're such a pain. When are you ever going to start being responsible? We're all working hard to make things right for you and you act like you don't even appreciate it."

Julian smiled sarcastically. They were working hard all right, but it definitely was not for him.

Elena was seventeen years older than he was and for as long as he could remember, even back in Cuba, she had been more like a dominating mother than a sister. Through the years he had just accepted it, but lately it was getting on his nerves. He was tired of being treated like an expensive piece of merchandise by members of his own family. Elena did not realize it yet, but he planned on making some changes.

Nicole discovered she could not dismiss Julian Marquez as easily as she'd planned. The minute she stepped onto the fourth floor, she realized he was still a patient. A burly security guard was posted conspicuously outside his door, which should have been a revolving one, because a steady flow of bodies kept moving in and out. She was only slightly relieved that he wasn't assigned to her tonight.

An hour into the job, she found herself alone at the front desk for what would probably be about a second, and took the time to peek at his chart. It was obvious why he was still there. The antibiotics he had been prescribed were not having the desired effect and he had been switched to a newer, more potent one. The last posted temperature check on him read 102.

"Nicole, Mrs. Hansen in 404 is calling for you again," Maria said, approaching the desk.

"I told her in fifteen minutes. It hasn't even been five." Nicole sighed and brushed back a stray lock of hair.

"I did tell her that, but you know how she is." Maria's eyes twinkled. "Julian's still with us. Poor baby."

"Idiots!" Nicole declared.

"Who?"

"The people who can't stay out of his room. They won't let him rest."

"Most of them are family," Maria said. "His brother-in-law is his manager, then there's his sister, nieces and nephews...that sort of thing."

Nicole inspected the syringe for Mrs. Hansen. "I saw at least four blue-eyed blond model types going in there. Don't tell me they were family."

Maria laughed. "Oh them... Well, You know how stars are. They gotta have their women."

"I think it's kind of pathetic."

"No problem for you tonight since he's not your patient."

"I know." Nicole breathed a sign of relief. "Thank God."

Maria responded by laughing heartily. Nicole looked up at her. "Did I say something that funny?"

"Oh no, not at all. I just find it a little odd that you know you're not assigned to Julian, but you were reading his chart."

Gotcha! Nicole felt the accusing finger of guilt stabbing at her. "I was just curious," she began. *Oh stop it! The more defensive you get, the more you incriminate yourself.* "Okay, enough already. You're right. He is very attractive, but he's also conceited and…"

"Hallelujah! You're human after all," Maria interrupted, then lowered her voice as two co-workers approached. Nicole discreetly put Julian's chart away and glanced at her watch. It was now time for Mrs. Hansen's injection.

Visiting hours were finally over and a relative peace had settled on the floor. Nicole had just exited room 402 and was walking down the hall when the security guard posted outside Julian's door beckoned to her.

"Excuse me, nurse. Mr. Marquez needs you."

She hesitated. "I'll tell Evelyn. She…"

"No. He specifically asked for you," the guard insisted.

Specifically asked for me? Her traitorous heart skipped a beat, but the initial emotion was replaced by annoyance. The nerve of that man—she was supposed to drop everything and run to do his bidding. What could he possibly want anyway?

She pushed the door open and entered the room to find Julian sitting on the edge of the bed, wearing the infamous tie-in-the-back hospital gown. But under it was a pair of jeans. He appeared to be in the process of getting dressed.

"Are you going somewhere, Mr. Marquez?"

Julian flashed his killer smile. "And good evening to you, Miss Nicole. What a pleasure to see you again."

She stood with her back against the door. "I guess I should repeat the question. Are you going somewhere?"

"Yes. As a matter of fact, I'm getting ready to leave."

She stared at him incredulously. "You can't be serious. The doctor advised you to stay for two more days. You're not well enough to leave."

"I'll survive," he said. "You know, it's really okay to come a little bit closer. I promise not to bite."

She resisted the urge to laugh at herself. Why was she standing so far away? Was she afraid of him or something?

"I would like you to get rid of this IV thing for me," he continued.

Nicole stood directly in front of him with her arms folded. "Mr. Marquez, you can't leave."

"Why not? Would you miss me?" His question sounded beseeching, almost childlike, but she knew he was just playing games.

"Miss you?" She felt confused, flustered. "I'm telling you this as a nurse to a patient."

His demeanor changed and she could see impatience on his face. "I have to be in New York by Friday because I have two sold out concerts and…"

"That's impossible!" she cried, with more anguish in her voice than intended. "You'll have to cancel it."

"I don't cancel concerts."

"Listen to me," she urged. "The infection in your lungs has not cleared and your temperature is still elevated. Why don't you just get back into bed."

His dark eyes were set in a stubborn gaze. "I guess that means you're not going to take out the IV."

"That's exactly what it means."

"Fine, I'll do it myself." He yanked out the needle without even a flinch. She flinched for him.

"Mr. Marquez, you're being childish and unreasonable."

"I seem to be famous for that."

Nicole turned to face the door. There was nothing she could do. It was a hospital and not a prison. She looked back at him once more. "I'll tell you exactly what will happen. If you attempt to do that concert, you will probably pass out on stage."

Julian smirked. "That's highly unlikely."

"What about your family? Do they agree with this decision?"

"It's their decision too."

His eyes looked enormous, and his expression tore at her heart. She wanted to say something kind and compassionate, she wanted to cajole him into staying, but the words that came out of her mouth were angry. "What kind of family do you have anyway?" She abruptly headed out the door, muttering.

"Nicole, wait." Julian stood up and started after her. He knew he had moved too quickly because the sudden motion caused the room to lurch and careen wildly about. He groped desperately for the wall to steady himself, but it was too far away and the next second the hard linoleum of the floor slammed up against him.

Nicole heard the thud just as she stepped out. Her heart leaped into her throat as she rushed back into the room. "Julian!"

She found him on the floor, looking dazed. Standard procedure would have her calling for help from one of her co-workers, but she was not feeling very standard this night.

"Julian, are you okay?" She dropped to her knees.

"I...I guess I must have gotten dizzy." His mouth curved slowly into a sheepish smile.

She helped him sit up. "Are you all right?" she repeated.

"Yeah, I'm fine...as fine as any jerk can be." He felt intensely aware of their close proximity. Her arm had looped around him and he caught the faint whiff of some enticing vanilla scent. He breathed in, closing his eyes. Her facial complexion was smooth with yellowish-brown skin, almost the color of butterscotch. Her auburn-tinged light brown hair was worn back in a chignon, but he suspected it was long and thick. Her arms were slender, but strong.

"Can you stand up by yourself?" she asked. "If not, I'm going to call for help."

"No. Don't do that. I can get up." The initial shock of being betrayed by the weakness of his own body was passing. Julian found himself reluctant to stand, because it would mean breaking their embrace. He silently reveled in the knowledge that she really was worried. But he could not remain on the floor. He rose slowly, with her arm around his waist, guiding him back toward the bed. He maneuvered his own arm carefully so that it went around her neck with his hand resting lightly on her shoulder.

Standing, he was about six feet tall. She was 5'7", so he didn't exactly tower over her, but Nicole could feel that he was extremely well built, with taut, sinewy muscles barely camouflaged beneath the thin material of the hospital gown. She did not want to reckon with the fact that her heartbeat had increased dramatically and she secretly enjoyed the closeness. It had been such a long time since she'd last felt the touch of a man, and Julian Marquez was quite a specimen. Even in his weakened state, he was potent and lethal.

"I'll be back in a second," Nicole said as Julian collapsed on the bed.

She was relieved to step into the momentary solitude of the bathroom, even if it was just to keep from hyperventilating. Pulling herself together, she washed her hands and returned to the scene for another round.

He lay motionless on the bed, apparently with all the fight knocked out of him. She began reinserting the IV, while he watched her with sparkling, midnight eyes. *He's actually about as helpless as a rattlesnake,* she thought. *Even with their heads cut off, they still bite.*

Nicole could almost see the converging blood of many nationalities in his face—

Spanish, Ethiopian, Mayan, even Egyptian. It was appalling, but she was having a hard time resisting the urge to stroke his rumpled, curly black hair; just the thought of tracing her finger lightly over the wickedly sensuous curve of his mouth was making her dizzy.

"Are you still planning on leaving tonight, Mr. Marquez?" She could not resist teasing him.

"What? Are we back to Mr. Marquez again?" He sounded genuinely disappointed.

"Julian," she corrected herself.

"Believe it or not, I actually can be rational sometimes. I figure if I can't even stand up, then I won't be going anywhere," he said.

"That is a very logical conclusion, and a wise one I might add." She flashed him a smile.

"Are you always this pleased when you're proven right?"

"What makes you think I'm pleased?" she asked.

"Because it's the first time I've seen you smile. You really should do it more often."

She felt relief upon observing that his eyes were about to close and she was not going to have to respond to that comment. She was also aware that he still had his jeans on under the ridiculous hospital gown, but she was not about to remind him to get undressed. Ten minutes of her time spent with Julian Marquez was more than sufficient. Evelyn would have to deal with anything else. He was her patient.

Leaving the room, Nicole nearly collided with a woman about to enter. "Excuse me," she said automatically, catching her breath.

The woman glared at her and firmly took hold of the door. She was medium sized, probably in her late forties, with bleached blond, permed hair, and she was wearing a gray linen suit and heels that were much too high.

Well, excuse me for living, Nicole thought. The near collision was more the woman's fault than her own. What was she doing there anyway? "Visiting hours are over," Nicole reminded her curtly.

"I am not a visitor," the woman retorted indignantly.

I don't care who you are, you don't belong here, Nicole was tempted to say, but she bit her tongue. Diplomacy was always best. "If you're part of Mr. Marquez's entourage, there has been a change of plan. He is staying." She realized that it sounded as if she were gloating.

The woman ignored her and entered the room. The door closed abruptly behind her. Nicole shook her head and looked questioningly at the guard who'd done nothing to intervene.

"That's his sister," the man informed her, displaying a foolish smile.

Sister? Nicole thought. They bore no resemblance whatsoever.

A quick glance at her watch revealed that the time with Julian had cut into her break. Almost all of it had been spent baby-sitting a patient who wasn't even hers. There were only a few precious minutes left.

CHAPTER THREE

Leaving the hospital two days later than he'd intended, and coming home without seeing Nicole again, had been a big disappointment for Julian. He realized that she was deliberately avoiding him, but he couldn't understand why. Equally baffling, though, was his own obsession with her. He tried to psychoanalyze himself, reasoning that it was only because she wasn't throwing herself at his feet that he found her intriguing, and maybe that was a little bit true, but his heart kept telling him there was much more to it.

The New York concerts had been postponed until December. Publicists and promoters had been upset, but so far not many of the fans seemed to be demanding refunds. The hometown Miami show in two weeks was still scheduled and Julian knew he would be ready for that one, if only he could survive the boredom of being at home for a few days.

Home was a sprawling Spanish-Mediterranean-style estate with numerous rooms, a tennis court, stables, and other rewards of success, all shared with his sister, her husband, two nearly grown nephews and his favorite, his eight-year-old niece Amanda. They occupied the front part of the estate, while Julian had his own section with a separate entrance, facing the ocean.

He paced around the spacious living room, then stepped out onto the verandah, which overlooked the swimming pool, acres of gardens and finally, the cerulean blue of Biscayne Bay, which emptied into the Atlantic.

It was warm and balmy outside. Julian leaned against the railing surrounding the deck and stared out into the infinite blue. The ocean always lured and tormented him simultaneously. If he stared at it long enough, he could almost hear voices, whispers from the past, carried on the ripples of the waves.

Cuba, the place of his birth, was only about 90 miles across that expanse, yet light years from his reach. As an exile, he had no desire to return, but the memories of what he'd left behind haunted him and evoked startlingly visual flashbacks. He could see himself as a child, strolling along the sea wall of the Malecon in Havana with his father, carrying a fishing pole that was almost bigger than he was. He could see his father playing the old guitar, and the people who gathered in the square to listen to his poetic boleros. He could remember his father trying to explain to him that it was more than just oceans that separated people, and finally, he could remember his father being taken away. He had cried then, and many nights after, because a part of his family had been lost forever.

He pounded his fist on the railing, breaking the spell. "Come on, Nicole, call me," he said out loud, gazing at the cell phone on the deck table, willing it to ring.

"Talking to yourself, man?"

Startled, Julian whirled around to see his friend Wade Simmons stepping out on the deck. Wade was a tall, brown-skinned Jamaican with dreadlocks down the middle of his back. He was bass player for the band and a long-time friend.

"I always knew you were crazy," Wade continued. "Just didn't realize how much until now."

Julian laughed. "How the hell did you get in?"

"The door was open. Don't you know that's the surest way for trash to get in?"

"My intention was to get the trash out," Julian said.

Wade ignored the remark. "Anyway, I was just passing through and figured I'd drop off those tapes, you know, the songs we were working on before you got sick."

"Trying to keep me busy, are you?"

" 'A mind's a terrible thing to waste,' " Wade replied. "So, how's it going? You look like crap, by the way."

"Thanks, bro." Julian had to admit Wade was right. He hadn't shaved in two days and was sporting stubble. His raggedy jeans, wrinkled T-shirt and worn socks also supported the description.

Wade deposited the tapes on the table and dropped into one of the deck chairs. "So who's this Nicole you were babbling about when I came in? Another one of your model babes?"

Julian straddled a chair, facing him. "No. She works in the hospital. She's a nurse. Gave her my number, but no calls, *nada.*"

Wade squinted in disbelief. "Works in the hospital? You must be slipping, Romeo. Long as I've known you, it's always been them glamorous Hollywood types."

"Well," Julian said defensively. "She is beautiful, looks like a model, but I suspect she's better." He took a deep breath. "I want something real, man. Incredible as this may sound, I actually do want to settle down...the wife...the kids, all that stuff."

Wade shook his head. "Never thought I'd hear you say that. So what's with this chick? What Latina would ignore you?"

"She's not a Latina, but that's beside the point."

"Really? Thought sure she would be since you're so serious." He shrugged. "Maybe she's married or got a boyfriend."

"If that's true, she sure doesn't love him," Julian replied emphatically.

"How do you know that?"

"The way she looked at me, like she was interested, but didn't want to be."

Wade drummed on the surface of the table. "Well, you're a star. Most women must look at you like that. But if it bothers you that much, just go see her and ask her out."

Julian smiled wanly. "See that? I'm up here agonizing over this thing and all I gotta do is what you said. I've been living such a crazy weird life that I don't even know how to act around a real woman."

"Then you better start re-wiring your brain." Wade stood up. "None of my business, but I don't think it's a good idea to date fans."

"She's not a fan. Never even heard of me until we met."

"This girl must be from Mars."

"She looks at me like I'm from Mars."

"Whatever. I'm out of here. Let me know what you think of those tapes. I made a few changes on the arrangement."

Julian remained seated and watched him go. She was not going to call. The next move was going to have to be his. Either that or forget her.

The phone rang. Julian seized it like a drowning man reaching for a lifeline.

"Hi baby, it's me," a distinctive female voice rang out.

The air went out of him like a pricked balloon. It was Jami.

CHAPTER FOUR

"Oh, come on, open," Nicole muttered as she fumbled with her key, trying to fit it into the hole while juggling a large bouquet of roses in her free arm.

The door swung open from inside and she almost pitched headfirst into the apartment.

"Oops!" Allyson exclaimed, side-stepping as Nicole regained her footing.

Nicole laughed. "I sure wasn't expecting you to be up this late." Her smile froze suddenly. "Is everything okay? Trey?"

"Don't be silly. He's fine, sound asleep as a matter of fact. I started watching this dumb movie and couldn't get away from it. That's why I'm still up." Allyson came closer to inspect the flowers. "These are gorgeous! Who's the guy?"

"There is no guy. " Nicole placed the flowers on the end table. "They came from one of the patients discharged two days ago. He gave a bouquet to every nurse on the floor when he left."

Allyson groaned. "I should have known. You really need to get a life." She inhaled the intoxicating aroma while touching one delicate petal. "Must have been a rich patient."

"Yeah," Nicole said. "He's a Latin pop singer."

She moved into the kitchen, feeling a little bit annoyed because it was late and her intention had been to come home, check Trey and go right to bed. She didn't feel like answering Allyson's questions.

"Which singer?" Allyson asked, following her into the kitchen.

"His name's Julian Marquez."

Allyson grabbed her by the arm. "You mean *the* Julian Marquez? Gorgeous voice...gorgeous everything?"

Nicole groaned. "Oh, you've heard of him."

"Heard of him! Nicole, what's wrong with you? Haven't you checked out my CD collection lately?"

"I never realized you were into Latin music," Nicole said flatly, pouring a glass of water.

"Well, excuse me. I've been here in Miami for six years now and it's kind of hard not to be into it. I've got Celia Cruz, Julian Marquez and a few others right up there with Mary J. and Luther."

"Okay, I agree with you," Nicole sighed. "I really am out of it. I'd never heard of the man until he was in the hospital."

"That's because you only play that jazz fusion stuff," Allyson said.

Nicole glanced at the clock. The little girl inside her was screaming to blurt out all the details. Details like how all the other nurses had received bouquets, but hers had been different, containing a single yellow rose in the center with an envelope wrapped around its stem. Maria had been quick to notice that and begged her to open it. She had pretended to be apathetic, but in a private moment, had opened the envelope to find four tickets to his upcoming concert and a hand-written note that said, *If you can't stand my singing, give the tickets to a friend, but call me.* His number was there. She'd felt elated for exactly five minutes—until reality set in and she realized that she would never call him. It was too risky.

"Why was Julian in the hospital?" Allyson asked, interrupting her thoughts.

"He had pneumonia, but he's recovering okay."

"Did you meet him?"

"Yes. Ally, give me a break. "You're starting to sound like Maria."

"Oh my God, no!" Allyson said, fluttering her eyelids and gesturing in an exaggerated Maria parody.

Nicole laughed and removed the tickets from her purse. She was not going to call Julian or tell Allyson about that part yet, but there was no reason why they couldn't go to the concert, especially since Allyson was a fan.

"Well, sis, since you like Julian Marquez so much, why don't we go to his concert in a few days."

"Girl, you must be kidding. The one at the Arena has been sold out for months."

"Not exactly." She waved the tickets in Allyson's face.

"Tickets!" Allyson exclaimed excitedly. "I can't believe it!" She practically snatched the tickets from Nicole's hand. "You've got four of them. Can Lynette and Donna come along? I mean, unless you have someone else…"

"No. They can come. I would ask Maria but she bought tickets months ago."

"Nicole, is there more you're not telling me?" Allyson asked suspiciously, recovering from her excitement. "He didn't give these to everyone on the floor, did he?"

Nicole's eyes sparkled mischievously. "I don't know for sure. Maybe he did."

She saw no point in saying anything else, or the whole story would come out, so she left Allyson standing there with her mouth open and went to check Trey. His curly head was facing her and he had a tight grip on the pillow. The dog, lying on a mat at the foot of the bed, wagged its tail.

"Hey, Shane," she whispered to the vigilant animal, then leaned forward to plant a kiss on her son's forehead before retreating to her room.

Lying awake in the dark, she reflected on the things in her life that had to be changed. Being a nurse was too demanding and too time consuming. Her son needed her, and it was unfair that Allyson had rearranged her life around them. She had no life herself and now she was infringing on her sister's life.

As sisters, they had always been close, although very different in personality. Allyson had been the go-getter. She'd confounded and frustrated their parents, especially their mother, at every turn. As a teenager she'd had numerous boyfriends and later a marriage that had lasted for only a year, followed by another which had lasted a few months. The amazing thing was her resilience. Allyson always knew how to bounce back and find laughter and joy in her life. It was a quality that Nicole admired.

Nicole had drifted far away from her original goals and most of that had been Warren's doing. Her college major had been English, and her original goal had been to go into journalism, but they had been young and anxious to buy a house and start a family. He had insisted that she needed a real job and she had agreed.

If only she could have foreseen the future with Warren gone and the dream house sold, but there was no point in thinking about that now. She was thirty-one years old and it was time for her to find a new direction for herself and Trey. Someone had told her about an opening at the *Miami Herald* in the editorial department. The pay was nowhere near what she was making as a nurse, but the hours were good, and it was something to think about. She knew she should get started on a résumé.

The next morning, Nicole took Trey to school and rushed about trying to get things done. There was the never-ending laundry, followed by a stop at the bank and the post office. It was well into afternoon when she finally got back home, just in time to answer the ringing phone.

"Hello," she said breathlessly, shoving aside the laundry basket.

"Nicole, is that you?" It was her mother.

"Mother…," Nicole answered, surprised that she would call at this time when she knew Trey was in school and Allyson was working. "Is everything okay?"

"Everything is fine here. What's wrong with you? You sound like you've been running."

"I just got in the house and the phone was ringing," Nicole said. "I had to run to answer it."

"I just wanted to tell you that your father and I have decided to take that cruise to Jamaica."

"That's really great, Mom. What made you change your mind?" Nicole knew that all her life her mother had harbored a fear of water and of flying.

"Your father really wants to go and now that we're both retired, we should do things together."

"When are you going?"

"At the end of this month. The ship leaves from Miami. What we figured we'd do is come down and stay with you all for a week ahead of time."

"Oh, yes. Of course, that's a wonderful plan." Nicole nearly choked on the words because she knew Allyson was not going to be thrilled with having their parents for a week, especially her mother.

"Where's that sister of yours?" her mother asked, almost on cue.

"She's at the salon, working."

"And where's my grandson?"

"Trey's in school. I told you that this school starts sooner than the public one."

"How's he doing?"

"He's…well, at least he's not getting in trouble like last year," Nicole said.

"I still think you should come back home. Your father and I could help."

"Thanks, Mom, but we're doing okay here. Allyson helps a lot with Trey."

"Is Allyson seeing anyone?" her mother asked suspiciously.

"She hasn't been serious about anyone for a while," Nicole replied, trying to avoid a direct answer. Her mother did not fall for it. "Oh, but she *is* dating then?"

"Really, Mom. Ally and I are grown women, but if you must know, we don't have a lot of men running in and out of our home."

"That's good. Tell Allyson we'll be coming."

She wasn't asking. It was a command. Nicole smiled sardonically and allowed the conversation to ramble on until her mother reminded her that the call was long distance and they had better hang up. After putting the receiver down, Nicole laughed. Her parents were reasonably well off, with good pensions, but it didn't prevent her mother from hanging on to every penny. How on earth had her father ever convinced her to go on a cruise? She was going to have to question him about that one.

Nicole decided to use the time remaining to work on her résumé. In less than three hours she had to go reclaim Trey. Seated at the desk, she found it extremely hard to concentrate because her mind was not on what year she had graduated from college, what her previous jobs had been, and what her current objective was. She was thinking about her son's needs and her own desires.

Trey did not like the new school. It was true he was not acting up or being disruptive, but this new apathy he'd adopted was even more disturbing. He no longer even tried to interact with other children in school or out of it. His whole world consisted of herself, Allyson, and the dog.

She was furious that he had literally been forced out of public school because the teachers had shown little patience in dealing with his problem. Somehow, she had the feeling that Trey was angry with her for having given in and placing him in a school for the handicapped. At only six, how could he understand how hard she had fought against it? What was she going to do now?

Sighing, she rubbed her eyes and stared at the potential résumé in front of her. The problem could only be solved one step at a time and this might be the first step. A different, less stressful job, would definitely allow her more time to spend with him.

There were other problems too. For the last few weeks she had become more and more aware of how much she missed a reassuring male presence, someone to hold her as Warren had, someone to tell her that everything was going to be okay whether or not there was a solution. Having someone to share the good times and the bad times would make a world of difference. As though possessed, her hand opened the desk drawer and came out with the scrap of paper that had Julian's phone number on it. She fingered the paper, then rolled it up into a ball and laughed. Julian Marquez was not the answer.

CHAPTER FIVE

The sun had just begun its ascent as Julian completed his two-mile jog. His niece, Amanda, riding piggyback, had her arms tightly looped around his neck. The eight year old had given up trying to match his pace after the first mile. He glanced over his shoulder to see that Jami was far behind, obviously not doing much better. He ran a few more yards.

"Uncle J, slow down! Jami's calling you." Amanda's breathy little girl voice tickled his ear.

Julian responded by running faster, causing Amanda to giggle deliriously. She didn't really like Jami anyway, and it was fun being part of a conspiracy.

Finally Julian stopped running. He didn't want to admit that he was exhausted. "Okay, babe," he said, kneeling down to free Amanda. "You gotta walk now."

Jami seized the opportunity to catch up. "Julian, didn't you hear me?" she gasped, out of breath. "I was yelling for you to stop and you just kept going."

"Must've been the wind blowing," Julian said as Amanda stifled a giggle. "Didn't hear a thing."

She placed her hands on her hips and pouted in self-righteous indignation. "What wind? It's perfectly still out here. In case you forgot, you've only been out of the hospital for two weeks and I don't think you're supposed to be run…"

"Stop," Julian interrupted. "Two weeks is long enough. I feel fine."

He knew Jami was more upset that Amanda had followed them on their run than she was worried about his health, because she had expressed no such concern until the child had appeared. She was right that Amanda should have asked her parents' permission to join them, but the jogging trail was in their own neighborhood and Julian didn't see it as a big deal. He'd spent all last night with Jami anyway and was determined that this was the last time.

"Well, sun's up. Might as well head back," he concluded, looking at the sky.

"Can't we run a little further?" Amanda pleaded.

"No. You never told your mother you were coming with us, remember? I hope she's still in bed when you get back."

"Damn," Amanda swore.

"We'll have none of that, *chica*. No cursing until you're old enough to really sound like a moron."

"I'm sorry." Amanda tugged at his arm. "C'mon, race you back!"

She took off, feet flying. Julian started to follow her but Jami grabbed his arm.

"No! Let her go. This is supposed to be our time."

"Look, we were together last night. I thought you had a good time."

She let go of his arm. "I think we have to talk about us."

Julian felt elated. She had finally gotten the hint. Their relationship had ended a month ago as far as he was concerned, but he always preferred to let the woman be the one to officially end it. Things were less complicated that way.

"I think we should stop seeing each other," she hesitated, "at least for a while."

Nice touch, Julian thought. *Break it to me gently.* "And last night wasn't fantastic?"

"It was good. It always is, but that's all. A relationship should be more than just...," she fumbled for the right word, "physical."

He forced himself to look disturbed. "I understand. I suppose you're right. We should stop seeing each other." He abruptly motioned to Amanda who had gotten quite a distance ahead.

Jami flinched, realizing that he had agreed with her too quickly. She wanted to discuss it in more depth, but before she could even open her mouth, he had raced off in pursuit of his bratty niece. Whatever they'd had was definitely over.

Back at the estate, Julian watched as Jami's Porsche pulled out of the driveway. He'd managed to sneak Amanda back in with no one the wiser. Elena would have been appalled had she known. She didn't approve of her child hanging out with her infamous uncle and his whores, as she liked to label every girl he'd ever dated, except the ones she'd selected.

Standing on the verandah, he peeled his damp T-shirt off and tossed it onto one of the deck chairs. For a brief moment he felt bad about breaking up with Jami. Despite his exaggerated reputation, he really didn't enjoy using people. Then he recalled how young and flirty she was. There would be many empty passions in her life before she was ready to settle down.

It felt good knowing that his doctor had declared him physically fit again, but he was disturbed that the nurse named Nicole had never called. There was only one more opportunity to either connect with her or forget it. He had given her free tickets to his concert for the third row—well within his sight. If she showed up, it would indicate that there was at least some interest on her part. He would take it from there.

They had arrived early, but the huge arena was rapidly filling up. Nicole could feel the crowd's eager enthusiasm as Allyson led the way to their seats, third row from the front of the stage. It was a good spot, although a little bit too close. She found herself on the end with Lynette and Donna sandwiched in between.

The three were chattering incessantly about some obnoxious customer at their shop, while Nicole remained relatively silent. She was friendly with them but they were definitely a part of Allyson's clique.

"Looks like we're the only ones not speaking Spanish here," Donna said, sitting on the edge of her seat, twirling an extended braid around her finger. "What do you think? He's gonna sing and speak Spanish the whole show?"

"Probably," Allyson said. "Won't bother me none."

"Yeah," Lynette agreed. "That man could sing in tongues and you'd understand. Don't worry, Donna, you'll love the show."

Nicole settled back in the chair, crossing her legs. She wore an olive-green blouse with ivory-colored, khaki slacks. Her hair was meticulously french-braided and pulled back, with a whisper of a bang framing her face. She had checked and double-checked her appearance before arriving, as though it was somehow extremely important that she look good even though dressed casually.

As the show was about to start, stage lights dimmed, then came to life in a flash as the object of the crowd's passion strolled out to thunderous applause and a booming drum roll. He quickly launched into a salsa-tinged dance number that was currently number one on the Latin charts. The mostly female fans went wild, screaming and whistling, rendering homage to a celebrated icon.

Nicole's eyes were riveted on Julian, who wore a white rib-knit shirt, so tight it seemed sprayed on, along with white pants that set off his raven-black hair and mocha skin. There was no denying he had a great voice, which seemed to be naturally tenor, but capable of many ranges and nuances. She was having a hard time coming to grips with the fact that this was the same man she'd attended in the hospital.

Her attention drifted back to her companions. Allyson, Donna, and Lynette were virtually gyrating in the aisles. Nicole looked at them in amazement and resisted the urge to laugh. It was kind of embarrassing, or maybe she was the one being foolish for sitting stiffly in her seat.

Julian ended the opener and spoke in Spanish to the audience. Women screamed louder. The lights dimmed and his next number was a less frenetic, jazzy piece that everyone except Nicole was familiar with.

And then it happened. Their eyes met. He smiled. The smile was directed at her alone. Nicole felt the blood rush to her head and she self-consciously tried to avert the gaze by looking at Allyson. Her sister was completely oblivious, which was a relief. Maybe her eyes were playing tricks on her and she'd just imagined the whole thing. Yes, that had to be it. There was no reason why he would single her out in a vast auditorium filled with thousands of adoring fans.

As Julian moved cat-like across the stage, stalking, he turned to face his band and gave a wink that was just short of lewd.

"Hit it, Wade," he said.

The bass player to his left, a handsome man with long dreds, winked back and thumbed the opening chords. It was a booming, sensual sound, accompanied by drums and soon an acoustic guitar. Julian moved with the music, seizing the microphone. The audience screamed its approval.

"'*You're the love of my life,*' " he sang in a low-pitched sexy growl, his dark eyes riveted on Nicole.

"He's looking this way!" Lynette shrieked.

He couldn't be. Nicole tried to deny the obvious, but his eyes remained fixed on her, while he moved in a sinfully seductive manner and sang words in English that left little to the imagination. Mercifully, the song ended before she melted into the floor.

"You all were right," Donna gushed. "He really is to die for."

"And he can dance too," Allyson said. All three of them laughed, but Nicole was in another world. Allyson leaned over and poked her. "Did you see that, Nicole? He was looking right here in this row."

"It could have just appeared that way," Nicole said lamely. "I'm sure he was really looking at the whole audience."

"Get out of here! He was looking at us," she insisted.

"Hope he does it again," Lynette chimed in. I want to see those gorgeous eyes."

Julian had reverted to Spanish again, introducing his band and the four back-up singers.

"That bass player is awful cute too," Donna whispered.

"That's Wade Simmons. He did studio work with Bob Marley," Allyson said.

"Marley's dead. Guess that means he's pretty old," she replied, sounding vaguely disappointed.

The next song was another dance number, loud and colorful with confetti flying, strobe lights and choreographed dancers. Despite all this, Julian remained the focus with his magnificent voice, magnificent even when he abused it.

About midway through the show, he emerged wearing all black— a V-neck shirt and leather pants, which caused Nicole to flinch. She detested men in leather, even if the wearer was a celebrity and had the body of a male model.

Julian announced that he needed a girl from the audience, and many eager candidates volunteered, screaming and waving their arms in an attempt to get his attention. He teased them mercilessly, scanning the crowd for the right one. His eyes met Nicole's again. She recoiled in horror. *Oh God, no way am I going up there*, she thought, petrified.

When he selected a tall, big-breasted blond in a hot pink halter top, Nicole breathed a sigh of relief, yet felt strangely annoyed at the same time. As Julian serenaded Ms. Voluptuous with a ridiculously seductive song, the girl practically entwined herself around him, her hands wandering over his body, coming to rest on his backside.

"That had to have been rehearsed," Allyson said.

Nicole laughed out loud and the others looked at her. "Well, it's so tacky it's funny," she said, irritated that she had even bothered to explain herself.

After that foray, Julian took a break and relinquished the spotlight to a shrill-voiced diva, who could hit notes high enough to rupture eardrums.

When Julian returned, his costume was quite a contrast to earlier. He was now attired in a traditional tux, complete with black bow tie. The band had grown significantly, and the songs that followed enthralled her, classic love songs, sung in the style of Johnny Mathis or

Nat King Cole. His voice transformed into a very smooth falsetto that seemed effortless and completely natural.

After two songs, and after he managed to lose the jacket and bow tie, the lights dimmed into an eerie shade of blue, and Julian faced the audience with his white shirt halfway unbuttoned. Someone in the shadows handed him a plain, old-fashioned guitar with a shoulder strap, and the audience became so quiet that a cough or sneeze would have sounded like thunder.

He introduced the song in a barely audible Spanish whisper. He said something about *mi padre,* which Nicole understood to be in reference to his father, and then he stroked the first mesmerizing flamenco chords on the guitar. She knew it was a love song, but there was a tragic element to it. His face, bathed in the blue light, was haunting, as was his impassioned voice. There were a few echoes from two female back-up singers under a pale yellow spotlight and the subtle refrains of a saxophone. Julian closed his eyes.

Nicole looked away. Tears had started welling up in her eyes and she was fighting to control them. It was useless. The anguish resonated in his voice and Julian and the stage swam in her watery, distorted vision. The walls were caving in, and the morbid eulogy of "Taps" was being played at Warren's funeral. A folded flag was being handed to her...the snow was falling...lingering guilt over things said and not said. She stood up abruptly.

"Nicole," Allyson began.

"I'm going to the ladies' room," she said, trying to sound normal.

She remained there, locked in the stall for what seemed an eternity, with the sound of the crowd in the background. *Stop it!* she commanded herself, stabbing at her eyes with a handkerchief. If she didn't come out soon, Allyson would come looking for her, and it would ruin the show for them.

Taking a deep breath, she stepped out of the stall and stared at her reflection in the mirror. Her skin looked pale and her eyes wide and hollow; despite her actual age she looked like a demented teenager.

Carefully, she patted cold water over her face and quickly reapplied some lip-gloss.

When Nicole returned, Julian had just finished his last encore. Donna and Lynette glanced at her questioningly, but taking Allyson's cue, said nothing about her departure...yet. She knew that status would change the minute she got home and Allyson lit into her.

They left during the applause to avoid getting the full impact of the departing crowd. The trio chattered non-stop during the entire ride back, mostly about the concert, all giving raves to Julian. Nicole was impressed too, but somewhat subdued after the flashback episode.

Once the others had departed, and Nicole and Allyson were alone in the kitchen, lingering over coffee, the questions started. "You missed a whole half hour of the show. What was that all about?" Allyson asked.

Nicole stirred at her coffee mechanically. "It just got really hot in there and..."

"You're too young for hot flashes. It was that song, wasn't it?"

There was no point in lying to her, Allyson already knew. Nicole sighed, "Yes, it was weird. All of a sudden it just gave me a flashback. I started thinking about Warren and the funeral."

"Well, it *was* a really moody piece, but other than that, what did you think?"

"Think?" Nicole looked confused.

"About the show. I was blown away. He's even more talented than I thought."

"He is," Nicole admitted. "And it didn't even matter that he sang in Spanish."

"Not *everything* was in Spanish," Allyson reminded her. "What about that one song he did in English, the one where he was looking right at you."

"Do you really think he was looking at me?"

"It was pretty darn obvious. I mean, it was the only song in English and he was doing it for you. I didn't mention it before, 'cause I didn't want Lynette and Donna in on it."

Nicole stood up and put her cup in the sink. "Okay, suppose that's so. It doesn't mean anything. I'm just the nurse he remembered from the hospital."

"Sis, you are completely hopeless," Allyson declared, shaking her head.

"So what would you do? Go in hot pursuit of him, camp out at his mansion?"

"Good, I'm glad you asked. I would call him," Allyson said.

"Call him?"

"Don't give me that blank look, Nic. I was cleaning out the desk drawer the other day and I found his number."

Nicole was speechless. How could she have been so careless as to leave that number in the open? Why hadn't she thrown it away?

"You *should* call him. The phone number is still there."

Nicole found her voice. "Listen, if I had wanted to call him I would have. I'm not interested in being used by some...some celebrity. I'm still not quite sure I'm over Warren. I probably never will be."

"You won't let yourself get over it!" Allyson shouted. "He's been dead for three years and you haven't even dated since you moved down here. All you do is work, work, work and take care of Trey. What kind of life is that?"

"I call it a *responsible* life," Nicole shot back. "I've had enough of this...this conversation. If you're so in love with Julian Marquez, *you* call him." She walked out of the room.

CHAPTER SIX

Every time he put down an empty glass, someone handed him another. Julian wasn't sure how many shots he'd consumed at this point, but he knew he wasn't drunk. At any rate, he'd better leave before he really was.

The music was loud and the dance floor was crowded with jet-set revelers. They were celebrating. Actually he didn't remember what they were celebrating. But it was one of those hot nightspot parties on South Beach that Luis had told him it was good to be seen at. Well, he had been seen.

Quickly, Julian eased past a flock of sparkling, sequined women, and blinked as a camera flashed in his face. It would be nice if he could get away without catching the eye of Natalie Gennero, the famous movie producer's daughter. The girl looked like Jami. Even the guys looked like Jami.

The night air was humid as he slipped out into a sea of Ferraris, Porsches and limousines. He slid into his modest Lexus and watched the lights fade in the rear view mirror.

He'd just returned from Brazil a few hours ago, where he'd been filming his latest music video. There had been a lot of partying down there too, and he was amazed that his brain was still functioning, if indeed it actually was.

The hot night screamed in his head. He wanted to press the accelerator to the floor and launch the car forward like a NASA rocket, complete with flames and smoke spewing from the exhaust. He wanted to break the sound barrier and then drift gently down into a quieter, less chaotic world.

It was nearing midnight and he found himself on the north side of Miami, cruising slowly through a peaceful, middle-class enclave. He swung left and entered the gates of Vista Condominiums. This was it. This was where Nicole lived.

He drove through the grounds and parked the car in a space that was near section 4B. Yawning, he cut off the motor and sat there, bathed in darkness, waiting. Waiting for what?

She would probably appear soon, because she got off work at midnight. It was insane, but he *had* to see her. Observing her at the concert had confirmed it even more. It baffled him that he had spent almost the entire show watching her, and suddenly she had bolted from her seat and vanished. It was actually kind of insulting. Most women did not run away from him.

The minutes ticked away, and it dawned on him that she might not appear. Maybe she hadn't gone to work that day. Maybe she was on vacation. "You're totally losing it, man," he told himself. He felt oddly like an obsessed pervert, but something had convinced him it wasn't all one-sided.

Two days after the concert, he'd gotten a message on his answering machine from a woman claiming to be Nicole's sister. She'd told him that Nicole was definitely interested, but there were complications in her life that caused her to avoid relationships. She had added that Nicole was about to give in and call him soon. The call had never come and he was tired of waiting.

Julian got out of the car, went inside, and climbed up a flight of stairs. He stopped at 4B and looked down. There was a light shining under the door. Someone was up.

He lifted his hand to press the bell, then hesitated. *These are regular people, not creatures of the night like you. Regular, sane people do not appreciate visitors after midnight.* He knocked anyway.

"Nicole, is that you?" a voice rang out from inside. Before he could even think of a reply, the door opened and he was face-to-face with a woman who bore a striking resemblance to Nicole, only she had darker hair, cut in a short, chic style. She looked as if she were about to scream and go into cardiac arrest simultaneously.

Nicole had gotten off from work an hour earlier, had gone home briefly to check on Trey, and then gone to Allyson's salon, taking the dog along to keep her company. There were some financial matters that had to be taken care of and it was best done at night when no one was there to interfere.

Allyson and Lynette were great at cosmetology but their business skills left something to be desired. The inventory count of supplies did not tally and the bookkeeping was shoddy. It would be even worse if she didn't occasionally check up on it.

She punched the figures into the computer and the cursor blinked a negative response. Angrily, she stabbed at the keyboard again. The spreadsheet came up.

"Shane, Ally doesn't have a clue what she's doing," Nicole said to the dog lying at her feet.

Shane pricked up both tawny ears and seemed to agree. She was glad he was with her because it was a little unnerving to be alone in the shop at this hour. The only thing keeping her awake was the now cold cup of coffee.

Suddenly, the dog bristled and stood up. He released a low growl and started backing away from her desk.

"What? What is it, boy?" Nicole asked, and then she heard someone knocking. Her heart leaped into her throat. Who would be knocking on the door of a closed shop? She was way in the back office with only a dim light on. No one could tell she was here, unless it was the police.

She opened the door of the office and Shane burst out into the salon area, now barking furiously. He stopped at the main entrance, scratching and snarling, prepared to attack. Nicole followed him slowly.

"Who is it? What do you want?" she yelled, trying to raise her voice above Shane's ear-shattering barking. She gripped him by the collar and turned on the outside light.

A tall man was standing there. A man with very dark hair and equally dark, penetrating eyes.

"Julian?" The shock registered on her face.

"Can I come in?" he shouted.

She unlocked the door and held it slightly open so he wouldn't have to yell. With her other hand, she fought to control the dog.

"What in the world are you doing here?"

"I want to talk to you. I was told I could find you here."

"Told? Who told you that?"

"Does it matter? Can't we just talk...please?"

"Yes, it does matter," she said. The shock of seeing him was starting to turn into irritation.

"Okay, okay. I met your sister. She told me. Now can I come in? Unless you're planning on letting your bodyguard have me for supper."

"Considering what time it is, that might not be a bad idea," she said, wondering how Allyson could do this to her. *I'll kill her,* she thought.

Julian was unfazed. "I might add that your sister is a lot friendlier than you are, and she's got a really cute kid."

"The cute kid is mine."

"Does the cute kid come with a father?"

"The cute kid's father is dead," she retorted. She silenced Shane's growling and stepped back, allowing him to enter. At the back of her mind a little voice cried out in protest. *Why are you letting him in?*

"I'm sorry about your...husband," Julian said, entering a bit cautiously, glancing around in the dim light. "What happened to him?"

"I don't care to talk about it," Nicole said.

The nerve of him, she thought, and then she looked at him hard. He was as handsome as ever, in a silvery gray silk shirt, a darker gray tie and black pants, but this was not the same icon she had watched on stage. This was closer to the vulnerable man she'd met in the hospital. His eyes looked tired.

Julian got down on his knees in an attempt to make peace with Shane. He scratched the dog behind the ears while talking to him. Nicole observed, with shock, that he was successful. Her once faithful guardian was now fawning all over the enemy, kissing his face with his tongue.

Julian stood up. "Nice dog."

Nicole folded her arms defensively. This whole scene was pointlessly ridiculous. She had work to do and she didn't want to spend another hour here. "Julian, would you please tell me what you're here to talk about?"

He smiled disarmingly. "I came to ask you why you haven't called me. You did get the note?"

She rolled her eyes. "Yes, I got the note. Oh, thanks for the flowers by the way. The rest of the staff thanks you too."

"Why didn't you call?" he repeated.

"Do you always make a personal appearance to every girl who doesn't call? Or is it that they usually do?"

"They usually do," Julian admitted, without mincing words. He began looking around. "Your sister has a nice place here."

Nicole was frustrated. She turned away, motioned for Shane, and started for the back office again. If he wanted to hang out here that was his business. It had occurred to her that he might be slightly inebriated. Famous people were known for their vices.

Julian followed her. "How about if I take you to this little place downtown. It's open all night…"

It's after midnight," she interrupted him. "And I think you've had enough to drink."

She sat back at the desk and fixed her eyes on the computer screen. Julian paced around and then came close to her.

"I did have a few drinks, but I'm not drunk. Just got back from Brazil on business, then there was this party I absolutely had to appear at. All this traveling and the different time zones can be tiring. I…"

"Poor baby," she murmured aloud, toying with the keyboard. She really had no clue what she was doing, but she didn't want him to realize it.

He stood so close that she could smell his cologne. She took a deep breath. He smelled sinfully intoxicating. Was this really happening? Or was she so tired that she was having delusions?

Mercifully, Julian stepped back and wandered down the hall, opening the door to the room where there was a couch and a television. He turned left and glanced in the bathroom.

"Nice set-up. It's even got a shower," he commented. "Mind if I use it?"

Nicole didn't know whether to laugh or scream. She didn't look at him. "Why don't you go back to your palace and take a shower?"

"That would be pointless. I have no one to annoy there."

She pushed back a stray lock of hair. "You poor thing…all alone in a glass palace."

"I'm not alone. My sister and her family live there."

"Really? Not quite what I would expect from a superstar and swinging single."

"You don't know me, Nicole, you just think you do."

"True," she admitted. "I don't."

His eyes twinkled. "I'm giving you the opportunity."

"Julian, I'm trying to add these figures, and you're distracting me."

"Well, excuse the hell outa me." He vanished into the bathroom.

She gave a sigh of relief. How could she of all people, find herself alone in an empty salon with Julian Marquez taking a shower? A shower? She heard water running full force. *The man is nuts.* She knew that a lot of famous people were eccentric, but this was bizarre. He had shown up out of the blue, babbled a few pointless words, and then ended up in the shower. She didn't really know what she was supposed to do next because he was too unpredictable.

Nicole leaned back in the chair and closed her eyes. She could virtually feel the steam in the room, see the cascades of water running down his lean, sinewy frame, feel his strong, wet hands on her shoulders as he pulled her into the swirling mist.

The door opened and she nearly choked on her coffee as he stepped out naked, except for a towel tucked loosely around his waist. Short spirals of wet black hair clung to his forehead; his midnight eyes shimmered, along with the gleaming muscles on the exposed parts of his body. And what a body! Broad chest, flat, well-toned mid-section, and narrow hips.

Her mouth opened, closed, and issued forth no words. He gazed at her nonchalantly, as if it were the most natural scene in the world. "I'm gonna crash on the couch for a few minutes, wake me when you get ready to leave."

The words still did not come as she watched him vanish into the tiny lounge room and close the door. She slapped her palms against her face and screamed inwardly. What should she do? What should she say? It was even more apparent that the man was insane, drunk, or both. But who was really crazy? She couldn't deny that she was both offended and charmed by his behavior.

She glanced hopelessly back down at the computer. It had frozen into a loop, not moving.

"I hate you!" she shouted, and gave it a hard whack.

The screen went completely black except for the leering cursor. It was time to go. She stood up and cautiously approached the door of the room into which Julian had vanished. She could not will herself to open it. Turning, she nearly tripped over Shane and went into the bathroom.

His clothes were hanging neatly on the towel rack. Impulsively, she yanked them off and returned to the office where she balled up his Armani...Versace, whatever, and crammed it all into a paper bag.

"Let's go, Shane," she said, glancing once more at the closed door.

She locked up the shop, seized the bag with Julian's clothes, and left with the dog trotting beside her. She passed his silver Lexus parked near her car. *I'm being cruel,* she thought to herself, *but I don't care.* She tossed his clothes into her trunk.

"Now greet the morning in your birthday suit, Romeo," she declared aloud, while Shane panted his agreement.

HAVANA SUNRISE

A sliver of sunlight pierced the tiny window. Julian came awake with a start. For a couple of seconds he had been dreaming he was lying next to a certain slender green-eyed, mocha-skinned beauty. Then it all came rushing back. Feeling foolish, he got up and looked at his watch. It was almost seven o'clock in the morning. Alarmed, he flung open the door. Why hadn't she wakened him?

"Nicole!" he shouted, but there was only silence.

The towel he was wearing dropped to the floor. Quickly, he tied it back on and stumbled out, vaguely remembering where the bathroom was. It was clear that Nicole had abandoned him, and since this was a place of business, he probably didn't have much time to get out before people started coming in.

There was only a lone towel hanging on the rack in the bathroom. Where were his clothes? He looked all around…nothing. He went into the office and searched everywhere, under the desk, in the drawers…nothing. A wave of embarrassment washed over him. She had gotten him really good.

Think, man, think. His mind raced. Fumbling with the main entrance door, he scanned the street. A few cars were passing, but there were no people walking. He would have to move now. Barefoot, wearing only a towel, the great Julian Marquez rushed to his car.

"Yes!" he declared triumphantly as he reached for his key, but his hand touched the terrycloth of the towel, and he remembered the key was in the pocket of his missing pants.

Nicole had won.

CHAPTER SEVEN

Maria was off duty that evening, and her replacement was Nurse Ann Robinson, a rather obese sixty-year-old veteran who normally worked the day shift. Nicole was escorting an elderly patient back to her room when Ann waddled up, her shoes making swishing sounds on the linoleum floor.

"Nicole, when you're through, there's a handsome young man who wants to see you. I told him to wait in the solarium."

"Uh oh," Nicole gulped. She knew who that handsome young man was. "Thanks, Ann."

In the morning, she'd had Allyson both mortified and rolling on the floor laughing when she'd related what she'd done with Julian's clothes. Now that she was about to face him, it didn't seem so hilarious. But the truth was she'd had no recourse except to defend herself. He deserved what had happened. She approached the room.

Julian had slipped anonymously into the hospital with nobody recognizing him. It sometimes worked out, especially at night or very early in the morning, because fans did not expect to see him moving around in ordinary places without an entourage.

He was standing in the sitting room, staring out at the panoramic view of the city from the large bay windows, when he heard her quiet footsteps approaching. He turned to face her with a sardonic smile etched on his face.

"Well, if it isn't my favorite nurse. You really got me last night."

Nicole leaned in the doorway, folding her arms, faking the self-confidence she didn't feel. "You were such easy bait," she said. "I suppose you're here for your clothes."

"Please don't tell me you threw them out. My car keys were in the pants pocket."

Ouch! She hadn't realized that. Horror upon horrors, she giggled, and then caught herself. "Well, I have a few minutes. Let's go outside. They're in the trunk of my car."

"That's not the main reason I'm here," he said, regarding her closely.

"Oh?" She looked at him quizzically, noting that he was wearing a black pullover sweater and khakis, like any ordinary man.

"First, I'm not apologizing for showing up last night, but I am sorry for the way I acted. I was totally...totally out of it."

Nicole wanted to ask him why he'd been so out of it, but nervousness was making her impatient, and the less said, the better. There was no reason not to forgive though. "I guess we're even," she said, glancing at her watch. "I really don't have much time. Let's go to the car."

He started to say something else, but she was already moving, so he followed her out to the parking garage. She unlocked the trunk, pulled out the bag, and handed it to him.

"I'm afraid everything's in a thousand wrinkles," she said.

"Doesn't matter. Before you go rushing off back to work, I want to ask to see you tomorrow." He held up his hand upon observing her expression. "I mean at a reasonable time. No games. I promise. I'm too old for games."

Instincts told her to decline, but he was very appealing in his sincerity. "I accept," she said softly. "But only if I get to name the time and place."

He smiled. "Whatever you want."

"I still have your number, so I'll call you later tonight."

"I'll hold you to that," Julian said. "And I want the call to come from you, not your sister."

She laughed. "It will come from me."

He walked back with her to the main entrance and held the door open. She stepped inside, and he walked away. Impulsively, she turned to watch him go. Even his walk was impressive, like that of a determined panther stalking his prey—enthralling to watch, unless she was the prey.

Early next morning, Nicole pulled her car into the lot outside the mall. She entered the building through Wellington Bookstore, and started to browse the shelves. There was a tiny café located within the store, where she planned to meet Julian in ten minutes. It was a far cry from where he had suggested taking her, but she liked having the advantage of keeping him within her territory. He seemed less threatening that way.

She had come right after driving Trey to school and was feeling stressed. Her son had not been in the best of moods and had put up some resistance, indicating he did not want to go. She had wheedled and cajoled, until finally he gave in. But as he got out of the car, he'd turned to look at her with an expression that was a cross between bitter disappointment and anger.

It would almost be a relief if Julian did not show up. There was the possibility he wouldn't. After all, why would a star want to have coffee in a bookstore café? Wasn't he worried about being harassed by fans?

Shoving Julian to the back of her mind, she gravitated toward the education section and selected a book on home schooling children. It seemed that more and more people were choosing that option lately and she wondered if maybe that might be a solution for Trey. The more she read, the more engrossed she became. If home schooling were possible, she could still keep her present job and devote the hours during the day to her son. There were a lot of state qualifications to be met, but she did have a college degree and both her parents had been teachers.

A shadow fell over her, and Nicole turned with a start to see Julian standing behind her.

"Hey," he said. "Did you think I wasn't gonna show up?"

"It did enter my mind." She started to replace the book, but he picked it up.

"A parent's guide to home schooling," he said, reading the title. "Got something against public education?"

"As a matter of fact I do, but my son is in a private school." She took the book away from him and put it back on the shelf.

"Your son? Oh yes, the kid I saw the other night. How old is he?"

"He's six," she said, not hiding her irritation. How could he have forgotten being told about Trey? It also reminded her that she'd never asked Allyson what Trey was doing up way past his bedtime on that stupid night.

"He looks like you," Julian said, drinking her in with his eyes. "It's good to see you without the uniform."

She couldn't think of anything to say to that, but she was aware he was looking at her with an expression that was nothing short of intense. It made her feel self-conscious, as though a button had suddenly come undone on her pink blouse. She wondered if the jeans she wore were too tight, because they felt like they were melting under his gaze.

"Let's go for coffee." She knew she would have to take charge of the situation or it would get completely out of control. Already she was getting lost in his hypnotic eyes, and a few people passing by seemed to be staring at them. She hoped she was imagining that.

They climbed the stairs to the café. Julian pulled out a chair for her and asked what she wanted. When he went to the counter to order, Nicole noticed the cashier give him a double take. Hopefully the girl would conclude that he just *looked* like the famous singer. It felt very weird to be a part of this scene. Julian was obviously a man who was used to being waited on and here he was in a little self-serve café.

"Are you sure that's all you want?" Julian asked, setting the cappuccino in front of her.

"Yes, I'm sure, thanks," she murmured, stirring distractedly at the hot beverage, noting that he had chosen black coffee. She was also noting his skin-tight aqua T-shirt.

"Do you always drink coffee plain?" she asked in an attempt to break the awkward silence.

"Yeah. It's usually the Cuban variety though. Have you ever had Cuban coffee?"

"No, can't say that I have."

"Next time," he said.

There would be a next time? She had never been so tongue-tied in her life, because she did not know what they were supposed to be talking about. Gazing at him, she could tell that he was not the least bit bothered by the silence. It was as if they both had all day to sit there.

Julian did not find the setting uncomfortable. He liked being in a casual, unpretentious place, looking at a woman who was beautiful, not because she was wearing the latest designer clothes, not because she'd had her makeup done at some chic salon, but because her reddish-brown hair was long and thick, restrained only by a simple barrette, and her lips were not flaming red, but delicately pink, with just a touch of gloss. He also knew she had more on her mind than self-gratification.

Perhaps a bit of humor was needed. Humor at his expense, Nicole thought. "Julian, I'm dying to know what exactly did you do that night when I left you at the shop?"

A slow burning smile crept over his face. "Oh, it was one of those truly great moments. I realized that I had to get out of there before someone came to open the shop. I checked outside to see if anyone was looking and then I sprinted for the car. About that time I realized my keys were missing.

She laughed. "Continue."

"Well, there really isn't much else. I called a friend and he came and picked me up."

"Did anyone observe this?"

"Probably, but at least it was early, not too many people out."

He *didn't* tell her that he'd rushed back to the shop to make the phone call, only to find that the door had automatically locked, leaving him with no recourse except to beg a passerby on the street for money in order to use a public phone. Hopefully the observers had not known who he was.

Nicole was even more puzzled by him. She had expected that they would spend their few minutes together talking about his career. Most famous people loved to talk about themselves. She had been prepared to just sit, nod her head, and look awed at the appropriate time, but it appeared that he was forcing her to ask.

"You must lead a very exciting life," she said

Julian shrugged. "I get to travel a lot, meet fascinating people. It's not really all glamour though. Sometimes it's just plain tiring. I've been on tour since spring."

"Are you on a break from touring now?"

"The tour is over for this year, thank God, but I still have some promotion stuff to do. I'll be in the studio working on my new CD. Next year I'll be touring to promote that one."

"What's your new CD going to be like?"

"It's supposed to be a big one. Up until now, I've only recorded in Spanish. The record company wants me to do a crossover in English this time."

He would definitely be a success in English, she thought. "I'm sure that won't be a problem for you," she said. "I...I was at your concert and it was really great. You have a terrific voice."

His eyes narrowed. "Oh? Is that why you walked out in the middle of my song?"

He seemed to have the advantage now. She'd slipped up and given him an opening. "It was a beautiful song, but it reminded me of something that...that happened in my past and...I know it's silly, but I just couldn't..."

"I understand," he said. "That song has a personal meaning to me too."

She wanted to quickly ask him what the song meant to him, so she wouldn't have to explain herself anymore, but she wasn't fast enough.

"You did tell me that your son's father died. Does it have something to do with that?"

"Yes." She could not lie. "My husband was a cop. He was murdered right in front of our son." And the torrent was unleashed. Julian remained absolutely silent as she related the whole story, hardly pausing, hardly even breathing. When she stopped talking, she only hoped that she had made some sense.

"Life can be really cruel sometimes," Julian said slowly. "I'm very sorry about what happened to you and Trey."

Nicole sat up straighter and pushed her cup away. Bitterness started to creep in. She was angry at herself for having revealed so much. So what if he was sorry? What did he care about her problems?

"It's been three years," Nicole said, ready to leave. "Life goes on."

Julian took a deep breath. "Yeah, life does go on all right, but the past makes us who we are. We don't really forget. We *never* forget."

We? She drifted out of her own head and looked directly into his eyes. They looked haunted, as if he were reflecting not only on her pain, but his own as well. She started to question him, but again he spoke first.

"So what're they saying about Trey? Will he talk again?"

She told him about the endless therapy sessions, the heartless teachers in the public school, and the fact that he was now in a school for the handicapped.

"I'd like to see you again," Julian said. "And I'd like to meet Trey."

"Oh, no, I don't think so. Trey's kind of shy,"

"That's okay. I like kids. Besides, how's he going to get over his problem by avoiding people?"

That wasn't really what she meant. She did not consider Julian to be like regular people, and she had assumed that this would be their last meeting. She did not want her son involved in this game.

"How about Saturday…you, me, and Trey," Julian offered. "We'll go skating early in the morning. I know this great diner where we can have breakfast. It's real kid-friendly. He'll enjoy it."

She couldn't believe what he was saying. She laughed. "You mean you want to hang out with a six year old?"

"Sure. He's probably better company than some of the adults I usually hang with. This Saturday, before seven, I'll pick you up."

"Okay, sounds like it could be fun," she murmured, wondering who this woman was who had agreed to such a thing.

"I thought you looked beautiful doing your nurse thing, but you're even more beautiful now," Julian said.

"Thank you," she said, blushing.

Out of the corner of her eye, Nicole noticed the cashier whispering to a co-worker, and then they were both looking at Julian.

"Uh oh, I think your cover has been blown," Nicole said.

They both rose simultaneously and went down the stairs. Julian felt slightly irritated by the intrusion, but maybe it had come at the right time. He wanted to spend the rest of the morning with her, but he realized that Nicole had revealed a lot, making herself vulnerable and if he pushed harder she might retreat.

"See you Saturday," she said, approaching the bookstore's exit.

"Don't forget your skates," he said.

CHAPTER EIGHT

Later that day, as Julian wandered through the studio, he reflected on how rapidly their musical enterprise had grown. It was jointly owned by Luis and himself, and was housed in a large office complex. Already it had become the studio of choice for a lot of popular recording artists. Luis was starting to get involved with the management of other artists, and in the future, Julian intended to get more involved with the business side too. If he could help it, he did not want to be a performer for the rest of his life.

He glanced into his manager's office, but Luis was not there. He went inside and scanned the desk to see if he'd left a certain demo tape on it. It was nowhere in sight. Luis probably had it with him. As he turned to leave, he heard the distinctive sound of footsteps, footsteps in high heels rapidly approaching. He groaned.

"I have been looking all over for you," Elena said, entering. "Where is Luis?"

"Somewhere in the building I guess," Julian said.

She's trying too hard to disguise the fact that she's forty-nine, he thought. Her harsh makeup and bleached hair actually made her look older. Her hair had been permed so much that it had lost all luster and was as dry as hay, but no one could tell Elena anything. It always had to be the other way around.

"I have something to talk to you about," she said, and slapped a magazine down on the desk.

"A tabloid?" Julian said. "Thought you didn't read this stuff."

She ignored him. "Turn to page three."

Frowning, he turned the page to stare at a big picture of himself standing at an open phone booth, wearing a towel. The caption under the picture read, "What's it all about, Julian?"

"Would you care to explain this lunacy?" Elena demanded.

"Well, let's see." He rubbed the side of his face. "I was taking a shower and then I decided I had to make a phone call."

"I don't think that's very funny. Maybe your simple-minded girl-friends find it cute, but I've told you over and over again about this kind of behavior. You…"

Julian shoved the tabloid aside. "Look, I know it was stupid, but I have no intention of explaining anything. Just let it go, will you? At least I wasn't naked."

"You have a responsibility!" She practically jabbed her pointed finger in his face. "Young people emulate stars like you. I do not want to hear about any scandals in this family." She was in full-blown, self-righteous mode now. "You had better get control of that drinking problem."

"I don't have a drinking problem."

"And just what were you doing in *that* part of town anyway?" she continued.

He tossed the magazine into the trash. "Maybe it's because I'm *that* kind of person."

"Oh, don't start on me with that crap. We've had this conversation before, only you were much younger. You've become the success you are by not hanging around with…with minorities. *They* are not your audience. There is no reason for you to capitalize on the fact that your father was black. The Cuban community and other Hispanics have supported you."

Julian struggled to contain the anger he felt. "The Cuban community and *others* are not blind. Maybe I don't completely look it, but most people know that I am also black."

"Oh, so you want to get in touch with your distant roots, do you? Are you planning to do rap music on your next CD?"

He had to laugh. He did listen to hip-hop occasionally, but for him to do a rap recording would be nothing short of a joke. "You're such a bigot, Elena."

"That's a lie and you know it! This is about business."

"Yes, it's *always* about business. I am not going to argue with you, but this is my life and no one is going to dictate to me who my friends should or shouldn't be, or tell me what part of town to avoid."

"I am not trying to run your life. All the things I've told you have always been for your own good. You should realize by now that things go smoothly when you listen to sound advice. You always wind up in trouble when you start getting strange ideas."

The best way to deal with her is just to shut her out. She will continue to think the way she always does no matter what say I say, he thought.

Elena took his silence as an indication that he agreed with her.

"Remember it's for your own good," she reiterated.

Julian walked past her and left the room.

The stars were twinkling in the velvety night sky and the light from the crescent moon reflected on the rippling waves. Julian sat on the dock at the end of his property, closed his eyes and remembered.

"How many fish are in the sea, Papi?"

"Oh…billions and billions. You could never count them, son."

"You mean like the stars? I can't count them either."

"Yes, like the stars."

"Papi?"

"Yes, Julian."

"Why is Mama so sad?"

"She sees things differently from other people, and when things do not go the way she wishes, it makes her sad."

"Why can't things be like the way she wishes?"

"Ahhh, you are so young. You have many questions."

"Why, Papi?"

"You will understand when you grow up, but you will grow up in Miami, not here."

"Are you coming to Miami with me, Papi?"

HAVANA SUNRISE

"Yes, son. I'm coming."

Julian opened his eyes and realized they had gotten misty. He had come a long way since Cuba, but the images and his father's voice were so real. He definitely did not miss the place, but he did miss the feeling of having once been loved and cared for.

It hurt that he could not remember his father Enrique's face. He did remember a tall, solid man with large brown hands and a gentle voice. He remembered Enrique's hands on his own smaller ones, teaching him how to play the guitar, showing him how to throw a baseball, drying his tears. He could remember the essence of the man who had loved and cherished him for seven short years, but without having any pictures, he could not visualize his face.

He could still smell the aromatic scents coming from his Aunt Alma's tiny kitchen, and he could picture her face with its chocolate-colored skin, honey-brown eyes, and the way her long, thick-textured hair framed it. Once he had believed that she was really his mother because she'd always called him her baby and she was always buying him things and giving him hugs and kisses.

He had never hugged his real mother. His memories of Felicia were of a pale, sickly woman who had always been in bed every time he had been taken to see her. The visits had been few, because his father was not married to his mother and she was unable to take care of him. She was legally married to Elena's father, Jorge Diaz, an abusive man who hated Enrique and had threatened to harm Julian when he was a baby, which was why he lived with his father and his aunt.

Felicia had been separated from Jorge for three years at the time she'd fallen in love with Enrique. They'd met when she'd been a patient in the hospital for the emotionally ill, where he worked as an assistant pharmacist. Enrique's being a descendant of African slaves, and Felicia's being a mix of white and Hispanic, had not been an issue in general society, but her estranged husband had detested the relationship out of jealousy, even though he lived elsewhere with another woman.

Julian remembered how his father had grown tired of Cuba's communist policies and because he could not outright oppose the government, had taken to writing and performing poetic protest songs. People would gather to listen to him in the public square, until the government became incensed and eventually put an end to his activity.

Enrique and his sister Alma applied to get out of the country legally with Julian, but Enrique's request was turned down. Alma was allowed to leave and join her husband, who was already living in the United States. Although Enrique requested that she take Julian with her, Felicia refused to go along with the plan. She could not raise her own child, but she wanted him to stay in Cuba near her. Alma departed tearfully, and Julian remained with his father, who was still trying to find a way for them to leave.

When Julian was six, his father was falsely accused of stealing drugs from the hospital pharmacy and selling them. He was sent to prison. Julian was returned to his mother, who still could not take care of him, so the job fell to Elena who was already burdened with caring for their mother. She was a strict disciplinarian and harshly critical of him, but she did what she had to do, and she protected him from her own father, whom she herself hated.

A month later his father died in prison. They were told he'd had a heart attack. Shortly after that, his emotionally fragile mother committed suicide.

"Julian, listen to me. You, me, and my boyfriend Luis, are going to America tonight," Elena had told him about three months after his mother's death.

"Are we going on a boat?"

"Yes. You can take only one thing with you, and it can't be anything big. Now hurry."

He remembered being upset about not being able to take his toys, but the one thing he had grabbed was his father's guitar. Elena had told him no, that it was too big, but he had become hysterical and Luis had consented. For some strange reason, he hardly remembered the illegal crossing in a rickety fishing boat, but he remembered the hard feel of the guitar pressed up against his chest.

"Are you coming with me to Miami, Papi?"

"Yes, son. I'm coming."

The humid night air was starting to suffocate him. Julian stood up and began walking back to the house. He felt ashamed that he had allowed Elena to change his name from Sanchez to Marquez when he'd first become famous. Even then, she'd been trying to erase the memory of his father, and although he'd casually acquiesced, the memories lingered on like a ghost image burned into the visual screen of his brain.

It had been a while since he'd had such vivid recollections of the past, and he was intensely aware that they had not started until the very first day he had gazed into Nicole's green eyes. He did not completely understand why she had this effect on him, and he was not sure he even liked it, but there was something deep in his heart and soul that compelled him to pursue her. Maybe if he could find real love among the people of his lost culture, he would start to remember what his father's face looked like.

She could still cancel the date. Nicole was on a break, sitting at the front desk, staring into space. Hours after meeting with Julian, she was even more annoyed with herself for telling him so much. She had blabbered away her private life story, and he had revealed nothing about himself at all—nothing that the whole world didn't already know. There was no reason for him to meet Trey. What could a millionaire performer have in common with a little boy who could not talk?

"Nicole...Earth to Nicole...*Hello.*"

She jumped with a start to see Maria standing over her. "Maria! Are you trying to give me a heart attack?"

"Maybe. I think you need something to wake you up. I was telling you about the patient in 407."

"Oh, sorry. What about him?"

Maria sat near her. "Never mind him. What's wrong with you? You've hardly said anything all night."

"Nothing's wrong. I was just thinking about someone."

"Ooooh, a new love?"

"Well, I'm not sure he's a love yet, but he's getting to me."

"What's his name?"

"Julian Marquez."

"Whaaat! You mean it's true? You're actually seeing Julian?"

Nicole sighed. "I have a date with him on Saturday, just a fun thing. He wants to meet Trey."

"Oh my God. This is serious. Julian wants to meet your family. What's your secret, Nikki?" Maria paused to come up for air. "You are serious, no? You're not just kidding with me, are you?"

"Nope. This is no joke. The scary part is, I wish I were joking."

"You're something else," Maria said. "You've been down here three years and if you've ever dated anyone, I never knew about it. When you finally do, it's Julian Marquez."

"Life can be bizarre," Nicole said, rising. "I'm going to check on 407 now. Oh, and Maria, please don't tell everybody about this. I'm sure Saturday will be the last date with him anyway."

"If that's true, I think you're crazy, but my lips are sealed."

The whole hospital will know about it in thirty minutes, give or take, Nicole thought as she walked down the hall.

CHAPTER NINE

"Man, would you look at this guy?" Julian said to Trey, gently turning the little boy around so he could inspect Trey's wild tropical print shirt and baggy khaki shorts with cargo pockets. "You make me look like a real nerd. I bet you're tough too."

Trey bit his lip shyly, and then offered Julian a watery smile.

"He is tough," Nicole said, encouraging the byplay. "The other day I couldn't get the lid off something, but he was able to do it."

"Bet you can do lots of things," Julian said to Trey. His eyes twinkled as he looked at Nicole. "It was one of those child-proof bottles, wasn't it?"

She laughed. "As a matter of fact, I believe it was."

"Amanda gets me with that one all the time."

"Amanda?" she questioned.

"That's my niece. She's not much older than Trey." He turned his attention back to the boy. "Let's see those muscles."

Shifting from one foot to the other, Trey shoved up his sleeve so Julian could inspect. Nicole laughed as Julian looked truly amazed.

"I'm scared now," Julian said. "I'll try to be on my best behavior, so you won't have to take me out."

Trey giggled. *He's good with kids,* Nicole thought. It normally took Trey a lot longer to warm up to strangers. Julian opened the door and lifted Trey up into his shiny, silver Explorer.

"What? No Lincoln Navigator?" Nicole teased.

"I left that at home with my Rolls and my private jet," he said, helping Trey buckle the seat belt.

Nicole wasn't sure if he was joking or not. Looking up, she noticed the curtain part a little inside their apartment. She smiled to herself. Allyson was snooping. Nicole felt as if the whole world were watching her, but that was silly and paranoid. The sun had not even risen yet and most people were still in bed.

Wearing jeans and carrying a canvas bag containing Trey's skates and hers, she climbed into the front passenger seat of the Explorer, next to Julian.

"Are you a good skater, Trey?" Julian asked.

Trey nodded confidently. Nicole resisted the urge to correct him. Trey was not a good skater and she was only adequate herself. Allyson was the skating enthusiast in the family. She would have to mention that fact later.

Once Trey got over his brief indignation at having to wear a helmet and kneepads, they hit South Beach, flying, sailing past the closed shops, the alfresco restaurants and the historic rows of art deco hotels. Julian made skating an art form, and even with Trey holding on to his hand, Nicole had to struggle to keep up with them.

Julian suddenly swooped Trey up so he was perched on his shoulders, a move that almost caused her to protest, because it could be dangerous, but the little boy was smiling so broadly that she didn't have the heart to say no. He extended his arms like an airplane and pretended to soar high above the ground.

They left the main street and skated as a trio, with Trey in between them on a path that ran parallel to the ocean. Finally, they came to a stop and collapsed on a bench. Trey tugged eagerly at Julian.

"Trey, please. No more. I have to rest," Nicole gasped.

"Yeah, sport, your mom is too old to keep up with us," Julian said, and then noticed Nicole glaring at him. "I mean, your mom and I are too old to keep up," he corrected.

"That's better," she said.

By the time they resumed skating, the sun had risen in all its ferocity and they headed for a little diner with a Spanish name. Nicole was relieved that they would be able to sit down.

"This is a Cuban diner," Julian said. "But don't worry, they serve American food too.

"Uh, Julian. Our shoes are in the car," she reminded him.

"No problem. We can just take the skates off inside."

"Eat in our socks? Won't that be a little odd?"

He laughed. "You worry too much. I know the owner, and the place isn't officially open to the rest of the public until seven-thirty."

The air conditioning felt like heaven in the charmingly old-fashioned place with red vinyl booths. She and Trey sat side-by-side, while Julian conversed in Spanish with a short, heavy-set man wearing an apron. The owner seemed overjoyed to see him. Julian returned to the booth and sat opposite them. Observing this, Trey scrambled over her and sat next to Julian.

Little traitor, she thought, amused. They had known each other for only an hour, and her shy, silent child couldn't get close enough. He was, in fact, squirming about, poking playfully at Julian, who in turn, kept tickling him.

"Julian, where are the menus?" she asked.

"Don't need them. I ordered already."

She gulped. Trey was extremely picky, and she wasn't really in the mood for trying anything exotic herself, not so early in the morning anyway. The food arrived, Trey's favorite, pancakes.

"How did you know?" she asked in surprise.

"Trey told me," Julian said, with a sly smile.

Trey imitated his smile, and there was nothing for her to do but laugh, and wonder about the weird chemistry transpiring between them. They all had pancakes and chocolate milk.

"When I waddle out of here looking like a hog, I'll know who to blame," she said to Julian.

He laughed. "A few pounds wouldn't hurt you at all." He insisted she try Cuban coffee, which was served in a little tiny cup. "Go on, try it."

She took a sip. It was the strongest concoction she'd ever tasted. He was amused by her reaction.

"Now I know why this stuff is served in small cups," she said.

"I used to work in this diner when I was a kid," Julian said. "That's how I know Rafael, the owner."

"Really? That's so…so ironic. What did you do?"

"Washed dishes and bussed tables," he said.

It boggled her mind to think of Julian Marquez doing dishes and cleaning up tables, but beneath his public veneer, she was seeing a lot of humility. How many big stars would return to some little tiny diner where they'd once been employed, and still be friendly with the owner?

"I'm really nothing but a hometown boy in this neighborhood," Julian said. "I like it that way."

"You're amazing," she said, and meant it. Nicole leaned back against the cool vinyl of the booth. She stretched out her legs and her feet brushed against his under the table. Something akin to an electrical jolt pulsed through her, causing her heart to beat faster. Julian, though, toyed with his coffee and seemed unaware of the contact.

She loved his long eyelashes and the precision cut of his sideburns. She liked the way the white of his T-shirt set off his tan skin, and she even liked watching him eat. Unconsciously, she allowed her wandering foot to slide lightly over the curve of his ankle.

Trey had finished his portion and some of hers. He was now using his straw to enthusiastically blow bubbles in his chocolate milk. The bubbles were threatening to spill over the edge of the glass, and before she could reprimand him, he impulsively lifted the straw out and blew a stream of milk right into Julian's face.

"Trey!" she shouted, appalled by her child's behavior. "Julian, I…"

She stopped short, because Julian was laughing. He plunged a straw into his glass and shot it back at Trey, who gleefully armed himself again. An artillery of milk shot back and forth between them.

"Stop it! Both of you!" Nicole yelled, simultaneously charmed and shocked by such childishness. "This is ridic—"

Before she could even finish the word, the weapons launched chocolate milk at her; she ducked, throwing up her arms, as milk splashed over them. She laughed and screamed for mercy. It was as if they had all gone completely insane.

"Look at the mess you all made," Nicole spluttered when the nonsense had ceased.

HAVANA SUNRISE

"No problem," Julian said, cheerfully wiping milk off the back of the seat. Rafael knows I'm crazy."

They all joined in cleaning up. Afterward, they reclaimed their wheels and skated back to the car a few blocks away. While Nicole and Julian were putting their shoes back on, Trey started to skate away from the car. Julian caught him and rolled him back.

"C'mon, Trey. Stop it," Nicole scolded. "We've had a good time but now we have to go home."

"It doesn't have to end yet," Julian said, his eyes intently on her. "You can come to my place for a while."

Nicole fell silent for a moment. What was wrong with that request? Trey was with them. Nothing was going to happen on his territory with a child between them. Besides, she was secretly dying to see where he lived.

Trey looked at her pleadingly, and that did it. She caved in. "Okay, just for a little while."

Trey's smile blazed. He hugged her, and she wrapped her arms around his sturdy little body, and then removed his helmet and skates. Eagerly he bounded into the car.

They were in for a surprise. Julian drove to a marina, and they got out on a pier where many boats were docked.

"I could cross over the private bridge to the island, but I think Trey would like the boat ride better," he said.

"What?" She stared at his sleek, blue and white cigarette style speedboat awaiting them. Aha! The real Julian had surfaced. Trey's eyes were wide. He was in his glory.

"I don't know," she balked. "We've never been on a speedboat before. I don't think…"

"There's a first time for everything," Julian said. "It's nothing, just a fast car on the water."

He leaped down into the boat, and Trey jumped down into his arms. He held out a hand to her. Reluctantly she took it, and joined them. The brilliance of the white leather interior dazzled her eyes, but her attention was on Trey as Julian outfitted him with an over-sized life jacket.

The wind whipped at her hair as the engine roared and the boat skimmed the water, plunging and rising, creating the sensation of a roller coaster. They were going way too fast for her comfort, but not for Trey, who was at the helm with Julian, convinced that he was helping navigate. She opened her mouth to protest, but the wind literally sucked her breath away.

As they approached a private dock, she could see a thin strip of beach and rolling stretches of emerald green grass. Beyond that was a towering villa-like estate. The tourist in her made her wish she had a camera, because Allyson would have loved to see this home.

With Trey's help, Julian tied the boat up, and they crossed the beach and went up a flight of stone steps.

"This is all our property," Julian said.

"The beach too?"

"This section of it anyway."

They passed through a lush park-like tropical garden before they reached the sprawling Spanish-Mediterranean estate. "I live on this side," Julian said, leading the way up the granite stairs. "My sister, brother-in-law, and the kids live on the other."

"Kids?" Nicole was trying to restore the wreckage of her hair. "How many does your sister have besides Amanda?"

"Two boys. They're big though. One's in college and the other is seventeen."

As he opened the door, a very tall, large-boned woman in a maid's uniform stepped out. Julian acknowledged her with a casual nod. Nicole smiled and said, "Good afternoon."

The woman looked at her with a dour expression, twisting her mouth into a mockery of a smile, and continued on her way to attend to other business.

"Pleasant," Nicole said.

Julian laughed. "Pay her no mind. Gretchen's been here for years. She's a good worker, but she's got her quirks."

The interior of the home was what Nicole expected, but she was still awed by it. Standing in the foyer, she noted that the floors were a light-colored, glistening marble and the ceilings were high and vaulted. The area was filled with light and mirrors. Her eyes fell upon an end table with stacks of unopened mail.

"What's with all this mail?" she asked.

"It's mostly from fans."

"Do you actually read all this?"

"Some of it. It's supposed to go to the fan club's post office box, but a lot of the people know my home address…" He paused to acknowledge Trey, who was tugging at his arm. "Come on, I'll show you guys where the bathroom is."

"Mind if I look at one of these letters?" Nicole asked as he started down the hall.

"Help yourself."

A large purple envelope among all the white ones caught her attention. She selected that one and opened it as she trailed Julian down the hall. At first she thought it was a child's drawing, but she gasped when she realized that on the piece of notebook paper was a lewd cartoon depiction of someone meant to resemble Julian doing something unspeakable with another man.

He glanced over his shoulder as Trey shot in the bathroom. "What? What's wrong?"

"This." She thrust the paper at him.

Julian looked at it and smirked. "Of all the letters, you *would* pick that one."

"It was in a purple envelope."

Julian ripped the drawing up and threw it in the trash. "That's just some loony. Every now and then I get those."

"Doesn't it…well…isn't that kind of scary?"

He shrugged. "It happens when you're in the limelight. That wacko has been writing me for years. When he first started, he was giving me advice, telling me who I should date, what kind of music I should sing, and stuff like that. I've never answered any of his letters, but he just keeps sending them. Through the years they've gotten more bizarre."

"Isn't that kind of like stalking? You should tell someone. Stalking is a crime."

"Actually I don't even think about it. I don't consider it stalking," he said. "If I got upset over every psycho who sent me stuff, I couldn't stay in the business." He placed both hands lightly on her shoulders and looked into her eyes. "You really do worry too much."

"It seems to go with my territory," she said.

"Your turn," Julian said, as Trey popped out of the bathroom. "When you come out I'll give you a little tour around."

"Trey," she started.

"There you go, worrying again. I'll watch this guy."

His *apartment* had three stories. The ground level had an impressive game room that would enchant any child or childlike adult. Trey had to be dragged out. Also on the ground level was a spectacular indoor pool, a gym, and a small recording studio. The main floor had a library, a mini movie theater, and a gorgeous kitchen and living room.

She stood in that living room, clinging tightly to Trey's hand, and looking around. That space alone could hold her entire condo. The room was a brilliant white, with marble flooring, custom-designed furniture, and built-in ceiling spotlights. Numerous tropical plants gave it an airy, almost Caribbean feeling. It was all so beautiful, but she felt as if she were walking through an expensive hotel instead of a home. She could not help wondering how much of this he could actually enjoy when most of his time was spent on the road.

"The bedrooms and other guest rooms are on the top floor," Julian said.

She nodded, grateful that he didn't offer to take them up there. She was overwhelmed and frankly, exhausted. Her legs ached from all the skating, and she wanted to go home so she could just sit back and savor the moments of the day.

Julian led them out onto the verandah for a spectacular view of the ocean. He was surprised to find his niece sprawled in one of the deck chairs, her nose buried in a book.

"Amanda, what are you doing here?"

She let the book drop. "It's nice and quiet here," she said, with a pleading let-me-stay look in her eyes.

"You're not hiding from your nanny again, are you?"

"Nope. She knows where I am."

"Come over here and meet my friends."

Nicole smiled as the little girl approached. She had long, damp brunette tresses, and big almond-shaped hazel eyes. She was wearing a multi-colored bathing suit.

"Nicole and Trey, this is Amanda," Julian said.

"Hello, Amanda. Have you been swimming?" Nicole asked.

"Uh huh," Amanda replied, without a trace of shyness. "You should see me dive. I'm really good, almost better than Uncle J."

"I'll bet," Julian said with a laugh.

Nicole noticed that Trey had moved behind her, trying to make himself invisible. Julian reached for the reluctant boy's arm and tugged him out front.

"This is Nicole's son, Trey. Trey's not ready to talk yet, in English or in Spanish, but someday he will. When he's ready."

Trey squirmed, wanting desperately to be out of the spotlight, and Nicole was instinctively about to come to his rescue, when Amanda spoke. "That's okay," she said. "Sometimes I don't like to talk either. Do you like horses, Trey?"

Trey nodded, brightening.

"Uncle J, can I show Trey my pony?"

"Yeah, but no riding though."

"We won't. I promise. C'mon, Trey."

"Julian," Nicole objected. "This is Trey's first time here. I don't think he should go wandering off without supervision."

"It's perfectly all right," Julian insisted. The stables are not far from here. Amanda's a great big sister. She'll take care of him."

"We'll just go look at the horses and we'll come right back," Amanda said, pulling a wrap over her swimsuit and shoving her pink-toed feet into sandals.

Nicole reluctantly gave in. "Okay. Trey, make sure you don't get too close to the horses."

He nodded, suddenly eager to be off on an excursion with someone closer to his own age—even if that someone was a girl.

Nicole strolled closer to the railing and looked down at the gardens and a massive lagoon-shaped pool. She looked up at Julian who was standing beside her.

"Your niece is really cute, and so grown up," she said.

"Isn't she? Spoiled rotten too."

She laughed. "I'm sure you're the one spoiling her."

"I do my part."

Nicole took a deep breath and inhaled the rose-scented breeze drifting up from the gardens below. There were things she desperately wanted to know about this paradox of a man who engaged millions with his beautiful voice, had a disturbing reputation as a shallow Casanova, and yet liked to have food fights with children. She also wondered why his niece, or the woman she'd been told was his sister, did not physically resemble him at all.

"You must be very close to your sister, since you all live within this villa."

"Close?" An ironic smile flickered across his face. "We're a family. We do what we have to for each other."

She detected the resignation in his voice even more than the actual words. "You almost sound as if you were adopted."

Julian looked at the sky. "Both my parents died back in Cuba when I was very young. My sister Elena and I had the same mother, but different fathers. My father was black."

That explained a lot of things she thought, but she wondered what his father's being black meant to him.

"Do you remember your father?"

"Yes, a little bit. He was a singer and a poet." His eyes looked even more distant. "Anyway, after my parents died, Elena became my guardian. She was a lot older than me. She and her husband Luis took me with them to this country."

"How was the crossing?"

"We came illegally on a fishing boat. I really don't remember the details."

Nicole shuddered at the thought. Miami was a mecca for both Cuban and Haitian refugees. She recalled a young patient, a Haitian woman, who had nearly drowned when the makeshift boat she and hundreds of others had been on, capsized. The woman had been taken to the hospital with severe dehydration and other problems, only to be returned to Haiti when she was well. The Cuban refugees who survived were usually allowed to stay because their reasons for escape were political.

"How old were you when you came here?" she asked.

"About seven. We started out living in a New York suburb with some of Luis' relatives. I was in this school...couldn't speak a word of English. I was laughed at, picked on. You know how kids are."

"Yes. I know that all too well," she said, recalling Trey's dilemmas in the public school.

"Anyway, the relatives got sick of us, and I know they didn't like me, didn't want this little mulatto boy around with their kids or something. Eventually Luis found a job in Florida and we all moved down here," Julian said.

"How were you treated by Elena and Luis?" Nicole asked.

"I was fed and had a roof over my head. Luis was pretty cool, but when I was small, Elena used to beat the crap out of me when I misbehaved. She always had me doing a lot of chores and things. It wasn't *that* bad until she had her two boys. After that I became a babysitter and house servant."

Nicole flinched at the thought and waited, but he did not elaborate. She was conscious of the fact that Julian had moved very close, and that his arm had slid around her waist like an anchor. It did not feel oppressive yet.

"So how did you become famous?"

"Well, I always had this music thing in me. When I was about thirteen, I started hanging with these guys who were a lot older. We formed a band and we would play at clubs and weddings. It was a great escape for me, especially when we started getting a lot of gigs. We were pretty popular locally."

"And Elena allowed that?"

"No. I was a teenager and I was kind of going through a rebellious period. In other words, I was out of control and she really didn't know what to do about it. Anyway, a few years later, Luis got to be manager of a record store, and a lot of popular performers would come around to do promotions, record signings and stuff. He gave one of them a demo tape of mine and he in turn showed it to his producer. They liked the tape and the rest is history."

His arm tightened around her, and she looked into the velvet depths of his eyes. There was still a lot he had not said, but if she used her imagination she could almost see the dark-eyed seven-year-old with no parents in a strange land, being raised begrudgingly by a sister who had her own family and probably resented being saddled with the additional responsibility of a little brother.

She imagined what it must have been like when little brother became the star and the family cash cow. She was sure Julian was paying for everything they had, including the education of his sister's children. That was all very generous, nice and well, but what was Julian getting out of it? He didn't seem very happy. Did they even care?

"You didn't have much of a childhood," she murmured. "That's sad."

"Other people have had it much worse," Julian said. "I'm grateful."

They were so close that their lips melded together in slow motion. Nicole closed her eyes and savored the kiss. She felt herself drifting farther and farther away from the safe shore. She wanted this man. She desired this man. She had never felt such a powerful physical attraction before, not even with Warren—definitely not with Warren.

"Uh…Julian…no." She planted her hand firmly on his chest, and pulled away.

The unjustified comparison to her husband was too much. How could she feel more attracted to a virtual stranger? Julian did not protest, but his eyes were questioning.

"This is silly," she said, looking over the verandah, relieved to spot the returning forms of Trey and Amanda at a distance.

"Silly? It felt pretty natural to me," Julian said.

"That's probably because you've had a lot more experience." She regretted saying that, but it was too late. The words were out.

"Okay," he admitted. "I have been with a lot of women, but I am not experienced with one who is afraid of me."

"Afraid of you? If I were afraid of you, I wouldn't be here alone with you on *your* verandah, separated from the mainland by a bay."

"I don't mean *that* kind of afraid. I mean afraid of intimacy."

No! She did not want to get started on that line of conversation. "Look, I just want to say thanks for a really wonderful day. I've had more fun than I've had in a long time. I especially thank you for being so wonderful to my son. I'm sure he'll always remember this. You really impressed him."

"I was kind of hoping I'd impressed his mother."

She took a deep breath, and then said, softly. "You impressed his mother."

Now let's just leave it at that, she thought desperately. *Please do not ruin a beautiful day by getting all passionate and talking about intimacy.* She did not feel ready to handle that and was not sure she ever would be.

The journey back home was much more subdued, with conversation that was trivial and safe. When she reached her humble condominium, she felt as though she'd returned from a trip to Mars. Trey was fighting exhaustion, and she was relieved that he would be taking a nap, because it would give her a chance to reflect and unwind.

As soon as Trey had vanished inside, a painful silence took over. She gazed into Julian's eyes, knowing she wanted to say more, and knowing he felt the same way. Instead, she simply thanked him again for the day, and turned to go.

"Don't forget. You still have my number," he said, aware that his voice sounded hollow.

Julian backed the Explorer up and as he was leaving the parking lot, he could see Nicole in the rear view mirror, still watching. She looked hauntingly vulnerable and so refreshingly beautiful. He gripped the steering wheel hard. It was all he could do to keep from turning the car around and running back to her. He wanted to grab her, despite her feeble objections, and convince her to stay in his world.

CHAPTER TEN

"It's been a week. When are you going to see him again?" Allyson asked.

"It's not entirely up to me," Nicole replied, placing a folded sheet in the linen closet.

"It *is* up to you. He made the first move. Now it's your turn."

Nicole did not want to think about Julian at this moment. Their parents would be arriving from Chicago the next day and she was trying to prepare things. She had taken off all of the coming week so she could spend time with them. The brunt of that responsibility was going to fall on her, because she knew Allyson was going to shirk it.

"Did you hear me, Nic? I said it's your move."

"I'm not going to make a move." Nicole extracted a pillowcase from the laundry basket and tossed it at her sister. "Here, fold this."

Allyson caught the pillowcase and glared at her. "Say what?"

"You heard me. If I never hear from Julian again I will be disappointed, and I will always wonder about him, but life will go on and I will survive." She noticed Allyson's expression and continued. "Look, I know you think I'm crazy, but get real. The man is a celebrity. What possible use could he have for little Nurse Evans and her son? He's got countless other women, women more like him, who are more used to his lifestyle."

"Do you remember that movie *Coming to America*?" What if Julian is like the prince?"

Nicole laughed. "Listen to yourself. When we were kids you used to always call me the dreamer, the one waiting for the knight in shining armor. Well, this is no movie and Julian Marquez may be rich, but he's no prince."

Allyson had no reply for that, although she hoped Julian would take the initiative again, since it was clear Nicole had no such intention. She focused her attention back on what her sister was doing. "Hope you're not planning on using that sheet for them. You know Mom will hate it,"

Nicole finished folding the navy blue sheet. "Never, nothing but light colors for her. And I think you better take that bible of yours from down off the shelf so Mom will think it's being used."

Allyson laughed. "Should I dust it off?"

"You're terrible. When *was* the last time you were in church?"

"Last Christmas, and you shut up. You only go because you take Trey."

That's not quite true, Nicole thought, but neither of them was as devout as their mother. Eleanor Whitfield had always insisted that her girls attend church when they were young. She'd read bible passages to them at night instead of bedtime stories, and she had always insisted that they be chaste and virtuous young ladies. Now that she was retired from teaching elementary school math, she devoted most of her time to religious pursuits, sponsoring youth groups, teaching bible classes, and singing in the choir.

The differences between her and their father, James Whitfield, were so obvious that it was amazing the marriage had survived. The only thing they had in common was that they had both been teachers. James had been a professor of political science at the community college. He was also something of an agnostic and an avid civil rights activist, having participated in countless sit-ins, marches and demonstrations back in the early sixties before the girls were even born. Eleanor had lived in constant fear that he would be killed or arrested, but surprisingly Nicole and Allyson's early lives had been relatively sheltered, unaffected by the turmoil of the world around them.

Nicole remembered the quiet suburban neighborhood they'd grown up in, and the racially mixed but predominantly white school they'd attended. The only time she had ever been called by a racial slur it had been from someone of her own race. Only after becoming an adult had she realized that her life had been relatively unscathed by racial injustice because of the collective efforts of her father and other courageous pioneers.

James Whitfield's retired life was a lot quieter now. He had passed the torch on to the younger generation, but he still occasionally conducted seminars and gave lectures. In his seventies, he had also acquired wisdom and tact, and was known as a diplomat and negotiator in the community.

"Are you going to tell them about Julian?" Allyson asked.

"Of course not. And don't you mention him either."

"Me? You don't have to worry about that. I plan on limiting my conversations with Mom."

Nicole closed the closet door. Her mind drifted wistfully to Trey, who was in school. If her son could talk, he would be the one blabbing all her secrets to his grandparents.

The Marlins had come from behind and in the final inning they'd struck out all of the opposition batters. Wade was elated as he and Julian left the stadium through a private exit.

"Maan, that was some play. Did you see when—?" He interrupted his own outburst of enthusiasm when he noticed that Julian was a million miles away, with thoughts that had nothing to do with baseball.

"So what's up with you?" he asked as they crossed the parking lot to his car.

"Up?" Julian looked puzzled. "Oh yeah, great game."

They both got in and Wade started the car. "You aren't thinking nothing about the game. It's that Nicole woman again, isn't it?"

Julian switched the radio on to a jazz station. "She told me she had a good time that Saturday, but it's been a week. Don't you think she could at least call?"

"I *tink* that woman done put a hex on you," Wade said in Jamaican patois.

"I *tink* you may be right. Don't know what *appnin* to me, *mon*," Julian replied.

"Don't know what *appnin* to you either, but I do know you make a lousy Jamaican." Wade reached up with one hand and smacked the Marlin cap off Julian's head.

Julian laughed, and then stared at the passing traffic. "Tell me, did Yvette play this hard to get when you were going with her?"

Wade reflected on the courtship of his wife, nearly twenty years earlier. The situations could not be compared. Yvette had come from Jamaica too; they had also had music in common. In fact, they had met in a recording studio when she was doing back-up vocals for another artist.

"It was nothing like that," Wade admitted. "Yvette and me always had a lot in common. She trusted me and I trusted her. You and Nicole can't even share the music. She's a nurse, a nurse with a kid who's got a problem. It's not an easy thing dealing with someone else's kid."

Julian folded his arms behind his head and stretched. "I think what you're really saying is that you're too damn old to remember dating Yvette. You only remember her as your wife."

It was Wade's turn to laugh. He did remember it very well, and it made him feel bad for Julian. They were both artists, but his friend was a star and that prevented him from having a normal life.

"Do yourself a favor and just forget Nicole. What's wrong with Lydia? She's Cuban. Your family likes her."

Julian flinched. "My family? Are you going crazy too? This is *my* decision."

"I know that," Wade said, concentrating on the road. "I totally agree with you, but I hope you're prepared to deal with the consequences."

Julian could already foresee the consequences of marrying Lydia Ramos. She was the daughter of Elena's best friend, Carmen, who had come over with them to America on the same fishing boat. Lydia was a pretty girl, and a nice one, but she was barely twenty-one and so shy that he'd only managed to maintain direct eye contact with her after their second date. He had only dated her because Elena had insisted that she was the one. Lydia was an only child who had gone to a private Catholic school and had not even been allowed to date until she was twenty. As a wife she would do exactly what she was told and he could continue touring and having affairs with other women while she'd quietly pretend nothing was going on. If they had children, neither of them would have an active hand in parenting them, because Elena would hire a nanny to do it, and Lydia would never raise her voice in protest. She would forever be the good little girl who stayed in the background. That was not what he wanted.

Julian turned the radio up louder. "I probably should have thought about consequences before I sold my first record."

"Don't say that, man. You know you never could live without music."

Wade was right. The music had always been his. No one could ever control what he wrote or the passion and emotion he ignited on stage. The music had been his father's escape from political and emotional turmoil and now it was his legacy. If anyone was controlling him in a negative way, it was only because he was allowing it.

CHAPTER ELEVEN

Allyson had gone to the airport to pick up their parents and Nicole was in the kitchen hurrying to finish the preparations for supper. Trey came rushing in with Shane chasing him. They raced around the island countertop, nearly knocking a chair over.

"Out! No playing in the kitchen," Nicole shouted in aggravation. They ran out, making such a racket that she didn't even hear the doorbell ring. Trey heard it and raced back into the kitchen, with Shane barking behind him. He tugged at her arm.

"Not now, Trey. Can't you see I'm busy?"

Trey shrugged and went back out. Shane was still barking, and she wished she could temporarily muzzle him. *Why do German shepherds bark so much?* She seized a cucumber and began chopping it up to put in the salad.

"Hey, easy with that thing. No point in getting psychotic," a familiar voice said.

Nicole whirled around to see Julian standing there, escorted by a beaming Trey. She was speechless. The man had done it again, another one of his impromptu surprise appearances that always put her at a disadvantage, even in her own home.

"Julian…" Her hand flew up to brush back a stray lock of hair, leaving a streak of flour on her forehead.

"Whatever you're cooking smells really good. You didn't have to do all this for me," he said, entering the kitchen soundlessly, like a panther treading on a mossy jungle floor.

"I didn't," she said, trying to recover. "Julian… Why are you here?"

"I missed you and this guy." He held a laughing Trey in a headlock.

Nicole wiped her hands on a towel. "You know, this is a really bad time. My parents are coming from Chicago. Allyson just went to pick them up at the airport. They'll be here any minute."

"That's cool. Can I meet them?"

She wasn't sure she'd heard him correctly. "What? Meet them? You want to meet my parents?

"What's wrong with that? I promise I won't drool, pick my nose, or do anything else unacceptable."

She had to laugh. "I don't mean *that*. What I mean is you don't know my parents…"

"I know that. That's why I want to meet them."

"Will you please let me finish. My mother is very strict, strict to the point of being insensitive. If you're here, it will be awkward. How am I supposed to introduce you?"

Julian shrugged. *What about as your boyfriend?* he thought, but did not say it. He could see that the timing was bad. "How about if you just introduced me as a friend of the family?"

Trey clung to Julian. She could almost hear him saying the words. "Please Mommy…Please let him stay."

"It would still be awkward," she said, wishing he didn't look so appealing in his faded denim shirt and jeans, a shirt that was unbuttoned just enough to expose a very slight dusting of hair on his chest. She swallowed hard.

"No problem," Julian said. "Maybe I'll get to meet them some other time."

"Yes, maybe."

"Are you sure you don't want some help in the kitchen?"

Help? From him? Good Lord, please get this man out of my house before I do or say something I'll regret, she thought.

"No, thank you. I don't need any help."

"I'll leave only if you promise to call me sometime this week."

"My parents are going to be here all week. Oh all right, I'll try to call."

"Sorry, *amigo,*" he said to Trey. "I'll make it up to you another day. How about a basketball game, our Miami Heat. You like basketball?"

Trey nodded in excitement.

"If Mom says yes, I'll take you one night."

Nicole turned down the fire under the vegetables and glanced up just in time for Julian to kiss her lightly on the cheek. He then disappeared as abruptly as he'd arrived.

Her face felt flushed. It was more than a little disconcerting, the way he kept casually invading her life, demanding attention, insisting that she respond. And she *was* responding. But how much of that response was simply because he was famous? If he was just like any other man, would it still be that way?

Julian spent the next three days in England with other famous artists, participating in a benefit concert with proceeds going to the orphaned children in war-torn countries. Doing benefits was one of the highlights of his career. He enjoyed being able to give back to the world. The image of the selfish, materialistic star had never set well with him. Despising that image had also led him to secretly donate a great deal of money to other causes as well—most of them involving children. The opportunities to reach out to others also kept him from dwelling on his own problems.

It would be so great to be able to return home after touring, after traveling around the world, to have someone besides fans to sincerely welcome him back. Someone who would listen to him and share his passions. Someone who would caress him with warm arms and understanding eyes when he woke up nights agonizing over the fact that he could hear his father's voice but could not remember his face. Someone who would understand and never belittle the more sensitive side he tried to conceal from the world.

But as the plane touched down in Miami, the only embrace he received came from the press and the paparazzi, who were milling around, trying to get pictures and statements from him and the others. Julian managed to evade most of them.

In a few more hours, he would be told by Luis, Elena, or his publicist, what his next mission was supposed to be. He hoped there would be a call on his answering machine from Nicole, but it didn't seem likely.

Despite constant complaints about the heat, Nicole knew her parents were enjoying their visit to Miami, especially the time they spent with their grandson. In the last four days they had been all over the place, zoos, museums and beaches. They were now on their last evening before taking the cruise to Jamaica.

"Miami really is like Cuba before the revolution," James Whitfield said, glancing at the television.

"Yes," Nicole agreed. "Remember when we were in the Little Havana section? Almost no one spoke English."

"I don't think that's quite right," Eleanor said, fanning herself, even though the air conditioning was on. "When people immigrate to another country, I believe they should learn to speak the language of that country."

Nicole observed with amusement that Allyson rolled her eyes. They were all gathered in the living room after supper. The television was tuned to CNN, but no one was really paying much attention to it. Trey was on the floor, rolling a newly acquired Matchbox car around.

"The Miami Cubans have really built this place up. When I was down here in the seventies this place was falling apart," James said, reflecting. "It's a shame none of that progress has touched the African American community here."

I knew he was going to bring that up, Nicole thought. "It *is* a shame, Dad, but not all of us live in bad areas. There is a good, solid middle-class too."

"Yes," Allyson agreed. "There is diversity in our neighborhood. Everyone gets along with everyone here. I don't hear a lot of complaining about social issues from the people who come to my shop."

"What kind of people come to your shop?" Eleanor asked.

"What do you mean, what kind of people? They're regular people, Mom—black, Hispanic..."

"Are they Christian people?"

Allyson groaned, and Nicole laughed. The two of them were always pushing each other's buttons. Eleanor had never forgiven her oldest daughter for leaving Chicago and starting a business so far away from her influence. She could not understand how she could have given birth to a child so unlike herself. She was also constantly worrying that Nicole would be influenced by what she called Allyson's worldliness. Her fears were totally unjustified.

"Oh, by the way, I brought this here with me 'cause I thought you would like to see it," Eleanor said, rising and going towards the bedroom. She returned with a small red-covered photo album, and resettled herself on the couch, patting at her short, silver-frosted curls. Nicole knew that the album contained pictures of herself and Allyson when they were little.

Stirred by curiosity, Trey rose from his play and came to have a look. Shane, who was banished to the sun deck because Eleanor didn't like dogs, started to bark. The doorbell rang.

"I'll get it," Allyson said. "Probably Lynette."

Trey pointed to a picture of a little girl with long pigtails, playing on a swing.

"That's your mother when she was about your age," Eleanor said to her amused grandson.

Nicole leaned forward to see. The picture had been taken in their backyard, and it brought back memories.

"Mom, Dad, this is Julian. He's a friend of...ours," Allyson announced, returning to the room.

The now familiar feeling of anticipation and dread swept over Nicole as she looked up to see Julian standing beside her sister. Her father turned away from the news and her mother looked up. Trey abandoned the photo album and ran to him.

"I just happened to be passing by so I thought I'd drop this off," Julian said, his eyes fixed on Nicole. He handed Trey a small *Star Wars* figurine. "He must've left it in my car."

Trey eagerly accepted it and showed it to Nicole. She flinched. Her son had never even indicated the toy had been missed. "That was very nice of you, Julian," she said tightly. "Thank you." *Now please go,* she thought.

Allyson glanced up at Julian. "We're just kind of hanging out here tonight. Why don't you stay for coffee...a drink...whatever?"

Nicole glared at her sister.

"Yes, that would be nice," Eleanor said, inspecting Julian as if he were some rare exotic breed. "I'd like to get to know some of my daughters' friends."

"You have two very beautiful daughters," Julian said. "I can see where they get their looks from."

Her mother actually blushed, Nicole observed. The Marquez charm was getting to her too. It wasn't even so much in the words he'd chosen, but the way he looked when he said them.

"I only hope that my two daughters have inherited more than beauty," Eleanor replied, having recovered.

"They definitely have." Julian looked directly at Nicole, who averted her eyes from him. "I'm not a parent, but I'm sure it's every parent's goal to raise children who are intelligent and have principles. I'd say you both succeeded."

"Umm, well, I hope so."

"Oh, Mom, please," Allyson interrupted. "I'm sure Julian doesn't want to hear about how we were raised."

"Sit down and stay a while, Julian," James said. "My wife and I will be leaving on a cruise to Jamaica in the morning. We're not going out anywhere tonight."

Julian's eyes sparkled. "Which ship are you going on?"

"I think it's called *Rhapsody,* Eleanor, is that the one?"

"Yes, something like that."

"You're going to enjoy it," Julian said. "I played on a cruise ship once. It was fun, but being a passenger is better."

"Played?" James quizzed. "What business are you in?"

"I'm a musician. I used to be part of a Latin jazz band."

"No kidding? What do you play?"

"Well, I sing mostly, but I started out playing guitar, then drums."

"Are you successful at this?"

Julian shrugged. "I do all right."

Nicole could not believe it. She was not surprised that her father didn't know who Julian was because, musically, he was still in the Dizzy Gillespie, Count Basie era, but she couldn't figure out why Julian didn't just admit to being internationally famous and wealthy.

"Is that so?" James was interested now. "When I was young, a very long time ago, I used to play drums. Never actually did anything with music though."

"I was wild about anything percussion. Kind of dreamed I'd be the next Tito Puente," Julian said.

"You're into rock now though, I would assume," James said, clearing his throat.

"Actually it's more like Latin pop."

James laughed. "I know. You young people have to go where the profit is."

"Dad, could you excuse us for a minute," Nicole said. It was time to get to the point. "Julian, would you come with me to the kitchen?"

He knew she was going to try to get rid of him now. He excused himself and followed her. She glared at him accusingly.

"Didn't I tell you this was a bad time? I told you my parents would be here all week."

Julian rubbed the side of his face. "I was in Europe. I kind of forgot." He held up his hand. "No, that's a lie. The truth is, I missed you and I kept seeing your face. I had to come."

It made no sense that he should feel that way. She had absolutely nothing to offer him, but still he kept coming back. If it really was just a game he was playing, what was he getting out of it? She knew that her own resistance was about to break down, and that she was the one most likely to get hurt, but the romantic side of her was captivated and mesmerized by him. She surrendered.

"I...I missed you too. It's okay."

"Your parents don't seem that upset," he commented, leaning against the refrigerator.

"I *said* it's okay." She watched his white collarless shirt part slightly as he leaned. It exposed a thin gold chain around his neck, from which some sort of emblem dangled. What was it? She moved a little closer, and could see that it was a tiny gold dolphin.

"My father gave that to me when I was small," Julian said, aware of her attention. "He used to wear it...said it would protect me out at sea."

"I guess it worked," she said softly "You came here from the sea."

"He should have kept it. He was the one who needed protection." There was a controlled tightness to his voice.

"What do you mean?"

"Nothing. I don't really believe in that sort of thing. Do you?"

"No, I don't, but other people's beliefs are fascinating."

And you are even more fascinating. She reached up impulsively and traced her finger lightly across the velvet of his eyebrow. Julian caught her hand and brought it to his lips, planting a whispery kiss on it. She trembled as he lowered her hand so that it was resting on his chest, over his heart.

"Nicole, is there any beer in there?" her father called from the living room.

Her sanity returned. At any minute one of her parents could come walking in. Reluctantly she stepped back.

"Yes. I'll bring you one," she called, and then turned back to Julian. "What are you having? Coffee? Tea? Or my father's favorite, beer?"

"I'd like your father's favorite daughter."

She smiled. "Now, now. I think you're going to have to settle for the beer."

Julian looked disappointed as he extracted two cans from the refrigerator. He returned to the rest of the family, and she followed him slowly. The conversation about music continued.

"So you're not only a singer, but you're a songwriter as well," James said.

"Yes, as a matter of fact I'm working on a piece right now. If you all don't mind being my audience, I'd like to test it out."

Allyson looked absolutely dazzled. "Oh yes! We'd love to hear it."

James and Eleanor nodded in agreement. Julian went outside to get his guitar. When he returned, the room grew silent as he sat and played the first few chords. It had a slightly flamenco ring to it. He had said it didn't yet have a title, but as he started singing it, Nicole could hear the phrase *when I dream*, repeated a lot. Even without the orchestra and backing, it sounded as beautiful as one of his concert songs. She glanced at Trey. Her son looked spellbound.

Everybody applauded very loudly when he finished. "That was beautiful," Eleanor said after a long silence. "Unlike my husband, I'm not really into popular music, but that was very…very moving."

"You've definitely got a voice," James said. "If there is any justice in this world, you should go far, but you *do* know how hard it is to make it in the music industry…"

"Dad," Allyson started, but was silenced as Nicole bumped her.

Julian's eyes twinkled. "It is hard, but a lot of times it's all about being in the right place at the right time."

He put the guitar down and immediately Trey picked it up.

"Trey, put that down," Eleanor commanded before Nicole could speak.

"It's okay," Julian said. "He's not going to hurt it."

Trey sat on the couch near Julian, who showed him how to hold the guitar. Nicole watched them and found herself drifting into the past. Her son moved closer and Julian lightly looped his arm around the boy's neck, his hands on Trey's smaller ones, guiding his fingers to the proper chords. Together they pieced out the tune of "Jamaica Farewell." Trey smiled up at Julian with such adoration that her heart ached. Her son needed a father. She needed a ... *Get real!* her mind snapped back.

Everyone applauded for Trey. Julian finished his beer and announced that he had to go. Trey tugged at him in protest, and to Nicole's embarrassment, offered him the previously forgotten photo album.

"What's this?"

"Those are just some family photos," Eleanor said. "Mostly of the girls when they were little."

Julian looked interested. "Mind if I take a quick look?"

"Go right ahead," Eleanor obliged.

"You don't really want to look at those," Nicole protested feebly.

Julian ignored her. He turned the page. Before him were images of two beloved little girls. He knew which child was Nicole without being told. She was the demure looking one with the long braids. He saw them at play, in school, on family vacations, and with grandparents and other relatives. He turned a few more pages. He saw them approaching adolescence. He saw the family all together, hugging one another—the closeness—the rich tapestry of familial bonding. He had seen enough.

"You've absolutely got to see this one of Allyson and Nicole when—" Eleanor started, but Julian interrupted.

"Maybe another time. I really have to go. It's been nice meeting all of you." He moved to the door.

"The pleasure has been all ours," James said.

"Thank you. Have a good time on the cruise."

Julian leaned against his car and took a deep breath of the hot night air. Everything had been perfect until he had looked at those photographs; it was then that he'd felt as though the walls were closing in on him. He had no pictures, no visible evidence that anyone of his own blood had ever loved him, and it hurt, even though he knew it shouldn't. He was, after all, a grown man.

"Julian, why did you leave like that?"

He felt Nicole's hand on his shoulder, and he turned to look into her green eyes. "I thought you wanted me to go."

"It's a woman's prerogative to change her mind. What's wrong?" she pressed.

He wanted to tell her, but if he did, he knew it wouldn't make any sense. He looked into her eyes again. They were misty, and they were not judgmental or callused. "I...," he started. "Nothing. There's nothing wrong."

She sighed. "Why didn't you tell my parents the truth?"

"Truth about what?"

"The truth that you're wealthy and famous."

"I don't know. Somehow I figured you didn't want me to."

"Is mind reading another one of your talents?"

"Well, it's not an exact science, but sometimes it works." He gazed up at the moonless sky. "Your father is pretty cool."

She laughed. "I don't understand you at all."

"You don't have to. I just want to keep seeing you."

His eyes met hers with an intensity that was hypnotic, and he had a firm grip on her arm.

"Just say when," she whispered, and for the second time that night, he held her close, as close as a heartbeat.

She wanted to do more than just *see* this man. She wanted to be lying on the ground in some hot steamy jungle, with his lean, panther-like body draped over hers. She wanted to whisper sweet nothings, share his every breath, his dreams, his passions...

"Nicole! Are you coming in?" her mother's voice rang out into the night. "That program you wanted to see is coming on."

Julian laughed, and Nicole's laughter joined with his. "That's my mom...you gotta love her."

"I'm surprised you didn't become a nun."

"Are you happy I didn't?"

He nodded but he looked at her long and hard. *Are you sure you aren't?* he thought, but didn't say.

She watched him slide into the Explorer and she remained standing there until he'd vanished from sight.

"Nicole!"

"I'm coming, Mother, I'm coming."

CHAPTER TWELVE

A faint breeze rustled gently through the fronds of the palm trees and fresh air drifted down below. Nicole welcomed the breeze as she and Trey sat on a bench in the courtyard of the condo complex. Shane was anchored to the bench, languidly pawing at an escaping lizard.

"Come on, Trey, pay attention." She took a quick look at the diagram in the book of sign language she was consulting and then imitated the gestures so he could see. "Here's how you do it. I...love...you." She waited for him to respond.

Trey stared up at the sky and pointed at an airplane flying over-head. Seizing the opportunity, Nicole thumbed through the book and found the hand signal that indicated airplane. "Airplane," she declared, making the sign. "Like this, Trey."

Trey made a face at her, then slid off the bench and began pulling up clumps of grass, which he proceeded to throw at Shane. The dog, sensing a game, leaped up, snapping vigorously at the grass and dirt flying at him. Nicole caught her son by the wrist and turned him around.

"Trey, I want you to pay *attention*. You can play later."

He laughed and tried to throw clumps of grass at her. Nicole wanted to just give up, take advantage of the beautiful day and have fun, but the long-term consequence of Trey's inability to communicate would be devastating.

"Honey, if you listen to me for just a half an hour, we'll go out for ice cream later."

Trey leveled an almost adult expression of aggravation on her, making her wonder if her child thought she was completely nuts—she was definitely starting to feel that way.

Midway through the week, she had received a report from one of Trey's teachers, informing her that he was not paying attention in class, that he seemed bored and distracted and was not following even the most basic commands of sign language. The report had angered her. The new school year had barely started and already there were problems.

She had been hoping that he could at least make it through this year. The next year they would try home schooling, but if right now was any indication of her skills as a teacher, it was going to be a struggle. Trey seemed determined not to learn sign language.

"Come on, Trey, please. Let me see *I love you.*" She repeated the sign once again.

Trey shook his head negatively and stared at the tips of his grass-stained sneakers. Completely frustrated, Nicole grabbed Trey by the arm and pulled him close to her. "I love you!" she practically screamed, manipulating his fingers into the proper position.

Trey whined and struggled to break free. She released his fingers and gripped him tightly by both forearms, in a face-to-face position.

"You listen to me right now! You're getting too big to act like this. If you can't talk you're going to *have* to communicate with your hands." She took a deep breath and more anguished words poured out. "Do you think *other* people are going to care about you, pointing and whining? Do you think the world will?"

Trey went limp in her arms and squeezed his eyes shut. *My God, what am I doing?* Suddenly she remembered a similar incident when Trey was three, not long after Warren had died. She had shaken Trey and screamed at him, demanding he talk, because she knew he could. Shocked at his mother treating him that way, Trey cried hysterically, making her feel like the worst kind of criminal. She had vowed to never repeat that kind of behavior—and now it had almost happened again.

"I'm sorry, baby," she whispered, hugging him tight. "I am so, so sorry." She could feel the first traces of her own tears as she clung to him, rocking back and forth.

Trey opened his eyes and looked at her. He reached up quietly and tried to wipe the tears from her face. She stroked his curls.

"It doesn't matter," Nicole said haltingly. "I will always love you, even if you never talk."

He moved slowly out of her embrace, then turned, smiled and held up his hand, his fingers forming the *I love you* sign.

In the evening, Julian sat in his car waiting for Nicole to leave the hospital. It was almost midnight, so she should be out at any minute. This meeting would be no surprise, because she had agreed that he could come pick her up after he left the studio. They would talk on the way home, and if he was lucky, maybe there would be more than just talk.

This woman is really making a fool out of me, Julian thought. *Here I am catering to her every mood—even playing chauffeur, and she never initiates anything.* If he suddenly decided to stop pursuing her, she probably wouldn't even question it. She would just continue on in her little world as if they had never met.

So why am I doing this? He knew the answer. Nicole still attracted and intrigued him, and her son had added another dimension to the appeal. The night he met the whole family, he'd felt a bonding with Trey that was even stronger than the day they'd gone skating. The way the boy responded when he introduced him to the guitar had reminded him of himself and his father, only this time the roles were reversed.

"Hi," Nicole said, sliding into the car.

She looked exactly the way she'd looked when they first met. Her crisp white uniform clung to her lean, willowy body, and it rose well above her knees as she settled into the car. Her hair was held back by a barrette, as usual. He wanted to reach up and undo it so he could watch the thick shimmering tresses tumble down below her shoulders. She was so beautiful and half of that beauty was hidden behind her stiff professional veneer.

"Hey, babe," he said. "Busy night?"

She sighed. "It was bad. A patient with no history of heart trouble suddenly went into cardiac arrest."

He shook his head. "An elderly person?"

"No, middle-aged, maybe fifty."

"Will he be okay?"

"He was taken down to ICU. He was stable the last time I heard."

It was a sobering thought, but Julian really did not want to be depressed this night. He concentrated on the road, driving slower than usual so as not to get her home too quickly. He wondered if she realized what he was doing. Studying her out of the corner of his eye, he decided to be impulsive.

"How about coming to my place tonight?"

She wanted to. He knew she did, but she shook her head negatively and sat up straighter. "I can't do that. I have to be home for Trey."

"He's in bed. Your sister is with him."

Her voice sounded agitated, disturbed. "Well, I have to be there when he wakes up, to get him off to school and..."

"I'll get you back before he wakes up," Julian insisted. He knew that he had made progress with her during that last visit. There was no question that she was attracted to him. What was the problem? "I can have you back home before sunrise. I have to be in the studio by—"

"I said no!" Her response came out angrier than she had intended. Feeling embarrassed, she averted his eyes and looked out the side window. She tried to sound calmer. "Look, you offered to pick me up and take me home. I didn't ask you to do this. If you have other plans, fine. Just drop me off near a convenience store and I'll call a taxi."

Darn crazy woman! He bit his lip to hold back the harsh words that threatened to come out. What did she think he was, some kind of deranged date rapist or something? He gripped the steering wheel harder. "Fine, whatever you say, Miss Daisy. I will take you directly home—no conversation—no pitstops. I will keep..." He stopped in mid-sentence. She was laughing.

"Julian, I'm sorry. I didn't mean to be so rude. It's just that I have a lot on my mind and..."

"Trey?" he asked, resigning himself to reality.

"Yes. He's having problems with sign language. He doesn't really want to learn it."

Julian looked frustrated. "Why does he have to learn it? Why is the kid in a school for the deaf anyway? He can hear perfectly."

She rubbed her forehead wearily. "I know that, you know that, but the rest of the world just doesn't give a darn. They don't want to deal with him in regular school. He can't talk, so he has to learn to communicate in some other way."

Julian took a deep breath. "Do you really believe that he'll never talk again?"

"I don't *want* to believe that, but the awful truth is it's been three years. I really don't know, so I have to make plans based on the possibility that he might never talk again."

He made a quick left turn through the gates of the now familiar condo complex. "I understand what you're saying, but I wouldn't give up. Maybe Trey doesn't want to do the signing thing because deep inside, he knows he can talk. Maybe he doesn't want his mother to give up on him either."

Touched by his surprising insight, Nicole struggled to find words. "You...you're very intuitive, but as I said before, it's been three years and there's not much else I can do about the problem."

"I don't think he's in the right school," Julian said.

"What?" They were parked in the lot next to Allyson's car. She knew she should get out. "What would you suggest?" she asked, looking directly at him.

"My niece goes to Harmon Academy. It's a private school for regular kids. They have only about ten kids to a classroom, so he would get more attention than in public school, but he'd still be treated like every other kid. The teachers would be patient with him there."

Nicole shook her head incredulously. "Harmon Academy would be perfect…if I took home a six-figure salary."

Julian remained silent for a moment. He glanced at his watch, then back at her eyes. He knew what she was going to say even before he spoke.

"I could help."

"No." She toyed with a bracelet on her wrist. "That's very sweet and generous of you to offer, but I could never accept *that* kind of help. Trey is my son, and my responsibility alone."

"Not quite true," he reminded her. "I'm sure you've heard the saying 'It takes a village to raise a child.' "

"A village, yes, but one very wealthy man, no."

He rubbed his eyes and stared out the window at the stars sparkling in the ebony sky. At one point, Trey had simply been a bridge to Nicole, but the short time he'd spent with the child had affected him more deeply than he wanted to admit. He wanted to be involved.

"Well, if you won't allow me to help financially, then how about in a different way?"

"What way?" Looking deeply into Julian's eyes, Nicole saw no cynicism or opportunism. He looked and sounded sincere. She listened.

"I'd like to spend time with Trey, take him places. Movies, basketball games—stuff like that. You're a great mother to him, but…"

"He needs a big brother, father figure," she finished, flatly. "I know, I've heard…"

"It's got nothing to do with how you're raising him," he began, and was interrupted.

"You're right," she said. "Don't think I didn't notice how quickly you and Trey bonded. That night when you were playing the guitar with him, the way he looked at you. It was almost eerie." She shook her head, and gazed skyward. "I love my son. I want the best for him. If you think you can help, then I'm going to have to let you try."

He breathed a sigh of relief. She held up her hand. "Just one thing. I don't want you to talk to him about his father, or about anything concerning death. I'm his mother and I'll handle the heavy stuff."

Julian nodded, but he wondered just how much Nicole had actually discussed his father's death with Trey. From past experience, he had learned it was best to handle the reality of death by dealing with it head-on, not pretending that it had never happened. *Stop it!* he told himself. *Do not bring your own agenda into this. She's allowing you access to her dearest possession, her child. Don't blow it.*

"I'll be in Mexico for a few days, but the next Saturday I'm free. I promised Amanda I'd take her to the ice show. Will it be okay if Trey comes along with us?" he asked.

She thought about it for a minute. "That sounds nice. If I have to change the plan, I'll call you."

"Good." He glanced at her. "You can come too."

She sighed again. "I wish I could, but I'm afraid I have to work that Saturday."

"Let me know when you've got vacation time and we'll make plans."

"Yes. I'll let you know." She started to get out of the car, but hesitated.

"Uh, Julian, there's something else, something important I have to say."

"I'm listening."

"I like you a lot, maybe even love you, but right now we can only be friends."

He rolled his eyes, hating the implication of that last word. He knew he wanted more. "Why does it have to be that way?"

"Because...because we are very different people. You have your priorities and I have mine. I just can't deal with anything more than friendship right now."

Right now? He hung on to the words in his mind. It was the second time she had said that. Did it mean she would be ready at a later date? Ready for what? He knew his feelings for her had gone beyond physical desire. If that was all he had wanted, he would have pulled out a long time ago. Just how involved did he really want her in his life? They definitely did have different priorities, and she would not be able to easily adapt to his world.

"All right," he said slowly. If that's the way it is, I'll go along with it for now."

"Thank you," she said.

"Nicole…"

"Yes?"

"Don't wait too long. I can't promise you I'll always be here."

She leaned forward and brushed his lips lightly with her own. "I know," she said, her voice barely a whisper. "No one can promise that."

CHAPTER THIRTEEN

Nicole was dreaming. She could feel the wind stinging her face and she could taste the salty spray of the sea. The speedboat was skimming the surface of the ocean and suddenly it swung into a sharp curve and went careening madly out of control.

"Julian!" she cried.

He turned to face her, but the man at the helm was not Julian. It was Warren.

"Don't worry, hon, everything's under control." He took his hands off the steering wheel and came toward her.

"But the boat, you're not steering it!" she shrieked.

"I told you it's okay," he said nonchalantly.

She could see cliffs up ahead. They were heading straight for them—at over seventy miles an hour. Desperately she grabbed the wheel.

"What the hell do you call yourself doing!" Warren yelled, trying to forcibly reclaim control as she struggled to turn the boat away from sure disaster.

Behind her, she heard laughter, and with the wind screaming in her ears, and Warren's powerful hands preventing her from turning the wheel, she looked over her shoulder to see Julian calmly sitting in the back seat.

"Julian, help!"

"It's your decision, take control," he said.

The cliffs loomed up ahead—solid and lethal. They were going to crash! They were going to die! With every ounce of strength she had left, she yanked the wheel.

Sunlight streaming through the bedroom window nearly blinded her as she sat bolt upright in bed. *Oh no! it's after eight. I've overslept,* she thought, trying to will her heart to stop beating so fast. It took a few minutes before she actually remembered that it was Sunday and Trey did not have to go to school.

Slurp! Shane's tongue caught her right in the mouth. "Ugh," she frowned, pushing the fuzzy face with the cone-shaped ears away. Not the least bit deterred by her response, the animal panted heavily and wagged his tail, letting it thud against the dresser. She laughed.

"You're such a clown," she said, hugging the dog. "But I know you have ulterior motives. Ally hasn't fed you, I'll bet."

Shane collapsed on the floor with a grunting noise and waited for her to get up. In the kitchen, Allyson and Trey were having breakfast. They looked up when she entered.

"Kind of late for you, isn't it?" Allyson said.

"I was having this really weird dream," she replied, ruffling Trey's hair in passing.

"What about?"

"I don't know, but it was really awful."

"Couldn't have been that awful if you don't even remember it."

"Believe me, it *was* awful."

"So what's up with you anyway? We've both been so busy coming and going, we've hardly talked. How's Julian?"

Nicole noticed Trey look up at the mention of that name. She would have to be careful what she said about him around her son.

"Julian? He's okay, I guess. You know how it is with him—always traveling."

"Did I tell you that Mom called at my shop yesterday? She asked about him," Allyson said.

Nicole rolled her eyes. Of course her mother would find Julian a hard man to forget. After his visit she had demanded to know what was really going on. She had gone on to remind them both, because she wasn't too sure which one of them Julian was seeing, that he was a very handsome man, and that handsome men were the types one should stay away from. She had also reminded them that coming from Cuba, he was probably Catholic, and his culture was very different from their own. She and Allyson had laughed themselves silly over her paranoia.

"What did Mom say about him?" Nicole asked.

Allyson shrugged. "Nothing much. She's just being nosy, that's all."

It had been a week since their parents' trip to Jamaica. Both had enjoyed it immensely and said they were planning another one next year. They were now back home in Chicago.

For a brief moment, Nicole felt homesick. The calendar reminded her that it was October. In Chicago it would be accompanied by multi-colored leaves, the scent of wood burning in the fireplace, and the sound of children hurrying to get home from extracurricular activities at school, hurrying before the darkness of shortened days overtook them. None of this would happen in Miami. It was the worst part about living in Florida. She missed the seasons.

Shane bumped up against her. "Ally, did you feed *your* dog?"

"You can feed him. I fed *your* child."

Nicole laughed. "I guess that means I get to walk him too."

"He likes walking with you."

After feeding the dog, she attached his leash and led him outside. Trey eagerly accompanied them. He was eager because she had not suggested going to church. If she hadn't overslept, that was exactly where they would be going. Trey needed to be around people, even if they, in their ignorance, tended to treat him as though he didn't exist.

The bright sunlight filtering through the palm trees annoyed her terribly. Did the sun really have to be that luminous? Couldn't the stupid trees show some respect for autumn by at least altering their color?

Her thoughts drifted back to Julian and his plan to take Trey to the ice show. Trey had been excited when she told him about it, but had shown some trepidation when he realized that she wouldn't be going. He had quickly recovered, though, and indicated that he still wanted to go, regardless. She had offered him no encouragement, had left the decision entirely up to him.

As Shane sniffed the ground, and Trey ran a few yards ahead, elements of the nightmarish dream returned to her. What was the dream saying? Was she really supposed to take control? If so, control of what? Maybe she had never been in control of anything, at least in her marriage, because she had left everything up to Warren.

She was just plain not ready for a physical relationship with Julian or anyone. For a long time she'd tried to forget the fact that sex with Warren had always been a *wifely duty*, not an act of love. He'd always been the one to initiate everything—the one who was literally always on top, doing what he wanted while she just accepted and went through the motions. No wonder he'd so often accused her of being frigid.

Somehow she had managed to put up with it because he had been so great in other aspects—a great father, great provider and strong decision-maker. He had also been the only man she'd ever dated. Now here she was, feeling things for Julian that she had never felt for her husband. What kind of woman was she?

There were other issues that were barring her from Julian too. She did not believe in casual physical relationships between people, relationships without commitment. If she gave Julian what she thought he wanted, he'd reject her if she was as terrible as Warren had claimed, and if she kept pushing him away, the results would be the same. *How on earth did I get into this dilemma?* she wondered. Why couldn't Julian have met Allyson first? Her sister shared none of her hang-ups.

That same morning, Julian was fighting the urge to bodily remove Elena from his apartment. She was violating his space and, as usual, treating him like a slightly retarded child.

"You know you have to be in Mexico tomorrow," she reminded him, waving an envelope containing plane tickets in front of his face.

"I'm not senile yet." He snatched the envelope.

"No need to be nasty. You have a way of forgetting things. Maybe I should keep those tickets until you get ready to go. That way you won't lose them."

"I'm not going to lose them."

It was still early, and one of few days that he had nothing planned. All he wanted to do was go back to bed and listen to the morning chatter on TV—instead, he had to contend with her.

"Oh, Luis asked me to deliver these." She dropped a folder down on the end table.

"What's that?"

"The proofs for your new album cover. I already selected the one they should use, but Luis wants you to look at them too."

"How thoughtful of both of you." Julian sat down on the couch and opened the folder. The photographs spilled out. His own face stared back at him, big eyes, pale skin and a pathetic expression.

"That's the one we picked," Elena said. "You have this vulnerable thing going. The fans should like it."

He rifled through the other photos. All of them looked better than the one she had picked. He plopped them back on the table without making any comment. Elena usually selected what went on the CD covers, because he had never considered himself to be a good judge of his own appearance. He suddenly wondered which one Nicole would pick if he asked her.

"Make sure you don't lose those tickets," Elena said, finally moving toward the door. "Oh, one more thing. You better start working out, because you're getting kind of fat."

"Maybe you should change your glasses," Julian retorted, holding the door open so she could exit. He knew for a fact that he'd recently lost four pounds.

Once she was gone he felt too wired to return to bed. Pacing around, he ended up in the foyer. Sure enough, another stack of mail greeted him. Wearily he shuffled through it and unceremoniously dumped it in the trash.

It still made him feel guilty doing that. After all, the letters were from fans, and they were the ones who bought his records. He recalled how in the early stages of his career, he'd tried to answer each one personally. It had been impossible. Now members of his staff were paid to go through the stuff and send out autographed pictures. The mail was supposed to be going to a post office box and not to his house. It was a little disconcerting to realize how many strangers knew where he lived.

One piece of mail missed the trash and landed on the floor. It was a purple envelope. Julian laughed. Of all the letters, *that* one really belonged in the trash. He picked it up and it joined the rest.

CHAPTER FOURTEEN

Nicole reached for the telephone, then hesitated. "What's wrong with you? Go on, call him," she muttered to herself. Julian had told her that he would be back from Mexico on Thursday, and she was in the habit of always calling friends who went away, to make sure they got back safely. *He is a friend, isn't he?* she thought.

Without even having to look it up, she dialed the number and waited for the answering machine so she could leave a message. It continued to ring. Nicole started to hang up, but than a strained, barely audible voice answered.

"Hello," she said uncertainly. "I...I'm sorry. I must have the wrong number."

"Nicole, is that you?"

"Julian? You sound weird. Did I wake you up?" It suddenly dawned on her that it was only eight o'clock in the morning. She had just gotten back from dropping Trey off at school, and it didn't seem early to her, but a lot of people liked to sleep late.

"No. You didn't wake me," he said.

"Well, I just called to make sure you got back safely. I was expecting to leave a message."

"But luck wasn't with you," he interrupted, his voice still sounding odd. "Instead, you got me live and in person."

She shook her head. There was definitely something wrong with him, but shouldn't she expect that kind of behavior from a celebrity? Maybe he was drunk. A wave of anger and disappointment swept over her. *And this is the irresponsible person who is going to take my son out Saturday? We'll see about that,* she thought.

"I'm glad you're back," Nicole said, crisply. "I'm going to let you recover..."

"No! Don't hang up yet. I know what you're thinking. I'm not drunk. I sound like this because I was sick all last night. I think I'm about over it now."

"Sick?" Nicole repeated, feeling ashamed of herself for immediately jumping to negative conclusions about him. "Julian, what's wrong?"

"Nothing much. Just a case of food poisoning or something." He described some of the unpleasant symptoms.

The nurse side of her took over. She wanted to see him and make sure he was going to be okay. After that episode in the hospital, she had reached the conclusion that he was the type of man who would not take his own health seriously.

"Are you alone?" she asked, wondering if some woman might be there with him.

"Yeah. Actually I'm glad you called. Kind of reminded me to get my act together…got to be in the studio by noon."

"Don't you dare go anywhere. I'm coming over. I think I might have the perfect cure for you." She let the words escape quickly so she wouldn't have time to think the offer out and take it back.

"I'm sure not gonna argue with you," Julian said. "But I want you to know, it's not like I'm dying or anything."

"Now I'm *really* worried. I'll be over in about thirty minutes."

"Take the causeway," Julian said. "It's the private road off…"

"I know. It's the only way I could get there without a speedboat."

"Good. I'll have Carlos unlock the gate for you."

"Carlos?"

"He's the security guard."

After she hung up, she sat there for a few minutes wondering what she had gotten herself into. What if he was just faking, and wanted her alone at his place? What if he—never mind about what he might do. The question was whether she could keep her hands off him much longer.

"Do I always have to be sick in order to get your attention?" Julian asked.

"You're kind of cute when you're vulnerable," Nicole responded, staring at the puffy white clouds in the sky.

"I'm usually never sick, but this year has been bad."

"It's probably because your resistance is low after that bout with pneumonia. It wasn't that long ago," she reminded him.

Nicole had been there for a while and it was nearing noon. She had arrived with a care package consisting of two bottles of ginger ale and green tea, some of which she had actually cajoled him into consuming, since he hadn't been able to eat or drink anything for almost twelve hours.

He had granted her permission to roam around his place at will while he slept for two hours on the living room couch. She'd spent most of the time strolling in the garden, until she'd had a near collision with the fear-inspiring maid, Gretchen. After that she'd gone off to peruse books in the well-stocked library, discovering that they were mostly American and Latin history texts, historical autobiographies, the writings of Jose Marti and literature by Gabriel Garcia Marquez. While selecting an anthology of Latin poetry, she noted the glaring absence of Langston Hughes and James Baldwin.

Julian was now wide-awake, and feeling a lot better. He had joined her out on the terrace, pleased that she had chosen to stay. He studied her, observing that her hair, pulled back as usual, looked lighter in the sun's rays. Her natural unspoiled beauty never ceased to amaze him. Even the mannish white oxford shirt and jeans she wore could not obscure the feminine curves and nuances of her lean, slender form.

"Why are you looking at me like that?" Nicole asked, disconcerted as she glanced up from her book.

"Because even the clouds and the ocean can't compete with your kind of beauty," he said, aware of sounding corny, but meaning every word.

Nicole blushed. He was definitely feeling better, and it was probably time for her to make her exit. Instead she put the book down and glanced at the man sitting near her. His coloring was no longer as gray as the tight T-shirt he wore, and his eyes had their devilish intensity back.

"Flattery," she said, rising, "will get you another cup of green tea."

He laughed. "I wasn't flattering you. I was telling the truth, but if you're going to punish me with more of that damn tea, I'll remember not to do it again."

"Don't curse at my tea," she declared, hands on her hips. "It seems to have worked wonders. You even managed to keep it down."

"Yeah," he admitted. "You're right. Suddenly the thought of food isn't making me sick anymore. Maybe I..."

"Sorry," she interrupted, "no food for you today, unless you have a taste for Jell-O. I made some while you were asleep.

"Made some?" he repeated, amazed by her revelation. "I do have a cook. You didn't have to do that."

Nicole smiled. "It wasn't a problem. I make it a lot since Trey is crazy about the stuff." She *didn't* tell him that it had also been a pleasure working in that beautiful kitchen.

She found herself inadvertently studying his long out-stretched legs encased in blue denim, and then her attention drifted to his feet, which were sockless in deck shoes. This was one of the few men who would probably still look attractive in shorts and sandals, she thought, then tried to take her mind and eyes off his body.

"I did get to speak with your cook," she told him. "She's now under strict orders not to feed you anything solid."

"Why is it my fate to always be around bossy women?"

"I'm not trying to be bossy," Nicole said quietly. "I...I just care about you. Is that wrong?"

"No, not coming from you," he said slowly.

Julian suddenly envisioned Nicole in his life permanently. He'd detected complete honesty when she said she cared, and that was so unlike any other woman he had ever known. Her caring had nothing to do with his money or who he was. It was just simple, pure and honest. It felt good for a change.

She abandoned the terrace for a minute, and then returned, handing him a glass of ginger ale. "No more tea torture, but I'm serious. You'll have to drink a lot today, or you'll get dehydrated."

He silently took the glass and watched her sit down. The expression on her face was reflective. She picked up her book and then put it back down.

"Julian, can I ask you something?"

"I'm at your mercy."

"Have you ever been married? I mean you have what everyone thinks they want—fame, wealth. I would think some woman would…"

He didn't let her finish. "Never been married. Never been *that* much in love with anyone."

"Never?" she looked surprised. "I mean never been in love?

He ran his fingers wearily through his hair and leaned back in the chair. There had been someone a very long time ago.

"I guess maybe once," he said, staring at the distant blue of the ocean. "But I was a teenager, might not count."

"I think it counts," she said gently. "Could you tell me?" He knew so much about her past that it seemed logical he should share some of his.

His eyes reflected poignant, maybe painful memories of the past. "Her name was Linda Medina. She was nineteen…I was eighteen. My career had just taken off at that time, and Elena didn't like our relationship."

Nicole rolled her eyes. *Elena again.* "Why?"

"Because Linda was an employee. She was an illegal immigrant from Honduras, who Elena hired as a maid."

"What did she look like?"

He looked surprised. "Why do you want to know that?"

In truth, Nicole didn't know why she had asked that. "Well, since you said she was your only love, I was just kind of curious."

"Actually," he said, with an ironic laugh, "she looked a little like you. Well, her hair was redder, and she was short, but she had green eyes, like yours."

"Really?" Nicole wondered if there was any significance to that disclosure. "What happened to her?"

"She got pregnant. We planned to get married, but Elena thought it was ridiculous. She thought we were too young—that I would ruin my career, and a lot of other crap. Anyway I was sent on a promotional tour for two days, and when I got back, Linda was gone." He took a deep breath and looked at Nicole's questioning eyes. "Elena paid her off and she went back to Honduras. I never saw her again."

Nicole cringed. "That's terrible. You have a child somewhere that you'll never know."

He closed his eyes for a second and then looked at her. "There is no child. I discovered receipts from the gynecologist. Elena paid for her abortion too."

She was speechless, feeling his pain, loathing this tyrannical sister called Elena. Was there any justification for ending a young love in such a cruel way?

"I, well, I can kind of see why Elena would have thought you were too young, but she had no right…that was awful. You must have hated her."

"At the time, I did hate her, but I was a naive kid. I realize now that Linda never really gave a damn about me. If she had, she couldn't have been paid off."

He has never known any kind of love that can't be bought. How sad, she thought. No one deserved to be treated in that way.

"I caused a lot of trouble back then," he reflected. "Ran away from home, got an apartment in New York, basically tried to hurt Elena by throwing my career and her money away. In the end, Luis talked me into coming back. I was only hurting myself and I really couldn't abandon the music."

Nicole shook her head. "This is none of my business, but I hope Elena doesn't have *that* kind of control over you now."

"No. She still tries, but basically she just makes a lot of noise. I kept Luis as my manager because he's got a good business sense, and I like him."

"Does Luis control everything, I mean, financially?"

Julian laughed. "Fortunately I've learned *not* to be one of those artists who get ripped off by unscrupulous managers and record companies. When I was about twenty-one, I took a career hiatus for two years so I could go to college. I majored in business and marketing, with a lot of accounting thrown in."

Nicole breathed a sigh of relief. "Good for you."

"At least that's one smart thing I did that paid off. Elena and Luis fought me tooth and nail over the college issue too."

"Why?"

"Lots of reasons—one being that music fans are fickle. They figured that in two years I'd probably be forgotten."

The other reason being that if he knew too much, they wouldn't be able to take advantage of him as much, she thought, but did not say.

"I am proud to say that I'm totally 'hands on' with the financial aspects of my career now. I know where the money is going."

But most of it is going in the pockets of Luis and Elena, not because you're being ignorant, but because you are allowing it, she thought.

"I suppose I'm a little too generous with Luis and Elena," he said, reading her mind, "but they're all I have as far as family goes."

The few hours she had spent taking care of him and listening to him talk had drawn her more into his world than she'd ever intended. She had the feeling that there was still so much more to his story, that he'd only scratched the surface. *But his life is really none of my business. Why am I being so nosy? Why am I, of all people, feeling sorry for him?*

"Julian, It's getting late. I really should be going."

Should be? She wasn't sure? he thought, rising from his seat. He looked at his watch. "It's only twelve-thirty. Before you go, I just want to show you something."

They both returned to the living room, and he handed her a port-folio. "These are some potential covers for my new CD. Just tell me which one you think is best."

Surprised, and admittedly honored that he would ask her such a thing, Nicole looked through the photographs. Most of them were good, except for one that didn't resemble him at all. "This is it," she said, selecting one where he looked darkly handsome, and had a mischievously suggestive smile.

"Really?" He looked at the picture she had chosen.

"Actually, they're all good, except for this one. Are you sure that's you?" She held up the pale-faced, big-eyed portrait that Elena had selected.

He laughed. "It does look kind of weird. I think I'll consider the one you picked."

She felt childishly proud and honored again as she watched him put the folder away. There were a million more questions she wanted to ask him, and a million more things she wanted to do, none of them in keeping with the image of nurse, mother, and widow.

"I really have to go now. Make sure you drink plenty of liquids and eat the Jell-O," she said.

"You could stay for lunch. The cook will…"

"No thanks. There are things I have to do," she insisted.

"Thank you for coming and being a…friend." he said, impulsively pulling her close and planting a lingering kiss on her lips.

The *kiss* was not the kind you'd give a friend, Nicole realized as she left the prince in his lonely palace.

CHAPTER FIFTEEN

In about an hour, Trey would be going to the ice show with Julian and Amanda. Nicole sat at the nurses' station, worrying because Julian had informed her, at the last minute, that three of Amanda's school friends were also going. Four children would probably be intimidating to a child who was more comfortable with one or two people. She was debating whether she should call Julian and tell him not to pick Trey up.

Plop! A magazine dropped down on the desk near her. She looked up to see Maria standing there.

"It's sure quiet tonight," Maria said.

"Sure is," Nicole agreed. "I hope it's not the calm before the storm."

Maria opened the magazine. "You're worrying about Trey, aren't you? You shouldn't. Julian's good with kids."

"And you know Julian personally?"

"No, but you do. Give yourself some credit. You wouldn't trust Trey to just anyone. He's gonna have a good time, believe me."

"I hope you're right." Nicole sighed and looked down at the magazine.

"Maria, why do you buy these gossipy things?"

"I didn't buy that one. It was in the solarium."

A patient anchored to an IV approached the desk. Maria immediately abandoned the magazine and turned her attention to him.

Nicole absently turned the page and was about to shove the tabloid to one side, when the picture of someone familiar caught her eye. She looked closer and saw Julian wearing swimming trunks and strolling on a beach with his arm wrapped around a nearly nude blond in a thong bikini. The caption read: Latin singer Julian Marquez and actress Dana Reid are inseparable in Acapulco.

So that's what he did in Mexico, and I, like a fool, spent my precious time worrying about him and taking care of him, when he probably deserved to be sick. Angrily, she ripped the picture out of the magazine and tore it into tiny pieces.

Of course she knew there was no justification for her feelings—hadn't she told Julian that they could only be friends? Hadn't she sworn to herself that she wouldn't read about, think about, or question anything pertaining to his illustrious sex life? All of these things she had vowed, but there was no denying the fact that she was still upset.

Hanging out with four giggling eight-year-old girls and one silent little boy, was not the best way to spend a Saturday evening, but for Julian it had been something of a diversion. At first, Trey had seemed unnerved by the group, but he'd let the boy sit on the end of the row near him and he'd managed to convince him that it was their job to look after the girls, since they were the only guys. The concept worked and in the end he knew Trey had enjoyed the show.

It was now late in the evening and the other kids had been dropped off at their homes. Julian was back at his estate with Trey and Amanda. There was no reason to return the boy immediately because Nicole didn't get home until midnight, and he was sure her sister could use a break from watching him. As far as Amanda was concerned, Julian was convinced that she would always be at his place if Elena didn't intervene.

"Can we watch *The Lion King?*" Amanda asked, bounding into the living room, with Trey following.

"Yeah," Julian said, taking the disc from her. He popped it into the DVD player and both kids flopped down on the floor to watch the wide-screen TV.

Julian wandered off to the music room, relieved that Amanda and Trey had discovered something to amuse themselves with. The little boy had been glued to him for almost the entire evening.

He sat down at the gleaming, black Steinway piano and played a few notes—trying to add on to a song he'd been mentally composing. The guitar was his instrument of choice, but some things just required a piano.

An hour later, Amanda silently entered the room and sat down on the piano bench beside him.

"What's up, *chica?* Where's Trey?"

"He's watching the movie," she said, swinging her legs back and forth.

"And why aren't you?"

" 'Cause I hate that part. You know, when the little lion's father dies. It makes me cry."

Little lion's father! Amanda's words struck him suddenly. He had seen the movie a while ago and had since forgotten that the animated film contained a rather powerful death scene. It was probably a movie that Nicole wouldn't want Trey to see. He rushed back toward the living room and then hesitated as he noted that the boy was so riveted to the screen that he was unaware of being observed.

Julian took a deep breath and watched as the cartoon lion cub walked around with drooping ears, obviously in mourning. Despite the intensity of his concentration, Trey did not seem overly disturbed by what he was seeing. It would be ridiculous, and possibly more damaging, if he were to come rushing in to turn the TV off.

"Is it over yet?" Amanda asked, coming up behind him.

He nodded and quietly returned to the music room. It was so hard to know what was going on in the mind of a child who could not speak. In truth, he really didn't know enough about Trey to reach any conclusion. What had Nicole told her son about death? Had he attended his father's funeral? Did he actually remember his father? He had been only three at the time, but it had impacted him so much that he'd lost his voice.

Even though he didn't know enough about the case, Julian felt that if Trey's emotions had been dealt with immediately after the trauma, he would have gotten over it better. He didn't think it was Nicole's fault because she had been in too much pain herself.

The insight he had, if that's what it was, came from his own childhood memories of life and loss. Strangers in uniforms had taken his father away in the night. No one had explained anything to him. Soon after that, he'd been told one second that his father had died and in the next that his mother was dead too. He had not attended any funerals for them. When Elena and Luis had taken him to the United States, he had secretly been hoping that his father would be there waiting for him.

He remembered the painfully shy child he used to be—the one who always felt inferior to everyone else. The one who was either laughed at or ignored, and finally the one who learned to listen to his father's voice in his heart, and discovered the music that gave him wings to fly.

The memory disturbed him. From where he was now, he did not like to admit having been so vulnerable, but he knew that child, still very much alive within him, fueled his passions, his emotions and his humanity. That child kept him from flying too high, and that child would not let him forget who he was or where he had come from. It was Nicole's fault that the child was getting louder and louder.

Trey entered the room and Julian quickly came back to the present. He looked at his watch and noticed it was eleven o'clock. "Ready to go home, *amigo?*"

Trey shook his head in a negative response, and moved to the corner of the room. He cautiously touched the guitar that was propped up against the wall. He glanced at Julian.

Julian smiled. "You want to play it? Bring it over here."

Eagerly, Trey came forward with the guitar, handing it to him. "Oh no, you don't," Julian said. "I'm not going to play it. You are."

The child laughed. Julian held him close, guiding his fingers on the guitar strings, as he'd done the night he'd met Nicole's parents. The first tune that came to his mind was one of the first his father had taught him, an old Spanish tune called 'Guantanamera.' After a few times going over it, Trey could play the opening chords by himself.

"Man, you're really good," he told the smiling boy. "When I was about your size, my father taught me to play that song. I don't think I caught on that quick."

Trey looked at him as if he wasn't quite sure he could believe that. "It's true," Julian insisted. "My father taught me how to sing too. Bet you can't beat me at that."

The child studied him incredulously while Julian pretended to ignore the expression. Trey played the opening chords again and Julian sang the first lines. "Your turn, Trey."

He felt a sudden rush of exhilaration as he noticed Trey silently mouthing the words, but it ended when Trey suddenly stopped playing and started to throw the guitar to the floor. Julian caught it just in time.

"Hey, it's okay. It's okay. You don't have to sing if you don't want to," he said, hanging on to the child who was struggling to get away. "A lot of really great musicians can't sing, but if you're angry, don't take it out on the guitar. It didn't do anything. It just wants to be your voice. If you're mad at me for asking you to sing, let *me* know. Make a mean face of something, but don't throw things."

Trey stopped struggling, realizing that this man was stronger than he'd even imagined. He was much too strong to get away from. Surrendering, he looked worriedly up at Julian's face, and was relieved to find no trace of anger there. He hung his head.

Ironically, Trey's downcast expression reminded Julian of the lion cub in the movie.

"Nobody's angry at you," he said softly, putting the guitar aside. He placed his hand under Trey's chin and lifted his head. "I hope you had a good time tonight. Did you like that movie?"

Trey responded by nodding his head eagerly.

Julian knew he was about to commit a breach in confidence. Nicole had asked him not to discuss anything concerning death with Trey, but the words escaped anyway. "That was sad when he lost his father, wasn't it? When I was little I kind of felt the same way he did when my father died."

He could almost feel the intensity of Trey's undivided attention.

"I thought it was my fault," he continued. "I was walking around looking all sad with my head hanging down, didn't want to talk to anyone. But after a while I started to realize that there really was nothing I could have done to change things. The world is both good and bad. Sometimes really terrible things happen to good people; but you know something, Trey? The people you love don't really leave you even when they die. Oh, it's true you don't see them anymore, but sometimes you hear them in the voices of other people who love you, your mother, your grandparents, even your friends."

He took a deep breath. Trey's golden brown eyes were wide and attentive, understanding as much as a six year old could, and he was bonding for reasons that were possibly more intense than Julian even thought.

"My father loved the ocean," Julian murmured, his arms around the boy. "Sometimes when I'm alone, walking on the beach, I listen to the sound of the waves and it's almost like I can still hear him. I hear him in the music from my guitar too."

He sat up straighter on the piano bench, bracing his back against the instrument, noting that Trey, still in his arms, showed no sign of wanting to escape.

"All fathers don't like the same things, though. I'll bet your father liked…" He tried to imagine what Nicole's late husband would have enjoyed. "How about baseball?"

Encouraged by Trey's smile, he ventured further. "Imagine this— you're watching your favorite player hit a home run, and everybody's cheering. In the roar of the crowd, you can hear your father cheering too. Better yet, suppose it's you. Trey Evans up at bat."

Trey laughed at the imagery.

"Your father's rooting for you, Trey. He's right there with you— cheering louder than everybody else, and you don't have to be a baseball player. You can be whatever you choose, doctor, architect," he noticed Trey pointing at the guitar, "or musician. He just wants you to be the best you can be, and your mother and grandparents want that too."

And what about you? Trey's eyes asked him wistfully. *Is that what you want me to be?*

"Me too," Julian concluded.

He suddenly felt deflated. Nicole would no doubt be appalled by the conversation. He was about as far from Trey's father as anyone could get, yet the boy was clearly trying to see him as a potential substitute and he had been willingly falling for it. Breaking the spell, he reached for the guitar and placed it in Trey's arms.

"Okay, maestro. Let's hear "Guantanamera" one more time so you don't forget."

Obediently, Trey repeated the chords he had learned.

"Excellent! Now it's time for you to go home."

Amanda had fallen asleep on the floor in front of the television. Julian woke her up, despite her protests, and they all stepped outside, to be immediately caught up in the glare of headlights from an approaching car.

Julian flinched in irritation as Elena and Luis stepped out, both attired in formal wear. He wondered what pretense-at-charity, high society social affair Elena had talked her husband into this time.

"My goodness, Elena exclaimed, spotting her daughter. "Amanda, what on earth are you doing up this late?"

"Mommy, it's okay," Amanda said. "Nanny said I could. We were just watching a movie."

"Well, into the house, right now, young lady." Elena glared at Julian. She would have to have a talk with Amanda's nanny.

Amanda hurried to obey. Luis flashed Julian an apologetic look, then put his hand on his wife's arm in an attempt to guide her inside. But Elena halted, noticing Trey for the first time. "Why, hello there. Who are you?" she asked.

Julian opened the door of his Explorer for Trey to get in, and the little boy averted eye contact with Elena completely as he scrambled inside.

"Julian, whose child is that?" Elena demanded, the irritation at having been snubbed, apparent in her voice.

"He doesn't talk, Mommy!" Amanda yelled from the doorway, before Julian could answer.

"Doesn't talk," Elena repeated, then impatiently snapped at her daughter. "Amanda get inside and go to bed right now!"

She turned her attention back to Julian who was about to get in the car. "Who's the little boy?"

"The son of a friend," Julian said nonchalantly. "What's the big deal?"

"Your friends allow their children to stay up all night?"

"Elena," Luis tried to intervene. "This is not your business."

"He's my brother. Don't tell me that he's not my business! Julian, have you lost your mind? Don't you remember what happened to that other singer who liked hanging around children?"

"Elena, why don't you just..." He stopped himself, remembering that Trey was in the car. "That doesn't deserve a reply."

Julian turned the key in the ignition and glared back at her through the open window. He was completely disgusted by what she had implied, although certainly not surprised. He knew that she had always considered him to be a talented, hopelessly immature person, who was also brainless and inferior, but accusing him of being a pervert was something new.

"Julian, ignore that," Luis said loudly. "You know how your sister is. She doesn't mean it."

His words fell on the retreating headlights as the car pulled off.

CHAPTER SIXTEEN

"Hello, Julian. This is Nicole." She tried to control the irritation in her voice, but she couldn't completely obliterate it.

"Nicole," he said, sounding pleased. "Can you hang on a few minutes? I'm in the studio.

Hang on? I'd really like to hang you at this moment, Nicole thought as she held the phone to her ear.

"Okay. I'm in the lobby. I can talk," he said.

"You let my son watch *The Lion King* last night after I told you not to…"

"How do you know that?"

"I asked him. Trey draws pictures and sometimes we communicate that way, but that's beside the point. I told—"

"It wasn't intentional," Julian interrupted. "It's Amanda's favorite movie. She wanted to see it and I wasn't even thinking until—"

"You're the adult. You're supposed to think," she reminded him curtly.

"What's the problem? Did he seem upset by it?"

She was taken aback. "Well, no. He didn't seem to be." She was the one who was upset. Trey had been quite pleased with the entire evening.

"I didn't think so," Julian replied before she could get another word in. "How about coming with me to Barbados next weekend?"

The man never ceased to amaze her. Nicole shook her head in despair. She was still annoyed by what had happened with Trey and wanted to discuss it further, but typically he'd made light of her irritation and had the audacity to throw in an invitation. Of course she couldn't just drop everything and go to Barbados. Normal women didn't do such things unless they were hopelessly in love.

"I know what you're going to say, but I won't take no for an answer. I'm sure you can get Friday off from work. You must have a lot of unused vacation days," Julian continued.

She found herself taking offense. She was not some publicity-starved starlet dying to be in his presence, but her response came out like a weak excuse. "Julian, even if I could, I can't leave Trey with my sister. She has a date."

"I told you I'm not going to take no for an answer. Trey can come with us."

Why don't you ask Dana? she thought, but bit her lip to keep from saying it. The remark would sound just like something a jealous lover would say, and Julian was only her friend. She wasn't above lecturing her friends when they needed it, but she never got offended over what they did with their personal lives.

She had been to some of the other islands but never to Barbados. She desperately needed to break up the routine of her life and three days away would not hurt, especially because Trey would be with them. What harm could it possibly do?

"But isn't Barbados a little far to travel for just three days?" she asked haltingly.

"No. It's roughly a two-hour flight, and it's one of my favorite islands, real nice and low-key. I'll pick you up in the morning. Just bring passports or birth certificates."

They arrived at the airport on Friday and Nicole was shocked to discover they were not going on a commercial airliner but a private Learjet. Julian assured her that their pilot was one of the best and was also a friend whose services he used while on tour. Another surprise was that Amanda and her fiftyish *au pair*, Michelle, were also accompanying them. Julian explained that Michelle would look after both kids, leaving them free to pursue more adult things. His clever plotting unnerved her a bit, but it was too late to back out.

The flight was smooth and it was around noontime that they landed at the airport in Barbados, to the tune of an obligatory welcoming steel drum band. After passport checks and customs red tape, a chauffeur picked them up for the ride to the hotel.

Nicole would have been even more unsettled had it not been for Amanda's persistent chattering, bringing her back to reality. Trey, who had a fascination with airplanes, continued to watch the airport's landing strip until it vanished from sight.

They had a suite in a first class hotel, with the largest room going to the kids and Michelle. Nicole and Julian had their own separate rooms.

"Any complaints about the accommodations?" Julian asked.

"No. This is more than perfect." She wandered about, pushing open the sliding doors and stepping out onto the balcony, which overlooked gardens and a fountain. In the distance she could see the ever-present turquoise sea.

Julian retreated to his room to make some business calls, while she checked out the large living room and dining room. The master bathroom had a Jacuzzi. She realized that after having seen his Miami home, she was no longer dazzled by opulence. This definitely was befitting a celebrity, but it paled in comparison to his place.

Trey trailed around after her because Julian was temporarily off limits. Nicole noticed even more that her son was really getting attached to him, and she wasn't sure it was a good thing. How was Trey going to handle it when the roar of the crowd and the glow of the spotlight took his current hero away permanently? How was *she* going to handle it?

A maid served lunch in the dining room, without being obtrusive. She simply set everything up and left as quickly and quietly as she'd appeared. Amanda and Trey attacked the food ravenously, as though they'd been starving for days.

"Hey, you two, easy," Nicole said laughing. "Save something for the rest of us."

"There's a lot," Amanda replied, her mouth full.

Michelle lightheartedly reprimanded Amanda for her uncivilized behavior, then announced that she would take the children out for a walk around the grounds. She told Nicole everything they planned to do. She was not the least bit uncomfortable with Trey's silence. Nicole could tell that Michelle was a very capable woman, and she had no cause to worry about Trey being under her care.

Trey was not so thrilled with the plans. He wanted to be with Julian. Amanda whispered something in his ear and abruptly his attitude changed and he seemed content to go. She would have to question Amanda about that later on.

Nicole retreated to her room. What she really wanted to do was take a quick walk on the beach and wade in the water. From her open suitcase, she selected one of two bathing suits she had brought. They were both scoop-necked, one-piece styles similar to the types Warren had liked on her. In private, he had preferred her in a bikini, but in public he had always made an issue over the imagined notion that other men were looking at her. It annoyed her now when she thought back on it.

She remembered a vacation in Bermuda. She had left Warren in the hotel room and gone walking on the beach wearing a turquoise blue bikini, her hair in long cornrow braids, searching around for exotic shells. There were other scantily clad people swimming and sunning around her but not intrusively. Warren had appeared, carrying a long cover up skirt, suggesting that she wear it. Nicole had objected.

"I don't see anyone else wearing cover-ups. Why should I?"

"If all the guys gawking at you knew what I had to put up with, they wouldn't find you so sexy."

The words had hurt. She remembered not speaking to him for the rest of the day and becoming even more infuriated when he seemed to have no clue what he'd done wrong.

Why am I thinking about that? she wondered. It was an annoying flaw, but it wasn't all his fault. Warren had been raised the oldest child in a single-parent family consisting of a mother and four whining sisters. He'd worked at a young age to support the family when his high school dropout mother couldn't get a job. Even after his mother died and the sisters were adults, they'd always come running to him when they needed something. He'd learned to view women as indecisive and weak, always needing a man to advise them, and he had taken that attitude into their marriage.

Resolved not to think about the past anymore, she selected the yellow-gold suit, and after showering, she slipped it on and checked herself out in the full-length mirror. Fortunately she did not see any unsightly bulges or sagging skin. Not bad for a woman who was no longer in her twenties.

She knew that Julian was going to be observing her and it was going to feel awkward. He had never seen her in so little clothing before. She felt naked. Maybe he wouldn't pay that much attention. After all, he was used to ethereal beauties like Dana and countless others. She was just an ordinary, tall, leggy woman with flaws—just his friend. It would be okay.

She tied on a tropical-print wrap-around skirt with yellow patterns that matched the top of the suit. She loosened the bonds holding her ponytail and shook out her long ripples of hair. The tresses fell halfway down her back, covering the exposed skin. Methodically she slathered sun block on her face, legs and arms, recalling that Michelle had remembered to do the same for Trey and Amanda.

"You fool," she muttered aloud to herself as she sprayed on a lightly scented cologne and inspected herself one more time. What exactly were her reasons for all this agonizing and primping? She rarely spent more than ten minutes in front of a mirror normally.

There was a light tap on her door. "Vacation's officially started," Julian said. "How about a stroll on the beach?"

"My plans exactly. I'll be out in a second," she called back.

HAVANA SUNRISE

Julian surveyed the banquet spread on the dining room table, sampled some of the hors d'oeuvres, and waited. He felt slightly agitated. Would Nicole finally drop some of her reserve? Would the beauty of the island cast a spell? They only had three days, counting this one. The awful truth was he didn't really know if he wanted her to completely drop her reserve. It was one of the things that intrigued him. She made him feel as if he were courting a girl from another era. Even the notion of *courting*, if that really was what he was doing, seemed strange.

Nicole breezed into the room and turning to look at her, he was rendered speechless by her exotic beauty. She tossed the tube of sun block at him and he caught it.

"You look stunning," he exclaimed.

She pretended to ignore his comment. "The sun can be extremely damaging to skin. Why is it that most men always forget that?"

"Elena reminds me constantly," he replied, his eyes still glued on her.

"This time Elena is right." Nicole said.

To placate her he smeared the stuff on. Nicole sampled the fruit punch on the table, watching him out of the corner of her eye. It was funny because he kind of made her think of an outrageously handsome boy in his black v-necked T-shirt and fluorescent, aqua swimming trunks that came just above the knee—Trey all grown up. He would probably be appalled if he could read her mind.

"All done, Mom," Julian said, handing the tube back to her.

He took her hand and gently pulled her close to him, so close that she could feel both of their hearts beating. Instantly all of her visions of him as a young boy fled. He brushed her lip with his finger, sending tremors up her spine.

"Let's take that walk now," he said.

CHAPTER SEVENTEEN

The white sand shifted under her feet as they walked hand-in-hand, skirting the tide. The water was several surreal shades of blue. A few palm trees dotted the beach but they didn't provide much relief from the blazing sun.

"Julian, are there places in Cuba that look like this?"

"I have no clue what Cuba looks like at this point," Julian said, squinting in the sunlight.

"I know you haven't been there for years, but what do you remember?"

"There are good beaches at Varadaro. Mostly Canadian tourists go there now, but before the Soviet Union fell, it used to be a hang-out for the Russians."

"What about the Cuban people?"

"They mostly work there."

He was not going to elaborate on that subject, she noticed. He released her hand and stripped the T-shirt off over his head, tossing it on the sand, where they had placed their towels, far from the tide's reach.

"I never did ask you if you can swim. Can you?"

"Yes," she replied. "I wouldn't exactly call myself a good swimmer, though. I usually restrict myself to pools."

He looked thoughtful for a moment. "Well, just don't go in too deep. We're on the Atlantic side of the island. The water here can be a little rough. The Caribbean side is a lot gentler."

Nicole undid the skirt and tossed it where he had thrown his shirt. Julian's eyes appraised her. He gave an audible sigh of relief.

"What was that for?" she asked nervously.

"I'm just grateful that you're not wearing one of those old lady suits with the skirt."

Instinctively she slapped him. "I'm not sixty yet."

"That you definitely are not."

His attention was more than unnerving. She tried not to blush. "Of course if you were expecting a thong, I'm not sorry to disappoint you."

"I did buy you one," Julian said.

"You better be kidding. I'm not Dana." *Ouch! I had to let that slip,* she thought.

"Dana?" Julian quizzed.

"Dana Reid," Nicole said wanly. That model...actress you were with in Mexico. It was in the gossip column."

Julian seemed amused. "It's all just publicity. Famous people like to be seen with others who are. It attracts attention. Dana Reid means nothing to me."

Nicole shrugged, trying to sound nonchalant. "Your hand was on her backside."

He laughed. "She put it there just when she noticed the photographer. Why are we talking about Dana? You are more beautiful than she is, even if you're not wearing a thong."

She rolled her eyes. "Oh, please. I don't even compare. It's her job to look beautiful. I'm just average."

"Her job?" Julian repeated. "You're absolutely right. It *is* her job. I prefer natural beauty, though. As they walked slowly into the water, his arm encircled her slim waist. "You must look at yourself in some kind of distorted mirror, like the kind in a fun-house, because what you see is definitely not what other people see. You're a gorgeous woman."

Nicole felt the urgent sweep of the cool waves inching up her legs. She tried to laugh. "I think the beauty of Barbados and the sun have gotten to you."

His eyes twinkled. "That and the fact that Elena's going to have a stroke if she finds out that I took her daughter with us."

"She doesn't know?" Nicole looked surprised.

"No. Elena's in San Diego visiting some relatives. Luis said I could take Amanda since she kept begging to go."

"Well, Luis is her father. He's the one who'll be in trouble if she finds out. She really shouldn't be all that upset. I mean, Amanda's nanny is here too. She's probably with Amanda more than her mother is, right?"

"Probably," he admitted. "I sometimes think Amanda sees Michelle more as her mother."

"Is that what your future children have in store for them?" Nicole asked. "That is, if you decide to get married and have a family."

"No. There may be a nanny to help out, but my wife will take care of our children. I will also be involved in their lives as much as I can. I don't see any point in having children if someone else is going to raise them."

I totally agree with you," Nicole said. "But things happen, things you don't plan, like suddenly your wife or husband dies."

Julian turned to face her. He felt the urgent force of the waves pushing against his back as he placed both hands on her shoulders. "I believe a good parent has the ability to adapt and do the best they can in whatever situation they find themselves. You are a good parent."

His lips brushed hers and she smiled slowly. He took her hand. "Coming?"

"No. I think I've gone far enough. I'll watch you." She stood in the swirling water and watched him swim with effortless strokes. "Don't go too far!" she yelled.

Nicole waded around in the surf for a while and then went back to the beach. She sat on a towel under a palm tree and looked around. It was the hotel's private beach so there were only a few other people swimming and walking around. A tiny crab scuttled by and she watched it burrow itself into the sand.

Julian returned, beads of water clinging to his mocha skin. What an arresting presence he was, with his blue-black hair and sinewy athletic body. Nicole noted that a few bikini-clad women were watching him from a distance. He seemed oblivious. Together they walked back across the beach toward the hotel with his arm around her once again.

He surreptitiously allowed his hand to slide down a little so it touched the smooth, firm skin of her outer thigh. Pleased that she didn't object, he entertained other thoughts. They were two adults far away from home—from bonds and restrictions. They were now in a fantasy world. Maybe tonight would be the night. Maybe she'd allow him to…

"Oh, look," Nicole exclaimed, interrupting his thoughts. "Isn't this a beautiful shell?" She knelt to pick it up, freeing his hand.

"It is," Julian said, trying not to sound deflated as she offered him a perfectly formed, pearly-white shell with an underside that looked like shimmering, pink marble.

Back inside, Michelle and the kids had not returned, so they changed clothes and had lunch together in relative silence. Nicole wondered what he was thinking about because his eyes suddenly seemed distant. She didn't break the silence until after they had finished eating.

"Oh, I almost forgot to tell you that I was in the record store the other day and I spotted this tape by some artists I'm sure you'll like." She went to her room to fish it out of her bag and returned, handing it to him.

Julian inspected the tape. It was a recording of a group of old-time Cuban musicians still living in Cuba who had been brought together by an American producer who had visited the island for that purpose.

"I've been listening to it and it's got some really fascinating sounds. There's an old-timer who can really sing," she said. "It's a shame that the rest of the world has been deprived of them for so long because of politics."

"They are good," Julian said abruptly, rising from the table, abandoning the tape there. "I'll listen to it later."

Nicole stared at him. He was completely brushing off her gift, as though she'd handed him a bag of garbage. His response was like a slap in the face, and the reason was just starting to dawn on her.

"Oh, I guess you're following *that* agenda too, she said, not bothering to conceal her sarcasm.

His eyes narrowed. "What agenda?"

"Boycotting artists from Cuba because they chose to remain there."

Julian looked annoyed. "How I think or feel politically has nothing to do with us, but yes, I do have personal opinions."

"They're artists, Julian! Artists like you." Her voice rose. "Art should not be a political issue. Why is it that you and a lot of Cubans in Miami get so, so hysterical over these things when your generation has grown up in America?"

"Nicole," Julian said firmly. "I would prefer not to go there. As far as *hysterical* is concerned, that's an exaggeration. Even if I did try to explain, you wouldn't understand."

She sat down on the couch, crossing one tawny leg over the other. "Try me."

He paced around. "We lost our inheritance to a tyrannical charlatan. The United States is our adopted country. It has become home, and it's good to us, but our hearts are still in Cuba. We had to leave so many things behind there."

Nicole sighed. "I hear you, but from what I understand there was nothing so great about pre-Revolutionary Cuba either—especially for someone of color. You would have been considered a mulatto in that time. There was a lot of racism. Black entertainers had to go through backdoors into clubs just as they did in the South of the fifties and sixties."

"There was a lot of that American South influence in Cuba at the time," Julian admitted. "But as bad as all that was, at least living within a democracy there is a blueprint for change. You *can* speak out and protest. Communism is kind of like robbing Peter's wealth just to pay Paul peanuts. It makes everyone a slave except for the tyrant who instigates it."

She detected that he was still holding back something—something even more personal than what he'd revealed. "But what does all this mean to you as an individual? How does it affect you personally?"

"How does it affect me?" Julian's eyes became deep pools of reflection. "It means that I will never be able to say to my children or grandchildren that this is the park I used to play in, this is the school I used to go to, or this is where your great grandfather is buried. It means that all I can show them is a map of an island in the Atlantic that looks like a wound waiting to be sutured...closed...healed. But as time goes on, the wound only festers and deepens."

His emotional words struck her. The things he'd spoken of were things she took for granted. His nostalgia could only be compared to her enslaved ancestors longing for Africa. But Africa was vast and diverse and centuries removed from Nicole. With the blood of Europeans flowing through her as well, Nicole felt only a kinship, not a longing for Africa.

She no longer wanted to continue the discussion. Everyone had a right to their own feelings, and while she definitely did not believe in communism, she could see some of the reasons why the revolution had occurred. It was a fascinating chapter in history to her, but for him it was a chapter of his life.

"I'm sorry," she said, not knowing what else to say. "Actually what happened in Cuba is not much different than the history of the whole world. It makes one wonder if mankind in general really has the capacity to govern itself." She smiled ironically. "Maybe you'll agree with my mom's Bible philosophy."

"What is your mom's philosophy?" Julian asked.

"That the whole world is in the power of Satan, the wicked one. One day God will cleanse the earth and he will set things straight."

Julian smiled slowly. "I think your mom might have a valid point."

"And she'll clobber anyone who doesn't agree that she's right," Nicole added.

"Your mom's an intense lady, so's her daughter."

"Intense?" she quizzed. "Is that how you see me?"

Julian was relieved that he didn't have to reply to that because Michelle and the children entered, noisily. Trey ran to Nicole to show off a bag of interesting shells he'd collected.

"I've got some really cool ones too," Amanda declared, offering them to Julian.

Michelle kept the children occupied that evening, long enough for Nicole and Julian to have dinner in the hotel's exquisite restaurant; afterwards there was dancing to a reggae band. Nicole was a little overwhelmed by Julian's dancing finesse, but he held her in such a way that she had no choice but to move with him. She soon discovered that it was almost too easy to lose herself. She could not remember having had so much fun in a long time—the kind of fun only a man and a woman could share.

Julian became even more aware of the fact that he was tired of her friendship restrictions and tired of his own fear of completely revealing his feelings about her. He wanted her so badly that he knew he was going to slip up at some point and become blatantly obvious. And why shouldn't he? She *had* to feel the same way about him, despite the fact that their cultures were so different. The game they were playing could not go on indefinitely.

His grip tightened around her as they moved across the dance floor. They were two adults on vacation, away from their usual surroundings. Maybe, just maybe, she would cast aside her rigid inhibitions and succumb to the sensual spell of the island.

Julian did not get his wish. Nicole returned to her room late and found herself sharing it with Trey, who insisted on being with her. She was not surprised by his reaction, because he was only six and had rarely spent nights far from his bedroom at home.

The next day Amanda insisted that she and Trey did not want to spend the rest of their vacation time with Michelle. Nicole and Julian ended up indulging them in the usual tourist entertainment, like a submarine dive on the *Atlantis,* a cruise on a mock-pirate ship called

The Jolly Roger, snorkeling, swimming, and a bus tour around the island.

The kids had a great time, and although Nicole was secretly sorry that her private moments with Julian had been forfeited, she was also relieved that she would not have to compromise or confront her worst fears about being lured into intimacy with him. There were many things that went way beyond physical appeal that she admired and loved about him and just one of those things was his great patience and tolerance in dealing with children.

On the last evening, Julian was out strolling around the beach and hotel grounds with Trey and Amanda, while Nicole sat quietly on the well-lit terrace. The night air was warm and balmy, but not oppressive. Now and then she could catch a whiff of the intoxicating aroma of the flowers in the garden below, the scent being driven by a gentle breeze off the ocean.

"Hope I'm not intruding," a familiar voice with a slight French accent said.

Nicole looked up to see Michelle standing there in a long print dress, her frizzy brown hair confined to a pinned up chignon.

"Oh, no. Of course you're not intruding," Nicole replied quickly, smiling at her.

"It's such a beautiful evening," Michelle said, helping herself to one of the deck chairs. Her perceptive gray eyes scanned Nicole. "Oh, I've been meaning to tell you what a delightful little boy you have. He is so bright." She hesitated for a moment as if unsure whether to go on. "I...don't mean to be nosy, but is Trey currently seeing a speech therapist?"

You are being nosy, Nicole thought, but swallowed the sarcasm. It was only natural that a woman who spent her life working with other people's children would ask. "He has been to so many that I've lost count. None of them were of much help. They reached a point where they just gave up on him."

"That doesn't seem very professional," Michelle said. "No one should give up on a child."

"I couldn't agree more, but I've battled, screamed, ripped my hair out for years over the dilemma. I will never give up on my son, but the system just doesn't cooperate and Trey doesn't make it easy. He has been known to become hostile when too much pressure is applied. It's even caused one fool, who's supposed to be educated, to imply that Trey might be autistic."

"It must be terrible for you," Michelle said empathetically. "Raising a little boy without a father is extremely difficult anyway."

"I definitely can't argue with that," Nicole said, suddenly wondering just how much Julian had told Michelle about Trey and herself. She had nothing against the woman, but she didn't want her life dissected either. It was time to turn the conversation around. "So, Michelle, tell me, how long have you been working with the..."

"Torres family," Michelle filled in, realizing Nicole didn't know Amanda's surname. "I've been with them for about seven years. Amanda was a year old when I came. She's a darling, but a real handful at times, very headstrong and self-willed."

A faint smile crossed Nicole's face. "Would you call that a family trait?"

"Definitely. Amanda's mother is not an easy person to work for. As a matter of fact, she told me she hired and fired at least eight *au pairs* before I came along."

"I guess I'm not surprised," Nicole said. "I don't know Julian's sister, but I've heard things."

Michelle smiled reflectively. "Julian is nothing like any of them. It is because of him that Amanda is *not* an incorrigible little tyrant. She adores him, you know. I think she loves her uncle more than her own parents. Despite what some people might think, Julian is a very kind man. He always treats his employees with respect, no matter what positions they might hold. I have never heard even one of them say anything disparaging about him."

"He *is* very generous," Nicole admitted.

"I only wish he would find that special someone and get married," Michelle concluded.

"Married? Why? He seems okay as the swinging bachelor."

"He's good at pretending to be a swinger, but he is really very unhappy and his family doesn't treat him right."

Nicole sighed. "Julian's a grown man. He doesn't have to put up with that if he doesn't want to."

"That is true, but Mrs. Torres has some kind of strange control over him." Michelle's eyes searched the sky, and then riveted back on Nicole. "Julian seems to think you're special."

"He told you that?" Nicole felt her heart throb impulsively.

"Not in words, but he is different around you, happier, more care-free. You are nothing like the women he usually goes out with."

Why, because I'm not Caucasian or Cuban? "Some men just like variety to spice things up," she said.

Michelle rose slowly. "I don't think that's true in this case, but it's really none of my business. I hope I haven't offended you in any way."

"I'm not offended. I appreciate your honesty, actually. Maybe we can talk again sometime," Nicole said.

"I would like that," Michelle replied, slipping back inside. "Enjoy the night."

"I will," Nicole murmured, fully aware that it was the last night.

CHAPTER NINETEEN

They returned to Miami in time for lunch at Julian's estate, without Michelle and Amanda, who reluctantly retreated to their own section. Nicole was intensely aware that it was Monday and she had to be at the hospital in just a few hours. If she were in any profession other than nursing, she would simply call in and say she would be in the next day. But people were depending on her and if she didn't show up, it would force someone else to fill in for her on short notice.

Julian and Trey seemed oblivious to her obligation, even though she had mentioned it several times since landing.

"Trey, I've got something I think you're going to like," Julian announced as they were sitting around in the living room.

Trey's eyes lit up in anticipation as Julian vanished from the room. He returned carrying a large box that he placed on the floor. Trey rushed forward, eager to open it. Nicole rose and glanced at Julian apprehensively. She hoped this was not something she was going to have to object to.

"Don't look so worried," Julian teased. "It's not a weapon of any kind."

A beaming Trey exposed a black leather guitar case, housing a brand new guitar. He pulled it out of the case and held it as though it was the finest treasure on earth. Nicole had to smile.

"All yours, but only if you practice playing every day," Julian said.

Trey nodded in total agreement, strumming the chords.

That's asking a lot from a six-year-old, Nicole thought. Knowing Trey, he'd probably be infatuated with the guitar for a few days and then it would be forever resigned to its case. "Julian, you shouldn't have," she started, then hesitated. "Trey, say thank you."

The brilliant smile still lighting his face, Trey gestured his appreciation in sign language.

Nicole glanced at her watch, noting that it was one forty-five. She paced around while Julian discussed music with Trey. Sighing, she stepped out into the foyer and immediately her eyes were riveted on a fresh batch of fan mail that would soon be in the garbage. She opened a few letters, knowing Julian wouldn't mind. A fan pledged her undying devotion to him, another one wanted a date, another raved endlessly about how gorgeous he was, and the last fan had written a song that she wanted him to record. At the bottom of the pile were two purple envelopes and one black one. Disgusted, Nicole picked them up. She had been hoping the lunatic had quit writing him.

"Nicole, come in here and listen to Trey," Julian called.

She unconsciously stuffed the envelopes into her purse and rejoined them in the living room, where she was delighted and pleasantly shocked to hear Trey actually playing a song. She clapped very enthusiastically for him.

"When did you learn that?" she asked, hugging her son.

Trey smiled at Julian.

"He picked it up that evening he was with me," Julian explained. He turned his attention back to Trey. "How about if I be your teacher for awhile? Not always, but while I'm not touring."

Trey tugged at Nicole's sleeve. How could she say no? It actually sounded like a great idea. It had been a long time since she'd seen Trey so enthused about anything.

"Well, if you can find the time. I guess it can be arranged, but right now we really, really have to go," she said.

"I know." Julian helped Trey put the guitar back in the case, and the little boy picked it up carefully by the handle. "I have to be somewhere myself in an hour. Max, my chauffeur, will take you guys home."

Nicole hesitated as she watched her son walk to the door with the kind of familiarity that suggested he was comfortable with the palatial surroundings, chauffeur and all. She looked at Julian.

"I want to thank you for three really beautiful days. It ended too quickly," she said.

The dark eyes assessed her. "We have to do it again *soon,* without the kids."

She nodded, feeling foolish, realizing that she was *supposed* to kiss him and wanted to, but because it was so obvious, she refrained. "Oh and for Trey. You seem to have such incredible insight. Thanks for the guitar. He's never even given me any indication that he might be musical. It's amazing." Her eyes shimmered. "It…"

"It's no big deal since I can't seem to give his mother anything," Julian interrupted.

Nicole flinched, knowing full well what he meant. "That's not true. You've given me plenty. Just having your friendship has been like a gift."

"Does that mean we're history already?"

She laughed in spite of herself. "Friendships don't end like that. They continue through the years."

Julian's eyes narrowed. "Do they ever evolve?"

Flustered, she averted the beacon-like intensity of his gaze. "I wish you wouldn't take every little thing I say so seriously, but yes, friendships do sometimes evolve."

They also "dissolve," Julian thought sarcastically as he watched her follow her son's path out to the waiting chauffeur. Barbados had been fun, although hardly the three days he'd envisioned. His frustrations had mounted to a new height. He was sick and tired of the word *friend.* If he never heard it from her lips again it would be too soon. He had sensed right from the start that she was terrified of being hurt, but in reality it seemed he was the one taking the abuse. He should probably just stop seeing her.

There were plenty of other diversions. He still had to put the finishing touches on his new CD and his publicist was after him about some magazine interviews she'd lined up. There was also the party scene, which brought with it women who were his eager accomplices, women he didn't have to fight with just to get a kiss. Of course the opposite end of the spectrum was he had to fight them for a halfway decent conversation.

The real problem was that Nicole was not a diversion and he knew it. There was something more he wanted and needed from her, her physical attributes were only a part of the desire. If he could completely come to grips with where his own heart was leading him, then maybe he'd know what the magic words were, what kind of key it would take to open her heart.

The regular routine quickly took over. Trey was back in school, hating it, but coping better than he had been. Nicole became totally immersed in caring for patients and dodging Maria's questions about Julian and Barbados. Her job did not allow her the luxury of daydreaming, except during breaks, but Julian still haunted her subconscious waking and sleeping moments. She used to wake up imagining that Warren was beside her, but now she was seeing Julian's eyes instead.

She was completely unnerved and disturbed by her own emotions. It didn't seem normal that a man she had known for such a short time could invade her life in such a way. He had agreed to their friendship, but she didn't know how long she was going to be able to stand it. Being around him made her feel like an adolescent madly in love for the first time—and she had never felt that way before, even when she had been a teenager.

Saturday was a day off, and she took Trey to the local park in the morning. The basketball court was empty and she shot a few hoops with him. He was pretty good for his age and she quickly became aware that she was badly suited for one of Warren's favorite sports.

"Trey, you go on practicing. I'll be right here under the tree, reading," she told him.

Trey nodded, racing around the court with the ball. Nicole left the enclosure and sought out shade. She sat down on the grass and extracted a magazine from her bag, hoping Trey would have at least ten minutes before the other kids started appearing. He always retreated when other people were around, no matter how much she encouraged him to stay.

Engrossed in the magazine, listening to the rhythmic thump of the basketball hitting the concrete, it suddenly dawned on her that there was a voice. Quickly she put down the magazine and looked toward the court. Trey was no longer alone. Julian was there playing with him. Her breath caught raggedly in her throat. The man had a way of materializing like a phantom at the most inappropriate and disconcerting moments.

A tinge of resentment sparked within her. She was not in the mood to have to deal with him right now. She drew her jean-clad legs up toward her chin and sat watching them. Trey was doing an expert job trying to block Julian's jump shot, but when the ball bounced off the rim of the hoop instead of going in, she knew Julian had done it on purpose. The two high-fived, and now Julian was down on his knees, more appropriate to Trey's height, trying to block him. Nicole could not resist laughing.

"Uh oh," she murmured aloud, noticing that three kids around Trey's age, maybe a little older, were approaching. They looked like brothers.

"Hey, guys, wanna play?" Julian asked.

Trey immediately dropped the basketball and started to walk away, but Julian draped his arm around his shoulders, pulling him back.

"No hablo ingles," the tallest boy replied, leaning against the fence.

Julian repeated the question in Spanish.

"Si," they all responded in unison.

Nicole couldn't figure out the rest of the conversation except that Julian sounded as if he were introducing them to Trey. She caught that their names were Carlos, Ricky and Roberto. Next Julian turned to Trey and said a few things directly to him. Trey nodded slowly and remained there as the three brothers entered the court. Julian shouted a few more things in Spanish and then he left the court, walking toward her. Nicole sucked in her breath. Trey continued to play with the other kids.

Julian's shadow fell over her and she looked up at him in his baseball hat, beige T-shirt and black jogging pants.

"What *did* you say to him?" she asked.

"It's a secret," he replied, helping himself to a spot under the tree beside her.

"You have to tell me. If it's got something to do with magic, I want to learn."

"No magic. It's just pure logic. Those kids can't speak English and Trey won't speak at all. So who cares if nobody talks. It's all about playing the game."

"Is that *really* all you said?"

"Well, maybe not in those words exactly, but something like that." He stretched out on the carpet of grass, folding his arms behind his head.

"Have you ever taken any courses in child psychology?" she quizzed.

"No. Maybe it comes from the Enrique Sanchez school of heredity," he replied and noticed her puzzled expression. "Enrique was my father. I just remember the way he treated me when I was little."

"He must have been very special," Nicole said, wondering idly why his father's name was Sanchez instead of Marquez.

"Oh, he was…what I remember of him."

"Is it possible that you were a little like Trey when you were young?" Nicole asked. "I mean I'm sure you talked, but…"

"I was a really shy kid," Julian admitted. "My father always encouraged me, not by forcing me to do things I was afraid of, but by motivating me. He always told me that if you have the ability and the talent, nothing is going to stop you. He talked me into playing my first guitar solo in a public plaza in front of about fifty people. I was five years old and terrified, but I did it." He closed his eyes reflectively. "Not far from the plaza, there was this great sea wall. The tide was coming in and the water kind of crashed up against it, making this incredible sound. I felt like an orchestra was backing me. My aunt was there that day too. She was clapping louder than anyone."

"There's nothing wrong with your memory. It's very good and visual," Nicole said after a long silence. "It makes me feel like I was there too."

She wanted him to continue talking, but he stared up at the sky and then at his watch, bringing her back to the present reality. Nicole glanced back at the children playing enthusiastically, before turning her full attention to the man beside her. "So, surely you didn't just happen to be here in this park. Were you following us?"

Julian's eyes slanted under the bill of the hat. "Actually I dropped by your place because there was something I wanted to talk to you about. Allyson told me where you were."

"And are you planning on telling me what you wanted to talk about?" She stretched out on the lawn too, raising herself partially up on her elbows.

"Don't rush me. I need to rest first. Trey gave me quite a workout and I'm not six anymore."

She pulled the hat down over his face. Julian made no move to pull it back up. Sighing, Nicole silently watched him breathe. He stretched like a sinewy cat and she noticed the T-shirt rise slightly and the sunlight play on the exposed part of his mid-section. Impulsively, she walked her fingers across his chest. He pretended to be unaware. Encouraged by the fact that she could not see his expression, her wandering fingers explored his torso, stroking the taut, slightly ridged muscles over his ribcage.

Julian's right arm rose and encircled her, pulling her effortlessly down on top of him. The baseball hat fell aside. He could feel her breath quicken, smell her warm enticing scent as her body pressed tightly against his. With his eyes shut, he kissed the silky skin of her throat, his lips parting the open collar of her cotton blouse, baring her shoulder, covering it with passionate kisses.

Nicole saw the warning lights flash in her head, but she shut them out. She felt the strength of his arms holding her and she reveled in it. Their lips sought each other's and connected hungrily, savoring the pleasure. She was even more aware of his hard body beneath her and she wasn't the least bit repulsed.

"Julian, please," she murmured, a vapid, feeble attempt at protest.

She squeezed her eyes shut as she felt his hands gliding like molten liquid up under her blouse. The straps of her camisole were about to melt away under his touch. The inner warning light went off again and this time she saw it.

"No!" The shouted whisper was so low she barely heard it herself. The flashing in her head grew brighter and a roar sounded in her ears as his fire was about to consume her.

"I *said* no!" she screamed, ripping herself away with almost the same kind of intensity she'd use to escape a predator.

Julian surrendered instantly, but she caught a glimmer of hurt in his eyes as she scrambled to her feet, stabbing the ends of her blouse back into her jeans. She did not want to focus on his reaction. How could she be so wantonly stupid?

"What?" Julian demanded, getting up. "What's wrong with you?"

His voice had a trace of anger in it now, and in a way it was a relief, because it made it easier for her to defend her actions.

"What's wrong with *me*? Have you lost *your* mind? We're in a park, for God's sake! My son is over there playing!" She spat out the words with ferocity, while backing up…into a tree.

As the solid bark slammed against her back, it almost knocked the wind out of her and she looked up to see Julian confronting her, cornering her. She did not like the feeling of being trapped.

"You're right," he said, his voice calmer. "It was indiscreet, but don't lie to me, Nicole, you were enjoying it as much as I was. I'm not a rapist. I wasn't going to hurt you."

"Then get away from me! I need some space," she shouted, struggling for air.

Julian stepped back, his expression a mixture of confusion and resentment.

She rolled her eyes. "This...this wasn't supposed to happen." She tested the words, trying to censor them. "I am not accusing you of being a rapist, but this can't happen again...ever. I don't just mean the timing."

He moved closer again, leaning slightly forward, blocking her exit with arms extended and both hands braced against the trunk of the tree on each side of her, forcing her to look at his eyes. "Why can't it happen?"

"Because...because I'm not like that." She folded her arms defensively against her chest and fought an internal battle for control.

"What are you so afraid of?" he demanded.

"I'm not afraid of you or anyone. It's just that I have rules...principles. You can laugh if you want, but I don't believe in sex outside of marriage."

"We didn't have sex," he said sarcastically.

"And we're *not* going to. Why are you looking at me like that? If you really must know the whole truth, here it is. I'm no good at it. As a matter of fact I'm terrible, rotten, lousy. I'm a prude and I'm definitely not what men like you are looking for!" The torrent of painful words came blurting out of her before she could stop them. The silence that followed was deafening.

"Who told you you're no good at it?" he asked finally.

"I know myself. Take my word for it."

"Who told you?" Julian repeated.

"What do you want me to say?" she cried. "I was married once. It was a good marriage and I loved my husband. He's the only man I've ever been with, but he said...he said..." Her tears were falling freely now and she could not continue.

Julian stepped back a little, giving her some space. "If he's the one who told you that, then he's the one who had the problem. What really shocks me is that you still believe him."

The rage flared up within her again. "You don't know a thing about Warren. There was nothing wrong with him! He was everything that you're not."

"If you give me a chance I can prove that what he told you was wrong," Julian said softly. "I can take you places you've never been—show you things you've never seen, and I don't mean here, but in another time, another place.

My God, what an ego, she thought, with growing repulsion. He had pushed her to the explosion point now. She had never intended to reveal such an intimate matter to him in the first place. Warren was dead and unable to defend himself, and here she was blubbering away all their secrets to a handsome traitor who'd now proven what she'd feared all along, that he only cared about sex.

Gathering strength, she planted her hands on his chest and pushed him away. "Just leave me alone! Go practice your expertise on all your other women."

She hurried back to her original spot, picked up her bag, and crammed the abandoned magazine into it. Shielding herself from the hypnotic glare of his eyes, she moved towards the court and motioned to Trey. She finally looked back at Julian.

"If we never say anything else to each other again, I just want you to know that sex is not a game or an afterthought to me. It's something that requires the kind of commitment that you're not capable of giving."

Julian stood there silently watching. *You know nothing about what I'm capable of giving,* he thought. He was not just seeking a physical entanglement with her, but his actions had certainly suggested otherwise. He cursed himself, but he knew those actions had not been his alone. She'd been a willing contributor too. Now she was talking about commitment. Was he ready for that?

He remembered that he had come seeking her out to discuss just where their so-called relationship was headed and now he knew. She had forced him to face reality and it hurt worse than he'd even imagined.

152

"Well, *adios* to you too, *amiga*," he said finally, trying to sound detached. "Thanks for making me see what a shallow fool I am. I was actually stupid enough to think you liked me."

Nicole's eyes shimmered with tears. "You thought I liked you? Do you *really* like me, Julian? Maybe that's the problem. You've never actually said it, not even one time. You...you've met my whole family. My son adores you, but do I really know anything about you that the rest of the world doesn't already know? The only person I've ever met in your family is Amanda. You've never even given the slightest indication that our worlds might converge." She turned away abruptly. "Trey, come on, *now.*"

Trey reluctantly joined her with the basketball tucked under his arm. He looked worriedly at her. She took his hand firmly. Trey balked, puzzled, and looked back at Julian.

"It's okay, hon," Nicole said urgently. "Julian has to leave. Nothing's wrong."

But everything was wrong. The whole world that just last week had looked so bright and promising was now shattered. As she walked swiftly toward the car, Nicole tried hard not to convey her emotions to Trey, but she knew he was far too perceptive to think nothing was wrong.

CHAPTER TWENTY

Allyson returned home at almost midnight from a date. Nicole, staring zombie-like at the television screen in front of her, heard the sound of laughter and the slam of the car door. Relieved that her sister was back, but not particularly wanting to talk to her, she quickly turned the TV off and retreated to her room. Shane left Trey's room and hurried past her to greet his owner at the door.

"Hey, Nicole. You up?" Allyson announced her presence.

"No. I'm in bed," Nicole said.

"You are not." Allyson flung open the door to reveal Nicole completely dressed, putting her hair in a braid for the night.

"Haven't you ever heard of privacy?" Nicole asked, flashing her sister a sardonic smile.

"Not in this family. Marc said to tell you hello, by the way, and before I forget, he kind of wanted a favor."

"What?" Nicole pinned up the long braid.

"You know that he's still with that jazz band. They have a tape and he was kind of wondering if you could let Julian listen to it."

For a brief second, Nicole had the urge to push Allyson out the door and slam it shut; instead she abruptly sat down on the bed, bit her lip and stared blankly at the wall. She slowly made eye contact again. "I can't do that."

"Well, I know it's a little like taking advantage but..." Allyson stopped. "Wait a minute...what's wrong with you?"

"Nothing. I just don't think I'll be seeing Julian anymore."

"You two broke up?" Allyson stared at her incredulously.

"We didn't break up. We were never actually going together to begin with."

Allyson sat down on the edge of the bed beside her. "Are you going to tell me what happened?"

Nicole sighed. It was hard to try to explain what had happened because she was angrier at herself than at Julian. What had he actually come to tell her anyway? Before her treacherous, wandering fingers had set in motion the whole disastrous chain of events, before she had started the whole thing. Still, she was desperately in need of consolation and wanted to talk to her sister who might understand, even though her better judgment was telling her to keep her mouth shut. She took a deep breath and in a rush, related some of the events that had occurred between them in the park.

After listening, Allyson stood up silently and paced around. "You know, sis, you have a real problem."

Nicole stared at her. Those were *not* the words she wanted to hear.

"The problem is you are just like Mom."

"I am not!" Nicole shot back in defense. She remembered Allyson and herself as teenagers, laughing and talking about how prudish and repressed their mother was—laughing because of her outrageously negative response to public displays of affection, and the fact that she wouldn't even kiss her own husband in front of her children.

"Yes, you are. *Just* like her," Allyson insisted. "No other woman would break up with a man like Julian over that. He's the best thing that could ever happen to you and you're too blind to see it. How could you be so angry at him just for being a...a man!"

Nicole glared at her sister indignantly. "You're right I am blind. I'm also insane because I should have known better than to expect sympathy from you. You're just totally captivated with Julian, aren't you? He's a star. He's good looking and he's got lots of money. Is that all it takes, Allyson? Is it?"

"No! That's not all it takes!" she snapped. "But I wouldn't look down my nose at all those things either. Even Trey likes him, and Trey doesn't like everybody."

"I've known him for only two months," Nicole retorted. "Why can't you understand that this is hard for me. I still think about Warren."

"Warren's dead, gone, buried. You have to go on. And let me tell you something else. I never could stand that man."

"What?" Nicole stared at her sister in shock. "You never told me that before."

"I never told you a lot of things before, because you were the one who married him. I would never have been able to stand a man like that. Warren was manipulative and controlling and you did everything he told you to because you couldn't stand up to him."

"That isn't true! You don't know anything! If it seemed that way, it was because we usually agreed on things."

"What things?" Allyson retorted. "He told you to take up nursing and you did, even though you always told me you wanted to be a journalist. He told you he would never leave Chicago, even though your dream was to live in California. Are you remembering now? Is your mind starting to come back?"

Nicole flung up her arms in frustration. "Those things I wanted back then were selfish, childish things. When you're married and have a family you learn to compromise."

"The only one who compromised was you. Warren never did."

"Oh stop it! Just stop it right now! You're just angry at me because you enjoyed the little fantasy of me going with Julian. Maybe you even thought that he might give you a Porsche for your birthday because I'm your sister." She was going strong now. "Just what would you do if you were me, Ally? No, wait, I already know. You'd flop down on the grass in the park and shout, 'Oh, Julian, take me! Take me!'"

The instant the last few words escaped her mouth, Nicole wished she could take them back, but it was too late. Allyson regarded her in seething silence. Finally she spoke. "So in your high-minded opinion, I'm some kind of whore."

"No! That isn't what I meant. I'm sorry if that's the way it sounded." Nicole wanted to scream. She had had enough confrontations for one day. She struggled for the right words. "It's just that I don't want to hear you talk about Warren in that way. So, he wasn't perfect. Who is?" She threw herself down on the bed, childishly shielding her face with a pillow.

Allyson approached slowly and sat on the edge of the bed. "Look, you're right. This whole conversation is plain stupid. What I thought about Warren is beside the point. You were the one who loved him." She remained silent for a few seconds before speaking again. "Maybe Julian is moving too fast for you. He does kind of have a reputation as a player, but come on, Nic. Can you really blame me for hoping?"

Nicole pushed the pillow away. "No. I can't completely blame you. On the surface, he's like every woman's dream, and he really is great with Trey, but think about this real hard. You admitted yourself that he's got a reputation as a player. Are players ever serious? What does Julian actually want? He can have just about any woman, and in that regard I'm pretty ordinary. I think that maybe he sees me as some kind of challenge. The minute he conquers that challenge he'll move on to the next one. Am I wrong for not wanting to be his springboard?"

"No. You're not wrong for being true to yourself," Allyson acquiesced.

"Do you still think I'm being like Mom?"

Allyson laughed. "Don't push me." She stood up and moved toward the door. "It's getting late."

Nicole sat up. "Oh come on, tell the truth. Am I?"

Framed in the doorway, Allyson folded her arms "Do you think I'm a whore because I *would* sleep with Julian?"

"Allyson!"

Allyson's eyes twinkled. "Like I said. It's getting late."

Sunday, returning from church services, Nicole watched Trey go racing off to his room to change his clothes. It amused her that she never had to remind him to do that. He hated having to wear a suit. She really didn't enjoy getting dressed up herself, but it was a small price to pay in exchange for giving a spiritual lift to the day.

She would have to go to work later and just the thought depressed her. Maria would be on duty too, and no doubt she was going to be barraged with *Julian* questions. She decided that the only way she could get through it would be to imply that she hadn't heard from him since the trip to Barbados. In a way it was true, because mentally she wanted to erase that ill-fated Saturday.

Nicole carelessly tossed her purse on the couch and some of the contents spilled out. Annoyed, she started to ignore it, but there beside her wallet were two glaringly familiar purple envelopes. She had completely forgotten all about having Julian's demented fan mail. She crammed the rest of the stuff back into the purse and started to throw the letters out. That was all she needed—more reminders of the man and his insane lifestyle—but instead of throwing them out she took them into her bedroom and methodically opened them.

There were no obscene sketches this time, only notes with short, clipped, typed statements protesting being ignored, arguing that the fan and Julian were made for each other. *Am I crazy?* Nicole wondered. *Why am I reading this garbage?*

As though being driven by some force, she reached deeper into her purse, remembering that she had taken more than just two envelopes. She extracted the black one, ripped it open, and gasped. Two close-up photographs showed Julian getting out of a car, and walking down a street. *You can't hide from me. My eyes are always on you, even when you're sleeping,* the attached note read.

If that was not called stalking, what was? Nicole knew she would have to tell him. On the other hand, Julian had said a while back that he'd been getting that type of mail for a long time. He would probably laugh and accuse her of overreacting. Photographers took pictures of celebrities all the time, with and without their permission. Still, there was something menacing about this. There was no way she could ignore it.

CHAPTER TWENTY-ONE

A fairly late-season tropical depression had formed in the Atlantic. The storm center in Miami was monitoring it closely because it was threatening to become a full-fledged hurricane. By mid-week it had earned a name, *Ivan,* and it appeared to be heading for Jamaica. The residents of Miami were hoping it would change course or die out, but there was a chance that it could hit the Florida coast.

The potential threat was only a passing thought to Nicole at this point. The last big hurricane to hit Miami had been *Andrew,* and that was before either she or Allyson had moved down. Since then, there had been many smaller storms and others that just blew over. She wished the storm called *Julian* would blow over, because that was the one constantly on her mind.

On Monday, as she was driving him to school, Trey, using a subtle form of sign language, reminded her that Julian was supposed to give him a guitar lesson that evening. Nicole's heart hammered.

"Well, Trey, I really don't know if that's going to happen. Julian's a very busy man. How about if I get another teacher for you?"

Trey glared at her indignantly and furiously signed *no.*

"Honey, sometimes things happen and people can't do the things they said they would."

But he promised, Trey's eyes told her.

"I know he promised, but..." She stopped abruptly. There really was not much she could say. The sooner Trey faced the reality about Julian the better. The hero worship could not go on. "Well, when the time comes we'll just see," she finished.

Trey seemed satisfied with that. He was absolutely positive that Julian was going to show up. She cringed to think about how disap-pointed he would be and she was going to have to come up with something to placate him. He had been sleeping with that guitar since it had been given to him.

Back home, Nicole yanked the vacuum cleaner out of the closet and started doing the carpet. There were several other things that needed to be done as well, laundry and food shopping among them. The phone rang. Switching the vacuum off, she picked it up.

"Hello, Nicole," a familiar voice said.

"Julian?" she questioned, nearly strangling on her own voice.

"I promised Trey that I would be by at around seven-thirty tonight, so if it's okay with you..."

"Yes...yes. Of course...I mean, I'll be working, but Allyson won't mind."

"Fine. Bye."

The distinctive click of his putting the receiver down echoed in her ear. Her elation upon learning that he had no intention of disappointing a little boy sank at the perfunctory tone he'd taken with her. "Well, what do you expect?" she chided herself out loud, still cradling the phone's buzzing receiver. She had wanted to quickly tell him about the ominous fan mail, but he hadn't given her a chance.

Two days later, Julian entered his home. He had just gotten back from headlining a music festival in Puerto Rico. After the show, the nights had been wild, and so had his behavior. He'd been drinking pretty heavily, but the odd revelation was that he was actually aware of it. He remembered every drink he'd swallowed, every woman he'd danced with, and the one who'd shared his hotel room. It was as if he had to be deliberately intoxicated in order to enjoy himself, and even then it had not worked. He felt miserable.

The air outside was hot and humid. It was almost as bad inside. Automatically he started to switch on the air conditioning, but then decided against it. At least the heat wasn't creating any illusions. It was just the dose of reality he needed.

"Nicole, Nicole. What are you doing right now?" he murmured out loud.

Whatever she was doing wasn't supposed to mean anything to him, but he couldn't hide the fact that it did. Those few short days in Barbados with her had been like heaven in comparison to his recent escapades. He hadn't even felt the urge to drink. It would be better to live in a cabin with her than in all the palaces of the world with another woman. So, why couldn't he just tell her that? Why was it so difficult to relegate his material world to second place and just accept her with the kind of commitment she wanted, no matter what the consequences?

He laughed at himself. How could he commit to a woman who was still in love with her dead husband, even if her love for his so-called memory seemed more like guilt?

He went upstairs to his bedroom and exchanged his clothes for a pair of swimming trunks, then hurried back down to the ground floor. Maybe a few laps in the privacy of the indoor pool would settle his mind. It was too hot to go jogging.

"Hey, handsome," a voice echoed throughout the cavernous room, resonating into the cool, blue water.

Julian swam to the surface and clutched the smooth, tiled edging of the pool. His eyes connected with a pair of high-heeled pumps attached to a pair of shapely legs belonging to his young, blond publicist.

"Gail," he exclaimed. "What's up? Wasn't expecting you today."

"Sorry about popping in on you like this, but you're a hard man to catch," she explained. "I've got some really great gigs lined up for you and I'd like to tell you before I go rushing off to a meeting."

Great gigs? Julian thought sarcastically. He hated doing interviews and she knew it, but being a professional, he realized it was an integral part of his success in the business.

He climbed languidly out of the pool, dripping water. She handed him a towel, which he blotted at his face, then draped around his neck. "Come on out to the deck," he said, touching her arm. He left the door to the pool area slightly ajar, assuming he'd finish his laps after she left.

The brilliance of the afternoon sun bore down on them as they sat on deck chairs and discussed various magazine interviews, including one for *Rolling Stone.* Julian listened to her ramble, until his attention was disrupted by the sound of Amanda shrieking in the garden below. He glanced over the verandah wall. The child was running at breakneck speed, attired inappropriately in some kind of party dress. A few feet away, Elena was trailing her, yelling at her to come back. The sight amused him immensely.

"Julian, this is *important*," Gail reminded him.

"Sorry, go on," he apologized.

A few seconds later, Amanda joined them, racing up on the deck with multi-colored ribbons billowing like streamers from her wild mane of hair, her bare feet slapping the terra cotta floor.

Julian caught her as she tried to dash by. "Whoa, *chica!* What are you doing?"

"Please, Uncle J, please let go. Mommy wants me to go to Megan's stupid birthday party and I hate her and all those stupid girls. I don't want to go. I hate 'em all. She can't make me!"

"Julian," Gail exclaimed urgently, irked by the intrusion, "I have to be at a meeting in fifteen minutes."

Reluctantly, he released Amanda. Let her mother find her. He didn't see any reason why the child was being forced to attend some party for someone she obviously didn't like anyway. Knowing Elena, this birthday girl, Megan, was probably the daughter of some socialite who held the symbolic keys to another highbrow club where she was seeking membership.

Gail ended her discussion just in time and was departing as Elena climbed the stairs to the deck. Julian focused indolently on his older half-sister as she breathed rapidly from the workout.

"Looks like someone needs to join an aerobics class," he said.

She ignored him. "Have you seen Amanda?"

"Yeah. She went streaking by a few minutes ago like a bat outta hell."

"I don't know what's gotten into that girl." She scowled at Julian, attributing her daughter's unruliness to him.

Julian shrugged and toyed with the towel that was still draped around his neck. Elena peered into the living room, framed by the sliding glass door. "Amanda, if you're hiding in there you better come out right now!" she shouted.

"She's probably long gone by now," he said.

Elena turned to face him with her hands on her hips. "Well, don't just *sit* there. Help me find her. *You* call her."

"I'm not calling her. She's your daughter. Try looking in the garden again." He got up and walked past her, heading toward the pool to resume his interrupted swim.

Halfway there, he noticed Amanda's muddy footprints on the marble floor. Frowning, he followed them to the poolroom's entrance where the door he usually kept locked was wide open. An unsettling chill passed through him as he entered.

"Amanda?" He looked behind some of the huge tropical ferns that decorated the room. Maybe she was hiding behind one. His heartbeat quickened. There was no trace of her, and the azure blue expanse of water beckoned. No. It was not possible—Amanda was a good swimmer—he'd taught her himself. In complete denial, afraid to look, Julian moved closer to the pool's edge and scanned the depths to see his worst nightmare materialize. A bundle of pink and yellow lay at the bottom on the deep end.

"Amanda!" His almost primal yell pierced the walls, echoing and tearing at the core of his being as he plunged into the deep end.

Working on sheer anguish and adrenaline, he raised her limp body to the surface and stretched her out on the floor, where he started CPR, alternating between that and mouth-to-mouth, willing life back into the child. He didn't even notice Elena rush into the room.

Elena's face instantly transformed into an unearthly pale. "No!" she screamed, falling on her knees beside the stricken child.

"Call 911!" Julian yelled, still working furiously on Amanda.

Elena became hysterical. "My baby! My baby!" she shrieked, trying to shield the child's body with her own, blocking Julian's efforts.

Julian's reaction was instant. He raised his hand and slapped her, hard, in the face. "I said call 911. *Now!*"

The force of the slap snapped Elena back to her senses. She rushed out and somehow managed to make the call. It all happened in seconds, but it seemed like an eternity to Julian who was not going to give up.

When Elena raced back into the room, she was elated to see that Amanda was breathing on her own and starting to regain consciousness. Shaking, Julian stepped back as she covered her daughter with a blanket and the paramedics arrived to take over.

"Oh, he's so cute. I love him," Amanda declared, hugging the large, stuffed polar bear Julian had given her "How did you know polar bears are my favorite?"

"Because I know lots of things about you," Julian said. "You are my favorite girl and don't you ever forget it."

"I won't," Amanda said, suppressing a giggle.

Julian lightly touched the tip of her button-nose with his finger, and then left her bedside to glance out the window of the hospital room. Reporters armed with cameras were there, lined up like vultures, waiting for a statement from him concerning the incident—lined up with no respect for his or his family's privacy.

He was beyond ecstatic that Amanda was going to be fine, but the doctors wanted to keep her in the hospital overnight for observation. Luis and Elena were down the hall having a discussion with her doctor, and he had deliberately seized this moment as an opportunity to come visit Amanda without having to deal with them.

Elena had told him not to come to the hospital at all, but there was no way he was going to just sit home and accept telephoned progress reports from them. He had to see his niece for himself.

"I saw Trey's mother," Amanda said suddenly. "She said she would come down and see me later."

"You saw Nicole?" The mere mention of her gave him a physical reaction. "When?"

"Before you came. Mommy and Daddy were outside. She came in and talked to me and said she'd come back. She's a nurse," Amanda added, seeming impressed by that fact.

News sure travels fast among the hospital staff, Julian thought. He turned his attention back to Amanda. "I never told you she was a nurse before?"

"Nope. Never. She's a real nice lady, Uncle J. You should marry her. I mean she's not like a model or anything, but she's a lot nicer and she's smart."

From the mouths of babes, Julian thought. "Tell me, *chica.* How'd *you* get to be so smart?"

Amanda folded her arms over her chest. " 'Cause I'm a girl. All girls are smart, much smarter than boys." An impish smile suddenly lit up her face as she had a revelation. "Guess what? 'Cause I almost drownded and I have to be in the hospital, I don't have to go to Megan's party anymore." She started to giggle.

Julian looked at her incredulously. "Amanda, don't you ever say..." He stopped in mid-sentence as she continued to laugh deliriously. "You are the wackiest kid I've ever met in my life."

"No, I'm not."

"Yes, you are." The whole trauma of the day had taken its toll and now he needed a release. He found himself laughing with her, just as Elena and Luis entered.

"What are you doing here? I thought I asked you not to come," Elena said.

Amanda squeezed her eyes shut. "Mommy, don't be mad."

"Yes, don't be," Luis agreed, putting his hand on Julian's shoulder.

Julian stepped back. "I'll be out in the hall."

"Daddy, look what Uncle Julian gave me," Amanda said, holding the stuffed animal in the air.

"That's real nice, honey," Luis said.

Julian stood in the hallway for a moment. There was really nothing to do but leave at this point. It was obvious that Elena resented his presence there and some of her reasons were valid. Where he went, the press followed.

"Julian, I need a word with you before you go."

Elena had joined him in the hall. "When you go outside, make sure you say nothing to the reporters. Just tell them you have no comment and keep walking."

"What did you think I was going to do, invite them over for dinner?"

"There is no need to be snide. Haven't you caused enough trouble today?"

He flinched. "Aside from the vultures outside, what's that supposed to mean?"

"You know exactly what I mean. Amanda would not be here if you had remembered to lock that door."

Her accusation stung as if she had suddenly pulled out a knife and stabbed him right through the heart. "I…" he started, but there were no words to say. He turned away, but she caught him by the arm.

"One more thing." Her eyes scanned the hall, noting that no people were present. "Don't you ever," her voice lowered into a seething, vehement hiss, "don't you ever hit me again. Do you understand?"

Julian yanked his arm away. "What the hell are you talking about now?"

"This!" She stabbed a finger at a spot on her cheek where her facial makeup was even heavier than usual because it concealed a red welt.

He took a deep breath and remembered. "I'm sorry about that, but I had no choice. You were getting hysterical and someone had to make the call." He glared at her and added sardonically, "Just in case you forgot, I was kind of busy."

She spun around on her spiked heels and clopped back into Amanda's room.

There was no way he could face the press now. His exchange with Elena had left him feeling vulnerable. He could easily imagine himself slugging the reporters and breaking their cameras. He needed time out. He needed to talk to someone who could be objective—someone like Nicole.

Compelled by an inner force, he moved toward the elevator that would take him away from the pediatrics floor. He pushed the button, eager to get away from the garish clowns, balloons, and other circus figures painted on the pale blue walls. The door slid open and he was face to face with a pair of angelic green eyes.

Nicole was just as startled to see him, although she had admittedly come down to pediatrics in hopes that their paths would cross; still the instant confrontation was disarming. She hesitated for a fraction of a second, then stepped out of the elevator as he moved back. "Julian...hi. Are you going up?"

"Not anymore. I was going up to see you."

"Oh." She breathed a sigh of relief. He had broken the ice and made it easier for her. "That's funny. I was coming down here hoping I'd see you."

"Amanda told me she saw you."

She noted his tired eyes, and the darkened stubble on his unshaven jaw. She reached out and instinctively took his hand. "Don't look so worried. Amanda is going to be just fine."

"Yes, I know. Thank God."

Nicole's eyes searched his. "What exactly happened?"

"She fell in the pool and almost drowned, because the *idiot* in front of you forgot to lock the door."

She winced at his words. "We definitely have to talk about this and *other* things. There's a conference room right down the hall and it's empty." Still holding his hand, she led him to the room.

He sank down on one of the couches and she sat beside him. "What are you saying?" she asked. "Even if you did leave the door unlocked, Amanda knew how to swim."

Julian took a deep breath and studied the linoleum on the floor. "It was an accident. She was running to get away from her mother. She ran into the room and she slipped and hit her head on the edge of the pool. She was unconscious. That's why she almost…almost…"

Nicole put her hand on his shoulder. "Almost didn't happen. The doctors and the paramedics said that you saved her life. You did all the right things."

"Except lock the damn door."

"*Enough* about that door! It was an accident!" she shouted. "Why was her mother chasing her anyway?"

Julian looked disgusted. "Who cares. It was over something stupid. You know how kids are. They don't always want to mind."

"Well, there's no valid reason to blame yourself. I think you're a hero, and so would anyone else in their right mind. Amanda could very well have had the accident in the outdoor pool, which doesn't even have a locked door. What would have happened then if you weren't around? Would her mother have had the presence of mind to do what you did?"

He listened to her, allowing the calming words to sink in. How could his life go on without her in it? She was kinder to him than he was to himself. He turned slowly and kissed her on the cheek. "It doesn't change the fact that I was irresponsible, but thanks. I really needed to hear that."

Her eyes searched his, with compassion and concern. "Are you going to be okay?"

"Yeah, but there's something else I have to say. I…I've missed you." She had reduced him to stammering and averting eye contact, because he was afraid of what her response would be.

Nicole inhaled and exhaled slowly. "I've missed you too."

"I think we should do something about that," he said.

A lingering silence ensued. Finally she spoke. "I want to do something about it, but I don't know what. We tried to be friends but *other* things just kept getting in the way. Oh, I'm not blaming you for what happened that Saturday, because it was just as much my fault. I know I'm not making a lot of sense, but what I said then still goes. I'm not ready." Nervously, she fingered her watch, twisting and untwisting the gold band. "There are things about you that I just don't understand. It's as if you don't really want me to know any more about the private you than the public does, and when I *do* find out things it's because I have to pry them out, and that makes me feel awkward and more involved than I should be." She took a deep breath. "I may not be as chic and sophisticated as some women you've known, but I'm not stupid and I'm not a masochist. I don't want to get hurt."

"I would never intentionally hurt you," Julian said. "And I'm not deliberately trying to hide things. Please try to understand that really trusting someone is all new to me. For the past ten or so years, my life has been nothing but a big, phony circus. My family thinks I'm a brainless source of income. Most of my friends tell me everything they think I want to hear, but never the truth and they're always hitting me up for favors." He stared up at the ceiling and then back at the floor. "The women you keep mentioning are really only like pacifiers, physical compensation for the fact that I've learned to keep a tight rein on my heart, because if I didn't, I'd never have been able to survive in this business. What I'm really trying to say is that even though our lives and circumstances are different, I understand your feelings. I'm afraid too."

"I kind of sensed that, but it's the first time you've ever *said* it." Her eyes shifted to the floor. "Considering everything you just told me, your fears and mine, why should we keep seeing each other?"

He reached up and placed his thumb under her chin, lifting her face to his level. "Because I think we're like the evening tide meeting the shore and when I look in your eyes and hear the music of your voice, I know the sun will still rise every morning, even if I'm not there to see it."

"You have such a way with words," Nicole murmured, scanning the liquid depths of his eyes and finding unbridled sincerity and vulnerability. He was not just quoting lines from some imagined book of quotes and come-ons. She took his hand and clasped it tightly. "I guess we're just going to have to take things one day at a time."

There was so much more that needed to be said, but Nicole realized her break had been over five minutes ago, and it was not like her to be so irresponsible. She had to get back to her floor now. There was no time to even mention the stalker. It would have to wait until later when she could be more convincing about getting him to take the threats seriously. Julian sensed her urgency and released her hand.

"We'll talk later," he said.

"Yes, and no more worrying about Amanda. They're only keeping her overnight as standard procedure. She's fine."

She felt rather than saw his slow-burning smile as she hurried to catch the elevator before the door slid shut.

Julian left the hospital and stepped outside into the waiting barrage of flashing cameras. He walked swiftly toward the parking lot, with the whole team in hot pursuit.

"Could you tell us what happened to your niece, Mr. Marquez?" a reporter asked. "One of the paramedics said you saved her life. Is that true?"

"How about giving us a statement on her condition?" another asked.

"My niece is doing fine. Thanks for asking," Julian said, getting into the car.

"What's it feel like being a hero?"

"Sorry, guys. I have no comment."

He started the car and carefully pulled out as they continued to snap pictures. *This life is just too crazy*, he thought, switching on the radio. He instantly turned the volume up higher to catch the tail end of the weather report. "Hurricane *Ivan* is expected to hit Miami over the weekend," it said.

CHAPTER TWENTY-TWO

"I'm not sure what to do," Allyson said. "Lynette wants Trey and me to come over to her house, but that would mean leaving Shane here alone. She doesn't like dogs."

Trey responded negatively by pouting and wrapping his arms around Shane's neck. He did not approve of abandoning his furry friend.

"You might have a mutiny on your hands," Nicole said. "But whatever you decide, you'd better hurry and make up your mind. The wind's starting to pick up and I have to be at the hospital in an hour. I need to know where you are going to be."

The skies were already darkening even though it was only afternoon. The storm was rapidly approaching, and knowing that she absolutely had to work was making Nicole nervous. There was no way any of the scheduled nurses could get off. They would be needed more than ever. Possibly she might even have to work in the ER.

Miami General was bracing itself for more than its usual share of human mishaps, illnesses and all sorts of injuries, many of which could be avoided if only people listened to the radio reports, followed instructions and stayed indoors.

Allyson had closed her shop early and had originally said that she and Trey would just stay home, but as the skies became more threatening, she suddenly wasn't too thrilled with the idea of being the only adult at home. Nicole couldn't blame her, but according to the weather reports, *Ivan* was going to be more of a nuisance storm than a disastrous one.

The phone rang and Allyson picked it up. "Nicole, It's for you." She batted her eyelids and looked dazzled. "It's our prince."

Nicole's heart skipped a beat as she rushed to the other room. "I'll get it in the bedroom. She took a deep breath and picked up the receiver.

"Just checking up on you," Julian said softly. Are you planning a hurricane party?"

She laughed. "Hardly. I think people who do that are a little wacky. Real people have to work."

"Guess it was wishful thinking on my part that you'd have the day off. When are you going in?"

"Probably in about a half an hour. I'm going ahead of time because it's starting to get bad out."

"I'll take you."

"What?" She'd heard what he said, but even though it was not the first time he'd volunteered, she still found the chivalrous gesture extraordinary because it was coming from him.

"I said I'll be your chauffeur."

"I'd love it, but that means I would have to call you to come back and that might be way after midnight, assuming I'm going to be working even later than usual."

"That's not a problem. Call me whenever you want. I've got no plans and it's kind of boring here alone."

There were probably half a million women who'd love to be alone with him and he'd chosen to ferry her around during a storm. She could only be impressed—and she was—but another thought raced through her mind and before she could stop herself, the words came out. "Julian, I know this is going to sound really ridiculous, but Ally wants to stay over with a friend and she's taking Trey. The problem is that she can't bring the dog. Shane likes you. Could you maybe keep him overnight? He kind of goes berserk when he's left alone, especially when there's thunder."

"I've got a better idea—how about if I just stay at your place overnight?" Realizing the possible implications of the suggestion, he added quickly, "I can sleep on the couch."

"Would you *really* do that? I mean you certainly don't have to sleep on the couch. You can have Trey's room. I'll just get rid of the cartoon sheets."

"Actually I like cartoons."

Nicole laughed. "I can't believe it. You've just solved my problem."

"Believe it. I'll be over in about twenty minutes."

The phone clicked as he replaced the receiver. He had a habit of ending calls abruptly, probably because he didn't want to give her time to change her mind. It would be annoying if someone else did the same thing, but coming from him she found it surprisingly endearing.

"Ally," Nicole said, rushing back into the living room. "You and Trey can go to Lynette's, I've found a sitter for Shane."

"Who? Julian's bodyguard?"

"No. The man himself."

"You're kidding. Julian's staying here? In our apartment?"

"That's what I said." She rushed into Trey's room and stuffed his pajamas, a washcloth and a toothbrush into an overnight bag. Allyson followed her into the room.

"Maybe I won't go to Lynette's now. Maybe Trey and I will just stay here and keep Julian company."

"Allyson! I *told* him you were going," Nicole protested.

Allyson laughed. "I'm just messing with you. We're going. You and Julian can do whatever you like." She shook her head. "And just think, I thought you two were history."

Nicole gave her sister a playful shove out of the way. "Don't get the wrong idea, Ally. It's not *that* kind of overnight."

The wind howled fiercely outside and the rain poured down in slanting torrents. Julian lay stretched out on the couch half asleep, until his dangling arm came in contact with something wet. With a start, his eyes opened to darkness and he became aware of heavy panting.

Instantly he remembered where he was, and that it was Shane's tongue he'd felt. The electricity must have gone out, because he'd left the lights on before he'd dozed off. Sitting up, he reached for the flashlight placed conveniently on the end table and looked at his watch. It was a quarter after midnight and Nicole had not called.

There had been a call at around ten o'clock, and thinking it was Nicole, he'd answered it, only to discover it was her mother. Mrs. Eleanor Whitfield had sounded shocked to hear a male voice. He'd calmly informed her that Allyson and Trey were out, that Nicole was working, and his only purpose for being there was to take care of the dog. Somehow, he didn't think she believed him, and he was amused by this, even though he doubted Nicole would be.

He could not actually see what was going on outside unless he opened the door, because the windows of the entire condominium complex had been boarded up by the maintenance people. The howling of the wind, though, pretty much told him what he couldn't see.

The phone rang, adding to the noise. He picked it up. "Hi, Julian. It's me," Nicole said. "I just called my sister. She and Trey are fine. Is everything okay there?"

"The electricity died, but that's about it."

He heard her sigh. "I just thought I'd tell you that I'll be off at two o'clock, but I've decided to stay at the hospital and come home when it's daylight. The storm should be over then."

Julian clenched his teeth. The whole point of his being there was because he wanted to be with her, not with a grunting, snuffling dog. "I *told* you that I'd come get you whenever you're ready."

"I know that, but please don't argue with me. The roads are probably bad. Power lines might be down. I don't want you to—"

"You just can't stop with the worrying can you? If the roads are bad I'll turn around and go back. Besides, the radio reports said that the eye of the storm should be passing through about then. Look for me at two."

"Julian!" Too late, he'd hung up. She didn't have time to worry about it, because someone was paging her on the floor. She'd been on her feet since arriving and was now on her last wind. She'd just returned an hour ago to her normal duties. Most of her time had been spent in the emergency room attending to heart attack victims, victims struck by flying objects and several involved in car accidents. The only encouraging thing was that so far there had been no fatalities.

Nicole stepped out into the lobby at two a.m. She was worried because she had not been able to contact Julian again. She hoped he was outside waiting. Her fears were immediately alleviated. He was sitting in the deserted reception area looking impressive, as always, in a pair of light blue jeans and a denim shirt that was a darker shade of blue. He rose to greet her.

"It's been a long night, baby," he said, handing her a bouquet of pink and white carnations. "These are for my favorite nurse, who's also a very special lady."

Nicole felt her exhaustion lift as she accepted the flowers and gave him a hug. "Oh, they're beautiful! I don't know what to say." She held the bouquet clasped behind his back in the embrace, basking in the distinctly masculine strength of his arms. Rain and wind intermingled deliciously with his own exotic scent. "Where on earth did you get flowers at this time?"

"One of the mysteries of life," Julian said, taking her hand. "C'mon, let's get out of here."

There was an unnatural silence outside. The wind had temporarily stopped blowing; it was no longer raining and the air felt thick with humidity. Without illumination from the moon or stars, the night seemed darker and more penetrating than Nicole had ever been aware of before. Tree branches, stones and other debris littered their path as Julian led the way to the car.

"So this is what's called the eye of the storm," Nicole commented as he opened the door for her.

"Yeah. Weird, isn't it? Hope we get back before it starts up again."

He didn't seem the least bit worried; therefore she decided not to be overly concerned either. She settled back and watched him navigate around flooded roads and other obstacles. They had to make a major detour at one point because a fallen tree was blocking the road.

They finally entered the house, armed with flashlights, knowing that the electricity was still out. Nicole patted an overjoyed Shane and put the flowers in a vase. Julian set a flashlight upright on the end table so it dimly illuminated the whole room. The immense shadows that their passing forms created almost caused her to laugh childishly, but she refrained. What was she supposed to do now? She was a woman all alone with a gorgeous man. She knew exactly what she wanted to do, but just entertaining that thought was tantamount to disaster. Her heart was so much more treacherous than her mind.

Julian sat down on the couch. She noticed he had swiped a pillow and a blanket from Trey's room. "Guess there's nothing to do except sleep until daylight," he said. "I know you must be tired."

"I definitely *should* be," Nicole admitted, but the simple fact was that his presence in the house was so overwhelming that sleep had become the last thing she wanted to do.

"Are you actually sleeping out here on the couch?" she asked. "Isn't Trey's room better?"

"The couch is good enough." He had tried sleeping in there earlier, but Trey's room reminded him too much of his own childhood room in Cuba. Trey had a passion for model airplanes, which were suspended artistically from the ceiling. His Aunt Alma, he recalled, had allowed him to do the same thing when he'd lived with her and his father. As he'd lain between consciousness and slumber, he'd almost imagined the faceless ghost of his father entering to sit on the edge of the bed, preparing to tell him one of his favorite adventure stories.

"You can have my room," Nicole said. "I can sleep in—"

"No. This is fine, really," he interrupted, not wanting to tell her the reason. "It's only a few more hours." He unbuttoned his shirt, stripping it off to reveal a white, ribbed tank top.

She sighed and regarded him with beautiful, soulful eyes. She seemed to be waiting for him to say more. Or was she waiting for him to do what he really wanted to do—which was to take her in his arms, kiss her endlessly, passionately, and set the night on fire.

"There was plenty of food in the refrigerator. I hope you ate something," she said.

Deflated, Julian laughed in spite of himself. "Good night, Nicole."

He's right, Nicole thought. *Just shut your mouth and go to bed.* But she lingered as he mechanically removed his shoes and stretched out on the uncomfortably narrow couch. Slowly, she turned away. Daylight would come quickly and she would definitely sit down and talk to him then. "Goodnight, Julian," she said.

She stepped into the bathroom, went through the usual rituals, and undressed for bed. From her dresser drawer, she extracted a sheer, lacy red gown. It was a garment that Allyson had purchased for her from Victoria's Secret. She had never worn it before, and had never intended to. Now she slipped the gauzy material over her bare skin, released the barrette from her hair, and stared at herself in the full-length mirror. A strange, nearly nude woman enshrouded in scarlet reflected back at her. The eerie yellow glow from the flashlight set off her complexion and made her almost unrecognizable even to herself. Her eyes glowed as though possessed. She laughed at the alien woman and slid into bed.

CHAPTER TWENTY-THREE

The wind was blowing fiercely. The whole building seemed to be trembling under the force of the buffeting. The howling grew louder, more intense. Nicole felt a rush of cold air filling the room and suddenly her bed started to rise. She was being lifted up with it and was about to be hurled up against the wall. A loud explosive sound erupted, shattering the night—a sound like glass breaking.

A muffled scream escaped her mouth and she sat up, gasping for breath, catapulting herself from the bed. "Trey! Ally!" she screamed, racing into the living room, straight into Julian's arms.

"Nicole, it's all right," he said, catching her, holding her close. "You were having a nightmare."

"But there was a big noise, like an explosion," she cried. "Did I dream that too?"

"No. There was a noise, but it was outside."

"What *was* it?" She struggled to contain herself.

"Baby, I don't know," he said, holding her even tighter. "When you calm down, I'll go check."

It had all been a terrible dream, except for the noise. She felt a great sense of relief, but as the anxiety dissipated, it was replaced with the embarrassment of reality. She was grateful for the room's dim lighting because her skin was flushing as scarlet-red as the gown she wore—the *barely there* gown.

"It sounded like a tree falling," Julian said. "Must've hit something, maybe one of the cars in the parking lot."

He felt no real urgency to investigate the crash, because he was distracted by what she was wearing—or wasn't. Even if a tree had landed on his Explorer and mashed it flat, it would seem insignificant.

Still locked in the embrace, he kissed her shoulder, his mouth brushing against the thin strap of the gown.

Stop it! he told himself, releasing her. They both stepped back almost simultaneously. "I...I'll go see about the noise," he said.

"Maybe you shouldn't. The wind's still blowing."

"It's all right, not as bad as it was."

"Please be careful," Nicole said, easing back into her room.

Furious at herself, she stripped off the offending gown and changed into a white sweatshirt and a pair of jeans. The battery-operated clock read five a. m. Daylight was only an hour away; there was no point in going back to bed.

Julian returned. "A tree did fall," he confirmed.

"Where?" she asked warily.

"In the courtyard. Some of the branches went through the living room window of one of your neighbors."

She gasped. "Oh no! Are they all right?"

"Yeah. Good thing nobody was in that room at the time. I'm going back out. Told the guy I'd help him saw off some of the branches so he can board the window back up."

He left quickly. Julian was relieved to be immersed in physical labor at the moment. It was just the sort of distraction he needed. An added plus was the all-too-rare feeling of anonymity—being just like any other guy.

When Julian returned an hour later, Nicole tried to persuade him into having breakfast, but he wanted only coffee and a roll. They lingered at the kitchen table.

"Well, here we are. Finally we have a nice non-chaotic moment and nobody's talking," she said lightly.

A slow burning smile crossed his face. "Does the silence bother you?"

"Well, no." She searched his eyes questioningly. "Not really."

"Maybe it's because there's so much to say that we're both overwhelmed," he offered.

She bit her lip. "Perfect description. There *are* a lot of things we should discuss, so I'll start." She stood up. "I'll be back in a sec."

She left the room and returned with a manila folder, which she handed to him. "The last time I was at your place I made this enlightening discovery."

Julian opened the folder and spilled the stalker's mementos out on the table. He looked at the photographs of himself.

"Well?" Nicole quizzed.

"Very bad pictures," he said. "All taken from the wrong angle. I never realized my nose was so big."

"This is *not* a joke, Julian!"

He slid the contents back into the folder. "If it worries you that much, I'll speak to my security people about it."

She folded her arms and glared at him. "Sometimes you make me want to scream. You're the one who should be worried!"

"I believe I told you once before that this sort of thing goes with the territory. I can't have everyone who takes pictures of me arrested."

"But you told me that this loony has been writing you for years. The fact that he said he's watching you sounds like a threat to me."

"You were once married to a cop," Julian said gently. "It probably makes you overreact."

Am I really overreacting? Nicole pondered. What he'd said annoyed her, but she did not want to get into an argument about it. "Listen, just promise me that you'll remember to mention it to your security."

"I'll mention it." He pushed the folder aside and leaned slightly forward. "Now that that's over with, let's talk about us. When we had that argument in the park, you implied that you were upset because I'd met everyone in your family and you didn't know anything about mine. Well, I'd like to change that. Ever since we came to this country, my family always gets together on Thanksgiving. I'd like you and Trey to come."

Nicole regarded him in silence. Coming from any other man, it was not an unusual invitation, but coming from Julian, it had a whole different meaning. It was a much more intimate and personal request than if he'd asked her to fly to Paris and have dinner at some expensive restaurant. It was more significant than their trip to Barbados even. She studied the rim of her coffee mug.

"Nicole, you're not saying anything. It's not a big deal, kind of boring actually. Just a bunch of aunts and cousins and stuff. It's really the only time we get together."

"I'd love to come. I'll be spending Christmas in Chicago with my parents, but I didn't really make any plans for Thanksgiving," she said.

"Good, we're on." He glanced at his watch. "Speaking of family, I forgot to tell you that your mother called last night."

Nicole flinched. "She did? What did you tell her?"

"That we were living together."

"Julian!"

He laughed. "I told her the truth, that I was dog-sitting."

Nicole rolled her eyes. "I'm sure she didn't believe a word you said. She'll be calling me up later for an explanation."

"Maybe she'll fly down here to check for herself."

Nicole laughed now. "Don't even *say* that."

She knew that he was getting ready to leave, but she didn't want him to go. "How's Trey doing with the guitar lessons?"

"Well, I don't think he's going to be another Segovia. He's kind of all over the place at this point, but he seems to enjoy it. How's he doing in school?"

"Actually he's doing much better. He seems more focused and he's…well, he's not resisting the sign language as much."

But he's no closer to talking. Julian read her mind. "Does he still go for speech therapy?"

"He's on his eighth therapist. She'll probably be giving up on him soon. It's getting near that time," she said cynically.

Julian took a deep breath and searched her eyes intensely. "I know this isn't your favorite subject, but I'd really like to know just how much you've talked to Trey about his father's death."

She felt her inner defense system kicking in and tried to control it. There was no point in pretending that Julian wasn't involved, because he was. It was pretty clear that he was having some kind of positive influence on Trey and she didn't want it to end.

"He was only three when it happened. I didn't talk to him imme-diately about it, but later on we did discuss it a lot, as much as I could with a child who won't tell me what he's feeling." She struggled for the right words. "I told you before about all the psychiatrists and—"

"Does he have any pictures of his father?" Julian interrupted.

"Yes, yes he does. I gave him some last year. They're in his room on the dresser."

Julian raised his eyebrows. "Funny, I was in his room. Guess I didn't notice."

"*Of course* they're in there." She rose abruptly and went into Trey's room.

To her shock, the two pictures, one of Warren in uniform, the other of herself, Trey and Warren, had vanished. Disturbed, her eyes swept around the room. She looked under the dresser, thinking that they had fallen, and saw nothing. Frantically, she searched through all the drawers and when she reached the bottom one, she noticed a shoebox partially concealed by clothing. She opened it and the photo-graphs stared vacantly up at her.

When had Trey put them away? Why? She noticed something else under the pictures. It was a folded news clipping from the local Chicago paper, a clipping that had been filed away in her room. Mechanically she unfolded it and stared woodenly at herself and other memories of her family at the cemetery, surrounded by police officers. She was holding a folded flag.

Nicole became aware that Julian had entered. He stood quietly behind her and placed both hands on her shoulders. "What? What is it?"

"Trey hid the pictures," she said dully. "I don't understand...and this." She let him see the news photo. "Why would he do that?" It was a rhetorical question.

"I don't see Trey in this funeral picture," Julian said after a long silence.

"He…he wasn't at the funeral. He was too young, too traumatized. We thought…I thought, it would be best if he didn't go."

"I remember when I lost both of my parents," Julian said, his voice sounding distant, reflective. "First I was told that my father died. Then that my mother committed suicide—"

"Suicide?" Nicole interrupted, her consciousness focusing back on him. "You never told me. *That's terrible.* What happened?"

"It was a long time ago." His voice switched to a nonchalant but impatient tone. "She always had a lot of problems. I wasn't very close to her."

"But she was still your mother."

"Yeah. Whatever. The point I'm trying to make is that Elena took me to stay with neighbors and I never went to her funeral. Soon after that, we were on a boat heading for this country, leaving behind my whole past. I was six or seven."

Nicole shuddered. "That must have been horrible."

Her words seemed inadequate, but all sorts of images were flashing through her mind— images of Trey cloaking himself in a defensive silence and images of Julian as a bewildered child being dragged heartlessly around like an emotionless puppet.

"Don't get me wrong. I definitely do *not* miss Cuba, not the way it is now," Julian continued. "But I miss that I never got to say goodbye to my parents. It was like they just disappeared into some kind of cosmic black hole." His eyes stared vacantly into space. "When I was first in Florida, I'd go down to the ocean and wait to see if a ship was coming that would bring my father back to me."

"Julian." Nicole's voice was a quavering whisper. "Is that what I've done to Trey? Given him no sense of closure? I mean, I came running down here to Miami almost immediately after Warren…"

"No. *Don't* do that," Julian interrupted, his reflective tone transforming into a consoling, sympathetic one. "It wasn't your fault. You were in a lot of pain yourself. We're only human and we don't always know what's the right thing." He slid his arms around her, holding her close.

Nicole closed her eyes for a second, burying her face against his chest, muffling her voice. "Maybe what Trey is doing with these pictures is a good thing. Maybe it's his way of wanting to move on."

"Sounds logical to me," Julian said. "Are you going to ask him about it?"

"No. I'm just going to leave everything exactly the way he had it." She slowly, deliberately placed the pictures back in the box and closed the lid. "I'm not even going to lecture him about snooping around in my room."

Julian stepped back reluctantly as she returned the box to the drawer. "Much as I hate to leave, I've really got to go. I'll be in Spain for a week or so."

"Spain?" she repeated, the concept not immediately registering.

"Yeah, promotional stuff for my new CD."

The words took her back to reality. "I really appreciate your staying here last night," she said, almost shyly.

"Don't thank me. I'm only being selfish," Julian said. "I'm starting to think of you guys as my family."

She smiled. There was really nothing else she could say on that matter. She was flattered, but she didn't want to seem too obvious. "Make sure you don't forget to speak to your security people."

"I'll give you my hotel phone number in Spain so you can call and remind me."

She followed him to the door. He opened it, letting in the radiantly blinding sunshine. Except for the uprooted tree and strewn branches, there was little evidence that there had ever been a storm. Nicole tilted her head toward the sky and could see the faint etchings of a rainbow.

CHAPTER TWENTY-FOUR

Trey rushed toward the ship's railing so he could get a good look at the ocean. Nicole hurried to catch up with him. It was amazing that he still had so much energy after an entire day spent at the zoo, the planetarium, Bayfront Park, and finally a tour of the cruise ship *Serenity*. She wished she had just half of his stamina.

The ship was docked at the Port of Miami, being prepared to set sail for Puerto Rico on Monday. Nicole and a group of other people had been granted free passes just to tour the ship. It was a promotional tool that the cruise line used in an attempt to attract potential customers in the future. It would be a long time in the future before she would even consider such a trip, but she knew that Trey would enjoy the tour.

A perky tour guide had walked them all over the floating hotel before finally abandoning them to their own resources on the massive deck. The blazing sun was merciless, causing Nicole to gaze longingly at the numerous tables with bright tropical-colored umbrellas surrounding an Olympic-size swimming pool. She wanted to close her eyes and take a plunge right into the cool, sparkling water.

Trey tugged at her arm, pointing excitedly at another behemoth that was getting ready to depart with the assistance of a tiny tugboat. She leaned over the railing with him, temporarily forgetting the heat. It was fascinating to watch the tugboats in action as they guided the cumbersome giants who couldn't maneuver without them. The tugboats were like metaphors for strength in unlikely sources—the mental and emotional strength of a slight woman among powerfully built men. She liked the image.

"Trey, you can keep watching," she said finally, when the sun became unbearable. "I'm going to be right here sitting under the umbrella."

He nodded. She adjusted the baseball cap on his head and started to move away just as his hands tightened around the railing and he made a motion to pull himself up higher.

"Don't you dare! No climbing!" she shouted.

I'm not climbing, his irritated expression informed her.

"Make sure you don't. I'll be sitting right here watching."

As she took a seat, Trey gave her another surly look, and she sighed. She wished he would just *say* what he was thinking, even if he was being bratty. It was disconcerting to realize that she was one of very few mothers who would be elated to hear any form of vocal disrespect from her child.

Nicole leaned back, removed her sunglasses and watched as a group of young people moved closer to where Trey was. They began shouting and waving at the other ship. Trey waved too.

Come on, Trey, let's hear you yell along with them, she thought wistfully. But the small figure in the over-sized T-shirt and shorts remained silent and continued to wave. The departing ship's journey had begun and it proceeded to let loose with a loud blast of its horn. The teenage onlookers clapped and whistled. Trey turned to flash her a smile. Nicole smiled back.

"Hey! One more time!" someone yelled.

The horn sounded again, a penetrating, booming wail that reverberated through her very soul. From where she was sitting, she caught a glimpse of the tugboat skimming the water, off to find another assignment. Trey remained watching and Nicole allowed her mind to focus on the tugboat metaphor again. Curiously, it made her think about Julian. She had not heard a thing from him since he'd left for Spain, but then he'd probably been very busy. She was sure he had a good reason for not calling—like maybe he'd met the love of his life, a beautiful senorita from Madrid, and would return to make the announcement that he was married. She laughed. It was just the sort of thing her mother would expect.

Her mother had called her only an hour after Julian had departed on the day after the storm.

"Nicole, are you there alone?" She had asked, without even saying hello.

"Hello, Mom. "Yes, I'm alone."

"I called you last night and that young man answered."

"Yes, Mother. Julian stayed to look after Shane because I had to work and Ally and Trey were at Lynette's."

"Was there any damage from the storm?"

"A little. Nothing serious "

"That's good."

A long silence had followed, as if her mother had been waiting for her to volunteer more, as if she were expected to explain or justify herself in detail. But Nicole remained silent.

"I know you *told* me that Julian was just watching the dog, but when you came back from work, you and he were alone together. Nicole, do I have to remind you about how that looks? I would expect *that* kind of behavior from your sister, but not you. You have a child to be responsible for."

Indignant at the accusation, but struggling to contain it, Nicole sputtered. "I am perfectly well aware of my responsibilities, Mother. I'm not doing anything that would hurt Trey. Julian is a very good friend, and I'm sure you'll be happy to know that ever since I've known him, Trey has been doing better in school. Julian's giving him guitar lessons."

"Really?" Her mother was speechless for a second. "Well, that's…that's nice. Nicole, are you in love with this man?"

"Mom, I really don't know. We're just taking it one day at a time."

Her mother sighed heavily. "Couldn't you have met someone else, someone in church who's more like yourself? This Julian is…is Cuban. What do you really know about him?"

Everything and nothing, Nicole thought. "He loves children. He's extremely talented, and he's been very kind to Trey and me."

"There are a lot of God-fearing men who are kind and love children."

A lot of African-American men, Nicole interpreted. "Well, Mom, it's not like I planned this. I haven't exactly been in the market since Warren died. Julian just happened."

"Well, I think you should talk to your father about this. He can tell you how men are."

Tell me how men are? "Mother, I'm not thirteen anymore. I was married once…hello."

"Nicole, I'm only telling you this because I don't want to see him make a fool out of you."

"Why do you always assume that someone is going to make a fool of me? It could be the other way around."

"You know good and well that the woman has more to lose." She shifted gears abruptly. "Are you and Trey coming up for Thanksgiving?"

Nicole exhaled slowly. "No. I thought I told you that before. We'll be coming during the Christmas holiday."

"Oh. So what are you doing Thanksgiving? Maybe your father and I can come down."

"Julian invited us to dinner with his family."

"Oh. You mean he wants you to meet his family?"

"That's what I said," Nicole replied irritably.

"Are they black or white?"

"They're *people,* Mom!"

"I know they're people. You don't have to get an attitude with me."

She almost laughed as she abruptly returned to the present when Trey plopped down on a chair beside her.

"Tired?" she asked.

He shook his head negatively. No matter what the circumstances, he would never admit to that.

"Well." She consulted her watch. "It's getting late and that means it's time for us to start back home."

The sun was starting to set as they made their way off the ship and entered the port's parking lot. For a brief second, Nicole hesitated, not remembering where she had parked the car. Trey suddenly reached out and grabbed her hand tightly.

"What? What's wrong?"

He stood still and looked around, squinting. She looked in the same direction, but only saw the retreating back of a person walking a distance away.

"That's not someone we know, is it?" she asked him.

Trey scowled and shook his head. He held up his hands and mimicked the motions of a photographer taking a picture.

Nicole laughed. "Oh, Trey, that's nothing. He's just a tourist. People are always taking pictures around here. There's so much to see in this spot. You know that."

Trey's scowl became fiercer and he bent down to pick up a stone. Nicole took him by his free hand and they moved swiftly toward their car. Once inside, she locked the door and searched her son's face.

"Trey, did someone scare you?"

Trey indicated in sign language that he wanted to go home and he did not want to talk about it anymore. His odd reaction was making her nervous. She glanced in the rear view mirror, but there was nothing out of the ordinary. A few people were passing, going toward their cars. A young mother was pushing a baby in a stroller. There were no shadowy figures or monsters waiting to pounce on them. Nicole started the car.

"Honey, are you sure you're okay?"

Trey shrugged, looked nonchalant and reached to switch on the radio. A raucous rap song disturbed the silence. It was not Nicole's favorite station and it was too loud, but it seemed to be pacifying him, so she didn't touch the dial until they were back home.

It seemed much later, but it was only around seven p.m. when Julian arrived back home. Spain's time was at least six hours ahead of Miami's and despite over a decade of constant European air travel, the varied time zones still had a disorienting effect on him. It was because of those differences and his hectic schedule that he had not been able to give Nicole a call. She had been on his mind constantly, though, and as he unlocked the door of his home he knew the first thing he was going to do was call her.

The whole concept of being excited about coming home was something new to him. In the past, when he wasn't touring, he'd immediately rush off to one of South Beach's hot spots and drown himself in wine and starry-eyed women to assuage his loneliness and feelings of despair. The hedonistic habit had never actually solved anything, but at least it had anesthetized his mind to the point where he no longer heard faceless voices from the past, and he didn't have to think about the lack of unconditional love in his life.

A neat stack of mail greeted him from the table in the foyer. He groaned. Some of the more intelligent fans were getting the point and no longer sending stuff to his home, but there would always be the diehards. He remembered Nicole's parting words to him pertaining to the alleged stalker. It had been at the back of his mind, but he had still not mentioned it to security. She was going to ask him about it and he was going to have to give her some kind of answer. Scowling, he rifled through the envelopes and stopped at the all too familiar purple one. There was only one—maybe that was a good sign.

He stepped into the living room, opening it. The phone was ringing and he started to go answer it, but he stopped dead in his tracks when he stared at the contents of the envelope. A photograph stared up at him—not a snapshot of himself, but a photograph of Nicole and Trey walking in a parking lot. His pulse surged and he felt the blood rush to his head. The phone stopped ringing as he continued to stare at the pictures. Nicole's expression revealed that she was completely oblivious to the invasion, but Trey seemed to be staring straight ahead with eyes that were far too knowing and cynical for his years.

"Damn!" Julian dropped down on the couch. He could feel both rage and panic wash over him as he turned the photograph over. Letters cut out and pasted on the back spelled out the spiteful words. *Your standards are slipping, and that could cost you.*

"What am I going to do now?" he murmured aloud.

Threatening him was one thing, but involving Nicole and Trey was another. For a moment he felt an all encompassing urge to announce that he wanted nothing more to do with show business, that he was planning to leave the country permanently, maybe even leave the planet. Just when he was possibly on the brink of finding someone he really cared about, and who seemed to care about him, it was all about to be destroyed by some lunatic.

"We'll just see who it's going to cost," he muttered fiercely. "You are *not* going to destroy us."

He realized that he was going to have to tell Nicole and the final decision was going to be hers and not his. The stalker had already scored a major victory, because he had destroyed his whole plan for the evening. He couldn't call Nicole now because he wasn't prepared for her reaction to the news, and he couldn't selfishly pretend he hadn't seen the photos because he was too worried and he wasn't that good an actor.

He would have to tell her tomorrow. Tonight he had some very urgent phone calls to make to assure that she and Trey were protected, and after that, the first phase of his plan would begin. Starting with tonight, he was going to have to spend some more shallow nights partying on South Beach after all.

CHAPTER TWENTY-FIVE

"What gives you the right to look so good in the morning?" Julian asked, embracing her tightly.

Nicole smiled. "I think that's entirely in the eyes of the beholder and his vision is a bit distorted by jet lag." She studied Julian's exotically handsome face. "It's been a while. How come you didn't call me?" She inhaled the scintillating scent of his cologne.

"Important things had to be taken care of," Julian said.

It was early in the morning and Nicole had just returned home fifteen minutes ago after dropping Trey off at school. Allyson was at work, and Nicole was secretly pleased that Julian had chosen this time to make an unexpected visit. Ever since the night of the storm, she no longer felt as uncomfortable as she had about being alone with him.

Dressed in a steely gray suit jacket, matching pants and a black silk V-necked shirt, he looked as breathtakingly handsome as always. Her hands ached to separate him from the jacket, and slide up and down the silk of the shirt, feeling the ridges and nuances of his sleek body. She remained in his embrace studying the enigmatic reflections shifting in his eyes and gradually surrendered to a reality that she wanted desperately to deny, but could not. There was a glimmer of something troubling within the windows of his soul.

"Julian, is something wrong?" She involuntarily stepped back a little. *It's coming,* she thought. *He's going to tell me that he met that senorita from Madrid.*

"Well, I'm afraid what I have to tell you is not good. I think we should sit down."

She allowed him to escort her to the couch and they both sat. The intensity of his gaze was too overwhelming now, and she avoided eye contact. Already she was feeling angry. Whatever they had shared was about to end. She had not wanted anything to get started and now the gorgeous devil was going to reveal himself for what she had known all along.

"What is it?" she asked impatiently. She had to meet with Trey's speech therapist, the laundry had to be done, and her life had to go on. He was wasting her time.

"It's about that stalker."

Her angry emotions dissipated instantly, leaving her feeling dazed and bewildered. Could it be that she was actually relieved? The stalker was definitely not good news, but at least it wasn't *adios, amiga*

Her tone softened. "What about the stalker?"

"Just listen. I know you are going to be upset…and you have the right, but please hear me out." He took a deep breath. "As a precaution, I have hired bodyguards to look out for you and Trey." He went on to tell her everything about the disturbing events.

Nicole's relief transformed into fear. "Oh, God." For a few moments she was absolutely speechless, and then she started babbling incoherently. "This can't be. I can't have this happen to Trey, not again. He knew something was wrong. I never saw anything the day that picture was taken but Trey saw it. My son saw it." She laced and unlaced her fingers, stood up and paced nervously around.

Julian sat up straighter. "Did you say that Trey *saw* this person? Do you think he could identify him?"

Nicole didn't hear a word he said. Images of hideous events, past and present, were swirling in her mind—threats, stalkers, bodyguards. She could not allow this. They had escaped from under the shadow of the evil predators of Chicago and now it was starting up again. Trey had to be protected above all else, including from her own selfish desires. If she had never met Julian none of this would be happening.

"Nicole." Julian stood beside her and placed his hand on her shoulder. "I know this is awful, but please listen. Did Trey see the person?"

She spun out on him. "Do you think I'm going to allow my son, who doesn't talk, to be interrogated by some investigators? This is *your* problem. If you had taken care of it sooner, it probably wouldn't have come to this!"

The wounded look in his eyes tore at her. "No, I didn't mean it like that," she stammered. "Please…I'm upset and I…I have to think."

Nicole rushed down the short hall and went into her bedroom, closing the door. If only she could just blink her eyes and erase the last few minutes.

"That's not what I was implying," Julian said from outside the door. "I certainly wasn't intending to have Trey interrogated about this. It's not even going to come to that. I have a plan that might work."

"What plan?" Nicole asked, refusing to come out of the room. "Bodyguards following me and my child around? We're not celebrities and we didn't ask for this. There's only one plan I can think of and that's ending our friendship."

"I agree with you."

"You do?" She slowly opened the door a little and Julian gently but firmly opened it wider and stepped into the bedroom. They stood face-to-face again, in the most intimate room of her home.

"I agree that we should stop seeing each other *temporarily.* My plan is to start being seen with a lot of other women again." He took a deep breath. "I don't want it that way, but it should throw the stalker off track. As far as all the security is concerned, it's really just a precaution. These people are very good. You won't even know they're around." He sighed. "Nicole, I feel terrible about this. What more can I do?"

"Nothing," Nicole said in a hollow tone. "There is nothing you can do because it's up to me."

"Please give my plan a chance," he whispered. He was standing so close that she could smell the warm, minty scent of his breath. "We won't see each other for awhile, but I'll still call you. Just one chance." His lips brushed hers.

Nicole felt the betraying waves of passion coursing through her soul. Julian was a victim. It was not his fault that there were lunatics in the world. It also dawned on her that had he been a lesser man he could have just kept the whole thing a secret and she would have been none the wiser. If they did go their separate ways, how would she explain the end of their friendship to Trey in a way that he would understand? He had been inquiring about Julian's whereabouts everyday while he'd been in Spain. And if she abruptly decided to send him back to Chicago to stay with his grandparents, how would his fragile psyche handle that? She had to face it; neither she nor her son was prepared to sever the bond at this point.

"Nothing bad will happen," Julian said urgently, persuasively. His arms enfolded her once more and she melted against his sinewy form.

In the midst of the emotional turmoil, her body was sabotaging her mind so much that she wished she could separate herself from it. She tilted her head up and started to speak, but his mouth bonded tightly with hers and they seemed to breathe as one. His tongue slid sensually across her anticipating lips. She tried to step back a little, but the calves of her legs brushed up against the bed. If he moved forward just an inch, she'd collapse right onto it.

"I'll go along with it," she whispered, her voice quavering.

Julian felt the heat. *Go along with what? The plan or what we're doing right now?* He wanted to close his eyes, shut out the world and break the crumbling walls that barricaded her heart. He wanted to give her that final push that would send her hopelessly into oblivion—the place where he wanted to be right now.

They moved sideways in a mesmerizing dance to music that played in their heads. He kissed her again and felt her urgent response, but he knew the dilemma facing them was far too real. He had to stay focused. Experience told him that she would only hate him later if they took that final step. The motion stopped and he leveled his eyes on her.

"This is going to be so hard," he said.

"What is?"

"Having to do the party scene again."

Nicole smiled sadly. She was aware that he had been the one to put the brakes on their little love dance and she was grateful—disappointed, but grateful.

"Well, as long as you don't start enjoying it," she said, taking his hand and leading him back into the living room. "I'll go along with what you're saying as long as you keep in mind that Trey is the top priority here, not the two of us. If he notices anything else and it starts to affect him, I'll—"

"You don't have to worry," he interrupted. "Trey will always come first. I understand that."

"I'm not sure what I should tell him about us," she said.

"Nothing. You don't have to tell him anything. He already knows that I have to travel a lot. That should explain why I'm not around that often." He noted the doubt lingering in her eyes. "Look, I'm in no way trying to make light of the situation, but I think we're both blowing it out of proportion."

"I hope you're right."

"I know I am."

Julian lingered for a few minutes and then announced that he had to be at a meeting in fifteen minutes. He kissed her goodbye. It was another long, desperately passionate kiss, which she reciprocated because she did not know when she would see him again.

When he left, Nicole tried to refocus on what she had been doing before he had arrived, but she couldn't. Something had definitely changed in the relationship. While she had been with him in the bedroom, she had not once thought about Warren and she didn't even feel guilty about not feeling guilty. The relationship between Julian and her was definitely evolving and that was disturbing, because she didn't trust him completely, even though she wanted to. He still had his way of stirring up a lot of turmoil and unrequited passion and then casually slipping back into his separate world, the one she did not belong in. She sensed that their two worlds were either about to converge or explode in the very near future and the realization was terrifying.

CHAPTER TWENTY-SIX

It was the last week of October and the holiday season was just around the corner. Nicole could feel it even in the balmy Miami air. Stores were actively hiring people in anticipation of more customers. Children and adults were chattering about Halloween, and in the hospital, as well as on the street, people were buzzing about how quickly the year had passed.

Nicole counted the days with eager anticipation that things would work out, and with an acute fear of the unknown. She had met the two bodyguards assigned to her and Trey, and had been surprised to discover that they were female. Julian had informed her that despite their low-key appearance, they were fully capable of handling any situation, and they were sensitively inconspicuous. Also true to his word, Julian did call, whenever he could. She was grateful that he always took time out to speak to Trey, even though he knew the child wouldn't answer. The one-sided conversation would have made someone else feel foolish.

The most difficult aspect of the separation was the weird sense of unreality that would consume her whenever she went shopping and noticed that almost every Spanish-language tabloid heralded Julian's escapades. She would stare at his handsome face smiling vapidly from the pages as he escorted an equally vapid-faced young beauty. Unfortunately, the prying press had also picked up the story of the stalker. It reported the increased security Julian had lately, and it also went on to tell tales about other stars who had been stalked in the past, some with tragic outcomes. Nicole made a concentrated effort not to look at the tabloids, but it was difficult when they were always right in front of her.

There were increasing moments when she would wonder how it was even possible that she knew the man. It sometimes seemed that he'd always been a figment of her imagination, created to ease the pain of a broken heart.

He was very real to Trey, though. She knew that her son eagerly anticipated seeing him again. It showed in the way his face lit up every time Julian called, and whenever his name was mentioned. Allyson had also informed her that Trey still played the guitar every night, and that he even slept with the instrument until she removed it from the bed.

It distressed Nicole greatly to see how much Trey wanted a father and that he was substituting a most unlikely candidate. She wanted to believe that it was just a case of hero worship, but she knew it was much deeper than that. Like mother, like son.

She watched Trey now, sitting at the kitchen table with a very serious expression on his face. He was drawing a picture and concentrating on which colors to use. He inspected the drawing, scowled, and then added some more detail.

"What're you drawing, Trey?"

He frowned and positioned his arms so that the sketch was concealed from her sight.

"Oh, come on. Why don't you let me see? I know it's good."

Trey slid the picture off the table, hiding it completely. *It's for Julian,* he signed and mouthed the words.

She hesitated for a moment. "Well, it might be a while before Julian gets to see it. Maybe I can just have a quick peek and tell you what he'll think."

Trey took a deep breath and reluctantly surrendered the drawing. Nicole gazed at a huge, green blob of a monster with wide, bulging red eyes, yellow fangs and fearsome claws. Very appropriate for Halloween. She smiled.

"That's quite a monster, hon. You're such a great artist." She studied it some more and added enthusiastically, "Such amazing detail. Julian will love this."

Trey scowled at her as if she had told him that the drawing was worthless garbage. She immediately concluded that her praise had not been adequate, and fought for the right words that would please him.

"I would give *anything* to be able to draw pictures like this," she gushed. "It deserves to be seen, so I'm going to put it right here." She hung the drawing in the center of the refrigerator, along with some of his other creative endeavors, securing it with a magnet.

He folded his arms across his chest, rolled his eyes, and shook his head incredulously. While she was trying to figure out what his negative body language meant, the telephone rang and the call turned out to be an old friend from Chicago whom she had not heard from in a while. She became absorbed in the conversation, but not so absorbed that she didn't notice Trey silently remove the picture from the refrigerator and rip it into tiny pieces that fluttered like weary moths into the garbage.

Trey hated the monster. It lived inside him. It was real tiny and squished up, stuck inside his throat, but if it ever got out, it would be *enormous* and slimy with fiery red eyes, like the picture he had drawn. The monster was very powerful and it could hurt people, even kill them.

The monster had taken away all his words. He would stand in front of the mirror sometimes and open his mouth trying to force them out, but the only sounds that would come were squeaks. The monster's grip was too tight.

When he was really little, right after it had killed Daddy, the monster was even more powerful than it was now. Back then, it wouldn't even let him cry. But Trey knew that the bigger and stronger he became, the weaker the monster was getting, and that was making the monster very angry. The monster didn't like it that he could laugh and that he could play the guitar. The monster didn't like it when he played with other kids, or when his mommy smiled. It did not want him to be happy, ever.

The monster hated Julian most of all because Julian knew all about it and was not scared. Trey liked it a lot when Julian made his mommy laugh, and when he talked to him as if he were a *real* boy instead of a weird one with a monster. He did not look at him in the funny way that other people did. When Julian talked to him, he would look at his eyes and stand close to him, because he wasn't afraid of catching the monster, like catching a cold. He didn't shout real loud as though Trey couldn't hear, and he didn't think it was so strange or terrible that he couldn't answer back. He *knew* about the monster. Trey was sure of that.

The stupid doctors his mommy made him go to did not know. They would ask him to play silly games with dolls and try to make him remember the bad thing that had happened a long time ago. Some of them would talk a lot, but they didn't act like they were really talking to him. Others would just sit back and stare at him and write down words on paper that they would not let him see. It made him angry. Once he had gotten so angry that he'd just sat on the chair and rocked back and forth, screaming with his eyes squeezed shut so he couldn't see or hear. Mommy had gotten very upset when the doctor told her that he was *ortistic* and should be sent to a special school that was far away.

Trey did not like to see his mommy sad, and he wished she could know that the monster was the one who made him do crazy things, like screaming while the teacher was talking, and fighting with the kids in the regular school who laughed at him. He wished she knew that it was all the monster's fault, but she thought he was just being bad, and that's why he now had to go to school with the deaf kids and learn sign language. He wasn't angry at Mommy, though, because she was a girl, and girls just did not understand monsters the way guys did.

A long time ago, he had gotten a really bad sore throat and Mommy had looked inside his mouth with a flashlight. He had held his breath and squeezed his eyes shut real tight, hoping she would finally see it. But the monster had made itself invisible. All she had seen

were little white spots, and then she had given him some yucky medi-
cine that he hated and the monster liked. Even now, she still didn't get
it. She'd hung the monster's picture on the refrigerator as if it was something nice. Julian would not have done that.

On the first of November, Nicole awakened in the dark of night,
to the sound of the phone ringing. Still half asleep, she reached for it.

"Did you hear?" Julian's voice came through. He sounded excited.

"Huh? What?" Nicole sat up straight. It was about two o'clock in
the morning and she'd just gotten to bed an hour ago.

"I'm sorry," he said, realizing. "Didn't mean to wake you. It's not
all that late where I am."

"Where are you?"

"I'm in LA. Did you hear about the stalker?"

She was wide-awake now. "I haven't heard anything. Tell me."

"Last week, some maniac scaled the wall of my place, armed with
a machete. One of my security guards shot him. Don't you listen to the
news?"

Nicole was too stunned to reply. She could feel her heart pounding
wildly and she wasn't sure if her reaction was from relief that the stalker
had been caught, or fear over the violent nature of the event.

"Nicole, are you still…"

"Yes. Yes, I heard you. Is the stalker dead?"

"No. He was wounded, but he'll live. Turns out he's some kind of
paranoid schizophrenic who escaped from a mental institution in
Georgia five years ago."

"Are you sure he's the one?"

"Well, I've been getting those *love* letters every week for at least five
years, and this week there were none, so I'm kind of reaching a conclusion. I would have told you sooner, but I thought you might have
heard." He hesitated because Nicole's silence unnerved him. Had she

decided that their relationship wasn't worth all the drama? "So, what do you think? Good news or no?"

She laughed, a short nervous laugh. "Don't pay any attention to me. I'm just kind of overwhelmed. Of course it's good news, but it's also horrible. Did you say he had a machete?"

"Yeah. Huge blade too." Julian laughed. "Guess he was looking forward to lopping my head off with one swipe."

"That's *not* funny."

"Sorry." He took a deep breath. "When I get back home I'll start downsizing the security troops. How's Trey?"

"Eagerly awaiting your return."

"Is Mommy eagerly awaiting too?"

Before replying, she laughed at the beseeching, childlike tone of his voice. "Yes, Mommy's eager too."

"Did you take my buddy out for Halloween?"

"No. My family doesn't do that ritual. Never did."

She wished she could have seen his expression when she said that, because he got really quiet. Then he laughed. "Baby, I like your family, but that attitude is totally un-American. What I'm hearing is that your family doesn't *do* fun."

"Well, excuse me, Mr. Cuban-American. I'm just expressing my *very* American right, not to participate in rituals that I don't believe in."

He laughed again. "That's what I love about you. You always have an answer. But I see I have a lot of work ahead of me. There is absolutely nothing wrong with having fun. I'm going to…"

He stopped talking in mid-sentence, and Nicole suddenly became aware of voices in the background. Obviously he was not alone. "Julian," she started.

"Nicole, I'm sorry. I really have to go now. I'll talk to you when I get back."

She barely got the word "goodbye" out, before she heard the click on the other end, and then she just sat there for a few moments, holding the receiver, listening to the infernal buzzing. Finally, she hung up and shook her head in bewilderment. The man she was in love with but didn't want to be was driving her crazy.

The illuminated dial on the bedside clock informed her in flashing digitals that it was now three a.m.; she was probably not going to get back to sleep.

CHAPTER TWENTY-SEVEN

There were no more threatening notes in purple or black envelopes. Upon returning to Miami, Julian talked Nicole into celebrating the resumption of their relationship by going out to dinner at an exotic Chinese restaurant with his band-member friend, Wade, and his wife, Yvette. It was a low-key event for Julian, but Nicole preferred it that way. She was delighted that Jamaican-born Wade and Yvette were both very down-to-earth people, a genuinely nice couple.

Wade did most of the talking, which was fine, because he had a wicked sense of humor that only Julian could match when he was in the mood. But that night Julian seemed quiet and reflective.

The following week, Julian told her that he would be in New York for two days, filming a video. There was a scene that required a chorus of children, and he wanted Trey to be among them. He told her that there would be a group of about thirty school kids, and they didn't have to sing, just lip-sync. Trey wanted to do it and Nicole gave her permission. Since she had that week off, they all flew to New York to stay one night in a hotel that overlooked Central Park.

The video was shot in Central Park, on a beautiful and unusually warm November day. The autumn foliage had peaked, but a lot of multicolored raiment still clung to the trees. The ground was a carpet of russet, red and gold.

Nicole enjoyed being a spectator, but she felt a bit lost among the sea of people and tons of camera equipment. It amazed her to see how much work went into making a video that was under five minutes long. Trey was incredible. He did exactly what he was told, didn't seem uncomfortable around the other children, and didn't even whine about the boring moments between cuts and takes. He had one quirk though. He had to be in the front row, standing close to Julian. No one argued.

The song was a breezy pop tune, tinged with elements of gospel and R&B. It played on a tape in the background for inspiration, but Julian lip-synched along with the others. He looked boyishly handsome, the centerpiece in a melange of adorable little faces of all sizes and nationalities.

Nicole woke Trey up early Sunday morning. They were booked on a flight back to Miami in the afternoon, so they had only a few hours to explore the park and enjoy Manhattan at a time when Julian was less likely to be recognized by fans. They met him in the hall and took the stairs down instead of the elevator.

"Think you could live in New York?" Julian asked as they ran on a path that paralleled the reservoir.

"In the suburbs maybe, but definitely not in the city."

She slowed down to look back at Trey, who had stopped running and was standing still with his face pressed up against the tall wire fence, gazing out at the diamond-spangled reservoir. The sun had just started to appear, hopefully to warm things up a bit. It was not as nice as it had been yesterday and the sky had a grayish pallor.

"Trey, come on. Let's keep up."

Julian stopped running and studied Nicole as she focused on her child. Her reddish hair, worn in one long braid, was backlit by the sun, which created an almost ethereal glow to her whole face. Dressed in a mauve colored fleece jacket, black stretch pants and sneakers, she looked like a teenager. She was so naturally, innocently beautiful, and so unaware of it, that he felt like taking her in his arms right at this moment and sweeping her off her feet, lifting her so high that she would never touch the ground again.

He smiled and watched Trey flapping his arms in imitation of a seagull flying overhead. Trey wanted them to be together, and in the uncluttered heart and mind of a child, there was no reason why they shouldn't be. It was just as natural as birds flying, the sun rising, or going to sleep at the end of the day.

His and Nicole's lives were far from being simple and natural. How could a woman who loathed or feared all things connected with being in the spotlight marry a man whose whole life revolved around it? How could a woman who seemed terrified of having a physical relationship learn to enjoy it? What if they got married and she really did hate sex? It would be appalling to make love to a woman knowing that she was only doing it to please him.

Marriage? Was he really thinking about marriage? He had only known Nicole for a few months, yet, amazingly, he was envisioning the consequences of commitment. Still, this reserved woman and her child made him feel more alive and needed than anyone else had, ever. They made him feel connected to a family again, and that was pretty special. But was it special enough to survive cultural, physical, and emotional turmoil?

"Julian, look. Have you ever seen one like this before?" Nicole presented him with a fiery red maple leaf with pronged tips of gold. "Trey found it."

"That's pretty spectacular," Julian said, ruffling Trey's hair. "Nature's definitely the best artist."

"This is what I miss most about up North," Nicole said. "When I was little my father would take Ally and me to one of the parks and we'd walk around just collecting leaves. I always found the best ones, but Ally would steal them when we got home."

Julian slid his arm around her and she in turn hugged Trey and huddled against him, lost in her reflections. "We had plenty to rake in our yard too. Ally and I would dive into these huge piles of leaves and bury ourselves. We'd have leaf fights with the kids next door." She breathed in the damp, chilly air. "It's funny, I'd never let Trey do that now. I'd be afraid of him getting bit by a tick and getting Lyme disease."

"Weren't there ticks back then?" he asked, staring up at the sky.

She hesitated. "I'm sure there were. We just know more about the dangers now."

"Oh, yes, modern man and his great knowledge," Julian commented as though he were about to make an eloquent speech. "The knowledge that takes all the joy out of life."

"That's true," she said softly. "But I guess we've compensated by learning to find new joys."

"I preferred the old ones."

"So did I." She hugged him and Trey tighter. "Now let's stop talking like this. We're not senior citizens yet."

She noticed again that whenever their conversations touched on childhood memories, he had a tendency to become silent and moody. She did not want to feel that way now. She wanted to enjoy their time together, because when it was over, she knew he would be the man she would be telling stories about to the other senior residents of whatever nursing home she ended up in years from now. He would be the man she would remember for the rest of her life.

New York was over in a heartbeat. Nicole was back in Miami working, and Trey was back in school. The video wouldn't be aired until early next year, when Julian's new CD was released, so Nicole had decided to hold off telling her parents about their grandson's participation in it. They still didn't know that Julian was famous, and she was still being close-mouthed about him in general. Her intention was to tell them more about him after Thanksgiving, after she met his family.

Julian had to be downtown in an hour to appear on *Rosanna,* a talk show that was Latin America's equivalent to *Oprah.* He had been on the show before, and knew he'd answer the usual questions about who he was allegedly dating, who his musical influences were, and how it felt to be considered a sex symbol. The latter was even more of a laugh these days since the woman he desired didn't seem to view him in that way at all. The fans in the studio audience would also get to ask him questions, and after that he'd sing his latest song and it would be over.

"Julian," an irritating voice rang out. Elena was in his apartment. He'd forgotten to lock the door.

"What is it?" he said from the bedroom. "I'm busy."

He had been avoiding her ever since the incident with Amanda. The child had not paid any impromptu visits since then either, because he was sure Elena was seeing to it that she didn't.

"This won't take long," she called. "I picked out what you should wear on the show."

Julian opened the bedroom door and came down in quick strides. "Forget it," he said, looking her squarely in the eyes. "I don't need your valet services anymore. You've been fired."

She studied him for a moment, as if she were not quite sure what to say, then laughed.

"Listen, I know that things haven't been right between us, but I want you to know that it's over. I forgive you. We are family and this…this avoiding each other is ridiculous and ignorant."

"You *forgive* me?" Julian repeated. "Well, now, isn't that big of you? Where's Amanda? Being held hostage in her room?"

"Can't you just drop the sarcasm? Amanda is in Orlando with her cousins."

"Really? For almost a month?"

"No. She hasn't been there for a month. If you must know the truth, I never did think it was proper for a little girl to spend so much time with her uncle. It's more acceptable this way, and it has nothing to do with what happened in the swimming pool."

Julian yawned and looked apathetic. "Whatever you say, Elena. She's your kid."

"You were *never* that close to the boys," she countered defensively.

"That would have been impossible," Julian said, with a quick laugh. "The boys were too much like you." He recalled the early years with his bratty nephews who when they were young, had treated him not like an uncle, or even an older brother, but more like a servant.

Elena sighed heavily. "Can't we ever have a discussion without insinuations? This nonsense has just got to stop. Next week is Thanksgiving and we're having our usual family gathering. Carmen and Diego Ramos are coming."

Julian studied his reflection in the mirror, trying to determine if he should wear a tie or not. "I thought this was just family."

"Carmen and Diego came from Cuba with us. As far as *I'm* concerned, they *are* family. I do believe they're bringing their daughter too. You remember Lydia, don't you?"

She was doing it again—getting to him in the worst kind of way. "Of course I remember Lydia. I went out with her a few times. She's a nice kid, but don't even *think* about it. I'm not going to marry her."

Elena looked flustered. "Marry? Oh, don't be ridiculous. Who said anything about that?"

"You did. You're so predictable that it isn't even funny."

"I'm just telling you that she's coming, that's all. I also think you should know that Lydia is *not* a kid anymore. She's a very pretty young lady and she might surprise you."

"We'll just see who's going to be surprised," Julian muttered.

"What did you say?"

"Nothing. If Lydia wants to come and be bored to death, that's her business. I probably won't even be at the gathering for more than an hour. I have other things to do."

Elena looked stricken. "But it's Thanksgiving! Don't you have respect for your family anymore? That's not how I raised you."

He picked up his car keys. "You didn't raise me. My father did." He walked past her as if she were not there.

Elena's mouth opened and closed soundlessly. When she finally found her words, she yelled after him. "Wait a minute. What are you doing? Isn't the chauffeur taking you?

"Why? I can drive."

"And you can't possibly be wearing that *hideous* suit, are you?"

Her words were drowned out by the sound of his departing car.

Nicole waited outside the hospital for Julian to pick her up. He had dropped her off at work and then told her that he'd be back from some business event at around the time she got off duty. It still felt odd having him pick her up, but with both of their hectic schedules, seeing each other was a juggling act.

The silver Lexus pulled up and she slid in. She felt even more misplaced when she saw that he was wearing a dark-colored suit with a burgundy silk shirt that was open at the collar.

"Are you coming from a fashion shoot?" she asked.

"No. I always dress like this. How about making a late-night stop at one of the clubs before going home?

She laughed, imagining them stepping into a nightclub with him looking like a male model and her still dressed as a nurse. "You better be kidding. Halloween's over."

He smiled. "What if I'm not? Actually I just left downtown. Had to present an award at a banquet for a friend."

Nicole studied him in silence as he drove. What she really wanted to do right now was go straight to his place instead of her own. She wanted to sip champagne until she became giddy with unrestrained passion. She wanted to forget all about time, space and consequences and just allow her intriguing Latin lover to do whatever he wanted— whatever they both wanted. She tilted her head back against the seat and closed her eyes. It was a good thing he couldn't read her mind.

"I've been thinking about Thanksgiving," Julian said as he pulled the car into the parking lot of her place.

Nicole kept her eyes shut. "Hmm it's next week. What about it?"

"Maybe we could do something special, like go to Aspen."

"Aspen!" Her eyes flew open and she sat upright. "But I thought we were going to your fam—"

"Yes, I did say that," he interrupted. "But I've been thinking that it's really going to be boring and..."

"It's quite all right." Nicole said stiffly, trying to conceal her hurt. "Why trouble yourself with Aspen? Trey and I will go to Chicago to be with my parents." She did not want to hear the rest of what he was saying. It was perfectly obvious that he did not want her to meet his family. As long as their friendship remained covert, everything was fine. She opened the car door.

"Listen, will you just wait a minute," Julian said. "I know what you're thinking and it's not true. I'm not changing the plan. I was only suggesting."

She glared at him with the door still open. "Why are you suggesting? If you really don't want me to meet your family, why don't you just come out and say so. It was *your* idea to begin with."

He started laughing. "That's right. It was my idea, and I haven't changed my mind. You *should* meet them."

Nicole took a silent breath and shook her head. There were times like this when she wondered if Julian Marquez was in his right mind. She didn't see anything funny about the discussion at all.

"Close the door," he said quietly. "I only suggested going away because I happen to enjoy our time together. Attending a family gathering isn't exactly enjoyable, especially when it's my family."

Nicole allowed the car door to close. She hated the way she was always so quick to jump to negative conclusions about him. He was probably just being honest. "Okay, I think I know what you're saying, but it's all right. I've been to enough family gatherings of my own. Let's see, there's Uncle Aaron who drinks too much, Aunt Millie who can't stop gossiping, the cousins who always fight. Should I go on?"

He smiled. "I see you get the point, but I'd take Uncle Aaron and the gossipy aunt any day. I care about my family, but sometimes we're really cruel."

"A lot of families are," she agreed. "I'm sure it's not intentional, but sometimes when people are familiar and comfortable with each other, they think it gives them the right to say whatever they want with no thought of tact or sensitivity."

Julian stared out the window at the stars dusting the ebony sky. Thanksgiving was certainly going to be an interesting day, but it was only a few hours. They'd get through it and move on.

"Julian?" Nicole asked questioningly, hesitating for a moment. "I know you told me before that your father is dead, but what about his side of the family? Are you in touch with them?"

"I have some relatives on his side, but the majority of them are still in Cuba. The ones here are mostly from my mother's side."

She caught the now familiar *I'd rather not talk about it* edge creeping back into his voice, but she was tired of all the mystery surrounding his past and she wanted to know.

"Could you please tell me a little about your mother? You said she took her own life. What exactly went wrong?"

He did not look at her, choosing instead to stare at the sky. When he spoke his tone was tight and clipped. "I don't know what went wrong. I guess today they'd label it manic depressive, bi-polar, north-polar, whatever. Anyway, it got so bad that she didn't want to live so she tripped out."

"That must have been very difficult for you to deal with," she pressed.

"Not really." He sounded angry. "I didn't *know* my mother. She was married, but separated from this…this communist jerk who was Elena's father. My mother and my father were just lovers who never got married, and I lived with my father and my aunt."

Nicole sat silent, waiting for him to continue, realizing there was a lot of anger and emotion that he'd kept bottled up since childhood. She didn't enjoy badgering him about it, but she knew all too well the effects of locked emotions. She thought about Trey.

"Whenever I had to visit my mother she was always in bed," he continued. "I used to try to make her smile, but she always looked sad.

She didn't care about me or Elena. All she thought of was her own suffering. Elena had to take care of her like she was the child."

"I'm sure she loved you and Elena," Nicole said softly. "She just couldn't help the way she was. She was sick."

"She was sick all right," Julian said. He unlocked the car door. "I don't really miss her. But I do miss my father and my Aunt Alma."

"Is your aunt still in Cuba?"

"She's not in Cuba." He got out of the car and opened the door on her side. "Nicole, do you realize what time it is? I'll walk you to the door."

That's right, walk me to the door so you can shut it tight, Nicole thought. Clearly he was not going to tolerate any more questions, and she was exhausted from prying. Maybe at the gathering she would get to meet Aunt Alma and others, and maybe they would be more open to discussion. Getting personal information out of Julian was like extracting splinters from a wound.

CHAPTER TWENTY-EIGHT

Thanksgiving Day arrived and Nicole glanced in puzzlement at Julian as he parked the car in the circular driveway in front of the estate. "I thought the dinner was going to be at your place?"

"It's always at my sister and brother-in-law's," Julian said. "I didn't tell you that?"

"No. You didn't."

It wasn't a big deal, but she already felt nervous, and being in unfamiliar surroundings increased her anxiety. She glanced in the back seat at Trey. Wearing his best blue blazer and anxious to get out of the car, he showed no signs of panic so far.

Julian opened the car door for Nicole, who got out carefully. Dressed in a long black velvet, spaghetti-strapped dress, with a jeweled choker collar around her swan-like neck, she was a picture of elegant perfection. Her hair was in a sophisticated upsweep, and he thought she looked like an Ethiopian princess.

She had asked him more than once before they arrived if she was overdressed, and he'd had to assure her that she wasn't. Dressing formally was part of Elena's stupid ritual, and was the reason he was wearing a black suit and a white shirt. Not wearing a tie was his own deliberate fashion faux pas. But it didn't compare to last Thanksgiving when he'd worn a T-shirt and jeans, upsetting no one but Elena. It was only because Nicole wanted to make a good impression that he wasn't doing the same thing this year.

The minute Nicole entered the Torres family dwelling, a chill literally went through her. The surroundings bore no resemblance to the interior of Julian's home, because it exhibited none of his artistic flair for light, open space and creativity. It was like stepping into a vault containing the dark woody tones of traditional, conservative wealth and power. The foyer was huge and intimidating with an impressive chandelier suspended above alcoved walls and a dark marble floor.

As they moved down the hall toward the sound of voices, she noted expensive paintings lining the walls. She could see a winding staircase, more chandeliers and finally they were entering the library, or family room, where everyone had gathered for hors d'oeuvres and drinks being offered by a roving servant. Instantly her attention shifted from the interior decorating to the people who were all around them.

Julian introduced her to some of the cousins, whose names escaped her the minute they were spoken. There were just too many people to remember, and she was distracted by Trey, whose enthusiasm had died. He was now clinging tightly to her. Had she been a kangaroo, he'd probably climb into her pouch and hide. She wanted to hide too, but the unyielding floor was not about to swallow her up.

Julian, the star in the family, was the center of everyone's attention and while he was talking animatedly to an uncle, Nicole quickly assessed the entire scene. There were no people of color in the room. Not even one person from Julian's father's side of the family appeared to be present and it made her feel even more disappointed than she knew she should be.

Out of the corner of her eye, Nicole noticed an attractive young woman lingering a distance away with her eyes focused on Julian. She had tawny, wheat-colored hair that flowed down to her waist. It was certainly not unusual that she would be looking at him, but the concentrated focus of her gaze was a little odd for a relative…unless of course she wasn't.

"Nicole," Julian said. "I want you and Trey to meet Luis, my brother-in-law and manager."

"It's so nice to meet you," Nicole said, smiling and extending her hand to the tall, pleasant-looking man with thinning dark hair and a mustache.

Luis Torres did not shake her hand. He kissed it, flashed a genuine smile, and spoke in heavily accented English, "It is always a pleasure to behold a beautiful woman. Any friend of Julian's is a friend of mine."

Nicole was embarrassed but touched that Mr. Torres showed no sign of animosity or reserve. He shook Trey's hand and didn't make an issue out of the boy's silence. He started to say something else but an elderly man interrupted to speak to him and a woman quickly stepped forward to address Julian. Nicole took a deep breath. The woman was none other than Elena, and Nicole wondered if she would remember her from their brief meeting in the hospital months ago.

"Julian, Lydia is here," Elena said, ignoring Nicole.

Looking somewhat agitated, Julian turned as the tawny-haired girl approached him with uncertain steps, nervously brushing back her hair.

"Excuse me a minute," he said to Nicole, then smiled at Lydia and escorted her to the far end of the room.

Flustered and feeling awkward, Nicole focused her attention back on Elena, observing that the woman was wearing an elegant and ostentatiously expensive designer dress. Her hair was pulled back and confined so tightly in a chignon that it stretched her skin and gave her eyes a slightly slanted feline appearance. The cat, although inches shorter than Nicole, had her claws unsheathed and loomed larger than anyone in the room.

"Hello, I take it you're one of Julian's friends," she purred. A cat with a Spanish accent. "I'm his sister, Elena. Have you met his fiancée, Lydia?"

"Fiancée?" Nicole tried not to look too bewildered.

"Yes, they've known each other for years. They make such a beautiful couple, don't you think?" Before Nicole could respond, she continued. "Oh, I didn't even get your name. Are you a model, dear?"

"My name is Nicole and I am *not* a model."

"No? How unusual. Julian's friends are *always* models." She looked down at Trey who was scowling and tugging at Nicole's arm. "Oh, I remember this little boy. He's the one who can't talk." She looked back at Nicole. "You are his mother?"

"Yes. I am his mother," Nicole replied icily. "Now if you'll excuse me I…"

"How is it that you and Julian became friends?" she asked, completely ignoring the fact that Nicole was trying to evade her. "You are in show business, no?"

"I am not in show business. I am a nurse at Miami General Hospital."

"A nurse?" Her eyebrows arched, then narrowed. "How interesting." Her false eyelids fluttered a mile a minute. "That's a very beautiful dress you're wearing. Did Julian buy it for you?"

Nicole was about to explode when she suddenly felt Julian's hand on her arm. As she turned to look at him, she also noticed Lydia quickly making her exit from the room, looking upset.

"I see you've met my conniving sister," Julian said, glaring at Elena.

He urgently guided Nicole and Trey away from the line of fire. They stepped out into the quiet hall.

"I think it would be a good idea if you just take us home right now, so you can have dinner with your fiancée," Nicole said angrily.

Julian laughed. "Nicole, listen to me. That girl is not my fiancée. She's just another victim of Elena's scheming. I've told you enough about Elena to..."

At that moment, Amanda came rushing out, looking like a little princess in ribbons and a red velvet dress. "Hi Trey!" she shouted.

Trey's bewilderment vanished. He smiled.

Julian knelt down to their level. "Amanda, why don't you take Trey over where the kids are."

Nicole opened her mouth to protest, but Amanda grabbed Trey by the hand and they ran back into the crowded room.

"Come on. Let's just go back inside and get this over with," Julian said tightly. "*You* wanted to meet everyone. As far as I can tell, Elena is the only one who's been rude to you. Surely you must have anticipated that."

"I did. It's just that she got me with that fiancée thing. If there is nothing between you and Lydia, why did she get so upset and leave? What did you say to her?"

"She was upset because Elena lied to her. I told her the truth. Let's go back in."

But what is the truth? Nicole wondered. "Julian, I'm not sure this is a good idea now. I...I was expecting some cattiness from Elena, but this... Did you hear what she asked me? She asked me if you *bought* my dress."

"I'm telling you, don't take her seriously. She's only being her usual bitchy self. Just give it right back to her."

Nicole sighed. "I should have reminded her that you probably bought *her* dress."

Julian grinned. "Now you've got it. Let's rejoin the circus."

Instincts told her that she should stick to her original decision, which was to leave immediately, but the optimistic fool in her allowed him to escort her back into the viper pit.

She met Julian's nephews, Raul and Ramón. Raul was a studious looking twenty-two-year-old law student and Ramón, four years younger, was his polar opposite with spiked hair and an earring. They were formally polite and didn't seem to be harboring ulterior thoughts about her presence.

She looked around and spotted Trey among the group of children. He did not look uneasy, and she noticed with further relief, that Amanda's nanny, Michelle, was present and supervising the children. Nicole decided to relax. She would not allow Elena to get to her again. If they exchanged any more words, she would just stand up to her. Why should she care what Elena thought? Julian had invited her.

Dinner was served after a long prayer spoken in Spanish by Luis Torres's elderly father, who sat at the head of a seemingly endless banquet table in a dining room worthy of royalty. To his left and right were all the grown children, grandchildren, cousins, aunts and uncles. Nicole and Julian sat to the left, directly opposite Elena and Luis. All of the children under fifteen were in an adjoining room, which apparently was the Torres family equivalent of the children's table. For once in her life, Nicole would have preferred to be there.

The food was typical Cuban fare, beans, rice, roast pork, along with the traditional American turkey with all the trimmings, but Nicole hardly tasted it. She was too distracted by the atmosphere around her, and felt like an alien who'd just crash-landed on Earth, because everyone was speaking in Spanish and she could understand very little of it.

Instead of being relaxed and at ease with his own family, Julian seemed to be in another world too. Nicole was disturbed by the fact that his mood had shifted abruptly from cordial, to stiff, cold, and indifferent. He was also drinking more than she thought he should be. Every few minutes she found herself glancing anxiously at him, wondering if he were still awake.

Nicole didn't realize the exact moment when the conversation switched over to English, but all of a sudden she understood everything being said and immediately regretted it.

"You know, this country would really be great if it wasn't for the liberals," Elena said, addressing an aunt, but eyeing Nicole. "Remember that election year when we had to wait a long time to find out who won the presidency because the liberals wanted to keep recounting votes even though it was obvious who won?"

"That was something," the aunt said. "I'm glad it didn't happen this time."

A steady buzz of conversation ensued. Nicole toyed with her rice and tried to plot an escape from the room.

"Something really should be done about the crime in this country," Elena continued. "The death penalty should be restored in all the states. It probably would be if it weren't for those liberal hypocrites. Just think, if they ever get voted into full power, this country could become communist."

"Oh, I don't think it will come to that, at least not in our lifetime," someone else said.

"No one thought Castro would take Cuba," Elena said.

That was over forty years ago, Nicole thought. *Why dwell on that?*

"I don't see this country going communist," the other person continued. "But you are right about the liberals. They should never be allowed to get out of control."

"It's been a while now, but I still can't get over what they did to that little boy," Elena said.

Not that again, Nicole thought. She remembered all too well the international custody battle over a little Cuban refugee, a boy Trey's age who had been found floating alone in the Atlantic, having lost his mother. His Miami relatives had wanted to keep him, but the U.S. government had intervened and he had been returned to his father in Cuba, angering the Cuban-American community.

Nicole took a deep breath and glanced at Julian, wondering if he was going to make a comment, but his dark eyes were fixed straight ahead, staring into a void of nothingness.

"It was a shame about the little boy," Nicole said before she could stop herself. "But who knows, maybe when he's old enough to decide for himself he'll return."

Elena glared at her. "Oh, so you really think it's that easy? Obviously you know nothing about what it's like to escape a communist country."

Here we go, Nicole thought. Earlier, the woman had been catty, but now she sounded downright hostile. "You're right," Nicole admitted, trying to modulate the tone of her voice. "I don't personally know what it's like, but there are things such as history books and I have listened to other people's accounts."

Elena ignored her as if she hadn't spoken at all and continued her diatribe with the others. "If the liberals ever get in again, who knows what will happen next? They will probably completely end the embargo and try to normalize relations with Cuba. Remember the eighties when they allowed that devil to dump his Mariel trash here?"

Several of the other relatives nodded in agreement. Nicole flinched. She knew a few African Cubans who had arrived during the infamous boat exodus who worked in the hospital. "All of them weren't trash," she said. "A lot of them were political prisoners, poets, writers and hard-working people who have gone on to do well."

"And a good portion of them are in America's prisons and mental institutions being supported by taxpayers' money," Elena snapped.

Nicole shrugged, trying to sound nonchalant. "Then I guess that means that the devil, as you call him, is very cunning."

Elena sniffed. "You think Castro is a hero, don't you?"

"I never said any such thing." Nicole glanced at Julian again and this time his silence angered her.

"Excuse me, Elena," Luis said. "It's not proper to discuss politics over dinner, especially on Thanksgiving."

The others buzzed their agreement, and the conversation shifted to sports and general gossip.

Julian struggled with an urge to get out of the room. The walls seemed to be closing in on him and the chatter sounded like the roar of the sea. It never failed. Every year, at every gathering, he would be okay for awhile and suddenly the flashbacks would start. This year was no different. In the past, the remedy had been alcohol, but this time it was not having the desired effect. He knew from experience how much he could tolerate without getting intoxicated, but lately his tolerance level had increased. It took more and more to get to a level where he could not be touched by the past. He wasn't naïve. He did know that alcoholic pacification was a dangerous remedy, but as long as he didn't need it every day, he knew it was still under control.

He saw himself, ten years old, in the kitchen of the neat but tiny house Elena and Luis used to have in Hialeah. He was standing at the sink washing dishes while the rest of the family had dinner.

"Julian, come here and take care of the baby," he heard Elena call out.

He remembered sullenly entering the kitchen and having the baby, Raul, thrust at him so he could change his diaper. He hadn't been allowed to eat until all the relatives left the kitchen, and he had to clean up after them while Elena and the others sat in the living room laughing and talking.

"You know, that boy is getting so tall and skinny. He doesn't look like Felicia at all," said Aunt Isabella, adding disparagingly, *"he looks more like his father."*

"Yes," Elena agreed. *"Julian's not as dark, but he's got a lot of his father's features."*

"He's very shy and backward too, isn't he?"

"I guess he's not all that bright," Elena said. *"But he's a good worker. Go finish washing the dishes, Julian."*

"I'm not backward!" he cried out into a wall of silence. *"I am bright. I'll show you...you'll see."*

"How was Spain, Julian?" A much older, wizened Aunt Isabella asked now.

Julian did not reply. He was still in the past. Concerned, Nicole nudged him. "Julian, your aunt's speaking to you."

"Huh? What?" The crash back to earth was jarring.

"How was Spain?" Aunt Isabella repeated, smiling. "You do so much traveling, I guess you must be exhausted."

Julian smiled ironically. "Excuse me. I was daydreaming. I really have no reason to be tired since I'm not touring right now." He went on to elaborate about his recent trip to Spain. Aunt Isabella and most of the others leaned forward to listen with rapt attention.

A servant entered the room and whispered something to Luis, who excused himself and exited to take a phone call. Almost immediately after Luis departed, Julian slipped back into his morose coma, and the incendiary political discussion ensued once again.

"The real problem with this country is that too much attention is paid to civil rights advocates," Elena said. "That thing they call affirmative action should definitely be done away with. Those people want everything handed to them without doing the hard work like everyone else."

Those people? Who are those people? Nicole thought, infuriated by the fact that Elena was deliberately baiting her, the only dark skinned, non-Cuban woman, who was all alone and defenseless in a room full of conservatives, while the man she thought she knew and loved drifted deeper into the twilight zone.

Someone else made a comment, but Nicole didn't hear it. The only voice seemed to be Elena's

"They are uneducated and lazy," the witch continued.

Nicole pushed her plate aside. "Listen, this is your home and you can spout off all the narrow-minded bigotry you like, but I'll have you to know that my father was a civil rights activist, and he was also an educator. He got his master's degree in political science without the help of affirmative action, thank you, and my whole family knows all about hard work." She took a deep breath. "It is the true mark of ignorance to stereotype people."

The silence that followed was deafening. Elena's younger son, the one with the earring, put his hand over his mouth to conceal a smile. Clearly, Elena had expected her to just sit and suffer humiliation in silence, because it took her a few seconds to deliver her comeback line.

"Well, it wasn't my intention to offend you, dear, but it does take a considerable number of people behaving in a certain pattern to start a stereotype in the first place. I know nothing about your father, but the majority of Negro civil rights activists in this country and some others are borderline communists."

Nicole clenched her teeth. Julian was not going to provide any backup. She had assumed all along that he was politically conservative, but she had also assumed, perhaps incorrectly, that his being biracial would have also given him insight into the other side.

His silence indicated to her that he agreed with his sister. She was on her own.

"I refuse to play your stereotype game," Nicole said. "I can only speak for myself and my family. My father was *not* a communist and neither am I." She sat up straighter. "But as far as other people are concerned, your narrow view refuses to see the human side. When one government oppresses people, they often investigate other forms of government to find something better. Castro appealed to some because he spoke against racial discrimination and there he was, one little man with a raggedy guerrilla army who defied a more powerful nation and won."

"You admire him, don't you?" Elena said coldly.

"I'm speaking in general, not about—"

"Yes, you do. You love him, and I think it's about time you learn some real history."

History.

Julian felt his father's hand on his shoulder as they walked down a narrow, stone road at night. The air was still and warm.

"Look at the stars, son. They are the same stars all over the world."

"In America too, Papi?"

"Yes, in America too. They follow us all, and it doesn't matter if you're rich, poor, black, white, free or enslaved. Everyone gets to wish on the same stars."

Julian's pulse quickened. For a moment he could almost see his father's face. *Everyone gets to wish…everyone gets to wish…black, white, free.*

The features blurred and vanished. Julian came out of his haze and looked around in bewilderment. The tension in the room could be sliced with a knife.

"You don't have to tell me anything about history," Nicole was saying loudly.

"That devil you people admire so much, is responsible for the deaths of many innocent men, women and children." Elena punctuated the air, raising her hand in a defiant gesture. "He killed Julian's father! Didn't you tell your little activist girlfriend that, Julian? Didn't you tell her that your father was murdered, beaten to death in one of her hero's prisons?"

A silence swept over the whole table like an engulfing wave. Nicole felt as if she were drowning as Julian's face turned a weird shade of gray.

The weight of the room hung heavily on her now and she felt like an insensitive fool. Why hadn't she just kept her mouth shut?

"I'm sorry," she said, rising from the table. "I…I didn't know."

"You have nothing to apologize about," said Luis, reentering the room on the tail end of the debacle. "Elena, I have seen your cruelty often, but treating a guest in such a manner is despicable!"

Julian found his voice. "Nicole, it's okay."

Nicole did not even hear him. She rushed out of the room. Julian hurried after her and caught up with her in the hallway. They faced each other. He gripped her forearms with both hands, forcing her to look at his face.

"You didn't tell me," she cried. "You just sat there like you were invisible and let me go on and on like a blabbering moron."

His grip became even tighter. "You're not the moron. Elena is. You stated your opinion and you stuck to it regardless of consequences. I think it's admirable."

"Who cares about that! Your father…"

"I'm sorry I didn't tell you." He relaxed a little. "It's difficult. It happened a long, long time ago."

"I don't understand you, Julian. Sometimes it feels like we're so close and then something like this comes and slams me right in the face. You *made* me talk about the terrible things that happened in my life, but you can't share your pain with me."

"I was going to tell you more detail. I was just waiting for the right moment."

"Where is my son?" Nicole asked, resignation in her voice. "It's time for us to go."

Julian did not want to lose her. He sensed that she was shutting down, pulling away, and he didn't blame her. The day had turned out far worse than he'd ever envisioned. They had to get out of the house. Maybe the air would clear his head.

"The kids are over at my place in the game room," he said, searching his pants pockets. "When I find my keys, I'll take you home. We can talk."

Nicole turned away. "We'll be taking a taxi. I don't think you should be driving."

I'm not drunk, he thought, but he could tell by the grim set of her mouth that she thought he was. "My chauffeur will take you. Please, just go wait at my place. I have to say something to my family and I'll be right with you."

The sunlight was blinding as Nicole stepped outside. She was starting to feel the effects of a headache, but other than that she felt strangely emotionless. "Go find Trey," she told herself. Hopefully her son had fared a lot better than she had.

She found him happily playing video games, surrounded by the other kids. Michelle was sitting on a couch, reading a book and keeping an eye on their antics. No one even noticed her standing in the doorway. The sight of her son eased her anguish a little. She stepped back into the shadows, preferring not to be seen, and sat in the living room.

What could be done about Julian's overwhelming problems? she wondered. How could he get to the age he was and still feel such anguish over the past? She knew now that there was no way she would ever be able to get along with Elena, and at this point, she didn't even see why it mattered. What baffled her was Julian's acceptance of her cruelty. It *was* possible that he viewed her as more of a mother figure than a sister, but even a mother shouldn't have that kind of control or disrespect for a grown son. Why did he set himself up to be mentally abused by her?

"What's taking him so long?" she muttered. In truth, it had not been long at all, but she was anxious to talk things over so she could get some real understanding of the situation. She glanced at her watch and decided to return to the scene of the crime to find him.

"I need to have a word with you…alone," Elena hissed, beckoning Julian into the empty library.

He had just informed Luis that he was leaving and was about to return to Nicole when Elena intervened.

"I have nothing to say to you," Julian said coldly.

"You have some nerve getting angry at me. You are the one who caused this problem. What on earth possessed you to bring that woman to our gathering? I told you that Lydia was coming." She paused for air. "Now I have to call her up and apologize for your rudeness. That poor girl..."

"I'm sorry if Lydia is upset, but it's your fault," Julian said. "I told you I wasn't interested in her."

"And you're interested in that...that black girl?"

"As a matter of fact, yes, I am."

Elena rolled her eyes in disgust. "I simply can't imagine why. Oh, on the other hand, maybe I can. It's about sex isn't it? Well, Julian, you have never invited any of your other whores to meet our family before, so why this one, and why now?"

"Nicole is about as far from a whore as you can get, so don't even go there."

At that moment, Nicole was searching for Julian in the hall, and ran into Elena's son, Ramón. "Have you seen Julian?" she asked.

"Yes. I last saw him near the library." Ramón hesitated, then spoke again. "I hope you're not too upset about this. I don't know what's with my mother sometimes, but I just want you to know that we don't all feel that way."

She smiled at him. "Thank you, Ramón."

Nicole started to enter the library when she heard Julian's voice and realized he wasn't alone. He sounded angry.

"I don't give a damn what you think anymore!"

"You better," Elena said. "If it wasn't for me you wouldn't even be where you are now. A whore is just what she is. A whore and a gold-digger."

Nicole froze in the hallway, shielded by the alcove. She knew she shouldn't be listening. She really didn't want to hear this exchange, but she felt paralyzed.

"That's not true," Julian shot back. "She's the most unpretentious person I've ever met."

"Oh, but of course. Men are so gullible. She's just letting you think that, and you're falling for it like a fool. If you were to actually get serious about a woman like that, she would ruin your career. All of your focus and all your energy should be on your music. This next CD of yours is crucial. You do want a complete crossover into the English market, don't you?"

"I want it, but there are other things in life besides fame and money."

"Did she tell you that? Are you falling completely for her liberal propaganda? Listen to me, and listen good. I know that you're weak and a dreamer just like our mother was, but you can overcome it if you take my advice. You do not need an ignorant black woman and her retarded son in your life. She doesn't love you. All she wants is your money, so she can take care of that child!"

Nicole gasped and the room lurched. Retarded son? The witch could call her ignorant all she wanted, but calling her beautiful, intelligent son retarded, and implying that they wanted his money? She did not linger to hear what Julian was going to say. She did not care.

Rushing outside, she returned to his apartment and burst into the game room. A startled Michelle looked up at her.

"What's wrong?" she asked.

Nicole ignored her completely and seized Trey by the arm. He balked and stared at her in shock.

"It's all right," she said, aware that she was frightening him. "We just have to leave right now."

"But we were just playing," Amanda exclaimed, equally puzzled.

"I'm sorry, Amanda, but you have your cousins to play with. *Now*, Trey."

He allowed himself to be pulled out of the room. They stood outside while Nicole furiously punched in the numbers for the taxi on her cell phone. She noticed a curtain move from inside the window and caught a glimpse of Elena's amazonian maid, Gretchen, watching them with a tight, smug expression on her face. She felt an uncharacteristically intense hatred for the weird woman. Even the housekeeping staff was entertained by her humiliation. It would be the last time. Holding tightly to Trey's hand, Nicole walked rapidly down the winding path that led away from the estate. She never wanted to see Elena, the surroundings, or Julian again.

CHAPTER TWENTY-NINE

Within an hour Julian was knocking on her door. Nicole sent Trey to his room and continued washing the dishes, ignoring the sound. Allyson, all dressed up for a date, scowled and shook her head.

"Aren't you at least going to answer it?"

Nicole washed the same dish over again for the third time. "No. After I just told you what happened, do you really think I want to talk to him?"

"Apparently not, but he's gonna keep knocking. You could at least hear him out."

"Ignore him," Nicole said.

"Sorry, can't do that." Allyson moved toward the door. "I'll tell him you just don't want to speak to him."

The dish hit the floor and scattered in tiny pieces. "Don't! I'll do it!"

Nicole went to the door and unlocked it, leaving the chain bolted. It opened partially and she peeked out.

"What can I do for you?" she asked in the same tone she'd use to address a salesperson.

"Aren't you going to let me in?" Julian asked.

"I don't allow strangers inside. Say what you have to out there."

"Nicole, what's wrong with you? I thought we agreed to talk. I came back to my place and Michelle told me that you practically yanked Trey out and took off. *Why?*"

"Because I don't ever want to see you again unless it's onstage. Now please leave."

He folded his arms across his chest and glared at her, bewilderment and frustration evident in his eyes. "Listen, am I completely losing it or are you? I know that dinner was a nightmare, but you agreed to discuss…"

"I *heard*," Nicole said bitterly. "I came back looking for you and I heard what your demented sister said about my son and me. You're nothing but a pawn and a puppet for her. You can't even stand up to her."

Julian stood in shocked silence, trying to remember just what she might have overheard. What he recalled was pretty ugly.

"What did you hear?"

"Enough."

"Maybe not *quite* enough. Do you actually think I believe Elena? I didn't just stand there and take it. I—"

"I don't care what you did or didn't believe."

"Please don't shut me out. We have to talk. I'll tell you why things happened the way they did. I'll tell you about my father."

She detected desperation in his voice, but she did not want to sympathize with him. She wanted him to just go away—vanish into the clouds. "I'm sorry about your father, but spare yourself. You don't have to go dredging up old wounds for my benefit. Trey and I don't exist in your life anymore. I refuse to be hurt and insulted by you and your vicious, bigoted sister anymore."

"Just let me come in and explain."

"No! I have my own family to care about. Sure, we argue, fuss and even fight sometimes, but at least we respect each other. Everyone is entitled to that. I hope one day you'll find what you're looking for, but that day will come only when you accept who you are, *every* part of who you are."

Nicole closed the door firmly and locked it. He knocked three more times and then she heard his angry retreating footsteps. She leaned with her forehead against the door and squeezed her eyes shut, as if that action could block the pain. It didn't. Her heart nearly erupted at the sound of his tires screaming as his car careened wildly out of the parking lot.

He called four times the next day—three while she was at home and once while she was at work. Each time, she said nothing, and quietly put the receiver down. It was not a hard thing to do because her actions had become mechanical. Her brain was finally taking precedence over her heart.

It *was* hard trying to explain the situation to Trey. She sat him down two days later and made an attempt.

"Honey, I want you to try to understand, but we won't be seeing Julian anymore."

But why? Trey signed, staring at her in disbelief.

"Because…because there are some grownup people who can be cruel and ignorant. They dislike all people who are different than they are." She wrung her hands together. It wasn't going well. Trey looked even more puzzled.

"What I'm trying to say is that ignorant people dislike others because they don't speak the same language, or have the same color of skin that they do. Julian's family is like that. They don't like us because they think we're different."

Why are we different?

"Because we don't come from Cuba and we don't speak Spanish."

"Julian doesn't care," Trey indicated.

"I know he doesn't, but Julian is a famous singer and famous people spend most of their time traveling and being around other people." She knew that no matter how she tried to explain it to him, he was still going to be upset. "Julian has other important things in his life that have nothing to do with us. We have to live our lives and he has to live his."

Trey wasn't falling for it. *He's my friend and I want to see him.*

"I'm sorry, Trey, but things just can't always be the way you want them to be." She hugged him consolingly. "Mommy is sad too, but we'll get over it. We'll find other friends. I promise."

I don't want other friends! The monster was laughing at them. Trey swallowed hard, but the lump in his throat would not go down and tears were coming out of his eyes like a baby. The monster was growing bigger and bigger and it was choking him. He yanked himself free of his mother's arm and ran into his room, slamming the door hard.

Nicole wanted to run after him, but she realized that at the moment he needed his space, and it would only make things worse if she kept talking. In truth, she couldn't even console herself because she felt as wounded as he did. It was another of those disappointments in life that would only ease with time.

Julian could not accept that it was over. He called Nicole consistently until it finally became inevitable that she was not going to respond. His feelings went through stages—first disappointment, then humiliation, and finally anger. Anger at himself for being more vulnerable than he wished, anger at his whole life, his family and at Nicole. He didn't blame her for being upset over what had happened, but he had taken her to be not only a sensitive woman, but also a compassionate one. If she really was compassionate, where was the forgiveness? Had he been *that* wrong?

Whatever the case was, he now seemed to need a drink just to wake up in the morning and another to go to sleep at night. He didn't even want to think about the waking hours in between when he indulged more than ever. It's okay, he constantly told himself. As long as it doesn't get completely out of control. He only needed it to help him deal with the invasive public and to go on with his business until Nicole was nothing but a fleeting memory.

He tried to devote all of his energy to his music, but the end results were less than satisfying. The recording sessions seemed long and arduous, the back-up singers were always off-key, the musicians weren't in sync and his own voice lacked its usual depth.

Everything seemed pointless. Other women were eager to fill the void, but they were now a source of irritation too.

Late one night he returned home from Los Angeles and stepped on a note that had been slipped under the door. Realizing what it was, he picked it up and read: *I hope that we are still friends.* For a brief second his heart beat faster. Could it be that Nicole had reconsidered? He read on. *If you feel like talking about anything, no matter what, I'll always be there to listen.* It was signed, *Gretchen.*

"Oh, man," he said aloud, and then laughed. Were his woes so obvious that even the maid was trying to placate him? He tore up the note and tossed it in the trash. "Sorry, Gretchen, we won't go there again."

He went to the bar, started to pour a drink, but thought better of it. Instead he went up the winding stairs and stretched out on the bed, fully clothed, and recalled his first encounter with Gretchen years ago.

Elena had hired her as a maid and most of her services were rendered to the Torres family exclusively, but every Monday she would empty the trash, water the plants and clean and dust the furniture in his apartment. On a rare moment when he'd been home and bored, he'd found himself sitting out on the deck, reading a magazine and observing the morose looking six foot-plus blond with the tight braid wound around her head as she watered the plants. Despite her looking and acting like an elderly woman, he could tell that she was actually fairly young. Her eccentricities had made him curious, so he'd inquired about her life.

Her response had startled him. Instead of the few mumbled perfunctory responses he'd anticipated, she'd almost too eagerly launched into her life story. As a young child she had lost both parents in an accident in Germany, and had been sent to the United States to live with relatives who didn't really want her. The story, somewhat similar to his own, encouraged him to share with her a tiny bit about his early life and they had bonded.

Gretchen had rewarded him by misinterpreting his casual interest, thinking that he wanted more. He still remembered that awkward night when he'd returned from a show and found her in his room, sitting on his bed wearing a robe. Her long golden hair was cascading down her waist, and she brandished a wine glass in eager anticipation as she waited. His response had not been what she wanted. He'd had to tell her the truth, that he was not interested in her in any kind of physical way and that he was sorry if he'd said or done anything that led her to believe that was the case.

He *knew* he hadn't done anything to lead her on and he'd tried to turn her down as sensitively as possible, but she'd been humiliated anyway and in the end she had apologized stiffly and immediately left. Ever since that day they'd never shared anything more than a hello and a good morning. She came to clean his apartment only when he was away.

Now she had written him a note.

He placed both hands over his eyes. If anything, it was a wake-up call. His drinking and associated behavior had to be getting out of control if Gretchen felt sorry for him. Probably the whole housekeeping staff knew a great deal about all of their lives. He wondered if they returned to their own homes and laughed at the rich and stupid people who employed them.

After breaking up with Julian, Nicole's carefully constructed world fell apart as Trey became incorrigible. Almost every day she received calls from his teachers, reporting on his disruptive behavior: Trey is not paying attention in class, Trey hit another child, Trey keeps walking out of the classroom without permission. The list went on. She talked to him endlessly, took away privileges and on one occasion even resorted to what she never wanted to do, which was spank him. Nothing worked. He simply looked at her with reproachful eyes and indicated that he would do better, but the next day the calls would start again.

As time went on, she was so stressed out and depressed that she was seriously thinking about quitting her job, taking Trey and moving back to Chicago. She was thinking about that now as she drove him to Allyson's shop after another long meeting with one of his teachers. For the fifth day she would be arriving late again at work.

Trey stared silently out the window, hugging the cased guitar against his chest, a tiny, but dominating figure in his baggy overalls and navy blue T-shirt. *A six-year-old boy is controlling me,* Nicole thought. *Is that pathetic or what?* She was going to have to do something about it, though, because she did not know how long the staff at the hospital would continue putting up with her tardiness.

Allyson's salon was even busier than usual. All three hairdressers, including Allyson herself, were working. At least five other clients were sitting around gossiping, reading magazines and waiting.

"You're running late again," Allyson said, looking up as Nicole shuttled Trey to the back room.

"Don't remind me." Nicole kissed Trey, who rewarded her with a surly look and then pulled away and switched on the television.

In truth, Nicole wanted to shake her little brat until his teeth rattled, but she chalked the thought up as one of those less-than-inspired parenting moments, and stepped back out into the salon area.

"Was my baby bad again?" Allyson asked, wrapping a woman's thick, unnaturally red tresses around a huge roller.

Nicole rolled her eyes. "To say the least. I'll tell you about it tonight. Gotta go before I'm fired."

"I'll talk to him," Allyson said sympathetically.

It won't do any good, Nicole thought, rushing out the door. She sat in the car for two minutes trying to calm down. "Get a grip," she murmured to herself. Last year, Trey's behavior had been almost as bad and neither of them knew anything about Julian, so all of this could not be attributed to him. Still, there was no denying that he had been the catalyst in setting off whatever was smoldering in the child's mind right now.

Julian. She squeezed her eyes shut and thought about how much she missed his enticingly masculine presence and how much she hated to admit it. Of course Trey was hurting. He was just a baby and he didn't understand. They both needed to get away. If Trey could hold out a little longer, until the Christmas holiday when she had three weeks off, they'd fly out to Chicago and recuperate.

Trey clutched the guitar tightly and stood in the doorway of the room, watching. The ladies were all talking loud and laughing. Aunt Ally was washing some fat lady's hair. They did not see him standing there. Quickly, Trey sprinted past them and rushed to the door leading outside. He glanced back. No had one noticed. He opened the door and ran outside. He didn't stop running until he was a few blocks away, standing at the bus stop with other people.

He had ridden on the bus not too long ago with his mother and she had pointed out the road that went to Julian's place. Trey was sure he remembered it. He also remembered that all he had to do was give the driver the money and it was okay not to say anything, because no one did. One price paid for all the stops.

Trey jingled the lunch money he'd saved in his pocket. It would be enough for the bus. He felt happy because so far his plan was working, but he was kind of scared. What if the bus driver said something to him? He didn't want to think about that. There was also the fact that Mommy would be mad when she found out, but Julian would understand. He had missed too many guitar lessons and he was not going to let it happen again.

The bus stopped and he got on so quickly that he almost tripped. The guitar banged up against one of the seats. The driver looked at him kind of funny, but he took the money and didn't say anything. Trey ran down the aisle and found an empty seat way in the back. He sat down near the window and pressed his face up against the glass. He had to watch carefully so he didn't miss the stop. It seemed to take forever until finally he started to see the ocean. He couldn't reach the bell and he had to stand up on the seat in order to press it. The bus stopped.

Lugging the guitar, Trey stepped off at the entrance of the bridge road.

"Do you know where you're going, son?" the driver asked.

Scared, Trey nodded and began to run down the private road. It was very long. He kept running. There were no cars here. He could even run right in the middle of the road if he wanted to, but he didn't do that. At the end of the road there was an old man who looked like Santa Claus wearing a police uniform and sitting inside a little building. He was sleeping. Trey sneaked past him.

He could see a lot of big, castle-like houses, but he didn't care about those. He wanted Julian's and he remembered that it was near the end of the street. He ran some more.

Julian had a dinner date with Lydia. The persistent girl had invited him a few times and he'd finally agreed. After all, she was certainly no worse than any other woman, and he no longer had any reason to decline. He'd be at her place for roughly an hour and then he had to go to Orlando on business.

The dinner date fell on the day that he used to give Trey guitar lessons. He had the feeling that he probably missed it more than the boy did. Nicole had probably gotten him another instructor. The thought bothered him because he had enjoyed his bond with the child and had foolishly hoped that he would be around long enough to hear Trey break his three-year silence. It had never occurred to him that Trey would never talk. In his mind it had always been a matter of time, time that he no longer had because Nicole and her son were out of his life.

He stepped out of the house and was about to open the car door when he heard a shout, and saw the security guard chasing after a little kid who was running straight toward him—a very familiar little kid, carrying a big guitar case.

"Trey!"

Trey dropped the guitar as Julian swooped him up in his arms and held him. The little boy was breathing rapidly and trying hard not to cry.

"It's okay, Carlos," Julian said. "I know this boy."

Carlos shook his head in bewilderment. "That's one fast little kid. Don't know how he managed to get over the wall."

"Over the wall?"

"That's right he..."

"Never mind," Julian interrupted. Trey was crying now. "I'll take care of him."

Carlos shrugged and went off to return to his post. Julian turned his complete attention back to Trey.

"Trey, what on earth are you doing here?"

Trey sobbed louder and Julian hugged him tighter. "It's okay, I missed you too. Let's go inside and get you cleaned up." He put him back down and Trey reclaimed the guitar. As they went up the stairs, Julian looked hard at him.

"Your mother and your aunt don't know where you are, do they?"

It was a rhetorical question. Of course they didn't. Trey hung his head and avoided eye contact. Julian took the guitar from him and opened the door. They both went inside, and he tried to piece together in his head what had happened. It was quite possible that Allyson had been so busy with customers that she didn't even know that Trey was missing. He frowned at the boy.

"What you did was very bad, but right now I want you to go to the bathroom and wash your face. When you come back we're going to have a long talk."

Rubbing his eyes and smearing the dirt on his face, Trey trudged off down the hall. When Julian heard the bathroom door shut he picked up the telephone. He dialed the number and got the answering machine. *Idiot,* he thought. Of course she wasn't at home. She would be at work. He called the hospital.

They paged her and Nicole answered. "Hello."

"Nicole this…"

Her coldest, most mechanical voice interrupted him. "Julian, I have asked you over and over again not to call me"

Resentment and anger boiled up within him as he sensed she was about to hang up. "Excuse me, Miss Perfect, I actually do have other things to do with my time, but I just thought you'd like to know that your son is here with me…at my place."

"What?" She sounded as if she had been struck by lightning. "What are you talking about? Trey's with my sister at her shop."

"Well, I guess he has a clone, because a little boy who looks exactly like Trey is my house with his guitar. Unless you want me to keep him, I think you better get over here and pick him up." He stopped and let some of the anger dissipate. He was surprised at himself for being so sarcastic. Normally he would volunteer to take him to her.

Her voice dropped to barely a whisper. "I…I'll be there as soon as possible."

"He's a little tired, but he's perfectly all right, so don't rush," Julian said.

Nicole put the receiver down. She could not believe what he had told her. How could it be? How could Trey have gotten all the way over to his place? Was it part of an elaborate scheme of Allyson's to get her and Julian back together again? She picked up the phone and dialed the shop.

"Allyson, what's Trey doing?"

"He's in the room watching television. Why?" She sounded genuinely puzzled by the question.

Oh please let this be a warped joke Julian is playing, Nicole thought. "Are you sure? Go check."

She heard her sister mutter something as she put the receiver down to go check. Voices echoed in the background. Allyson returned and her tone of voice completely changed. "Oh, my God. He's not. I'm…"

"Don't worry! I *know* where he is!" Nicole snapped, banging the phone down.

Julian walked outside holding tightly to Trey's hand as Nicole's car pulled into the driveway. He had given the child an intense lecture on obedience, and Trey was a little upset that things had not gone the way he'd intended. He watched Nicole get out of the car, looking even more upset than her son. She was wearing her nurse's uniform, and her once pinned up hair was now hanging long, straight and wind-blown. Her green eyes shimmered like beacons, attractive even in her agitation.

"Trey," she exclaimed, relief and apprehension evident in her voice.

Julian let go of him, urging him forward. Trey's hesitation vanished when he realized that there were tears in his mother's eyes. He ran to her. She hugged him tightly.

"Oh, Trey, how could you? How did you get here?"

"I believe he came on the bus," Julian said. "Pretty amazing when you think about it."

Nicole looked up at him. The man before her was impossible to ignore even if he never said a word. He looked as stunning as ever in a close fitting, black V-necked sweater and black pants. His eyes searched hers like a shark circling, looking for a weak spot. If she actually made consistent eye contact with him, she knew he would find it, because all her spots were weak. If she continued to stand there, hugging Trey under his giant shadow, she would forget everything that had happened and melt in his arms.

"Thanks for taking such good care of my son," she said. "I'm sorry for the inconvenience."

Don't give me that thank you, sorry crap. I'm not a stranger, he thought angrily. "So, I guess this is it," he said, stepping forward. Nicole released Trey and he knelt down to the boy's level. "You make sure you remember what I told you. Don't you ever do this to your mother again."

Trey nodded glumly, biting his lip. He knew that Julian had to know that it was because of the monster that he was doing bad things. He *had* to know that he couldn't fight the monster without his help, but now it seemed like he didn't even care anymore. He was letting everything be up to Mommy, who couldn't even see the monster. Trey blinked back tears and slowly turned away. He got into the car.

Julian picked up the abandoned guitar. "Hey, don't forget..."

Trey slammed the door and stared straight ahead.

"Trey!" Nicole shouted, shocked by his behavior.

"It's all right," Julian said.

"I'm sorry," Nicole apologized.

"No problem. I understand him perfectly." He caught her arm as she was about to get into the driver's seat. "It's his mother I don't understand."

Nicole pulled her arm away. "Please don't make this harder than it has to be."

"You're the one who's making it hard." He didn't want to say too much in Trey's presence, but it was difficult not to. "I don't see why we can't just talk this whole thing out."

Because if we do, I'll probably surrender, throw away what little self esteem I have left, and become putty in your hands, she thought. "There is nothing to talk about. I'm a grown woman, but I still don't understand the concept of bigotry. I don't want to understand it."

"I'm not the bigot."

"You condone it. That's almost as bad."

She closed the car door and started the engine, rolling the window down slightly. "Thanks again for taking care of Trey. I really appreciate it. And don't worry, it won't happen again. Bye."

The car pulled off. Julian clenched his fists in his pockets and turned away. For a moment, he couldn't remember what he was supposed to be doing, and then it dawned on him that he was very late for his dinner date with Lydia. He glanced at his watch. There was no point in going there now because he had to be in Orlando in two hours. He picked up the abandoned guitar and returned to the house. There was enough time to raid the bar for another drink, though.

CHAPTER THIRTY

"You're going to have to do something about this problem, because it's serious now," Allyson said.

"I realize that. I *am* going to do something," Nicole replied.

"Would you mind telling me what? Something terrible could have happened to him today, six years old and gallivanting all over Miami. I would have been responsible. I feel terrible *now*. I would never be able to forgive myself if anything happened to Trey."

"It's more my fault," Nicole said glumly. "I'm sorry for yelling at you before, but I was kind of upset…"

Trey had been sent to bed earlier than usual as part of his punishment. It was now rather late. Allyson had just returned from the shop a half-hour ago, and Nicole had lost the rest of the evening at work, much to the ire of the nursing staff.

"What are you going to do? Allyson pressed. "If he's going to keep doing this running away thing, I can't keep him at the shop. I have to work too."

"I'm going to quit my job," Nicole said. "I have enough savings to hold us for a while, but eventually we'll be returning home to Chicago."

Allyson sighed. "I was hoping you'd come up with something better than that."

"Like what? If you're thinking I should go running back to Julian…"

"No." She sighed again. "I realize that even if you did that, it's only a temporary fix. It's not like you and Julian were engaged or something."

Nicole laughed, although she felt sick. "Julian needs a Cuban wife. It might also help if she's a psychology major."

Allyson smirked. "Whatever. Look, don't quit your job. I can put up with Trey a little longer. I can keep the door locked from the inside, so he can't get out. I'll pay more attention to him."

Nicole wrung her hands together. "This is awful. I just don't know what to do anymore. Every decision I make is wrong."

"Give it some more time," Allyson urged. "I *know* you can't really want to go back to Mom and Dad."

"Another week. I'll give this mess another week, and that's it. I have the feeling that if I don't resign from my job, I might end up getting fired. I've been late every day."

Allyson switched on the evening news. "Maybe next week will be better." Nicole flopped down on the couch. "I don't think it could get much worse."

She was wrong. On Monday, Trey was expelled from school for almost setting his desk on fire. No one knew where he had gotten the matches. The same afternoon, Nicole approached her supervisor, informing her of her resignation. The response surprised her. No one wanted her to quit. Everyone on the board insisted that she take an extended leave of absence instead. They told her that she was one of their best, that they didn't want to lose her.

Touched that at least someone appreciated her, Nicole took the leave and determined that she would spend all her time with Trey and home school him. The teaching staff at the school he'd been expelled from suggested more psychological evaluations of him, but she had no faith left in psychiatrists. He had seen so many in the past that it was pointless. She believed his atrocious behavior right now was a cry for attention, and now he would get it.

During the week, a large package was delivered to her. It turned out to be Trey's guitar. She started to put it away in the closet, but instead she left it out in the living room without saying anything to him about it. Trey noticed, and while he didn't reclaim it, he didn't try to destroy it either.

Her mother called, and after asking about Trey, the first thing she mentioned was the Julian affair. Nicole had only hinted at the recent problems with Trey, assuming she would tell her more when they were together, but she blurted out everything about Julian, including the fact that he was famous and wealthy. It didn't matter what she said about him now, since they were over. For once in her life, her mother was silent for a good three minutes, never interrupting her as she talked.

"I...I don't know what to say. I had no idea," she finally said. "Nicole, why didn't you tell me all this before? Your father is going to be shocked."

"It's awful, isn't it? Imagine going to dinner and being treated like that. You were right, Mom. I should have lis—"

"Your father did say he had a feeling about Julian, that there was something special about him. I know he has a beautiful voice, but famous?"

"Mother!" Nicole exclaimed, mortified as it dawned on her that her normally holier-than-thou mother was taking her tale of humiliation lightly. "Did you hear anything I said?"

"I heard you, dear. It's a shame that that had to happen." She hesitated for a moment. "But I don't see why you and Julian can't still be friends. Trey loves him so much."

Nicole felt the urge to hang up the phone, either that or start laughing. "I don't think Dad will feel that way." She bit her lip. *I hope I'm not wrong,* she thought.

"I *do* understand how you feel," her mother said. "But you have to realize that we're all just human, we all make mistakes. It's Julian's sister who has the problem. Why should you let her—"

"Mom, I'm sorry I told you any of this," Nicole interrupted. "You're only making allowances and excuses for Julian because he's who he is."

"Is that what you think I'm doing?"

"Isn't it?"

"Nicole, I don't know how to talk to you anymore. You get offended so easily. I do know one thing, though. You're my daughter and I know for a fact that you are in love with him. I've never seen you this way since Warren. I don't really have any advice to give you except that you have to follow your heart. I do want you to be happy."

I didn't realize I was asking for advice, Nicole thought. "I know, Mom, but the heart is…"

"Treacherous," her mother filled in. "That's why I married your father. That's why I'm still with him after forty years."

Nicole surrendered and laughed.

"Make sure you and Trey come home for the holiday. I asked your sister, but she's got *other* plans."

"We'll be there," Nicole said. *I definitely don't have other plans.*

"Julian, there's something I want to ask you," Luis said late in the evening.

"What?" Julian was on his way out of the studio and had come up through the office section. He was surprised that Luis hadn't gone home.

"In here." Luis indicated his office. Julian stepped in.

"There's something we have to discuss, but first, are you and Elena at it again?"

"Hardly. I haven't spoken to her since Thanksgiving."

Luis sat down at the desk and rubbed his eyes. "Oh, then I guess she's just upset about the maid."

Julian glanced impatiently toward the door. "What maid? What's this got to do with me?"

Luis laughed. "Nothing. One of the maids, the German one, quit this morning for no reason."

Julian was about to ask him to get to the point, but instead he started at the revelation. "You're kidding. Gretchen's been with us for years."

"I know. I guess that's why Elena's upset."

Julian became impatient again. "Elena's always upset. What are you really after?"

"Any reason why you canceled that interview tonight?"

"I'm not in the mood. No big deal," Julian replied.

"I'm starting to worry about you," Luis said. "Things aren't going right."

"I know, I know. The album should be wrapped up by now. The big chief at Vista Records is going ballistic."

"That's only part of the problem. Would you just sit down for a few minutes?" Luis indicated the chair facing his desk, and Julian sat. "Something is wrong. Suddenly your heart doesn't seem to be in this project. You're canceling interviews, being sarcastic with everyone, and worse, you're drinking."

Julian laughed and glanced up at the fluorescent lights on the ceiling. "That's quite a revelation. I'm not drunk, though. Takes an awful lot to get me high."

Luis sighed. "Is that something to be proud of?"

"Yes. It's one of the crowning achievements of my existence."

"You're being sarcastic again. Look, I know something is bothering you. It's related to that young lady you invited over for Thanksgiving, isn't it?"

Julian shrugged. "It's not a big deal. We broke up. People do it all the time."

"I'm sorry. I've been meaning to apologize to you on Elena's behalf. She—"

"Will you stop apologizing for her!" Julian shouted. "You've been doing it ever since I was a little kid. Elena isn't sorry."

"You know it's an insecurity thing. She can't help it," Luis said.

"I don't care about Elena's insecurity problems right now. She isn't even the issue here. I'm tired of this business, tired of everything."

Luis took a deep breath and searched Julian's eyes. "What do you want to do about it?"

"I don't know yet. I need space, time to think."

"That shouldn't be too big a problem," Luis said calmly. "Go away for a few weeks. How about Aruba? It's quiet and relax—"

Julian interrupted by standing up and angrily pounding his fist on the desk "Who the hell am I supposed to go away with, huh? Some gorgeous, empty-headed bimbo? Or are you and Elena going to arrange an escort? Does Lydia sound good to you too?"

Luis stood up. "I have never felt that way and you know it. Your personal life is your own business as far as I'm concerned. Why don't you try to patch things up with...with Nicole?"

"I can't. She's not speaking to me. Do you blame her?" He started to leave the room, then paused. "It's my own fault for exposing her to our warm, loving family."

"How about if I try to talk Elena into apologizing to her," Luis suggested.

Julian laughed. "I don't know about you, Luis. I think you've been married to my sister too long. You're getting as crazy as she is. Even if you were able to talk her into it, she wouldn't mean it. Nicole isn't stupid. She can detect an insincere apology."

Luis shook his head. "Maybe you should..."

The telephone rang and Luis picked it up. Julian left the room while he was talking. He needed to get outside in the air. He didn't usually get headaches, but right now one seemed to be coming on. He couldn't get out of that stifling building soon enough.

It had started to rain outside, a damp, misty kind of rain. Julian glanced at his watch as he got in the car. It was ten p.m. and the sky was pitch black and starless. Downtown Miami was illuminated with sparkling red, green and silver Christmas lights. Under different circumstances, he'd have found the festive decorations appealing, but now they looked garish and tacky.

He started driving, leaving all the lights of the town behind, until he lost all track of direction and didn't have a clue where he was going.

HAVANA SUNRISE

The road he found himself on was a fairly deserted, two-lane stretch of winding asphalt. The only lights seemed to be coming from his car and those few in the opposite lane.

He thought about his past and future. There didn't seem to be a future. How much more entertaining and traveling could one man do? How much longer could he touch millions of people and never feel the warmth of a genuine embrace himself?

The speedometer indicated 80. It didn't feel like he was speeding. He felt like he was just doing 55. He knew he wasn't drunk, because he hadn't had a drink since early in the morning and he could really use one right now. Any bar would do.

Don't do it, the reassuringly familiar voice of his father whispered in his ear. *You have the opportunity to nip this bad habit right in the bud, now. Weak and hopeless people need crutches. I didn't teach you to be weak and you're certainly not hopeless. You are not like your mother.*

The urge started to diminish. A hopeless alcoholic was not the image he had of himself either. The last thing he wanted was to become the stereotypical celebrity checking in and out of rehab centers. Death before dishonor seemed a lot more appealing.

As the car whipped around the curves, he opened the window and felt the lash of the raindrops on his face. "Slow down," he told himself, noting that the speedometer now registered 85. He wasn't really ready to die yet. There were still other things left to do. So what if he didn't get everything he wanted? Strong people learned to settle, to adapt. Lydia wanted to marry him regardless of his flaws. He would never feel for her what he felt for Nicole, but he could manage. They would have a family and he definitely would love their children, that was a sure thing.

Suddenly as he was about to decelerate, blinding headlights loomed at the peak of the curve in the road. Instinctively he focused his eyes to the side, but the headlights persisted. They were coming right at him, head on. Julian did not have time to sound the horn; his last conscious moments were spent steering hard to the right. He felt the brakes clicking, screaming, and the car hydroplaning, sliding right off

250

the road. He had a sudden, bizarre out of body experience as if he were watching this happen to someone else. Then he heard a loud crash, and saw a billion flashes of light before blackness enveloped him.

CHAPTER THIRTY-ONE

Nicole felt numb as she positioned herself in the doorway of the waiting room of the intensive care unit. Johnson Memorial was a much larger hospital than the one she worked in and the lack of intimacy made the nightmarish scene even more unbearable. There were at least twenty people in the room, milling around, talking in muffled tones. Among the crowd, she recognized Luis sitting on the couch with his arm around Amanda. The child was crying.

Fighting back rising waves of panic, Nicole resisted the powerful urge to turn around and run away from the scene. She saw herself on that couch, holding Trey, trying helplessly to comfort him. She saw the doctor walk in, grim-faced. *"We're doing everything we can, Mrs. Evans, but your husband might not make it. His injuries are extremely critical."*

"Hey," a familiar voice said quietly. She looked up and recognized Julian's friend, Wade.

"I'm glad you came," he said.

"They wouldn't let me go in," Nicole said, aware of the strained sound of her own voice. "How is he doing?"

"I wasn't allowed in either," Wade said. "It's only family. They're telling me he banged himself up pretty bad, but the injuries aren't that serious. The problem is that he's been unconscious since they brought him in last night."

Nicole shuddered. That was not a good sign. "Who's in there with him now?"

"His sister."

Nicole winced. "That's a comforting thought."

"Maybe if you go over and talk to Luis, he might let you go in," Wade suggested. "I don't see how it could hurt."

"I can't, not now. I certainly don't want to cause any confusion at this time. I'm going out a minute. I know one of the interns who works on this floor. I'll try to find out more about his condition from her."

Nicole left abruptly. As she went down the hall she felt dizzy. The walls seemed to be closing in around her. *Oh, God, please don't let this happen again,* she prayed. *Please, not Julian. If I can have him back I'll never leave him again no matter what.* She stopped in her tracks. *What am I praying? I never had him in the first place.* She thought about it. It was true, but she still meant every word she had silently uttered.

There was actually no need to consult with Sabrina Wright, her intern friend, because she had done that already. She *knew* the extent of Julian's injuries—three fractured ribs, torn ligaments in his left knee, a possible back injury and head trauma. He'd been stitched up and taken to X-ray where he'd undergone various brain scans and MRIs. There didn't appear to be any brain damage and the other injuries were considered minor, but no one could explain why he wasn't waking up.

She had found out about the accident from Maria, who had called her an hour ago, asking her if she had heard the news. She hadn't, of course, and this time she'd been grateful that she was not the type who turned the radio on first thing in the morning. She had been preparing breakfast for Trey when she got the call and she'd taken it in her bedroom. It was not the sort of news she wanted him to hear.

It never even occurred to her that she should just call the hospital and ask for information on his condition. She knew she had to be there. Allyson, completely understanding, had called her friend Lynette to open the shop for her, and she was home now with Trey.

Feeling frustrated and helpless, Nicole stood in the hallway and looked out a window. Down below, she could see mobs of fans gathering, being kept back from the hospital's entrance by policemen. They were waving get-well signs and banners that read, "We love you, Julian. We're praying for you." *Nice,* she thought, *but bizarre.* She clenched her hand in a fist around her pocketbook. *She* was more than

just a fan, and she had a right to see him. With a new determination,
Nicole left the hospital.

She returned late in the afternoon, wearing her nurse uniform. No
one said anything. No one questioned or stopped her. She entered the
intensive care unit quickly and passed the central nurses' station that
dominated the large room where patients clung tenaciously to life in
adjoining cubicles. This area of the hospital did not respect wealth,
celebrity or social status. Everyone lived or died in identical surroundings.

Nicole entered Julian's cubicle and was relieved that he had no visitors at the moment. The sound of a ventilator and other apparatus
clicking and beeping enveloped her. They were all familiar sounds, but
so much more pronounced and poignant when they were sustaining
the life of a loved one.

He didn't look that bad. His face was turned toward the window
and partially illuminated by the sunlight, which gleamed off his blue-
black hair. A large white bandage was on his forehead, above his left
eyebrow. She moved closer. A half-dollar size bruise of angry red and
purple glared at her from his left cheekbone, marring his paler, but still
mocha-colored skin.

Careful of the network of mechanical lifelines connected to his
body, she gently touched the uninjured side of his face. "Hey, handsome," she whispered. "I know you can hear me. When you wake up
we're going to have that talk. I really *didn't* want us to break up either.
It's been miserable without you. It's just that I was hurt and thinking
only about my stupid pride. I'm over it, Julian. Please forgive me.
Please wake up."

She lowered her face to his, brushing his mouth gently with her
lips, then kissing him passionately, hoping childishly, foolishly, that
something magical would happen. But there was no miraculous

healing. The prince did not awaken from his slumber. She straightened up.

"Is there any change, nurse?" a voice behind her asked.

Nicole turned abruptly to confront a red-eyed, pale-faced Elena standing there. The woman, who had assumed that she was part of Johnson Memorial's staff, froze now, recognizing her.

"You don't work in this hospital," she said in a low, tight voice.

"I know I don't." Nicole stepped back quietly. "I know how you feel about me, but I happen to care very much about your brother. When you love someone, it's impossible to stay away from them."

Elena said nothing, but she didn't ask her to leave. She walked past Nicole and leaned over the silent Julian. She gently ruffled his hair and mouthed a prayer. Nicole remained standing, watching. *She does care about him,* she thought. *In her own manipulative, twisted way, she really does care, and she's devastated.*

"As a nurse, I've seen many cases like this," Nicole said softly. "Most of them recovered completely."

"He's just so special," Elena said, without looking up from his face. "I remember when he was a baby and my mother first brought him home from the hospital, all that curly black hair, those big, dark eyes. He looked like a beautiful doll. I can't lose him."

"No one is going to lose him," Nicole said, moving closer again. She reached for Julian's inert hand, and squeezed it. "I'll leave you two alone, but I will be back."

She was sure Elena didn't hear a word she said, but it didn't matter. Even if the spiteful woman had launched into a venomous tirade, nothing would prevent Nicole from returning.

The next day there was still no change. Julian's vital signs were all normal. The orthopedic surgeons wanted to fix his damaged knee, but they had to hold off because he was unconscious. The waiting game continued, further agonizing his family, and the fans who kept a faithful vigil outside the hospital.

Nicole told Trey, because she thought Julian would want him to know. She'd learned that keeping secrets about the health of loved ones from a child wasn't always the best thing.

Trey's reaction was immediate. He wanted to see Julian. Nicole tried to dissuade him because she didn't know if it would be allowed, but he was adamant. That morning, they both left for the hospital.

"Trey, come on, let's go," she said, holding open the car door, wondering if he was getting cold feet at the last minute.

Trey slid out of the car, holding tightly to his guitar. *You can't bring that*, Nicole thought and was about to open her mouth, but suddenly she just shut it and escorted him into the hospital.

There were two guards posted outside of intensive care. Nicole hesitated. Trey looked at her. "Trey, I'm sorry, but I don't think they're going to let us in."

Trey looked at her and abruptly yanked his hand free from hers. He ran right past the guards and into the room. One of them made a move to stop him.

"No! Nicole said in a loud whisper. "Don't you *dare* touch my son. I'll get him."

Not wanting to risk a scene with a mother and her child, he backed off. A nurse stopped Trey and just as Nicole was about to approach, Luis appeared from Julian's cubicle.

"What? What is this?" he asked, then instantly recognized Nicole and Trey. He turned to the nurse. "I know them. Please make an allowance for just a few minutes."

The nurse and a few of the others at the station looked flustered, but they nodded. Nicole breathed a sigh of relief. "Thank you," she said to Luis.

Julian looked the same as he had yesterday. For a moment, Trey just stood there looking at him with a mixture of bewilderment and trepidation.

"He can't talk because he's unconscious," Nicole whispered. "Remember what I told you before we left the house?"

Trey tugged at her arm. *Can I shake him and wake him up?*

"No. That doesn't work when a person is unconscious. You can…" She almost started to say you can talk to him, but of course Trey couldn't do that. "You can touch him, but no shaking."

Trey turned away and knelt down on the floor to open the guitar case. Nicole caught her breath but did not stop him. Luis returned and stood silently like a sentry, watching. Elena came and stood beside him, looking shocked when she realized what was about to happen.

"He can't do that," she declared in a loud whisper.

"Shhh!" Luis hissed. "I don't see why not."

Trey climbed up to sit on the edge of the bed, and Nicole guided him carefully. He held the guitar and started to play, a very serious expression on his childish face. Instead of looking down at the chords, he focused on Julian. Nicole did not recognize the song, but the tune had Spanish overtones.

"Stop this nonsense, now," Elena declared, stepping forward.

"No!" Luis held her back.

Julian did not want to wake up. He heard the music of the tide splashing up against the shore, accompanied by the distant cry of a lone seagull. He felt as if he were on a small boat, being rocked gently by the waves to the faint, but increasing sound of a guitar being played, a guitar being played rather badly. He tried to block it out and listened for the tide again.

Wake up, son, his father's voice said.

The guitar sounds intensified and became worse.

Trey continued to play and everyone literally stopped breathing as Julian's eyelids fluttered. Was it just an involuntary reflex action? No, it was not. He turned his head away from the window and faced Trey. His eyes opened. Trey smiled.

"Pretty good," Julian murmured in a hoarse whisper, and then his voice grew stronger. "But you messed up on the A chord. Once more and do it right."

Trey beamed and started to play the song again. Luis was grinning from ear to ear. Elena's mouth was open wide. Nicole rubbed away tears of joy. *And a child will lead them all,* she thought.

Trey finished the song and encouraged by Julian, was about to give him a big bear hug, but Nicole quickly, carefully, swooped him and the guitar off the bed. "Sorry, guys, but this is a hospital."

The small cubicle suddenly seemed to fill up with people materializing from the walls. The low buzz of whispered voices and tears of joy grew into a crescendo and the diligent staff moved in, ordering them all out.

CHAPTER THIRTY-TWO

"Thanks for bringing Trey," Julian said hours later when they were alone. He had been moved into a private room and was no longer hooked up to a respirator or a monitor.

"We had to see you," she said. "There was never any question about that."

He did not seem to comprehend anything behind what she said. "I hope you agree that I can keep giving Trey lessons. That little kid of yours is pretty special to me."

"Trey *is* very special," she agreed.

"Good. Now that we've gotten that straight, there's no need for you to waste any more time here."

Waste any more time? she thought, a sickening feeling creeping over her. "I'm hardly wasting my time. I care about you."

He shrugged. "I know, and I appreciate it, but I'm going to be all right. Don't you have to work tonight?"

It dawned on her what he was doing. She wanted to tell him that she was not working and that there was nowhere she would rather be than right here with him. She wanted to tell him everything, but it had been a long day. He was tired, probably in pain, and he was scheduled for surgery in the morning. It would be extremely irrational and stupid of her to expect his undivided attention.

She sighed. "I'm off duty tonight. I'm going to leave you now, but only because you need to rest. I'll be back tomorrow." She kissed him and he moved abruptly so that the kiss glanced off the side of his face instead of his mouth.

"Don't you get it, Nicole? You don't have to come back tomorrow, or ever. If you want to know about the surgery, just call up and ask."

Hurt, Nicole backed away. "I…I'm sorry for annoying you. If that's what you want, I will call and find out. Bye."

"Goodnight," he said, without looking at her.

Nicole left the hospital and did not cry until she was sitting in her car. Tears of joy that he was alive and would be okay mingled with her tears of pain at his rejection. She sat there clutching the steering wheel for almost an hour, drowning in pent-up emotions.

Julian stared at the endless array of flowers, cards and balloons all over the room. The scene was frighteningly too familiar. He wanted to walk out of the hospital immediately, but he couldn't. He felt as if he'd been run over by a truck, and despite the tranquilizers, his heavily bandaged knee throbbed painfully. The orthopedic surgeon had explained that there were no fractures, and they could easily repair the ligament damage. After that he'd have weeks of physical therapy. Just when life was bad, it always managed to get a little worse.

He was thankful to Luis and his publicists for masterfully applying press damage control immediately after the accident. The police had initially reported that he was drunk, speeding, and completely responsible for running the car off the road into a tree. After the investigation had been done, questions started coming up. There had been additional skid marks on the road indicating that another car had been involved.

Now that he was conscious, Julian's foggy memory of the events had returned. He had told one of the visiting detectives that another car had been approaching head-on before the crash. They were looking for that car now. No one was questioning his sobriety or judgment at this point.

He had also been told that if he hadn't been wearing a seat belt, or if the car hadn't had an airbag, he'd probably be dead. Would it really have been such a tragedy had that been the case? The pain was making him cynical again. Despite everything that had happened, he didn't feel the overwhelming gratitude for life that he knew he should be feeling. The only wonderful thing he recalled was waking up and seeing Trey's genuine smile as he played the guitar and Nicole standing at his side, until he realized that she was only there out of a sense of duty, like all the others.

The surgery was done the next morning and took roughly an hour. There were no complications and the doctors said that after routine physical therapy, he would be perfectly all right. The family celebrated. Julian tried to be happy, but what he really wanted was a drink. The only visitor who noticed his despair was Wade.

About five days after the accident, he was out of the hospital and back home. Elena tried to insist on hiring a nurse, but he turned down the offer. He claimed he was fully capable of taking care of himself. He wondered why no one believed him.

On Saturday, Nicole called the hospital and was told that Julian had been released. It was entirely too soon, but knowing him, she was not surprised. He had probably insisted on leaving. She wanted to see him, but after the last encounter, she wasn't quite sure how to handle his hostility. The decision to visit was determined on Sunday afternoon when she got an unexpected call from Wade.

"Nicole, I don't mean to put you on the spot, since I know what I'm asking might be awkward," he began.

"Yes?" She waited.

"Julian loves you, but he's just too damn stubborn to admit it. The point I'm trying to make is that he needs you. I'm worried about him. I was over by his place a few minutes ago, and nobody answered the door. There is no reason for him to be out. He's supposed to be home recuperating."

Nicole hesitated. She was worried, but did not want to jump to conclusions. "Did you ask Luis or Elena?"

"They're not home. I think Julian's there alone and drunk."

Depression and alcohol were a lethal combination. Fear for Julian overcame her reservations. She thought about that awful Thanksgiving and she recalled how he'd appeared to be in an almost dazed state of mind. There was definitely something wrong and it was not his fault. Suddenly she didn't care what negative thing he might say to her. She loved him and she was going to be there for him whether he wanted her to or not.

"Wade, I'm going to check on him, but I really *have* to know more. You two have been friends for a long time. Is Julian an alcoholic? I want to help him, but I need to know the truth."

"No. He's not an alcoholic yet. He gets depressed sometimes and drinks. I don't know how to explain this, but he's, well, he's an artist. He's got a strange mind. Sometimes he thinks more about things than he should, things that other people just let go of. My wife calls it sensitivity. I call it just plain crazy, but that's my man. He's always been there for me and my family, but it's as if no one can ever be there for him."

Nicole took a deep breath. "I hear you. I really do want to be there for him, but I can't help him if I don't know what the problem is. Would you know if Julian has ever been treated for depression?"

"Luis and his witch would probably know that. He's never discussed it with me."

"Wade, I'm leaving the house right now. Would you please come with me?

Wade gave an audible sigh of relief. "I'll meet you at his place."

They both arrived at the estate simultaneously. Nicole followed Wade up the stairs. The door was partially open.

"That's funny," Wade said. "It was locked before."

"Let's go in," she urged.

"Hey, Julian!" Wade yelled, loud enough to awaken the dead.

There was no answer. "I'll look down here," Nicole said, entering.
Wade nodded. "I'll check upstairs."

The beauty of the place eluded her now. It felt more like a prison.
The door leading to the pool was locked. No one was in the game room
and he was not out on the deck. She called his name several times.

"Not a trace," Wade said, reappearing. "Let's check around the
grounds."

It was a raw, gray day, with the sun an opaque blur in the dreary
sky. Nicole shivered despite the fact that she was wearing a heavy
sweater. It was not a day to be out strolling around, especially if you
had just been released from the hospital.

Wade walked a few paces ahead of her, and then he turned and
looked back. "I just thought I'd tell you about what kind of man Julian
is. Ten years ago we were together on a big tour in Japan. My wife was
home expecting our second daughter, Julie."

"Julie?" Nicole questioned, quickening her pace.

"Yeah, we named her after him. Anyway Yvette went into labor
prematurely. There were complications. I had to quit in the middle of
this big tour to come back to Miami. Julian came back with me. He
postponed the whole tour. Didn't have to do that, mind you. He could
have easily found another bass player. He sat in that waiting room with
me the whole time. Julie was born and she had a heart problem. He
helped us find the best specialist in the country. They operated on her
and she's been fine ever since. Julian was with us through it all."

Nicole felt her eyes getting mistier. "I understand. I know what
kind of man Julian is too."

Wade branched off in the direction of the stables and Nicole felt
compelled to search the dock area. The closer she got to the water's
edge, the faster her heart beat. He was there somewhere, she sensed it.

"Julian!" she shouted.

His name echoed on the waves and came back to her. She found
him lying sprawled face down on the dock, one arm dangling almost

in the water. A now familiar panic seized her as she dropped to her knees beside him. She felt for the pulse in his neck. It was there, strong.

"Wade!" she screamed, motioning with her arms. "Wade, over here!"

Gently, she shook him. He mumbled something incoherent, groaned and tried to shield his face with his arm. He was wearing only a sleeveless undershirt and navy blue, drawstring-type pants. She made a quick assessment of his injuries and noted that there didn't appear to be any additional damage. He was just drunk.

Wade appeared, ashen-faced. "He's okay," Nicole assured him. "Just cold and disoriented. We've got to get him back inside."

"I don't know about you, *amigo*," Wade muttered to Julian. "There are easier ways to commit suicide."

Between the two of them they managed to get him back to the house. It took a while because they had to be careful of his injuries. Wade literally carried him up the stairs and gently lowered him on the bed. "Should have just thrown you down, you crazy fool," he muttered. "You're gonna be paying my doctor's bills when I get a hernia."

Nicole laughed in spite of it all. She covered Julian with blankets. There was nothing to do now but wait for him to sleep it off. Wade said he had to leave and Nicole assured him that it was okay. She thanked him for everything and he thanked her.

"If you need me just call." He gave her his number.

"Oh, one thing. Do you think maybe you could make a raid on the liquor cabinet?"

Wade flashed a wicked grin. "Good idea. I'll take everything."

CHAPTER THIRTY-THREE

"I told my family that I didn't need a nurse," Julian said upon awakening and discovering her presence. He was clearly annoyed.

"You're right," Nicole said, smiling sweetly. "You don't need a nurse. You need a combination of babysitter, guardian angel and dare I say, mother."

"And you're wearing all three hats?" He tried to sit up, but couldn't because his head was pounding, not to mention the pain he felt everywhere else.

"I used to have problems wearing just one, but knowing you has sure changed that," Nicole said.

He groaned. "What day is it?"

"It's Sunday."

"What *are* you doing here?"

"Attempting to save you from yourself. Allyson took Trey out to see a movie, and that means I'm free to hang out and irritate you for as long as I like." She stood in front of him with her hands on her hips. "Are you going to throw me out? You don't look well enough. Would another drink give you your strength back?"

Julian rubbed his eyes wearily. "I don't understand you. You were the one who said you didn't want anything to do with me. Then I go and have this stupid accident, and you're back again. I don't need you. I don't need anyone feeling sorry for me."

"Actually, you're right, you don't need me to feel sorry for you. You do a fine job all by yourself. I'm here because...because I have this really terrible problem. I never wanted this dreadful thing to happen, but it did. The problem is, I love you." She didn't give him a chance to speak, but continued in a rush of words. "I don't know what you're thinking, Julian. I don't know if you feel the same way about me, because I can't read your mind. I'm still angry over what happened on Thanksgiving, but I was wrong for not hearing you out."

He made another agonized attempt to sit up straight. She assisted him by propping up the pillows. His piercing eyes searched her face. "When you got into that argument with Elena, you told her it was wrong to stereotype people, but that's what you've been doing to me from day one. The star, the player, Don Juan, not trustworthy. You can stop me whenever you want."

It was true. "Stop," she said weakly. "You're right. I did do that to you and that makes me a hypocrite, doesn't it? I stereotyped you because I was afraid to get too involved with you." She stared up at the ceiling and blinked back tears. "I lost Warren, I lost a big part of my son. I feel that Trey's losing his voice is my fault because I didn't do the right thing. You came along and made me feel for a moment that it wasn't all my fault, that maybe we could get him to talk again." She subconsciously stepped back, feeling overwhelmed, but she continued to speak. "I didn't feel I had a right to expect you to commit to that, because you had your own world that was *so* different from mine. I kept my distance to protect myself. It's a lot easier to reject a stereotype than a person."

Julian remained silent for a few moments, watching her. She had drifted to the far end of the room and was pacing around nervously. Her long ponytail was slightly disheveled and she was wearing a white cable-knit sweater with tight-fitting jeans that hugged the gentle curves and slopes of her statuesque body. He visualized her as a dancer.

"Nicole, come here," he said.

She glided soundlessly toward him and sat on the edge of the bed. Her eyes, misty and gazelle-like, mirrored his own. He reached for her hand and held it. "We're both guilty," he said. "Guilty of not being perfect."

"All I know is that things have gone from bad to worse. Trey's been expelled from school and I'm about to quit my job. What must we do to rid ourselves of this guilt?" Nicole asked.

"I'm not sure, but first we could try trusting each other more. It would also help if I stop acting like a stereotype. Haven't exactly been doing such a good job lately," he added wryly.

"I'm ready to listen, Julian. I don't care what your family thinks of me. This is about the two of us. You can tell me whatever you want about your past and it's not going to change the way I feel about you."

Julian folded his arms across his chest and flinched. "I guess I can start by saying that you ran out of the house so quick that day, you didn't even hear me tell Elena that I was madly in love with you, and that you were the woman I wanted to spend the rest of my life with."

She stared at him in stunned silence before finding her voice. "You told Elena that?"

"Yeah, I hope I wasn't too off-base. You kind of have to be in agreement."

She noticed him divert eye contact at that crucial moment and she put her hand lightly on the side of his face, hoping to bring it back. Her hand trembled. "I had…I had no idea. Oh, what a fool I am. I never realized that you could love me the same way that I loved you."

Julian studied her face again. He had always considered himself to be fairly good at reading women, but from the beginning, Nicole had been unpredictable. His fame, money, or even what some considered his good looks, had never impressed her. Was it really true that the simple words, *I love you,* were all she needed to hear? What if he said or did something else that she considered offensive? Would she run away again? He was tired of playing games. He had to know.

"I meant it then and I mean it now. I love you," he said.

He leaned forward, ignoring the pain in his ribs, and kissed her passionately on the mouth. She responded without reservations. *I shouldn't be testing her like this*, he thought, but his arm slid around her neck, drawing her closer and closer until she was literally on top of him.

The scorching passion consumed them. Nicole could hardly breathe, but it was a pleasant suffocation. The old warning bells went off in her head, and she felt the usual panic, but she did not attempt to stop him. He was kissing her neck, his hands everywhere, stroking. The hands glided like smooth velvet under her sweater, pulling her up higher with almost inhuman strength. He stopped.

Nicole's eyes searched his trustingly, questioningly. He gently nudged her away, smoothing down her sweater, brushing back the loose strands of her hair.

"You don't *really* want to do this now, do you?" he asked.

She smiled uncertainly. "I'm sure there's a better, more appropriate time."

"I'm sorry. I do remember what you told me before. If I force you to break your principles, it's destroying part of the reason why I respect you in the first place. We can wait."

"Thank you," she said quietly.

He laughed. "Don't thank me. I've also reached the conclusion that this would be a little too painful right now. My ribs ache and I feel like throwing up."

She arched her eyebrows in feigned astonishment. "How *unromantic*. Don Juan would *never* say such a thing."

Julian smiled wanly. "If I could have a drink right now, I'd make a toast to destroying all stereotypes."

"You can still make that toast, but only if it's with water. Wade swiped all the liquor from your bar."

Julian scowled. "I'll kill him."

"You'll have to kill me too, because I suggested it."

Julian looked sheepish now as he recalled his recent behavior. "I'm sorry about that scene. I don't usually get *that* drunk. I was just doing it to block the pain."

"Weren't you given a prescription painkiller?"

"Yeah, but I hate taking medication."

"That makes a lot of sense. You hate taking medication, but it's okay to drink yourself into a coma. What's this about anyway? I first noticed that you were overdoing it on Thanksgiving."

Julian sank back against the pillows and closed his eyes. "I always get like that at family gatherings. I start having crazy flashbacks about the past, stupid things about how I was treated when I was a kid, and then I start drinking to shut it out. It used to work, but lately it takes more and more."

"You've got to stop doing that," she said, squeezing his hand desperately "I don't want to believe that you're an alcoholic now, but that's the way it sometimes gets started. Please don't tell me you were drunk when you had the accident. You need to talk everything out instead of drink."

He smiled sardonically. "I *was* guilty of speeding and this homicidal maniac came right at me, but I wasn't drunk. Are you suggesting I should see a good shrink?"

"Well, they are helpful at times, but after my experiences with Trey, I'm not the one to recommend that. I think you should start by just talking to me. You're so guarded with your past. You keep everything locked up inside. It's not a good thing."

Julian closed his eyes. He started from the beginning. He told her everything he remembered about his early life in Cuba, dwelling a lot on his father and his aunt. He touched on his mother's mental illness and the fact that she hung herself after hearing about his father's death. He told her that Elena was the one who found her dead.

Nicole shuddered at the thought. Despite her dislike of Elena, it must have been horrific to come home and discover your mother dead in such a manner. She knew Julian was still uncomfortable talking about the past, but she had to know more.

"Who told your mother that your father was…was murdered in prison?"

Julian stared at the ceiling. "It was confirmed by a family friend who worked in the prison, but my mother's ex-husband, Jorge Diaz was the one who told her." He squeezed his eyes shut, clenched his teeth, and continued. "That evil bastard worked for the police. He was the one who set my father up on the false drug selling charges to begin with, and the government just went along with whatever he said because they wanted to get rid of my father for being a dissident."

Nicole felt sick inside as she tried to imagine herself involved in the events that had shaped his life. There was no way that he could completely shut it out even though he was an adult and far removed from that environment.

Julian went on in almost a monotone about how he left Cuba with Elena and Luis. He spoke in detail about what it was like being a child in Elena's family and how he had been treated like an inferior. There were moments when it seemed as if he had forgotten that she was even there and he was talking to himself. The tone of his voice became quieter now and he looked at her eyes.

"I miss not being able to see the African side of my family," he said softly. "The night the police came and took my father away, he told me that he would never leave me, and even though he died, he kept his word. He's with me all the time, in spirit, and in voice, but I don't remember what he looked like. I know it's crazy to obsess over that, but I do."

"It's not crazy," Nicole said. "He had a big impact on you. He was your father." She dabbed at her eyes with a handkerchief. "You told me that your Aunt Alma is here in this country. I don't understand why you've never contacted her."

"Because I was afraid to."

"Afraid?"

"When Elena and Luis took me to this country, they wrote Alma in New York and asked her if she still wanted me. She said she did. After that, I really don't know what happened. Elena discovered that I made a good little servant for her family, and we moved around a lot. She never wrote Alma again, and she couldn't find us to get in touch."

Nicole looked away. "That is so cruel."

"Alma did locate us again when we were living in Hialeah, and she wrote to me when I was about thirteen years old. Elena never let me see the letter. I found it accidentally two years later when I was snooping around in her room. At around that time, my music was starting to get noticed, and I realized that I had my own identity and that no one could use me unless I allowed it. I confronted Elena about the letter."

Nicole held her breath, listening intently.

"She had a fit of course, made a whole lot of excuses, and finally told me that Alma only wanted to use me. She told me that it was all about money and she didn't really care about me at all.

"And you believed her?" Nicole said.

"I didn't want to, but I kind of had that fear myself. I didn't want to find out that that's the way my father's people were too. In my heart I wanted them to be different. I had this childhood image of my aunt being unconditionally loving, accepting, the way I remembered her. I was afraid to find out that she might have changed."

"Maybe she *didn't* change." Nicole's voice rose. "If she was really interested in your money, why hasn't she contacted you since? You're in the public's eye. She must know how famous you are."

He rubbed his eyes wearily. "There are actually two reasons why. First, it's quite possible that she's no longer alive, and second, when it looked as if I might become famous, Luis and Elena suggested that I change my last name from Sanchez to Marquez ."

"Julian, listen. I think it's time for you to find out exactly what happened to her, because this is going to bother you for the rest of your life. Do you still have that letter?"

"Yes." His voice sounded uncertain.

"I'd like to have it. Maybe I can find her for you."

He looked frustrated. "Let's just leave it alone. That letter was written years ago. There was a phone number, and I did call it. The number was invalid."

"I'm sorry, but I can be just as stubborn as you are. I want to know myself what happened to your aunt. I need the letter."

"It's in a gold box on the top shelf of the closet," he said in one breath.

Nicole rose and entered the enormous walk-in closet. It was bigger than her bedroom. She noticed that he was fastidiously organized, suits all in one place, sports clothes, casual clothes. She looked on the top shelf. Sure enough, there was a large gold, metal box. With her heart hammering, she opened it. From the bottom she extracted the letter, yellowed with age—return address, Mrs. Alma Rivera, 15 West Fifty-seventh St., New York. She returned to the room and quietly slipped the letter into her purse.

Julian had now been sober long enough to take the pain medication without any ill effects, so she insisted, and he did not protest. She found herself in full nurse mode, checking his injuries, making sure he was okay. She changed the bandage on his forehead, noting painfully that his once perfect face was now branded with a glaring laceration, held together by ten stitches. It would fade in time though.

He was drowsy from the medication at this point, and had his eyes shut. She was just contemplating an ice pack for his knee, which looked more swollen than it should be, when she had the uncanny feeling that she was being watched. She turned around to see Elena framed in the doorway. Nicole did not know how long she had been there.

"I came back sooner than usual because I was worried about him," the woman said. "It seems I have no reason to be."

Nicole didn't know what she was implying at this point, but she tried to control the hostility she felt.

Julian opened his eyes. "I'm all right, Elena. It was your idea that I should have a nurse, so now I've got the best."

"I see," Elena said. "How convenient."

"And appropriate," Nicole added. "Julian's recovering just fine. You don't have to worry about him."

"I see," Elena repeated again. She turned away and closed the door quietly. Nicole heard her footsteps down the stairs.

"Julian," Nicole said irately, "Wade locked that door when he left. Why does Elena have a key?"

His eyes twinkled a little. "Are you angry at me again? Are you going to run out?"

She laughed, catching herself. "No. I'm not about to run out."

"She doesn't usually have the key," he explained. "I gave it to Luis because they were worried that I wouldn't be able to walk downstairs if they knocked at the door. They only wanted to…"

"It's okay," Nicole said in a whisper. "Of course that makes sense."

"Despite some of the terrible things I told you about her, I would really appreciate it if you don't get too upset with Elena. She has a story too. Luis and I both know that she can't always help it."

"Are you saying that she is ill?"

"In a way. Can you imagine what her life was like? She was a child with an abusive father, who had to take care of her own crazy mother, and after that, a little half-brother. She never had a childhood, and she was always afraid that she was going to become just like her mother. She protected herself by controlling others."

"I'm starting to see a clearer picture of her, but still, some of the things she did were inexcusable."

"At around the time Amanda was born, she completely snapped," Julian continued, "postpartum depression or something. Anyway she was hospitalized for months. She wouldn't speak to her own children or her husband, acted like she didn't even know them. The only person she seemed to recognize was me."

Enough, Nicole thought. She didn't say it, but she was overwhelmed by all the family revelations. How had Julian managed to stay as sane as he was with all the madness around him?

"I'm sorry. I'm probably telling you too much now," Julian said.

"No. It's okay. It's a lot to swallow, but I'm glad you're telling me."

"Anyway, after she recovered, Luis and I kind of formed a pact to let Elena always think she was in charge, even though that's not the case. Being in control seems to give her stability. She really gets on my nerves, but I don't want her to end up like our mother. The irony here is that Elena believes I'm the one who needs help."

"I...I don't know what to say." She stroked the side of his face with her fingertips. "You deserve a lot better, and I think it's about time you get it. You deserve to be surrounded by people who will really appreciate your generosity, really understand how self-sacrificing you've been." Nicole reached inside her purse and felt the letter from his aunt. "We both need to know that there are others."

CHAPTER THIRTY-FOUR

Julian's progress was phenomenal. Within days he was in physical therapy and anxious to be recovered enough to do the make-up concerts in New York that had been canceled when he had pneumonia earlier. Nicole thought his expectations were unrealistic, but she did not want to be discouraging.

She and Trey visited him almost every day. Her evening hours were spent at home scanning the phone book and the Internet, calling every person named Rivera in Manhattan. Julian did not take her determination seriously and thought she would never succeed, but she persisted anyway. It was a frustrating process, because Rivera was as common a name as Jones or Williams. She was not very optimistic herself, until Friday, the night before she was to leave for Chicago.

"Hello, may I speak to Alma Rivera?" she asked for the twentieth time that night.

"You have the wrong number," a woman's voice rang out. "I *do know* an Alma Rivera, though."

Nicole's breath caught in her throat. "Maybe you could help me out. I don't personally know Alma, but she came from Cuba and she has a husband named Alejandro—"

"My brother-in-law's name was Alejandro," the woman interrupted. "He's deceased, though."

"I'm sorry to hear that." Nicole's heart hammered. "The Alma I'm looking for also had a brother named Enrique and a nephew named Julian. Enrique died years ago in Cuba."

"That's *her.*" The woman sounded intrigued. "I'm her sister-in-law. Is there a message I can give her?"

Could this really be true? Nicole thought. Could the elusive Alma Rivera actually be within her grasp? "Yes…yes. There is a message. My name is Nicole Evans and I'm a good friend of her nephew. He's trying to get in contact with her."

"Oh my! Alma is going to be so surprised. I'll give you her telephone number."

"Thank you so much," Nicole said, and proceeded to write down the number.

Long after the call terminated, Nicole sat there staring at the number she had written down on a yellow legal pad. It seemed to shimmer and sparkle before her. Obviously some higher force had had a hand in this, because there was no such number listed in the book.

"I'll call tomorrow," Nicole murmured aloud. She didn't want to push her good fortune any more than necessary.

She didn't tell Julian anything about the discovery, but she made the call in the morning as she prepared to leave for the airport. Alma did not answer the phone, but a man's voice on the answering machine confirmed that it was the correct number. Nicole left a message, along with her phone number.

Julian wished he were well enough to join Nicole and Trey in Chicago because he wanted to get closer to her family, so that they could become his as well. It would somehow make his dysfunctional one seem less significant.

He felt a new zest for life and gratitude to the powers above that he had survived the accident without serious injuries. The maudlin person who'd flirted with disaster and secretly courted death was now a complete stranger. And it was all because of one special woman and her little boy.

The phone rang just as his physical therapist was leaving. Julian picked it up.

"Hi, Julian. I just called to say I love you, miss you, and it's snowing here in Chicago."

"Love you too, baby."

"I've decided to come back home a little bit earlier, but Trey's going to stay with his grandparents for a while."

"Sounds like a good idea. Maybe you can come to New York with me next week."

"Julian, are you sure you're going to be up to peforming?"

He laughed. "I can still sing. It'll just be a different kind of show, without a lot of theatrics. I really am doing good though. Went jogging this morning."

"Oh stop lying. You better not even think about jogging yet."

"Okay, okay, so I exaggerated a little. I actually can walk without limping."

"That's great. I'm so happy to hear that."

"How's Trey?"

"Fine. My parents are spoiling him rotten. He's been entertaining them with the new song he learned. He sleeps with that guitar, you know."

"I used to do that when I was a kid," Julian said softly. "My aunt was always taking it out of the bed."

His aunt, Nicole thought. That was part of the reason she was anxious to get back to Miami. She wanted to know if Alma had left a message.

After three days in snowy Chicago, Nicole was back in Miami, where the temperature was a balmy 80 degrees. The first thing she did was run to the phone and listen to the messages. Most of them were from friends at the hospital, but suddenly there was a new voice, a lyrical, sweet, Cuban-accented one. She listened with her heart pounding. Yes, Alma wanted desperately to see Julian. As a matter of fact there were three messages from her. On the last one, she gave her Brooklyn address.

Nicole wrote it down, stood up and paced around, excited and nervous. Julian still knew nothing about it. She was going to have to tell him and his decision would determine whether there'd be a meeting or not.

She made a pit stop at Allyson's salon, thinking it was about time for a new hairdo, something that would lift her spirits even higher, and something that she knew Julian would like.

"Sis, you not only need a new do, but you need the fashion police as well," Ally exaggerated. "Lynette, you take care of my sister. I'd do it myself, but she aint gonna give you half the trouble she'd give me." She gestured eloquently. "When you get back home, Nic, there's a hot little number in my closet that I want you to borrow. Make sure you put that on and then go see our prince."

Nicole laughed. "Well, as long as it isn't something I'd get arrested in."

"Girlfriend, you need to get arrested," Lynette said, laughing. "Come, get yourself in this chair."

When Lynette was through with hair and makeup, Nicole almost didn't recognize herself. Her thick, wavy hair was now bone-straight, the color of wheat, with auburn highlights. It slid, satin-like, well below her shoulder blades. The subtle makeup accented the jade green of her eyes and gave her a haunting, exotic look. Several women clients gawked in admiration.

Back home, Nicole tried on the dress and laughed. It was a tiny, tight, white, spaghetti-strapped number that hugged every curve on her body. She borrowed a pair of Allyson's stiletto-heeled sandals. The total view in the full-length mirror shocked her. She was staring at the woman who'd terrified Warren, the one he wanted only for himself, that he never wanted anyone else to see. This overly sexy fraud would not threaten Julian. She decided to keep the dress on, but as she started out of the house, she chickened out a little, and covered up with a blazer.

She arrived at his place and immediately became aware of increased security. There were other guards besides the familiar Carlos, who at first didn't even recognize her, and when he did, couldn't stop staring. *Men,* she thought, brushing back her shimmering hair as she ascended the stairs.

On the way up, she was met by Amanda, who was bounding down the stairs two at a time. She stopped and stared at Nicole incredulously. "Wow!" she exclaimed. "You're the bomb."

Nicole laughed at her expression. "The bomb? Is that good or bad?"

"It's good, but you don't look like you anymore."

"I'm still me, Amanda, just wearing different clothes."

Amanda considered this for a moment. "I don't know if Uncle J. is going to like it though. He like nurses better than models now."

Nicole laughed again, considering the brutal honesty of children. "Your uncle knows that I'm still a nurse. Even nurses like to dress up once in a while."

Julian greeted her on the deck with a kiss. He looked terrific in ivory-colored pants and a beige silk shirt, not tucked in. She wrapped her arms around him, holding him at arm's length. He was standing perfectly straight, without crutches.

"You look as beautiful as ever," he said, inspecting her. "But it's a little hot for that jacket."

She allowed him to slide it off, his smoldering dark eyes never leaving her. Julian gave a low whistle. Her disarming beauty did not surprise him, because he'd known she'd possessed it from the first day he'd seen her. He was surprised by the fact that she'd decided to display it uninhibited now. He drank in the visual image of her smooth, caramel skin, the gentle slope of her bare shoulders, and the firm, tightness of her ever-so- slightly revealed breasts. He wanted to slide the fragile looking strap of the dress down. His eyes flickered back to her beautiful face and shimmering hair.

"Your niece said I was the bomb," she murmured, slightly self-conscious by his attention. "Does that mean I'm supposed to explode at any second?"

"Just wait for me to detonate you, baby, and we'll both explode simultaneously."

"So…" She took his hand, trying to divert attention from herself. "You really are doing well."

"Not good enough for Princess Amanda, I'm afraid. She's bragging about how she can outrun me now."

They sat down at one of the deck tables, and were served lunch by the household staff. Julian didn't eat very much and that disturbed her. He looked good, considering what he'd been through, but he had lost weight. She sampled more of the fresh sliced fruit than she normally would have, just to keep it from going to waste. It was something she'd get after him about later.

"So how were your parents?" he asked.

"They're doing really well. I had a great three days back home."

"What have you told them about us at this point?"

"Everything."

"Oh?" He raised his eyebrows. "And your father hasn't put out a contract on me yet?"

She smiled. "Bigotry in any form doesn't exactly amuse him. He was remarkably understanding." She glanced up at the puffy white clouds and noticed a pelican soaring overhead, looking like something prehistoric "Anyway it doesn't matter. I'm the one who chooses who I want to be with." She glanced reflectively at the sky again. "It felt really strange," she mused. "When we were driving from the airport, I asked my father to go past the street where Warren and I used to live."

Julian listened silently, intently, as she continued. "We drove past the house and I looked at it and it looked pretty much the same, but I didn't *feel* anything. It was as if I had never lived there. Trey didn't have any reaction either. Isn't that odd?"

"Maybe it's good," Julian said.

A long silence followed and she found herself focusing on the uncovered scar above his left eyebrow. Oddly enough, it enhanced his sensuality, giving him a slightly dangerous appearance. She had the brief illusion of him starring in some vintage swashbuckling movie.

"Will you come with me to New York for the show next week?" he asked.

"I'd love to," Nicole said. "There's just one thing."

"Uh oh. What is that?"

"Would you mind very much if Allyson comes along? She has a friend living there."

Julian groaned. "You want a chaperone. You still don't trust me."

"Allyson? A chaperone? It's not that. It's not that at all. I *do* trust you," she hesitated. "Maybe I'm the one I don't trust."

"She can come," he said with a laugh. "But please, *not* the dog. Is there anything else? You look a little nervous."

"Shane's checking into a kennel." She looked down at her hands. "Yes, there is something else, a very big something else. Julian, I found your aunt."

She explained the details while he stared at her in shock. "She sounded really nice on the phone. While you're in New York, perhaps we can go…"

Julian shook his head. "I don't know." He stood up abruptly, flinching because sudden movements still caused pain. " I'm not sure I'm ready for that."

"You have to start somewhere. Can't you at least just give her a chance?"

"I…well, we'll see."

That was all she could get out of him. After all those years and intense childhood memories, discovering a fraud would be pretty devastating, but not knowing at all was equally devastating.

On New Year's Eve, the day before the concert, they flew to New York on the private jet, along with some members of Julian's entourage. It was snowing as the plane touched down on the tarmac. Nicole had a slight headache from listening to Allyson, who had been gabbing during the whole flight. Julian seemed amused by it. She also flirted shamelessly with his assistant/bodyguard, Alex West, who looked as if he could bench-press five hundred pounds without even breaking a sweat.

The snow was coming down heavily as the chauffeur delivered them to their hotel suite in time for lunch. Julian ordered room service and the three of them ate together. Then he was driven off to Radio City Music Hall for a rehearsal, leaving Nicole and Allyson free to do what they wanted.

The weather forecasters were predicting a lot of snow, so Allyson was chauffeur-driven to Long Island, early, so she could connect with some old friends for a planned New Year's celebration.

Nicole was grateful for the silence. As she watched the snow falling in Central Park from the hotel balcony, romantic illusions filled her head and she wished Julian were beside her to share them. He had not said anything about any special plans for the last day of the year, but it was just as well. He couldn't afford to be partying now, and she had never been a habitual reveler anyway.

Dusk was falling when Julian returned. He came in quietly, switched the dim light on in the living room, and sat on the couch, still wearing his long, black leather coat. He appeared to be lost in thought.

"Hey," Nicole whispered, coming out of her bedroom "How'd it go?"

"It went good. Everything's all set."

"Are you feeling all right?"

"Sure. I'm just sitting here daydreaming." He looked at her directly. "Do you think I should see her?"

His question caught her off guard. "What?"

"My aunt. Do you think I should see her?"

She sat down beside him, and silently began unbuttoning his coat. "You'll never forgive yourself if you don't."

She slid the coat over his shoulders and he shrugged it off and stood up. He paced around, limping slightly. "How about going later this evening, in a couple of hours?" he asked.

"Fine, if that's what you want. I'll give her a call and…"

"No. We won't call. We'll just drop in."

"But she might be out. It *is* New Year's Eve."

"If she's still the same Aunt Alma I used to know, believe me, she won't be out on this night. She was very religious. She didn't believe in what she called pagan celebrations. If she is out partying, then it means we weren't meant to meet."

"Oh, Julian! That's not being fair. She could be out with family or something. I didn't tell you this before, but there was a man's voice on her answering machine. Maybe she remarried."

"Don't care. That's the way it has to be," he said sharply, then modulated the tone of his voice. "I just want to get this over with."

Resolved, she sighed. "What time do you want to go?"

"Around nine."

That's kind of late, and during a snowstorm, she thought, but decided not to make any further comment.

Her heart went out to him, because he was really stressed out over the potential meeting and was acting like a terrified little boy—like Trey. She rose from her seat, and went to him, sliding her arms around his waist while he studied the snow falling outside the window.

CHAPTER THIRTY-FIVE

The building was a neat little brownstone, in a long row of similar dwellings on a one-way Brooklyn side street. All of them were illuminated with decorative holiday lights, and as the snow fell in a wind-driven, slanting motion, the whole scene suggested an urban Christmas card.

Rick Foreman, their Minnesota-born chauffeur, got out and opened the door of the silver Range Rover for them. Nicole thanked him and stepped out, grateful for the fact that Rick was an expert driver who claimed to love driving in snow. Julian said a few words to him and then he got out slowly, studying the neighborhood.

"Well, Aunt Alma's not on welfare," he said.

Nicole smiled, squeezing his hand. "That's a good sign."

They carefully ascended the snow-covered steps. Julian was relieved that there were not many, because his knee was rebelling. The hallway, with antiquated lighting, smelled pleasantly of cinnamon. They stopped in front of number four. Julian held his breath and pushed the buzzer once, twice.

"Who is it?" a woman's voice said from inside.

Julian opened his mouth to speak, but the words stuck in his throat and no sound came out. He glanced anxiously at Nicole, hating himself for appearing so flawed and vulnerable in front of her. She did not look surprised, bewildered, or ashamed of him. Instead, she spoke.

"I'm Nicole Evans from Miami. I'd like to see Alma Rivera."

A light came through the peephole on the door, followed by the sound of deadlock bolts turning and a chain sliding down. The door opened partially and Nicole was face-to-face with a petite, elegant looking lady with gleaming silvery hair drawn back behind her ears. Her skin was light brown and she had large, almond-shaped eyes that looked a lot younger than their years. The eyes appeared stunned as they focused on Julian.

"I know we should have called," Nicole said apologetically. "But Julian won't be in New York for very long and so..."

"Come in," the lady said in one breath. She unbolted the chain and Nicole entered first. Julian just stood there, framed in the doorway, staring at the mother figure he remembered.

"Julian!" she exclaimed, breaking the ice. "Dear God, is it really you?"

"Yes," Julian said, recovering his voice. He could not take his eyes off the almost surreal woman from his past. "You...you used to be taller," he stammered, then laughed at himself. "I'm sorry. I'm still seeing you with the eyes of a little kid." He smiled hesitantly.

Nicole did not have a clue what Aunt Alma said next, because the emotional outburst that followed was in Spanish. She hugged Julian joyfully and then led him into the apartment, clinging to him as if afraid he'd disappear.

The living room was warm and cozy, painted in earth tones, with many Aztec and African-inspired paintings on the walls. There was a shiny, wood-toned piano appropriately dominating one side of the room. It was very fitting that his aunt should be musical too, Nicole thought.

"Sit down. Please sit down," Aunt Alma said. "I hope you both are able to stay for a while."

Julian and Nicole sat together on the brown, velvety couch. Alma was still beside herself. "I can't believe it," she declared. "Enrique's son, after all these years." She put on her glasses and inspected him even closer. "You look so much like your father."

"Tell me about *you*," Julian said softly. "What happened after you left Cuba?"

"Well, you know that my husband was already living here in the United States. He sent for me to join him, and that crazy government finally consented. We had many good years here but we never had any children. We wanted you, Julian, and your father wanted you to be with us too. He knew…" She paused briefly because her eyes were filling up with tears. "He knew that he would never get out of Cuba, that he would die there."

Julian looked away. "I'm sorry things didn't work out the way my father wanted them."

Nicole sensed that Julian was still being somewhat guarded with his emotions. He was probably visualizing how different his life might have been had he been raised by Alma and Alejandro, yet he was also realistically accepting the fact that the past could not be altered.

"I wrote to you a few times," Aunt Alma said.

"I…I never saw the letters until much later," Julian replied, his voice barely audible.

Alma sighed. "I assumed that it had a lot to do with that half-sister of yours. She wrote me when you all first came to this country, asking me if I wanted to come get you. Alejandro and I made arrangements to come, but when we got there, you were gone and Elena's relatives claimed they didn't know where you moved."

"A lot of stuff happened," Julian murmured. "I'm sorry."

"You don't have to apologize. You're not too late. I may be an old lady now, but before I close my eyes in death, I can say that I was able to see my little boy all grown up into a handsome man. God is good."

Julian smiled. "You talk the same as I remember. You're still religious."

"Yes," she said. "My life is very quiet now since Alejandro passed eight years ago. I miss him, but I have two sisters living in this building. I go to my meetings all the time."

"Sisters?" Julian questioned.

"Spiritual ones from my church."

"So, you never remarried," Julian said. "I guess that was Uncle Alejandro's voice Nicole heard on the answering machine."

Alma smiled warmly. "Yes, that was him. When you're alone and a widow, you don't want everyone to know it Besides, I couldn't bear the thought of erasing his voice. I like to remember him."

"I can relate to that." Julian felt the past wrapping itself around him again.

"I have so much more to tell you, but I'd like to hear about your life," Alma said.

She acts as if she doesn't know, Julian thought. He really didn't want to talk about his life. He wanted to hear more about hers, but she was waiting. "A lot has happened in my life," he said slowly. "Some good, some bad. When Elena and I escaped Cuba, the only thing I could take was my father's guitar. It was as if he was telling me that that was the most important thing. I know now that there were other important things I should have taken as well, but it's too late." He took a deep breath. "I grew up in Miami and when I was a teenager, I kind of got involved in music and…"

"Excuse me a minute," Alma interrupted, rising.

Nicole thought that it was an odd moment for her to leave the room. She glanced at Julian. He had that far off look that was now familiar. Aunt Alma returned carrying a large, leather-bound scrapbook. She placed it on the coffee table in front of Julian and then she sat down beside him.

"Open it," she commanded.

Nicole leaned forward, holding her breath as Julian opened the book. The first picture, preserved under a plastic covering, was of him performing during his last Miami concert. He turned the next page and there was more concert footage, news clippings, articles. He kept turning. The pictures were all in order, starting with the most recent and going back in time. He stopped turning the pages and looked up.

"You knew," he said. It was all he could say.

"Of course I knew," she replied. "There is no way on earth that I wouldn't recognize my brother's son even if he did use a different name."

"I…" Julian started to speak.

"Shhh! You just keep turning those pages."

Nicole nudged Julian anxiously and he continued turning the pages with shaking hands. He was now near the beginning of his career, staring at a lanky, tousle-haired, somewhat effeminate looking teenager, who made them both laugh. The next page was blank, perhaps symbolic of the years not captured. He turned that page and right before him was a large black and white photo of a smiling man and a little boy standing near a stone wall. The curly-haired child was holding a guitar. He blinked in disbelief.

"Is this…is this?" he stammered.

"Yes, that's you and your father. You were six. I took that picture."

Barely breathing, Nicole wrapped her arm tightly around Julian. She stared over his shoulder at the man in the picture. He was handsome, tall, and darker complexioned than Julian and Alma, but his most defining feature was unmistakable. He had the same velvety black eyes that his son possessed. Nicole felt the warmth of joyful tears trailing down her face.

Julian continued to stare, mesmerized by the photograph. He knew that beyond that wall was the pounding surf of the Atlantic Ocean. He could hear the waves—he could feel his father's strong embrace. He remembered the day the picture had been taken.

"Julian, hold the guitar like you're getting ready to play it." Aunt Alma's voice, drifted hauntingly through his mind. *"Okay, smile for the camera."* He felt the balmy breeze and saw his father affectionately gaze down on him. He remembered his father laughing, and then he remembered the guitar falling down on the grass and himself being lifted and tossed high in the air, flying in the clouds.

"Enrique, *stop it! You'll drop him!"*

"He knows I'll never drop him. Right, son?"

"Yes, Papi. One more time!"

"There's more," Alma said, her whispering voice drifting into the past, bringing him back to the present.

Julian fumbled with the page. There were more pictures of his father and baby pictures of himself, along with aunts and cousins that he did not remember. But the greatest discovery was that he could clearly see his father now. Even if he closed the book, he could see that face with all its features. The mental block had vanished forever.

The pictures shimmered crazily and became distorted as his vision blurred. It took him a few seconds to realize that the blurring was caused by his own tears.

"I've waited so long for this moment," Alma said, her voice cracking. "I have always been so close to you, yet so far. I've gone to most of your concerts when you were here in New York. I've got videotapes, all of your records. When you had the accident, I even flew down to Miami, but I could not go into that hospital. Instead, I called from my hotel room and inquired about you. Julian, I prayed and prayed to God that you would be all right."

Julian was so stunned by her words and his own emotions that he was speechless again.

"You should have *insisted* on seeing him," Nicole exclaimed, struggling through her own happy tears. "You're his aunt, you had every right. Oh, but this is just so bizarre. All this time two people who wanted and needed each other kept apart. Why? Why didn't you insist?"

"Because I was afraid." She looked at Julian and addressed him. "At first I thought that maybe you didn't want to know your father's side of the family because of race, but then I noticed that in all your interviews, you never denied your heritage and you always spoke honorably of your father. Since I could see it wasn't that, I decided that you didn't try to reach me because you thought I would be another greedy relative interested in you only because of your money. That *is* why you haven't sought me until now, isn't it?" She waited for Julian to speak, but he was silent. "I wanted you to seek me when you were ready," she continued. "Oh, Julian, how could you not know that whatever you did, whatever you became, I would always open my heart to you, even if you were a beggar at my door, even if you wrote to me from a jail cell."

The silence that followed was overwhelming. Julian slid one arm around his aunt's neck and the other around Nicole's. The trio embraced tearfully without reservation. "I know the truth now," Julian said. "I'm sorry for being so stubborn. Thank you, Aunt Alma. You don't know how much seeing you and those pictures of my father means to me. I thought I had forgotten what he looked like, but now I realize that I always knew."

"Those pictures are yours. I've been saving them for you," she said.

They talked endlessly over coffee and homemade cinnamon rolls. Time honored them by standing still for a while, but it finally announced its return with the sound of fireworks, gunshots, cannons and distant screaming. It was midnight, the dawn of a new year and they had to get back to the hotel.

Aunt Alma did not want them to leave, but Julian assured her that he would visit her again before he left New York. He gave her his hotel phone number and his home number. "This is definitely *not* the last time," he stressed. "I've found part of my family and I have no intention of losing you ever again."

Outside it was like a child's winter fantasy come true. Everything was splendidly carpeted in white and fat puffy flakes were still tumbling from the sky. The snow on the ground sparkled like jewels under the glow of the street lamps and muffled the normal sounds of the metropolis. For an eerie moment, Nicole felt as though they had been transported centuries back to a time when Brooklyn was still rural.

She stood mesmerized while Julian placed the treasured photographs into the waiting car and closed the door without getting in. "Let's go for a walk," he said.

"A walk? Are you sure you feel like…"

"Yes, yes." Urgently he took her by the arm and they strolled slowly down the block.

"It looks so beautiful," she exclaimed, awed. "This whole street is so quiet and peaceful."

"Probably because most of the neighbors here are seniors." He squinted, shielding his eyes against the pelting snow. "I can't even begin to thank you for arranging this whole thing. "I also can't believe that it's a new year and I'm not out partying."

Nicole nudged him gently. "I hope you're not missing it."

"No way, never. This is the greatest New Year's Eve I can remember and I owe it all to you."

"You don't have to thank me. I'm as happy as you are that everything turned out so wonderfully. Your aunt is a beautiful lady and a very elegant one too."

"Yes, she is. Kind of reminds me of someone else I know."

"Really? Who?"

"You." He lightly touched the tip of her nose with a gloved finger.

"Me?" Nicole exclaimed, laughing.

"Yeah, you. I know you're still going to look beautiful when you're seventy. And I plan to be around to see you."

Before Nicole could even exhale, Julian wrapped his arms around her and guided her sideways until she was standing up against the street lamp, her escape route blocked by his body pressed up against hers. In the chill of the falling snow, she had no desire to escape and she welcomed the warmth of his presence.

He reached in his pocket and pulled out a tiny black velvet box. Nicole felt her heartrate increase and she watched, motionless, as he opened the box and presented her with an exquisite diamond ring. A mixture of exhilaration and apprehension gripped her. She gasped.

"Nicole, you've given new meaning to my life. I can't imagine the rest of it without you. Will you marry me?"

"Oh, Julian, I…"

"Please say yes." His smoldering eyes were wet, gleaming with an intense passion. "I would get down on my knees if I could. What I'm really trying to say is that I'm not perfect and I know we still have some things to get over, but let's get over them together." His body pressed against hers even tighter, sending heat waves strong enough to melt the snow. "My player days are over. You're the only woman I want and…"

Nicole pressed her mouth against his to silence him. After leaving Aunt Alma's, she hadn't realized she had any more tears left, but they were back, coursing down her cheeks. She withdrew her mouth from his. "Yes," she said softly.

He removed the ring from the box and slipped it on her finger—a perfect fit.

"Yes!" he shouted loudly. "Yes!" He grabbed Nicole, lifted her off her feet and swung her around in an exuberant embrace.

"Stop!" she screamed deliriously. "You're going to hurt yourself. Put me down."

The words were jolted out of her as they both collapsed in the snow.

CHAPTER THIRTY-SIX

I'm so terrified. What have I gotten myself into? Nicole wondered. She had just returned to Miami two hours ago and was sitting in the silence of her living room, surveying the homey familiarity, which after three days of opulence seemed foreign. *I'm a private person engaged to a public one. I'm so caught up in the pathos of his family—the drama and romance of it all—that I haven't really taken the time to think about how drastically my life is going to change.*

She reflected on the obvious security surrounding him the minute they'd gotten off the plane, more so than when they were in New York, and it disturbed her. But in the end she had to laugh at her own fears, because for once in her life it didn't matter how much she thought about it, her heart was going to win. She would simply take one day at a time and deal with each challenge when it presented itself, including Elena's reaction.

When she went to pick Trey up, she would tell her family. She was grateful that Allyson had decided to remain with her friends in New York for the rest of the week, because it would have been impossible to keep the secret from her.

Julian's two make-up concerts had been fabulous. His voice and his guitar had never sounded better. Even taking a low-key approach to performing, his artistry had shown through and the audience did not seem to miss the usual theatrics. Nicole was glad that it was over and he was back home with nothing scheduled for a while until his recovery was complete.

Back at the estate, Julian reflected on the fact that he could not remember a moment since early childhood when he had been happier. In the course of a few weeks, he had nearly lost his life, reconnected with the love of his life, mended the fragmented pieces of his past and was now on the brink of marriage to the most extraordinary woman he had ever encountered. His desire for Nicole was overwhelming and it extended way beyond the physical. It was a love so deep that it was spiritual. It all seemed too incredible to be real.

The concerts had been triumphant, even without all the showy dancing and pandering to the crowd. With a back-to-bones mostly acoustic performance, featuring one man and his guitar, he had felt an intimacy with the audience that he hadn't felt in years, and it was a direction he wanted to continue pursuing. The gratuitously sexy persona the world recognized had been Luis and Elena's successful but uninspired recipe for pop stardom. He had always secretly preferred to be recognized as an artist, even if it meant losing ground with the younger crowd.

As he sat alone in the darkened living room, he thought about how much he missed Nicole even though they had only separated a few hours ago. He had asked her to spend the night at his place, but she had declined, as he had expected. He hoped that she wouldn't use her time alone to reconsider his proposal and conclude that she wouldn't be able to deal with marriage to him. He had not indicated it to her yet, but he hoped that they would have a short engagement and a private wedding. The sooner they tied the knot the better for both.

Unable to control the urge, he picked up the telephone and dialed her number. It wasn't that late. She answered on the first ring.

"Were you expecting me?"

She laughed. "I hope you're calling from home. It's almost midnight."

"I'm home. You're making a homebody out of me." He hesitated for a moment. "Have you thought about the wedding date?"

"Yes," her voice was barely a whisper. "You did tell me that your new CD comes out in June. That means you'll be touring. I guess after…"

"The wedding will be whenever you want it to be, tour or not," he interrupted. "If you want June just say the word."

"Well, in that case it should be before June," she declared.

He could not believe what she had just said. "How soon?" he asked cautiously.

"How about April?"

"Sounds good to me. It can be as big as you want it to be and wherever you want."

"Julian." She said his name as though breathing. "I *don't* want a big wedding. I want ours to be as small and private as possible."

"Fine with me. We'll fly down to Vegas in the morning."

She laughed. "You better be joking. I have to think it out more, but I'd really like just the family, those willing to come, and a few close friends."

"Are you *sure* that's what you want? Money is no object you know."

"I was married before, but if you want something big, that's up to you. I don't want to be selfish. This is a first time for you."

"See, that's exactly why we're so right for each other," he said. "I really don't want a big wedding either."

Nicole gave an audible sigh of relief. She had let her parents and relatives get out of control with her wedding to Warren, and it had ended up much larger than she wanted. With Julian, there was the opportunity to really get ridiculous, but she loathed even the thought of a huge celebrity wedding. Media weddings always seemed garish, showy and pretentious, saying nothing about the sanctity or intimacy of the couple involved.

Elena was going to hate the whole deal, regardless of size, but a big wedding would justifiably upset her. She had never mentioned it to Julian, but in some ways she felt that Elena was right about his career. A big wedding would probably have a negative effect on his mostly female fans. They liked their idols to seem available, even if that was not the case. She never wanted to be directly or indirectly responsible for sabotaging Julian's career. It was the private person she loved and wanted. His music belonged to the world.

"I'm glad we've got that settled," she said. "There's something else that's kind of bothering me"

"Uh oh. What?"

"Maybe I imagined this, but there seemed to be a lot of security at the airport tonight."

"Oh, that. It's nothing, just the usual precautions."

"It wasn't *that* obvious in New York."

"Do you promise you're not gonna give me the ring back if I tell you?"

She gripped the phone tighter. "Please don't play games. What is this about?"

"When I had the accident, the other driver was never found. My security people are just a little paranoid. They think maybe I could have been intentionally run off the road."

"Why would they think that? Who would…?"

"I told you. My crew is paranoid. I don't feel that way at all. It was a rainy night. The driver most likely was drunk or he lost control of the car and then recovered it. He was probably scared after seeing what he did and just kept going."

"He? Do you remember seeing him?"

Exasperated, Julian laughed. "I just *said* he. It could have been a she. All I saw was a car."

Nicole started to say something else but abruptly shut her mouth. His explanation was logical. It was another problem she was just going to have to learn to deal with—like Warren's being a cop. She flinched at the comparison. It was the first time in a while that Warren's death had entered her mind and she didn't like the feeling.

Two weeks later, Trey was back home and well aware of the news. Julian stopped by in the afternoon, and following a few words with Nicole, he sought out the boy and found him sitting cross-legged near the stairs on the tiny patio deck, with his arm draped around Shane's thick, furry neck.

"What's up, *amigo?*"

The boy turned around, looked up at him and smiled slowly, his eyes partially obscured by the bill of his favorite baseball cap. Julian sat down on the top step near him and reached over to adjust the cap, but Shane turned abruptly and shoved his drippy nose squarely in his face.

"That's just what I need, a snotty-nosed dog," Julian declared, lightly shoving the animal's nose away, wiping the side of his face with the back of his hand.

Trey laughed and Shane retaliated by licking him on the ear. From inside the condo, Nicole glanced out the sliding glass door and saw them together. She smiled and lingered for a moment.

"Just wanted to ask you something," Julian said to Trey. "It kind of bothers me that I don't really know how you feel about me and your mom getting married."

Trey hugged the dog tighter, but studied him with intensely alert eyes.

"What I'm saying is that I don't want you to think that I'm trying to make you forget your father."

Trey blinked, and Nicole found herself eavesdropping even more obviously. She knew that Trey was happy about their announcement, yet she, too, had been aware that he'd suppressed his enthusiasm.

"I can't read your mind," Julian continued. "I sure wish I could, since you can't tell me."

But you can read my mind, Trey thought. *I know you can.* He was very happy that they were going to get married, because he wanted Julian to be his new dad, but he had been thinking about his father, the one the monster had taken away, the one whose face he hardly remembered except for the pictures hidden in his drawer. He wondered if his real father was sad about it.

"Your father will always be with you in spirit, just like I told you a while back, but since he can't actually be here in person, I think he'd like to have someone else teach his son how to pitch a baseball, tune up an engine, whistle at girls and all that other cool stuff. What do you think, Trey?" Julian hesitated for a moment. "I might not be as good as the real thing, because I've never been a dad before, but I'm going to try hard."

It's okay, Trey wanted to tell him. He knew now that Julian had to be right about this—he usually was. *I want you to be my new dad.* He opened his mouth, trying to make the strange words come out, but there was only a rush of air. The monster had gotten a lot smaller in the last few days, but it was still stuck his throat. He had to let Julian know what he really felt in some way. He didn't want him to think that being a dad was too hard and change his mind. Silently he reached over Shane's back for Julian's hand and it met his. The small hand and the larger one clasped tightly.

Julian grinned and prodded Shane. "Out of the way, dog breath." Shane rose, shook himself vigorously, and stepped back. Julian pulled Trey close to him and yanked the hat down over his face. Laughing, Trey pushed it back up and swung a wild punch at him. Julian ducked and grabbed the child by both arms, pinning them while Trey laughed and struggled to free himself. Shane decided he could use some help and joined in the fracas, barking and nipping at Julian.

Nicole turned away now, moving back into the kitchen. Julian had obviously scored another point with Trey and she was grateful. Some things were definitely looking up.

CHAPTER THIRTY-SEVEN

Nicole surveyed the breakfast table. A cereal box was overturned, spilling its contents onto the fancy place mat. Milk puddled around the bowl Trey had been using, and a dozen or so miniature toy planes were lined up and poised for flight off the edge of the table into the wild blue kitchen yonder. A dusting of sugar surrounded Julian's place and a brown ring of coffee formed at the bottom of his cup when she lifted it. Why were men of all ages such slobs?

She laughed to herself as she collected the dishes and put them in the dishwasher. It was Sunday morning and Julian had stopped by for breakfast. They planned to spend the whole day together, just schlepping around. At the moment Julian had gone out on a deli run with Trey.

There was something strange and unsettling about the day, but Nicole couldn't quite figure out what it was. She could only assume that it probably had something to do with her nerves. April was not that far off, her whole family knew about the engagement now, and plans were being made. Allyson was elated. Her parents were baffled by the suddenness of it all, but they were not opposed. Julian's family was a different story, of course. He had told her that he didn't care what they thought, and therefore he wasn't even going to tell them until the last minute. The only one who mattered to him was his aunt and she was happy for them, and planned to attend the wedding. Nicole wished there was more harmony on his side, but she was determined not to let the negative aspects get to her.

One thing really was bothering her, though; she was worried that once they were married, Julian would see her exactly as Warren had, an ice princess. What if making him wait for marriage backfired and he realized that she wasn't worth waiting for at all? She bit her lip and cleaned the surface of the table. *I guess I'm really going to have to perfect my acting skills now,* she thought.

There was an undeniable difference, though. She actually *did* have strong physical desires when she was around him, so strong that it sometimes scared her. It had never been that way with anyone else before. Maybe, just maybe, the acting wouldn't have to be so pronounced.

She mulled this over as she gathered up Trey's toy airplanes and carried them to his room. Sunlight streamed through the open curtain, bathing the whole room in a blinding yellow glow, highlighting the unmade bed and his dirty clothes lying on the floor. Frowning, she dumped the model planes into the open toy box, and knelt to pick up his clothes. She had told him so many times to put them in the hamper and could not understand why it was such a difficult task.

As she was about to leave the room, her breath caught in her throat. The pictures were back on top of his dresser. She hovered over the gold-rimmed photograph of Warren in his police uniform, staring out at her with distant eyes, and then her attention shifted to the family photo, with her smiling on the left, Warren on the right, and the then chubby, two-year-old Trey sandwiched in the middle. Barely breathing, she bent down and opened the bottom drawer. The shoebox was still there, but there was nothing in it. Closing the drawer, she returned to her own room and found the news clipping of the funeral back in the place where she had originally filed it, as if no little hands had ever taken it.

"Check out that Lamborghini," Julian said as he observed the flashy yellow sports car in front of them. "Is that cool or what?"

Strapped in the backseat, Trey leaned forward and nodded his agreement.

"I think we should have one. I'll take you out on some back road and let you drive it."

Trey beamed in anticipation, then turned to look at the traffic behind them. There were not a lot of cars on the road yet because it was still early. Sometimes he liked it that way, but there was something funny about this morning. Trey wasn't quite sure what it was, but he didn't like it. Anxiously he glanced at Julian and saw that he was watching the road in front of him. He didn't seem to think there was anything funny. Trey turned around again, straining against the confines of the seat belt and noticed that there were more cars in back of them now. He counted three.

Behind the number three car was some kind of van that was bigger than their Explorer. Trey unbuckled his seat belt and turned completely, pressing his nose up against the back window. The van was really dark colored and it was creeping along. He could not see the driver. Worriedly, he poked Julian in back of the neck and pointed.

"What?" Julian asked. He glanced in the rear view mirror and noticed the cars behind him. He didn't see what Trey saw. "I guess everyone's waking up now," he said. "Put your seat belt back on, please."

Reluctantly, Trey fastened the belt again, but he kept his head turned. One of the cars disappeared down a side street and now there were only two cars in front of the van. He still could not see the driver.

Julian signaled and began slowing the Explorer down. "I'm gonna stop in this store for a minute to get the paper. Wanna come?"

The words echoed in Trey's brain—they were words he'd heard before spoken in some other time, some other place. His heart started to beat really fast and his mouth got dry. His throat felt like it was on fire.

Julian glanced at Trey and noted that the boy was staring out the rear window, transfixed by something.

"Okay, you just wait here a sec. I'll be right back." He swung the Explorer into a vacant spot, pocketed the keys, and opened the door.

Trey watched the two cars pass and the van move closer. It was moving slowly. The windows were dark. He could see it clearly now and suddenly he knew why there was no driver. It was because the monster was behind the wheel and he did not want to be seen. Panicking, Trey watched Julian step out of the car as if he were sleep-walking. Immediately the monster roared to life. Its red dragon eyes gleamed and the horrible yellow fangs flashed in the sunlight.

A scream built up in Trey's throat and stuck there. *No!*

Julian turned to shut the door.

"Daddy!" Trey screamed, the sound of his own voice shattering the deadly roar of the monster, hurting his own ears. "Daddy!"

Julian heard the piercing yell and whirled around just in time to see a large, black van barreling down upon him. With split second reflexes, he seized the partially open door of the Explorer and leaped, catapulting himself over its hood, landing on the sidewalk. The sound of smashing metal rang in his ears as the van sheared off the Explorer's door and went careening madly out of control into a power pole.

"Trey!" Julian yelled.

Trey leaped out of the car and raced to his side. "Don't die!" he screamed, throwing himself on top of Julian who was still stunned. "No! Don't die!"

Julian grabbed onto Trey and held him tightly while the child sobbed hysterically.

"You talked!" Julian shouted deliriously. He felt a surreal and bizarre sense of elation.

"Don't die," Trey echoed again, his arms tightly wrapped around Julian's neck, afraid to let go, afraid to look.

Julian remained on the ground hugging the hysterical child until he began to smell the thick acrid scent of smoke in the air. Shielding Trey's face against his chest, he turned to look. A few feet away, the van that had nearly killed him was on fire and a crowd was gathering. He heard the wail of sirens.

What's taking them so long?

Nicole felt an eerie premonition of dread as the phone rang. Her hands shook violently as she picked it up.

"Don't get upset," Julian said. "We had a little…er…accident, but Trey is fine and so am I. Could you come pick us up right away." He gave the street address.

She was there in record time and met them a block ahead of a nightmarish scene of flashing lights and fire and emergency apparatus. Julian was holding Trey, whose face was buried against his chest. Nicole sprang out of the car and ran to them. Julian enfolded her in his embrace, looking slightly disheveled and a little shaken, but there was something very wrong with the picture. He was smiling.

"Great news," he declared.

"What!" she cried out, staring at him as though he'd gone completely nuts. "What's so great about it?"

"He…don't…die," Trey murmured haltingly, reaching out to her. It was barely a whisper, but the childish voice was the most incredible sound Nicole had ever heard.

"Trey," she stammered, fearing she'd imagined it. "You…you talked."

"I almost got killed," Julian interrupted. "But Trey yelled and saved my life." He tried to sound nonchalant. "Let's go home. I'll have to go back and answer some questions for the police, but right now we've both had enough."

Nicole quickly picked up on his psychology. Trey *really* had spoken and Julian did not want to exaggerate the fact, fearing it would deter him. There was also the other pressing issue—if they remained on the scene, people would realize who he was and they would be bombarded by the notorious press, another nightmare for Trey that had to be avoided at all costs. She took the child from him, embraced him tightly, and they quickly got into the car.

"Are you *sure* you're all right?" she asked Julian as she drove. "Maybe we should stop at the hospital."

"No," he assured her. "I'm fine."

At the police station, Julian, Luis, and Elena were informed that the driver of the van had been identified as ex-employee Gretchen Lindquist. She had been trapped in the burning van and subsequently died of her injuries.

In the trash at her rented room, the police had discovered hundreds of photographs of Julian, photographs taken without his knowledge—in the pool, on the tennis court, walking—photographs that went back at least eight years and continued to the present. Among the evidence were the remains of the last note she'd written him, the one he'd torn up and thrown away.

Julian stared vacantly at all the confiscated pieces of the mad puzzle, realizing that Gretchen had been the real stalker all along. She had left a suicide note and had planned to kill herself after killing him. He recalled that the same day he'd had the accident, Luis had informed him that she had quit her job. The tire treads on her van matched the skid marks found at the scene of the accident.

Elena was uncharacteristically speechless, while Luis simply could not get beyond it and kept repeating, "My God, my God," over and over again in Spanish. Julian wished he would just shut up, but it *was* devastating to realize that someone could build up an obsession to such an extreme that it could destroy their own life as well as the lives of others. On the other hand, there was the undeniable sense of relief that the nightmare was over.

"I *trusted* her," Elena said as they got into the waiting limousine.

"She's gone," Julian said. "Let it go."

"That…that psychopath almost killed you."

"Because of Nicole's son she didn't."

"You didn't tell us that part before," Luis said. "What did he do?"

"He yelled in time for me to get out of the way."

Elena looked puzzled. "I thought he was mute?"

"Not anymore."

He had the urge to tell them about the marriage plans right at that moment, but he remained silent. Enough had happened that day and he wanted nothing more than peace and quiet and to be alone with Nicole and Trey.

CHAPTER THIRTY-EIGHT

"You know, I'm really gonna miss you and Trey living here," Allyson said three weeks before the wedding.

"Really? I thought you would be glad to get rid of us," Nicole teased.

"Actually, I *am* glad to get rid of you. It's Trey and Shane I'm gonna miss."

"Gee, thanks." Nicole looked at her suddenly. "What do you mean about Shane?"

"What do you think I mean? He's Trey's dog now. Poor Shane would be miserable without him."

"You never told me…"

"Aww, come on. Julian won't mind. He's got a huge place, horses and everything. What harm can one tiny little German shepherd do?"

"Ally, I know you have some ulterior motive for giving Shane to us. What is it?"

"Well, it's not really ulterior. It's just that Marc's allergic to dogs."

Nicole laughed. *"Marc?* You are so bad, just can't wait for us to get out so you can move that man in. Wait till Mom finds out."

"He's only moving in temporarily, and Mom better not find out from you."

"My lips are sealed."

Nicole and Julian jointly decided that Trey would have a private tutor for the rest of the school year, but the next year he would be enrolled at the prestigious Harmon Academy. In the meantime he was seeing a good speech therapist every day. He didn't seem to be having any repercussions from the latest trauma, but Nicole spent a great deal of time talking to him, feeling him out, making sure she didn't see the need for another round with a child psychologist.

Trey thought his mother was being silly for worrying so much. There was nothing to worry about now because he and Julian had finally killed the monster. There were no more funny feelings in his throat and people didn't look at him like he was crazy anymore. He was kind of shy about using his new voice because it had been such a long time and now his words needed to catch up with his mind, but he was eager to learn and happy to know that he had both Mom and Julian to help him out.

Julian finalized his work on the new CD and the record company executives were pleased with the results. They predicted that it would be a hit when it was released in June. For once, Julian felt that even if it failed commercially it wouldn't make much difference to him, because he was about to have a family that was more significant than his career.

Nicole officially resigned from her nursing position at Miami General, and signed up for summer courses at the University of Miami that would further her interests in creative writing and journalism. Julian was a firm believer in the right to pursue one's dreams and she was overjoyed that for once in her life she was being afforded the opportunity to pursue hers without feeling guilt because someone thought her talents were better served elsewhere.

On April 24th Nicole and Julian were married at the home of her parents, James and Eleanor Whitfield in Chicago. The wedding took place in the evening and was officiated by the pastor of Eleanor's church. It was a beautiful, star-filled night, the perfect end of an unusually warm day.

In attendance were Nicole's immediate family, her friend Maria, Julian's Aunt Alma and all of his band members. Luis came with Amanda and his two sons. Wade was the best man, Allyson was maid of honor and Trey was the ring-bearer. A big surprise came right before they were pronounced man and wife when Elena entered stiffly and took a seat beside her husband.

The best part was that it was a small and extremely private affair. The rest of the world had no knowledge, because everyone in attendance had been sworn to secrecy.

When Nicole looked lovingly into Julian's misty eyes, right before they exchanged vows, she knew she would be gazing into those velvety depths for always.

"Do you, Nicole, take Julian to love and to honor until death do you part?"

"I do."

"I do," Trey echoed, unprompted behind her.

There was not a dry eye in the house.

EPILOGUE

Place: Villa in Spain

A warm floral-scented breeze wafted in through the open window. Nicole sat on the edge of the bed and watched the candlelights flicker in the softly shadowed bedroom. The door leading outside to the patio opened and Julian stepped in, looking sleek and panther-like, wearing a long black satin robe, and holding two tulip-shaped champagne glasses in each hand. He knelt down at her feet and handed her one glass. She took it and smiled down at him.

"Nervous?" he asked.

"A little."

"Don't worry. I am too."

"Are you serious? Or are you just saying that to make me feel better?"

"You're special," he said. "This is the first time I've been with someone that I've really loved. That's why I'm nervous." His dashing ebony eyes sparkled enticingly like the champagne in the glass.

Taking a sip of the bubbling wine, she ran her finger tips lightly through his raven ripples of hair, down the back of his neck and across the smooth solid symmetry of his bare shoulder. She closed her eyes and inhaled.

"That comes as even more of a surprise to me, but I don't think either of us should be nervous…I don't think we're going to have any problem."

He kissed her and the kisses began trailing downward, parting the tissue thin material of her satiny silver gown. Nicole held her breath and put the glass down on the night table. She felt the fervent blossoming of desire overtake her. Julian's strong hands were on her shoulders and she felt herself drifting down onto the mauve satin sheets. She felt her own hands sliding the robe further down his shoulder to expose the solid sculpture of his chest and the symbolic dolphin dangling from its gold chain.

Just as she was starting to feel a little overwhelmed, he wrapped his arms tightly around her waist and shifted positions so quickly, so fluidly, that she almost didn't realize that he was now beneath her.

"Listen," he whispered.

From the open patio doors she could hear the gentle strains of a flamenco guitar being strummed. Her eyes gleamed and she looked down at him. He smiled.

"Go take a look," he said.

Nicole rose, gathering the gown around her, and stepped out onto the patio. There were gardenias everywhere. She glanced over the railing and saw standing in the courtyard four flamenco guitarists, dressed in traditional garb, serenading them. A woman dancer with swirling skirts danced to the sensual tune of the guitars and castanets. Rose petals rained all around them.

"Like it?" he asked.

She sighed and leaned her head against his shoulder. "It's beautiful, so romantic, but not half as beautiful or romantic as you are."

Drifting on a sensual high, she turned in his arms, took his hand and they swayed together with the music of the night and the gentle Spanish breeze. She led Julian back into the bedroom. "It's time," she whispered. "Time to finish what we started."

They slowly, passionately, released all the desire and emotion they had restrained for so long until the first glimmers of dawn began peeking through the window.

"Listen," Julian said again. "Do you hear it?"

"The music?" she murmured.

"No, not the music, the sun."

She kissed his mouth. "You can't *hear* the sun."

"Yes you can. It's kind of a whispery hissing sound. You *must* hear it."

Nicole lifted her head from his chest and squinted toward the window. "Yes, I believe I do hear it. We're the only two people in the world who can."

Julian studied the misty green forests of her eyes. "If you lie very still and concentrate real hard, you can hear it rising in Havana too."

She smiled blissfully. "Yes, my love. Our sun is rising all over the world." She lowered her head once again and listened to the sound of their hearts beating as one.

ABOUT THE AUTHOR

Kymberly Hunt resides in the New York suburb of Rockland County. A lifelong lover of romantic fiction, history, and music, she is intrigued by all cultures and believes that everyone has their own unique story. She is currently working on her second novel for Genesis.

Excerpt from

LOVE ME CAREFULLY

BY

A.C. ARTHUR

Release Date: July 2006

PROLOGUE

December
Negril, Jamaica

"You know this is a million dollar deal you're messin' wit?" A six-foot-tall Rastafarian named Rohan stood on the terrace of his plush beach home. In the distance, palm trees and a never-ending blanket of sparkling blue beckoned the weary traveler, promising luxury and relaxation. The perfect getaway, the perfect escape.

"I know what I'm doing." The burly American sat in a chair on the terrace, thinking and re-thinking the plan that had been discussed. It would work, he knew it would. In six months he'd be safe in Negril, away from Baltimore, away from the accusations and speculation that had plagued him for the last ten years. He'd start all over again, leaving his sordid past behind him. Building a whole new life wouldn't be easy, he admitted, but at least he wouldn't be alone. He'd be married by the time the deal closed, and he and his wife would move to Negril and live happily ever after. That was the plan. That was his plan.

"Dat's a lot of ganja to move." His Jamaican accent thick and profound, the tall man lit a cigarette and took a puff.

"I don't have to move it. All I have to do is make sure it's delivered safely to Jones and he can take it from there." Dismissing Rohan's concerns with a flick of his wrist, the burly man sat back in the chair. "You just make sure Jones is where he's supposed to be, when he's supposed to be there."

"He'll be d'ere. Don't you worry."

"I'm not worried at all."

CHAPTER ONE

February

Baltimore, Maryland

Terrell Pierce had worked all night, his mind reeling with computer code and logistics. This had been his routine for the past couple of months. SISCO Engineering was a huge job that he was lucky to land as an independent contractor. By Christmas the re-design of SISCO's entire system would provide him with more than enough money to have him comfortably in his own home.

That went along perfectly with his timeline. His life had been planned and scheduled since the day he turned sixteen. He knew exactly what he wanted and wasn't about to stop until he had it all. The college degrees, the perfect job, the six figure salary, all that had come easily enough with dedication and determination—of which he had plenty to spare. Now he was moving towards the next phase of his dream.

He needed a family to round out his perfect scenario. He wanted the whole nine yards—successful career, a wife, kids, house and pets. That was where Tanya came in. She was beautiful, educated and classy. She would be perfect standing beside him as he continued his climb to the top. As soon as things slowed down a bit at work, he would propose and, hopefully, by this time next year they would already be on their way to starting a family.

Life was good.

Pressing the appropriate code, he gained entrance to the high-priced condo he leased. As if on cue, his stomach growled. He dropped his suitcase and headed for the kitchen. But then he heard something. His feet stopped, his ears perking up like those of a hound hearing a fox call.

Plush charcoal gray carpet lined the living room and dining room floors, so his steps were muffled.

The moaning he'd heard coming from his bedroom was not.

He moved quickly then, propelled by adrenaline. When he approached the door the moaning subsided. For one brief minute he thought he might have imagined it.

"Oh baby, I'm about to cum!" a male voice groaned.

His hand was on the knob, his imagination never having been that good. Shock didn't begin to describe what he was feeling the second he stepped into that room.

In the middle of his bed—in the middle of his king-sized cherry wood Signature bed—some guy's ass was moving in and out of some woman with the vigor of a champion stallion.

The female's feet bobbed on the man's shoulders and Terrell couldn't quite see her face.

"Oh yeah, come on, baby. Cum for mama!"

But he knew the voice—knew it very well.

Consumed with their activities, neither person heard him approach. He cleared his throat once, then again for good measure. They stopped mid-stroke.

He wouldn't overreact, wouldn't turn this scene into some drama-filled fight that his neighbors would hear and disapprove of, even though his frantically beating heart was trying to lead him in that direction.

"What the hell?" the man yelled.

"Terrell!" Tanya screeched.

With clenched teeth Terrell stood at the end of the bed, waiting to receive an explanation, which he doubted he'd understand. "Am I interrupting?" He stuffed his hands into his pockets to keep from dragging her from the bed.

The man jumped up, surprise and embarrassment apparent in his eyes. "I thought you said you lived alone." He looked at Tanya as he reached for his pants.

Tanya sat up on the bed, not the least bit bothered by her nakedness. "I can't believe you found your way in here. It's been so long since I've seen you in the bedroom." She crossed her legs Indian style, her palms on her bare thighs.

Terrell took in the display; after all, he was a man. But it was like looking at a stranger. Her usually neat and perfectly styled hair was in disarray, she wore no makeup, and her eyes were dark, excited. This was not the woman he'd known for the past nine months. The thought should have made him feel at least a little better about the situation, but really didn't.

He clamped his teeth down so tight he thought for sure he'd get lockjaw. He refused to talk to her until they were alone. The man was hastily getting his clothes on, looking from Terrell to Tanya, yelling expletives as though one or both of them should have been doing something other than staring at each other. In retrospect, Terrell figured the man was probably right. This had to be the worst busted lover scene in history. It was too calm, too quiet, but then that was the kind of man Terrell was.

"You don't even care, do you?" Tanya asked after her lover had finally gone.

Terrell took a deep breath. "Do I care that you're cheating on me, or do I care that you were tasteless enough to do it in our bed?"

She gave a wilted chuckle. "It would be more like you to be concerned about the bed than what I was doing in it," she spat.

He turned his back to her then, moved to stand near his dresser, his hands still stuffed in his pockets. Inside he was roiling with anger, and his shoulders stiffened as he replayed the visions of them together. Still, he didn't yell, didn't demand an explanation.

"Aren't you even going to ask me why?" she yelled from behind him.

"Is it going to matter?" he spoke quietly. In his book infidelity was a definite negative. At this very moment he was witnessing his dream begin to crumble, and, for once in his life, was powerless to stop it. He'd chosen her carefully, made sure she met every one of his criteria before asking her to move in with him. It was a sure thing with her, they were a sure thing; he'd already picked out the engagement ring.

Tanya jumped off the bed, pulled on his shoulder until he turned around. "This is it, this is the problem right here! This is why I've resorted to someone else. But a lot of good it's done me. You can't even muster enough emotion to fight to understand why this happened."

Terrell took a step back because her pulling on his shoulder had brought him dangerously close to shaking the hell out of her. She seemed to want a different reaction from him, yet he knew if he unleashed his fury things would go too far, he wouldn't be able to control himself. Distance was definitely needed. "Are you saying this is my fault?"

"You're damned right it's your fault. If you'd pay attention to something other than your computers and your money you would have seen this coming. You would have tried to do something to stop it."

He couldn't believe she had the audacity to try to blame her betrayal on him. "I am not going to take the blame because you couldn't keep your legs closed. That was your stupidity." He did raise his voice then, because the pain of still seeing her naked and writhing beneath that other man was all too real. "I gave you everything, anything you wanted and this is how you repay me. I'm working all night long to make things better for us while you're screwing some dude in our bed. How exactly is that my fault, Tanya?"

"I didn't ask for any and everything, Terrell. I only wanted to be with you. But you were so busy trying to own every damned dollar in the world that you couldn't see that. We didn't need anything else except each other." A lone tear slipped down her face streaking the smooth honey toned skin. "I needed you, not your money," she whispered.

"Well, now you'll have neither." There was nothing else to be said. If he couldn't depend on her loyalty, they had nothing. He would not listen to her excuses, would not give them a second thought. She was wrong, and now it was over.

He pinched the bridge of his nose, knowing a headache was inevitable, and moved towards the bathroom. Pausing at his dresser, he retrieved boxers and a t-shirt. "I'm going to take a shower. You need to be packed and gone by the time I finish."

Leah Graham refused to celebrate Valentine's Day, but she had agreed to go out with Leon on the night before Valentine's, tonight. She was already seated at the restaurant when he called her cell phone to say he was running a little late.

She had gone out with Leon Reynolds, a cool guy she'd met at a wedding show, at least half a dozen times, and they seemed to get along pretty well. Leon was the marketing director for Onyx Apparel, a black-owned and operated business specializing in business and business casual attire for the urban marketplace. He owned half the company, partnering with his brother, Calvin, who actually did most of the designing.

They'd met in Cleveland. He was vending the company's first evening wear line at the same convention. It just so happened that they both worked and resided in Baltimore.

Lately, Leon was hinting at taking their relationship to another level. Leah was hesitant.

To her, sex meant commitment. And commitment led to moving in together. And moving in together led to marriage. And Leah was never, ever, getting married.

When she was eight she had envisioned what her wedding would be like. She'd wear a long flowing white gown, with a glittering tiara and a seven-foot veil. She'd walk down the aisle of the church and meet her husband-to-be, who would be clad in a white tuxedo with tails, and a smile meant only for her. She'd take his hand and they'd recite their vows to each other. They'd go on a fabulous honeymoon to Hawaii and come back to Baltimore to set up house. They'd both have full-time jobs but would be home together at night. She'd have two kids and they would live happily ever after.

Yeah, right.

On her ninth birthday Leah's mother announced that she was divorcing her father. The word *devastated* did not describe how Leah felt. The thought of her father not being in the same house with her was a hard blow to take. Just days after her birthday all her father's things were gone, and so was he. A few months later she received a letter from him telling her that he was moving to Alaska to open up his own business. Leah had cried for days.

By Leah's eleventh birthday her mother had married again. A year later she'd had another baby. By the time Leah graduated from high school, her mother had married two more times and had two more children, thus proving to Leah that marriage wasn't the lifetime commitment she had first thought it to be.

As she grew up, however, she never lost her interest in weddings, their grandeur, the playing out of the ultimate fairy tale. She loved planning them, loved feeling like an artist unveiling a new painting, a director standing proud at his movie's debut. She'd become a wedding planner even though the institution of marriage held little personal appeal to her.

Leah sat back in her chair, sipped from her glass of white wine, and thought about Leon. She wasn't angry that he was late. Actually, she'd hoped he was calling to say he couldn't make it. No such luck, though. She took another sip.

Leon wanted to have sex. She knew that, had known that the last two times she'd been with him. But she wasn't there yet—didn't even know if she'd ever get there. Hell, kissing him had become a chore.

Damn. What was she going to do? She took another sip. She couldn't play coy—she'd never mastered the games some women played. She liked to be up front and brutally honest with the men she was dating, especially since she had no intention of being with any of them forever.

Looking up from her glass she saw Leon walking toward the table. All six feet, four inches of his ebony beauty approached in that cool swagger that let everybody know he was the bomb!

Damn.

"Hey beautiful," he whispered, bending so that his lips could brush hers.

Leah tried to calm her rampant thoughts. "Hello."

"Did you order?" he asked while taking his seat.

She nodded. "Yes, the waiter came over right after I spoke to you."

"Good. I want to get you home as soon as possible."

Tell me something I don't know. He licked his thick lips, not looking a bit like LL, she thought dismally. His eyes glistened with promises she didn't want to acknowledge, and his large hands reached for hers. "We could have had dinner at my place," she said, glad they hadn't. At least this way she could give him a goodnight kiss and go into her apartment alone.

"I wanted to take you out. We'll be alone soon enough." He winked at her.

No, he wanted to be in control. Leon thrived on control, and normally that was fine with her. She ran her business like a tight ship, but in her relationships, as few as there were, she was used to letting the guy take the lead—at least until she was finished with him. Then it became her show.

Leon liked to make the plans, liked to come up with the surprises, and for right now, she was simply a willing participant. She dated for entertainment purposes only. There would be no grand love affair happening in her life, so there was never a power struggle. He could do what he wanted as long as she allowed it. Tonight, however, she wondered how long it would be before Leon would use his control to try to bed her.

The food came and she grabbed the waiter's jacket sleeve. "Another drink, please." This was going to be a long night.

2006 Publication Schedule

January

A Lover's Legacy	Love Lasts Forever	Under the Cherry
Veronica Parker	Dominiqua Douglas	Moon
1-58571-167-5	1-58571-187-X	Christal Jordan-Mims
$9.95	$9.95	1-58571-169-1
		$12.95

February

Second Chances at Love	Enchanted Desire	Caught Up
Cheris Hodges	Wanda Y. Thomas	Deatri King Bey
1-58571-188-8	1-58571-176-4	1-58571-178-0
$9.95	$9.95	$12.95

March

I'm Gonna Make You	Through the Fire	Notes When Summer
Love Me	Seressia Glass	Ends
Gwyneth Bolton	1-58571-173-X	Beverly Lauderdale
1-58571-181-0	$9.95	1-58571-180-2
$9.95		$12.95

April

Sin and Surrender	Unearthing Passions	Between Tears
J.M. Jeffries	Elaine Sims	Pamela Ridley
1-58571-189-6	1-58571-184-5	1-58571-179-9
$9.95	$9.95	$12.95

May

Misty Blue	Ironic	Cricket's Serenade
Dyanne Davis	Pamela Leigh Starr	Carolita Blythe
1-58571-186-1	1-58571-168-3	1-58571-183-7
$9.95	$9.95	$12.95

June

Cupid	Havana Sunrise
Barbara Keaton	Kymberly Hunt
1-58571-174-8	1-58571-182-9
$9.95	$9.95

2006 Publication Schedule (continued)

July

Love Me Carefully
A.C. Arthur
1-58571-177-2
$9.95

No Ordinary Love
Angela Weaver
1-58571-198-5
$9.95

Rehoboth Road
Anita Ballard-Jones
1-58571-196-9
$12.95

August

Scent of Rain
Annetta P. Lee
158571-199-3
$9.95

Love in High Gear
Charlotte Roy
158571-185-3
$9.95

Rise of the Phoenix
Kenneth Whetstone
1-58571-197-7
$12.95

September

The Business of Love
Cheris Hodges
1-58571-193-4
$9.95

Rock Star
Rosyln Hardy Holcomb
1-58571-200-0
$9.95

A Dead Man Speaks
Lisa Jones Johnson
1-58571-203-5
$12.95

October

Rivers of the Soul-Part 1
Leslie Esdaile
1-58571-223-X
$9.95

A Dangerous Woman
J.M. Jeffries
1-58571-195-0
$9.95

Sinful Intentions
Crystal Rhodes
1-58571-201-9
$12.95

November

Only You
Crystal Hubbard
1-58571-208-6
$9.95

Ebony Eyes
Kei Swanson
1-58571-194-2
$9.95

Still Waters Run Deep –
   Part 2
Leslie Esdaile
1-58571-224-8
$9.95

December

Let's Get It On
Dyanne Davis
1-58571-210-8
$9.95

Nights Over Egypt
Barbara Keaton
1-58571-192-6
$9.95

A Pefect Place to Pray
I.L. Goodwin
1-58571-202-7
$12.95

Other Genesis Press, Inc. Titles

A Dangerous Deception	J.M. Jeffries	$8.95
A Dangerous Love	J.M. Jeffries	$8.95
A Dangerous Obsession	J.M. Jeffries	$8.95
A Drummer's Beat to Mend	Kei Swanson	$9.95
A Happy Life	Charlotte Harris	$9.95
A Heart's Awakening	Veronica Parker	$9.95
A Lark on the Wing	Phyliss Hamilton	$9.95
A Love of Her Own	Cheris F. Hodges	$9.95
A Love to Cherish	Beverly Clark	$8.95
A Risk of Rain	Dar Tomlinson	$8.95
A Twist of Fate	Beverly Clark	$8.95
A Will to Love	Angie Daniels	$9.95
Acquisitions	Kimberley White	$8.95
Across	Carol Payne	$12.95
After the Vows	Leslie Esdaile	$10.95
(Summer Anthology)	T.T. Henderson	
	Jacqueline Thomas	
Again My Love	Kayla Perrin	$10.95
Against the Wind	Gwynne Forster	$8.95
All I Ask	Barbara Keaton	$8.95
Ambrosia	T.T. Henderson	$8.95
An Unfinished Love Affair	Barbara Keaton	$8.95
And Then Came You	Dorothy Elizabeth Love	$8.95
Angel's Paradise	Janice Angelique	$9.95
At Last	Lisa G. Riley	$8.95
Best of Friends	Natalie Dunbar	$8.95
Beyond the Rapture	Beverly Clark	$9.95
Blaze	Barbara Keaton	$9.95
Blood Lust	J. M. Jeffries	$9.95
Bodyguard	Andrea Jackson	$9.95
Boss of Me	Diana Nyad	$8.95
Bound by Love	Beverly Clark	$8.95
Breeze	Robin Hampton Allen	$10.95

Other Genesis Press, Inc. Titles (continued)

Broken	Dar Tomlinson	$24.95
By Design	Barbara Keaton	$8.95
Cajun Heat	Charlene Berry	$8.95
Careless Whispers	Rochelle Alers	$8.95
Cats & Other Tales	Marilyn Wagner	$8.95
Caught in a Trap	Andre Michelle	$8.95
Caught Up In the Rapture	Lisa G. Riley	$9.95
Cautious Heart	Cheris F Hodges	$8.95
Chances	Pamela Leigh Starr	$8.95
Cherish the Flame	Beverly Clark	$8.95
Class Reunion	Irma Jenkins/John Brown	$12.95
Code Name: Diva	J.M. Jeffries	$9.95
Conquering Dr. Wexler's Heart	Kimberley White	$9.95
Crossing Paths, Tempting Memories	Dorothy Elizabeth Love	$9.95
Cypress Whisperings	Phyllis Hamilton	$8.95
Dark Embrace	Crystal Wilson Harris	$8.95
Dark Storm Rising	Chinelu Moore	$10.95
Daughter of the Wind	Joan Xian	$8.95
Deadly Sacrifice	Jack Kean	$22.95
Designer Passion	Dar Tomlinson	$8.95
Dreamtective	Liz Swados	$5.95
Ebony Butterfly II	Delilah Dawson	$14.95
Echoes of Yesterday	Beverly Clark	$9.95
Eden's Garden	Elizabeth Rose	$8.95
Everlastin' Love	Gay G. Gunn	$8.95
Everlasting Moments	Dorothy Elizabeth Love	$8.95
Everything and More	Sinclair Lebeau	$8.95
Everything but Love	Natalie Dunbar	$8.95
Eve's Prescription	Edwina Martin Arnold	$8.95
Falling	Natalie Dunbar	$9.95
Fate	Pamela Leigh Starr	$8.95
Finding Isabella	A.J. Garrotto	$8.95

Other Genesis Press, Inc. Titles (continued)

Forbidden Quest	Dar Tomlinson	$10.95
Forever Love	Wanda Thomas	$8.95
From the Ashes	Kathleen Suzanne	$8.95
	Jeanne Sumerix	
Gentle Yearning	Rochelle Alers	$10.95
Glory of Love	Sinclair LeBeau	$10.95
Go Gentle into that Good Night	Malcom Boyd	$12.95
Goldengroove	Mary Beth Craft	$16.95
Groove, Bang, and Jive	Steve Cannon	$8.99
Hand in Glove	Andrea Jackson	$9.95
Hard to Love	Kimberley White	$9.95
Hart & Soul	Angie Daniels	$8.95
Heartbeat	Stephanie Bedwell-Grime	$8.95
Hearts Remember	M. Loui Quezada	$8.95
Hidden Memories	Robin Allen	$10.95
Higher Ground	Leah Latimer	$19.95
Hitler, the War, and the Pope	Ronald Rychiak	$26.95
How to Write a Romance	Kathryn Falk	$18.95
I Married a Reclining Chair	Lisa M. Fuhs	$8.95
Indigo After Dark Vol. I	Nia Dixon/Angelique	$10.95
Indigo After Dark Vol. II	Dolores Bundy/Cole Riley	$10.95
Indigo After Dark Vol. III	Montana Blue/Coco Morena	$10.95
Indigo After Dark Vol. IV	Cassandra Colt/	$14.95
	Diana Richeaux	
Indigo After Dark Vol. V	Delilah Dawson	$14.95
Icie	Pamela Leigh Starr	$8.95
I'll Be Your Shelter	Giselle Carmichael	$8.95
I'll Paint a Sun	A.J. Garrotto	$9.95
Illusions	Pamela Leigh Starr	$8.95
Indiscretions	Donna Hill	$8.95
Intentional Mistakes	Michele Sudler	$9.95
Interlude	Donna Hill	$8.95
Intimate Intentions	Angie Daniels	$8.95

Other Genesis Press, Inc. Titles (continued)

Jolie's Surrender	Edwina Martin-Arnold	$8.95
Kiss or Keep	Debra Phillips	$8.95
Lace	Giselle Carmichael	$9.95
Last Train to Memphis	Elsa Cook	$12.95
Lasting Valor	Ken Olsen	$24.95
Let Us Prey	Hunter Lundy	$25.95
Life Is Never As It Seems	J.J. Michael	$12.95
Lighter Shade of Brown	Vicki Andrews	$8.95
Love Always	Mildred E. Riley	$10.95
Love Doesn't Come Easy	Charlyne Dickerson	$8.95
Love Unveiled	Gloria Greene	$10.95
Love's Deception	Charlene Berry	$10.95
Love's Destiny	M. Loui Quezada	$8.95
Mae's Promise	Melody Walcott	$8.95
Magnolia Sunset	Giselle Carmichael	$8.95
Matters of Life and Death	Lesego Malepe, Ph.D.	$15.95
Meant to Be	Jeanne Sumerix	$8.95
Midnight Clear	Leslie Esdaile	$10.95
(Anthology)	Gwynne Forster	
	Carmen Green	
	Monica Jackson	
Midnight Magic	Gwynne Forster	$8.95
Midnight Peril	Vicki Andrews	$10.95
Misconceptions	Pamela Leigh Starr	$9.95
Montgomery's Children	Richard Perry	$14.95
My Buffalo Soldier	Barbara B. K. Reeves	$8.95
Naked Soul	Gwynne Forster	$8.95
Next to Last Chance	Louisa Dixon	$24.95
No Apologies	Seressia Glass	$8.95
No Commitment Required	Seressia Glass	$8.95
No Regrets	Mildred E. Riley	$8.95
Nowhere to Run	Gay G. Gunn	$10.95
O Bed! O Breakfast!	Rob Kuehnle	$14.95

Other Genesis Press, Inc. Titles (continued)

Object of His Desire	A. C. Arthur	$8.95
Office Policy	A. C. Arthur	$9.95
Once in a Blue Moon	Dorianne Cole	$9.95
One Day at a Time	Bella McFarland	$8.95
Outside Chance	Louisa Dixon	$24.95
Passion	T.T. Henderson	$10.95
Passion's Blood	Cherif Fortin	$22.95
Passion's Journey	Wanda Thomas	$8.95
Past Promises	Jahmel West	$8.95
Path of Fire	T.T. Henderson	$8.95
Path of Thorns	Annetta P. Lee	$9.95
Peace Be Still	Colette Haywood	$12.95
Picture Perfect	Reon Carter	$8.95
Playing for Keeps	Stephanie Salinas	$8.95
Pride & Joi	Gay G. Gunn	$15.95
Pride & Joi	Gay G. Gunn	$8.95
Promises to Keep	Alicia Wiggins	$8.95
Quiet Storm	Donna Hill	$10.95
Reckless Surrender	Rochelle Alers	$6.95
Red Polka Dot in a World of Plaid	Varian Johnson	$12.95
Reluctant Captive	Joyce Jackson	$8.95
Rendezvous with Fate	Jeanne Sumerix	$8.95
Revelations	Cheris F. Hodges	$8.95
Rivers of the Soul	Leslie Esdaile	$8.95
Rocky Mountain Romance	Kathleen Suzanne	$8.95
Rooms of the Heart	Donna Hill	$8.95
Rough on Rats and Tough on Cats	Chris Parker	$12.95
Secret Library Vol. 1	Nina Sheridan	$18.95
Secret Library Vol. 2	Cassandra Colt	$8.95
Shades of Brown	Denise Becker	$8.95
Shades of Desire	Monica White	$8.95

Other Genesis Press, Inc. Titles (continued)

Shadows in the Moonlight	Jeanne Sumerix	$8.95
Sin	Crystal Rhodes	$8.95
So Amazing	Sinclair LeBeau	$8.95
Somebody's Someone	Sinclair LeBeau	$8.95
Someone to Love	Alicia Wiggins	$8.95
Song in the Park	Martin Brant	$15.95
Soul Eyes	Wayne L. Wilson	$12.95
Soul to Soul	Donna Hill	$8.95
Southern Comfort	J.M. Jeffries	$8.95
Still the Storm	Sharon Robinson	$8.95
Still Waters Run Deep	Leslie Esdaile	$8.95
Stories to Excite You	Anna Forrest/Divine	$14.95
Subtle Secrets	Wanda Y. Thomas	$8.95
Suddenly You	Crystal Hubbard	$9.95
Sweet Repercussions	Kimberley White	$9.95
Sweet Tomorrows	Kimberly White	$8.95
Taken by You	Dorothy Elizabeth Love	$9.95
Tattooed Tears	T. T. Henderson	$8.95
The Color Line	Lizzette Grayson Carter	$9.95
The Color of Trouble	Dyanne Davis	$8.95
The Disappearance of Allison Jones	Kayla Perrin	$5.95
The Honey Dipper's Legacy	Pannell-Allen	$14.95
The Joker's Love Tune	Sidney Rickman	$15.95
The Little Pretender	Barbara Cartland	$10.95
The Love We Had	Natalie Dunbar	$8.95
The Man Who Could Fly	Bob & Milana Beamon	$18.95
The Missing Link	Charlyne Dickerson	$8.95
The Price of Love	Sinclair LeBeau	$8.95
The Smoking Life	Ilene Barth	$29.95
The Words of the Pitcher	Kei Swanson	$8.95
Three Wishes	Seressia Glass	$8.95
Ties That Bind	Kathleen Suzanne	$8.95
Tiger Woods	Libby Hughes	$5.95

Other Genesis Press, Inc. Titles (continued)

Time is of the Essence	Angie Daniels	$9.95
Timeless Devotion	Bella McFarland	$9.95
Tomorrow's Promise	Leslie Esdaile	$8.95
Truly Inseparable	Wanda Y. Thomas	$8.95
Unbreak My Heart	Dar Tomlinson	$8.95
Uncommon Prayer	Kenneth Swanson	$9.95
Unconditional	A.C. Arthur	$9.95
Unconditional Love	Alicia Wiggins	$8.95
Until Death Do Us Part	Susan Paul	$8.95
Vows of Passion	Bella McFarland	$9.95
Wedding Gown	Dyanne Davis	$8.95
What's Under Benjamin's Bed	Sandra Schaffer	$8.95
When Dreams Float	Dorothy Elizabeth Love	$8.95
Whispers in the Night	Dorothy Elizabeth Love	$8.95
Whispers in the Sand	LaFlorya Gauthier	$10.95
Wild Ravens	Altonya Washington	$9.95
Yesterday Is Gone	Beverly Clark	$10.95
Yesterday's Dreams, Tomorrow's Promises	Reon Laudat	$8.95
Your Precious Love	Sinclair LeBeau	$8.95

Order Form

Mail to: Genesis Press, Inc.
P.O. Box 101
Columbus, MS 39703

Name _____
Address _____
City/State _____ Zip _____
Telephone _____

Ship to (if different from above)
Name _____
Address _____
City/State _____ Zip _____
Telephone _____

Credit Card Information
Credit Card # _____ ☐ Visa   ☐ Mastercard
Expiration Date (mm/yy) _____ ☐ AmEx   ☐ Discover

Qty.	Author	Title	Price	Total

Use this order form, or call 1-888-INDIGO-1	
Total for books	_____
Shipping and handling: $5 first two books, $1 each additional book	_____
Total S & H	_____
Total amount enclosed	_____

Mississippi residents add 7% sales tax